Get ou

The thought of tou... him with fear. If she woke up she would kill him in an instant. Seconds ticked by, how long he couldn't say, but somehow he managed to make his feet move.

Her arms were folded across her chest in a state of repose. He carefully lifted her right wrist up and froze. There was a second ring resting beneath her palm. His eyes flicked to her face and then back to the second ring. He stared at it, not really believing what he was seeing, then reached out and took it, half thinking that it would vanish the moment he did.

The familiar shiver coursed through his arm the moment his fingers came into contact with the rose gold . . .

## Praise for MITCHELL GRAHAM's *THE FIFTH RING*

*Books by*
**Mitchell Graham**

THE ANCIENT LEGACY
THE EMERALD CAVERN
THE FIFTH RING

# THE
# ANCIENT
# LEGACY

## MITCHELL GRAHAM

*An Imprint of HarperCollinsPublishers*

EOS
*An Imprint of* HarperCollins*Publishers*
10 East 53rd Street
New York, New York 10022-5299

Copyright © 2005 by Mitchell Graham
ISBN: 0-06-050676-8
Cartography by Elizabeth M. Glover
**www.eosbooks.com**

First Eos paperback printing: January 2005

HarperCollins® and EOS® are trademarks of HarperCollins Publishers Inc.

Printed in the U.S.A.

10  9  8  7  6  5  4  3  2  1

To my dear Mia ( Dr. Zannis),
who made the psychology classes fun
and Dr. Rodríguez's class in particular, bearable.

# THE
# ANCIENT
# LEGACY

The World of
# THE FIFTH RING

Moreland Bay

(Q
Pro

Taylor River

Stermark

MIRDAN

Toland

WASTED LANDS

The Great
Plain

Oglive Bay

Mardell

N

Gardic Ocean

SEN

Bar

Camden
Keep

100 miles

# PROLOGUE

HE HAD ALWAYS BEEN LUCKY WHEN IT CAME TO KILLING people. The space behind the wall was cramped and uncomfortable, a narrow, musty-smelling cubicle that hadn't seen a human occupant in years, and the man waiting there had discovered it quite by accident. He could only guess why anyone would have built such a room in the first place. Popular rumor had it the old king used it to enter and exit his mistress's chambers. Whether that was true or not made no difference to Bryan Oakes. He had been there for nearly an hour now. Waiting was part of his job.

The only light came from a tiny opening no more than an inch wide. Oakes shifted his position slightly and peered out through it. *Any night now.*

The princess would follow an established routine. Most people did. In return for a few kisses and some frenzied lovemaking, a maid had been more than forthcoming about her mistress's habits. His looks had always been useful.

The princess was a beautiful woman, and under other circumstances he might have tried to get to know her better. But it was dangerous to become involved with one's prey.

Delain's instructions had been very specific. *The rose gold ring came first. Killing her was only to be a last resort.* It was fine with him either way. His employers weren't offering any bonuses for her death. The fee was set. He had no complaint with the arrangement; they had paid him very well.

According to the maid, Teanna would have a massage after dinner, take a bath, then read on the terrace before retiring for the night.

*Perfect,* he said to himself.

When the door to the apartment opened, he recognized her voice immediately.

"You can send in the masseuse when she arrives," she said.

"Yes, my lady," the guard replied.

The door closed and a shape passed in front of the opening. Oakes watched Teanna d'Elso cross to the opposite side of the room and open the terrace doors. She stepped out onto the balcony and leaned against the railing, the pale moonlight framing her face.

*Poor sad little princess,* he thought.

He continued to watch her, appraising and measuring at the same time. She was easily taller than most men, with a fine athletic figure. He could see the resemblance to the woman whose painting hung over the fireplace. Both had the same raven hair and bone structure.

"A little closer," Oakes whispered.

He raised the blow pipe to his lips. It would take the poison less than eight seconds to act. First, she would lose control of her muscles; next, the respiratory system would collapse; and last, the brain would die from lack of oxygen.

*Not very pleasant,* he thought.

Since securing a position with the palace guard, he'd seen Teanna's famous ring a number of times, but his goal was the ring she had taken from Mathew Lewin years ago. It was just a matter of time until he found where she had hidden it. He had a good feeling that it would be tonight.

After several minutes Teanna came back in and began unbuttoning her dress. She shrugged out of the garment and tossed it on the bed. The rest of her clothes followed while Oakes watched. He felt no stir of passion at the sight of her naked body. Business was business, after all.

The princess went into her dressing room and came out

again wearing a silk robe. She was still too far away, he decided, and any mistake would be fatal. The blow pipe was only accurate to about twenty feet, and rumors abounded about what Teanna was capable of. One chance was all he was going to get.

*Just show me where you keep it, girl. It would be a shame to kill anyone as lovely as you.*

A knock at the door froze him.

"Just a moment," she called out.

Teanna crossed the room to a shelf of books, took one down, and opened it. The inside was hollow. Oakes held his breath as she slipped the ring off her finger and placed it in the book.

*Why thank you, my dear. That was most accommodating.*

He slowly lowered the blow pipe and a faint smile touched his lips. Patience was a wonderful thing.

# 1

## Coribar

HALFWAY UP THE HILL TO THE TEMPLE OF CORIBAR, Thaddeus Lane, second officer of the Felizian merchant warrior ship *Daedalus,* raised his hand, bringing the squad of sailors with him to a halt. The sound of an explosion reached his ears a split second before a blast of hot air roared down the hill.

*"Down!"* he screamed.

The sailors behind him dove for the ground and ducked behind trees and rocks . . . anything that would give them cover as the blast rushed toward them. One man, slower to react than his companions, was hit in the head by a piece of masonry traveling at a phenomenal rate and died instantly.

Lane checked to see where his men were and if any others were injured, then motioned to his coxswain, a heavily muscled man named Brown.

"We're too easy a target," he said. "Take half of the men and circle around to the back of the temple. I'll lead the others directly up the—"

A second series of explosions cut off the lieutenant's words in mid-sentence. He raised his eyes and stared at the top of the hill.

"What the devil are they doing up there?"

"No idea, sir," Brown replied, following his lieutenant's gaze. "It sounds like the whole place is coming down. One of the balls must have hit something."

Lane considered that for a moment. He was a tall, gangly looking young man in his early twenties, with intelligent blue eyes and thick, dark hair that came to the middle of his neck.

Brown was ten years his senior and had seen men come and go in the Felizian navy. This one was different. Lane had a confidence about him that inspired trust. Despite his age and a disturbing tendency to get seasick at the beginning of a voyage, he had proven himself in battle enough times to earn the crew's respect. Ship's navigator for the last four years, he made the right choices under pressure, and Brown was content to follow where he led.

Lane reached his decision. "I saw the temple from the ship. We don't have anything that could produce that kind of damage."

"Coribar folk are a strange lot, Lieutenant," a grizzled seaman spoke up from behind them. "That goes double for the priests. I was here ten years back. None of 'em are like regular priests. Like as not, they blew the building up themselves."

Lane frowned and looked up the hill again. "All right. I suppose there's only one way to find out. The rest of you men, look alive. I don't want any more casualties. No prisoners are to be harmed. Do I make myself clear?"

"Aye, sir," Brown replied.

Similar acknowledgments came from the other sailors. Satisfied, Lane rose to a crouch and drew his sword. Keeping low to the ground, he started up the hill with half the men. Brown and the remaining half angled toward the rear of the building. They numbered thirty in all.

When Lane reached the crest, he straightened and slowly put his sword back in the scabbard. Expressions of shock and disbelief came from all around him. The temple with its gleaming gold dome was now little more than a colossal wreck. From where he stood, he could see a number of white-robed figures partially buried amidst the rubble. It was a gruesome sight.

"Mr. Warrenton," he called out.

A red-haired youth of about fourteen years stepped forward. "Yes, sir."

"*Aye, sir,* in the navy, Mr. Warrenton," Lane corrected.

"Aye, sir," the boy stammered. He was staring at a man's leg sticking out from under a block of marble.

"Be so kind as to signal the ship and let them know that the temple is taken. Tell the captain there appear to be no survivors. We will search the area for anything valuable and return by midday."

"Aye, sir," the boy said. He saluted and began trotting toward the edge of the hill, carrying a boxlike contraption that was suspended around his neck by a leather strap.

"*Walk,* Mr. Warrenton. You are an officer and the men will be observing you."

Warrenton immediately slowed. "Aye, sir." He kept his eyes averted from the bodies.

Brown and his squad rejoined them a few minutes later. "Nothing to report, sir. Hell of a mess, isn't it?"

"Any sign of Mr. Fikes and his party yet?" Lane asked.

"No, sir. Shall I send someone to look for them?"

"That won't be necessary. I'm sure they'll be here directly."

Lane turned and looked at the *Daedalus*, whose tall masts were moving gently in the waters of the bay. Everything there appeared secure. He scanned the plateau for his first officer.

Elton Fikes was fifty-four and a man who wanted nothing more than to serve out his remaining few years and retire to a farm in his home province. Like most professional seamen in Felize's merchant marine, his personal fortunes had taken a substantial upturn when the Felizian government had rediscovered the cannon. Now, instead of merchant traders, Felize had a fleet of seagoing pirates.

In truth, Lane was stunned by what had happened. His stomach had nearly revolted at the death and destruction, but he kept his face neutral and moved methodically from body to body, checking for survivors. After making sure that no one was alive, he instructed Brown to take a party of men and give the priests decent burials. Next, he told Warrenton, who had returned from sending his heliograph message to the ship, to take the remainder of the men and begin combing the wreckage for any signs of treasure. The prospect of robbing the dead sickened him, but it was a role he had learned to play.

Lane picked his way across a pile of rubble and sat on the edge of a broken wall. He had signed on with the *Daedalus* when the ship visited Sennia. It was a calculated gamble at the time—he had desperately needed to escape the authorities who were scouring the land for him. Lane's real name was Mathew Lewin, and apart from Gawl, Sennia's king, his was perhaps the most recognizable face in the country.

At one time children had played games and pretended to be Mathew Lewin, holder of the famous rose gold ring, who had saved the West at the battle of Ardon Field. Drawings of him appeared in newspapers, minstrels told stories of his exploits in taverns, and merchants sold tin replicas of his ring—a ring he no longer had. It had been taken by Teanna d'Elso, the Crown Princess of Nyngary and conceivably the most powerful person in the world.

Mathew stared out at the sea. Nearly four years of hiding and maneuvering had brought him no closer to his goal. The ring was still gone, and his friends Father Thomas and Gawl d'Atherny were still prisoners. Edward Guy, the usurper who had wrested Gawl's throne from him, was still in power, and the world believed Mathew Lewin dead.

Those events were as vivid in his mind now as they had been four years ago. Without his ring he might as well have been dead, for all the good he'd been able to do his country and his friends. An echo from wearing the ring for so long had remained with him, but what power it could produce was inconsequential compared with the devastation Teanna d'Elso could unleash if she chose. The last hopes of the West had disappeared along with loss of the ring.

It had taken less than nine months for Elgaria to fall, and he had not been home since. The southern third of his country from Elberton to the mouth of the Roeselar River was now ruled by the Orlocks, a savage and cannibalistic race of creatures, as payment for Karas Duren's unholy bargain with them. Delain, the former king, still controlled the northernmost tip of the country with the remnants of his army, but they had been reduced to making periodic raids and trying to disrupt the puppet government Alor Satar had set up. The balance of Elgaria was ruled by the Vargothans, a ruthless lot who would kill without the slightest compunction to maintain order. That they hadn't succeeded in removing Delain completely was chiefly because Alor Satar had been stretched thin militarily and financially after the recent war.

The world had changed; whether in spite of him or because of him, Mathew didn't know. He only knew that the ring was gone. He no longer blamed himself for its loss. In the great scheme of things blame made little difference. Gone was gone, and he was no closer now to Teanna's palace in Nyngary than he had been when he started his journey. Thanks to the echo, he had a very good idea where the ring was being kept, but for all the good it had done him, it might have well have been on the moon. Mathew picked up a pebble and pitched it over the edge of the hill, listening to it clatter its way down the rocks.

The *Daedalus* had provided him the means he needed to get out of Sennia. Heeding Father Thomas's advice, he had changed his appearance. A dye purchased at the Stanley Market in Barcora had turned his hair black and another darkened his skin. There was little he could do about the color of his eyes, but the beard he had grown certainly helped. At six feet two inches, he was still slender, but had gained a fair amount of muscle in the last four years.

Mathew picked up another pebble and threw it.

"Home." He said the word quietly to himself and wondered what Lara Palmer was doing at that moment. He had left without a word to her, or to his best friend Collin Miller. That was the hardest part of all, nearly as hard as not contacting them in the succeeding years. It would have been too dangerous.

*You are our last hope, my son. The ring must be recovered at any cost,* the priest had told him.

*A marvelous hope I've turned out to be,* he thought bitterly.

The sound of a commotion at the far end of the plateau pulled Mathew back to the present, and he stood up to see what was going on. Seventy-five yards away he saw Elton Fikes returning with his landing party. Two white-robed priests were with them. Mathew made his way down the rubble and went to meet his first officer, careful to keep his pace moderate. An officer who moved deliberately and didn't become overanxious demonstrated confidence to his men and set a good example for the young midshipmen.

Fikes waved and Mathew waved back. Like Mathew, he was dressed in a coat and tie and white breeches, the uniform of the Felizian navy.

"All in one piece, Mr. Lane?" Fike asked.

"Aye, sir. We lost Swanton. He was our only casualty."

Fikes nodded and looked at what was left of the temple. "Bloody mess. They must have been storing black powder here. I never heard anything so loud."

"I suppose so. A secret like that is hard to keep, but it's odd that Coribar should have acquired it so soon."

Fikes shook his head. "This'll put the captain in a fine state. Have you informed him about what happened?"

"Aye, sir," Mathew replied as they began walking. "I had Warrenton bring the heliograph and we sent a message."

"Good. Any response from the ship yet?" Fikes asked.

"The captain wants us to examine the area for any—"

"*Plunder.* Yes, I know," Fikes said, with a look of distaste. "Have you found anything worthwhile?"

"I have two parties searching the area now."

"Filthy business this, Lane. Can't say I much care for robbing a church, even if it is one of theirs."

"The captain also wants us to examine the bodies for any jewelry or coins. His message said that we were to check the teeth for gold fillings."

Fikes stopped and turned to face Mathew, indignant. "The devil you say. We'll be robbing women and children next. This is too much. I'll be damned if I'm going to do any such thing."

Mathew stared straight ahead and dropped his voice. "We'll need to make a show of it for the men. There are toadies among the crew."

Fikes opened his mouth to say something and closed it again when he noticed that a bosun's mate named Pilcher was hovering nearby.

"What are you standing around gaping at, Mr. Pilcher?" Fikes snapped. "If you don't have sufficient work, I'm sure we can find something to occupy you."

The man executed a halfhearted salute and moved off.

Fikes watched him for a moment and shook his head. "We're going to have trouble with that one. Anyway, Thaddeus, thank you for the warning. I see you've already got some of our people at work on a burial detail."

"It seemed like the right thing to do," Mathew said. "Perhaps one of the priests will say a few words. I assume we're going to turn them loose once we're done here."

"What? Oh, quite right. I don't think the captain . . . what the devil, now?"

A loud argument had erupted between one of the priests and the sailors guarding them. The Felizians were attempting to remove something from a leather bag the priest was carrying, and he was protesting loudly. Fikes and Mathew exchanged glances and started toward them, but what happened next surprised everyone.

The sailor who was arguing finally succeeded in pulling

the satchel away and a small wooden box fell out, hitting the ground with a thud.

An expression of panic appeared on the priest's face. He reached down, snatched up the box and started running.

"Stop that man," shouted Fikes.

Mathew and four sailors gave chase. The priest ran like he was possessed and only came to a stop when the edge of the hill loomed in front of him. They were at the steepest part of the plateau, with the ocean a good two hundred feet below them. The sound of waves crashing against the rocks could be heard. Wild-eyed, the priest looked around for a means of escape.

Mathew took a moment to catch his breath and held up his hands in a placating gesture.

"Father, my name is Thaddeus Lane. I am an officer onboard the *Daedalus,* that ship in the harbor. I regret what has happened, but I assure you no harm will come to you. I give you my word."

The moment he took a step forward, the priest took a step back. The priest glanced over his shoulder at the rocks below.

"What's he carrying there?" asked one of the men behind Mathew.

"Quiet, men."

Clearly the small box of polished wood was of great importance to the priest; so much so that Mathew could tell he was thinking about jumping to his death to protect it. One look at the man's face was enough to convince him.

"Father," Mathew said, "this is not worth dying over. I don't know what happened to the temple, and I'm truly sorry for it, but—"

"Sorry? You come here as invaders and thieves, attack a house of God, then apologize for murdering your victims. Your sorrow is touching, young man, but my faith in miracles is already stretched to the limit."

"I'll bet he's got black powder in that box, Mr. Lane," a sailor said.

The rest of the men took a step backward.

"Stay where you are," Mathew snapped.

Elton Fikes and several other sailors reached them a few seconds later. "What goes on here, Lane?" Fikes asked.

"I was telling this gentleman that we mean him no harm. Father, this is my senior officer, Elton Fikes."

The priest looked from Mathew to Fikes and said nothing.

"He's trying to steal black powder, Mr. Fikes," someone said.

"Place the box on the ground and step away from it please, Father," Mathew said.

But the priest made no move to comply. He took another step back.

"He could be stealing treasure, Mr. Fikes," Pilcher said.

"Hold your tongue," Mathew shot back. "If we require your opinion, we'll ask—"

Mathew never got a chance to finish his sentence for without warning, the priest spun around and faced the ocean. He was clearly preparing to jump, and would have done so had not the hilt of a knife suddenly appeared between his shoulder blades. His back arched and the box fell to the ground. The priest staggered sideways, one hand reaching out for it. Too late Mathew lunged to catch him. Without a sound he toppled over the edge of the cliff.

Fikes dashed to the ledge and looked down. The priest's broken body lay on the rocks below.

"Dear God. Who threw that knife?" Fikes said, rounding on the men.

"'Twas me, Mr. Fikes," Pilcher replied. "I was just doing me duty to prevent him from escaping with any treasure, like the captain told us."

It was all Mathew could do not to knock the man down. But that was exactly what the captain had said.

Fikes rubbed his face with his hands. "Well, you've

done your duty. Now gather the rest of the men and make ready to return to the ship."

"But ain't we gonna see—"

"One more word out of you, Pilcher, and you'll find yourself lashed to the ship's wheel. Now get out of my sight."

Pilcher shrugged. He and the other men began walking back to what was left of the temple. Mathew waited until they were gone and picked up the box.

"What have we got there, Thaddeus?" Fikes asked.

Mathew tried the lid and found it locked. "I don't know."

"This was so important a man was willing to die for it?" Fikes said.

"It's a lockbox of some sort," Mathew said, turning one of the dials. He moved the box back and forth gently. "There's something inside."

"Can you open it?"

Mathew shook his head. "I've seen one of these before. The Vargothans use them to send messages. There's probably a vial of acid attached to the lid. Unless we open the locks in the right order, it will break and destroy whatever's in there, assuming it hasn't done so already."

Fikes frowned. "I suppose we should bring it to the captain and let him decide what to do."

"I suppose."

Mathew and his senior officer started back down the hill together.

## 2

# Corrato, Capital of Nyngary

ELDAR D'ELSO SAT WITH HIS DAUGHTER ON THE BALCONY that overlooked the palace's formal gardens. The sound of water could be heard coming from a magnificent fountain two stories beneath them. The fountain was a duplicate of the one Karas Duren had built shortly before his death. Despite the cost, Eldar had installed it at his daughter's request. Though she seemed quite taken with it, such things had never particularly interested him. His own leanings were more toward books and poetry, but he had a tendency to be indulgent where his only child was concerned.

The king watched Teanna as she stared down at the fountain. *So much like her mother,* he thought.

A pang of sadness touched him. Eldar smiled and continued to study her. His daughter was two inches taller than he was.

His wife and her insane brother, Karas, had wanted to unite the world under their banner, and they might well have succeeded had it not been for an Elgarian farm boy named Mathew Lewin. Now they were all dead.

*A terrible waste*, Eldar thought, not for the first time. "You haven't touched your eggs," he said.

"I'm not very hungry, Father."

"But you'll need your strength if you're going riding with Remy this morning."

Teanna made a face at the mention of Remy's name.

She took a deep breath and let it out. "I guess so," she added with little enthusiasm.

The king noted the tone in her voice and looked at his daughter more closely. Crown Prince of Sibuyan, Remy Chambertin was the fifth suitor to seek Teanna's favor in the last three years. The Sibuyan not only had a strong economy, they were a significant military presence. A marriage into their family would cement relations between the two countries and ensure the defense of Nyngary's northern border. Remy was a polite and charming young fellow, but Teanna had shown as little interest in his advances as those of his predecessors.

Twenty-three hardly qualified her as an old maid, but the king felt that it was high time his daughter got on with her life. It had taken her nearly a year to recover from the knife wound she'd received in Sennia. According to the physicians, it was a miracle she survived at all. The rose gold ring on her right hand had a great deal to do with that, of course. Eldar didn't understand the rings, nor how they accessed the Ancients' machine buried deep under the surface of the world, but he accepted their reality as a fact.

With Marsa, Karas, and the Lewin boy dead, his daughter was the only one alive who could now use it, giving her access to unimaginable power. She could bring entire cities crashing down with just a thought, if she chose. Strangely, after her trip to Sennia, Teanna had pulled more into herself. She was an observer of things, reserved in her speech, and generally gave little indication as to what she was thinking.

Eldar stood up, came around the table and held out his hand. He led Teanna into the drawing room, away from the distraction of the fountain, and they sat down on the couch together.

"Why don't you tell me what's bothering you," he said.

"It's nothing."

Eldar lifted one eyebrow and waited. Teanna met his

eyes for a moment and then glanced away. She curled her legs under her and rested her head on her father's chest. Neither spoke.

"I've been thinking about Mathew lately," she finally said.

"Ah."

"I had a dream about him the other night. Do you find that odd?"

"A little," Eldar replied, giving her shoulders a squeeze. "He's been dead for some time now."

"I know. It just *feels* different."

"Feels different?"

"When Uncle Karas died there was a finality. I knew it the moment it happened. I've never had the same feeling where Mathew was concerned."

"But wasn't the young man killed during the fighting in Sennia?"

"I thought so at the time, but I've never been completely sure. They never found his body, you know."

"I was under the impression that an Elgarian constable identified the remains," Eldar said.

"Cousin Eric was never positive about it either."

"Are you thinking that he might still be alive?"

Teanna shook her head. "I don't know. It's difficult to explain. It's just a feeling I get . . . but it's been growing stronger, I even had a dream about it last night."

"Do you want to talk about it?"

For a moment it looked as if Teanna was going to say something, but then changed her mind. "No, not right now. Do you mind, Father?"

"Of course not. It's just that you're my only daughter and I don't like to see you upset. I'll be here if you need me."

Teanna hugged him. "Promise. Promise you'll always be here, Father."

Eldar smiled and kissed the top of her head. "You have my word as the king on it. Am I correct that you had feelings for this boy?"

Several seconds passed before he got a response.

"I was a lot younger then. You do a lot of silly things when you're young. It's just that we were unique . . . the only two people in the world who had these." Teanna lifted her hand higher, until sunlight angling in from the balcony reflected off the ring's surface.

"That's true. But he killed your mother and uncle. It would be difficult to put that aside, even if he *were* alive. Do you find yourself thinking about him often?"

"Yes," Teanna said. "I know everyone in the family wants me to marry, and I will one day, but I want it to be someone I love and . . ."

"Respect, perhaps?"

Teanna looked up at her father and nodded.

"Well, respect is an important part of any relationship," Eldar conceded. "A partner is certainly preferable to a millstone. I take it none of the young men who've called on you in the past have met your expectations?"

Teanna shook her head slightly.

"Remy seems quite nice," Eldar said. "He's a handsome man and—"

"He has the brains of a doorknob."

The king pulled his head back a few inches. "A doorknob?"

"A doorknob," Teanna answered morosely.

Eldar d'Elso considered that for a moment. "Well . . . we certainly wouldn't want a *doorknob* for a son-in-law. I imagine we'll just have to keep our eyes open for a suitable candidate. There's certainly no rush. You still have a few good years left," he teased, poking Teanna in the ribs with his knuckle.

"What if I just stay here with you forever?"

"Forever is a long time. I'll send word to Remy that you're indisposed today. Will you join me for dinner later?"

The question was innocuous, but they both knew what the king was referring to. Over the last two years, and more so in recent weeks, Teanna had been spending more and more time in the underground town the Ancients had built. She had taken him there twice, but the Ancients' power source frightened him. His ancestors had failed to avoid their own destruction, despite unlimited power and knowledge at their disposal. What if whatever killed them were still there?

"No," Teanna said, drawing him back to the present. "I think I'll have something in my room and read for a while."

The corridors of the palace were lined with the portraits of Teanna's ancestors, and they watched the young princess solemnly as she walked by. Most days she barely spared them a glance. Dating back nearly two thousand years to the first Orlock war, they represented an unbroken line of succession on her father's side of the family. Her mother's people were descended from the Durens who had ruled Alor Satar for almost two centuries. For some reason, Teanna chose that day to stop in front of the painting of a middle-aged man named Tiglath d'Elso. His blue eyes were a family feature. They reminded her of Mathew's, but recollection made her uncomfortable, and she pushed it from her mind. She remembered her father once telling her that Tiglath had led the Eastern forces at the battle of Amon Plain when the Orlocks had finally been driven back. The following day a band of the creatures captured Tiglath as he was returning to the palace. He was never heard from again.

Teanna studied his face and could see her father as well as her grandfather there. *Strange how some things never change,* she thought. The jaw and cheekbones were the same, and of course there were the eyes. She stared at the portrait for several seconds before continuing down the hall.

How her uncle Karas had ever thought to make a bargain with the creatures was beyond her. In one breath he had managed to accomplish what they could not do for three millennia—all for the purpose of destroying Elgaria. In return for their cooperation, he had given them the lower third of the country.

The creatures now walked freely abroad, no longer confined to their caves and underground caverns. She considered it a blessing that they had stayed put. In the last few years there had been no reports of attacks of any kind. In fact, there had been no word at all about what they were up to, and that made her nervous. Sending a spy into their midst was out of the question, even if someone had been willing to go. A human would be recognized immediately . . . and Orlocks were cannibals. They were also far more intelligent and complex than either of her cousins, Eric and Armand, believed. One thing Teanna had learned was not to underestimate her enemies.

She could still recall the two giant statues that guarded the second entrance to the Emerald Cavern.

*Orlocks and humans together?*

It was incredible, given the enmity between the races, but the evidence she'd found in the old buildings all pointed to the same thing. She searched for the answer over the years, but had been unable to find out why, or even when, the schism had taken place. Records from that time period were notoriously scarce, which complicated the task.

Teanna had studied the old books and exhausted the resources available in Nyngary. Ultimately, she turned to the more extensive library in Rocoi where she had seen the first reference to the Ancients' underground town. The day it had happened was still vivid in her mind.

After the funeral ceremony for her uncle Kyne was over, she had decided to take a walk through the extensive grounds at Karas Duren's palace. Her thoughts drifted to the Ancients and what a town under the earth must have been like. A number of books referred to it, but there were no pictures. She recalled sighing and wishing she could see what the town actually looked like. Suddenly, and without warning, a white light enveloped her and she felt herself being sucked into a tunnel-like vacuum. It took all her willpower not to scream.

One moment she was sitting by the banks of a lake, and the next she was standing in the middle of a three-thousand-year-old town. At first she was in shock. It was like no place she'd ever been, or imagined could exist. The roads were wide and paved perfectly smooth. A yellow stripe ran down their middle. All around the square every blade of grass was green and cut to precisely the same height. They were perfect—almost. When she bent down to examine the grass, she pulled her hand back in surprise. It was not a living thing at all, but something made of a substance she'd never felt before.

She knew it was important that she calm herself and think clearly. Once she did so, she deduced that it was her own thoughts, channeled by the ring, that had triggered the transportation. Consequently, she ought to be able to return home the same way. A few cautious experiments in moving back and forth from one side of the square to the other proved her theory correct, and in the future, she resolved to be more careful about letting her mind wander.

Content that she was in no danger, Teanna had begun exploring. Hours passed as she came across one astonishing discovery after another—coaches with no horses to pull them; lights that went on when you entered a room; a building with a room containing a whole wall of clocklike things, except they weren't clocks at all. Each one had a single hand and a succession of numbers along the inner perimeter of its face. She had no idea what they represented. Then there were the homes—row after row of them containing the most unusual furniture. It was astonishing that any of the pieces had survived the passing of the ages, but they had. High up on the walls inside the homes, fresh air passed through small grill-like openings, and unbelievably, water ran from sink faucets when you lifted the levers up.

It was obvious that the Ancients had abandoned the town abruptly; she was certain of that. Kitchen tables still had place settings on them, and a number of homes had odd two-wheeled contraptions with seats that lay on their sides in the front yards. It was like stepping through a magic doorway into the past. Teanna strolled around, looking in the shop windows at the strange clothes her ancestors wore. Two of the manikins had dresses so short, her mouth dropped open in surprise the first time she saw them.

It was all so fascinating she could easily have spent a week there exploring and learning. But then she met the Guardian.

## 3

# On Board the *Daedalus*

MATHEW LAY ON HIS BACK CONSIDERING THE ODD BOX.
After he brought it on board, the captain looked at it for a
moment, tried the lid a few times, then handed it back,
telling him to see if he could figure out a way to open it.
Mathew had seen lockboxes before, but never one with
four separate dials. More confusing was that the priest had
been prepared to throw himself off a cliff in order to prevent it falling into their hands.

He put the box down, got up, and walked to the gun
port that served as his window. The cabin was slightly
more than ten feet square, and he shared it with a large
black cannon, a twenty-pounder. As a room, it left a great
deal to be desired, but he was grateful for a place of his
own. Privacy on a ship was a rare commodity, and during
those times when they were in action, both his cot and the
small desk were pushed to one side so that a three-man
crew could work the gun.

He looked out at the island of Coribar. An offshore
breeze drifted in, carrying a hint of jasmine from bushes
that grew wild along the coast. Mathew took a deep
breath, let it out, and rested his head against the side of the
frame. The temperatures had been dropping steadily for
the last two weeks, and the fresh air made the tiny cabin
seem almost tolerable.

Thus far the Felizian raid had proven spectacularly un-
successful. The temple contained little in the way of gold,

gems, or anything else of value, which had put the captain in a foul mood. It had been a costly venture in many ways. Two crew members were dead and another three had been injured. Fikes's party took what they could and carried it back to the ship. Their captain, Phillipe Edrington, was anxiously waiting for them. He took one look at what they had recovered, muttered something under his breath, and went down to his cabin with the ship's clerk to log the pieces in.

Under Felizian law, the royal family received twenty percent of everything their navy recovered. The rest was divided between the captain and crew, which in this case amounted to seventy-five percent of nothing. It was an interesting system, Mathew reflected, all made possible by the cannons and black powder. As a result, a number of ship captains had become wealthy overnight. Unfortunately, this was not the case with Phillipe Edrington.

He was the second man to command the *Daedalus* since Mathew had come aboard. A minor noble at court, Edrington purchased the ship, complete with its crew, from its previous master, who was now happily retired and living on an estate in the country.

Mathew cared nothing about the plunder. Serving on a ship was only the means to an end. The Felizians traded extensively with Nyngary, and that was where Teanna had hidden his ring. But every opportunity he'd had over the last four years to get close to it ended in failure.

He looked at the calendar. Now another opportunity was about to present itself, provided he could get the captain to land the ship in Vargoth in two weeks' time.

Mathew walked back to the cot, picked up the box, and turned the dials a few times. He listened carefully for the sound of a tumbler falling into place, but the wood was too thick for any noise to escape. After trying for several minutes, he gave up and went on deck.

His watch wasn't due to begin until four bells, and he

found it was easier to think outside the stuffy confines of the cabin. Elton Fikes was at his usual station on the quarter-deck, overseeing preparations for their getting underway.

Water and fresh fruit were always problems on a ship, and Fikes had the good sense to send a party out to refill their casks. The senior officer gave Mathew a smile when he saw him and returned his attention to the activity on the starboard side of the ship. There was a great deal of it going on.

Young Stanley Warrenton was in the process of tying alongside in the lighter. Mathew glanced over the rail and saw they were bringing back a number of crates filled with oranges and limes. Near the foredeck and amidships, different crews of sailors were busy mending sails and repairing frayed lines. Others, working under the guidance of Ellias Marsden, the ship's carpenter, were replacing a spar that had recently cracked in a storm off the Elgarian coast. It was as close as Mathew had come to seeing his homeland in nearly four years.

The experience had raised a hollow feeling in his chest. Through a series of careful inquiries, he managed to learn that Collin and Lara had made it safely back to Devondale. The knowledge, however, gave him little comfort. He wanted to contact them, needed to, but he knew it would have endangered his plans, not to mention putting them at risk. The northern two-thirds of Elgaria, where Devondale was located, was now ruled by the Vargothans. From time to time stories reached him of the atrocities being committed in his country, and the fact that he was powerless to do anything about it made him sick at heart.

The situation with Gawl and Father Thomas was not much better. As recently as six months earlier, when the *Daedalus* had visited Barcora, he'd overheard a merchant talking to a man in the Stanley Market. Apparently, the king was still imprisoned in Camden Keep. The men spoke in hushed voices, and while Mathew couldn't hear the entire conversation, one word did catch his attention. *Trial*.

Gawl had already been tried and sentenced to twenty years in prison. So why would the Regent want another trial? Some careful poking around in other taverns and shops over the next few days brought him the answer. Lord Guy was now satisfied with the high court's composition and was ready to remove what he perceived as the last threat to him. Gawl d'Atherny was far too dangerous an opponent to let live, even in captivity. The ex-king still held the people's love, though few were willing to stand up against the new government. Complicating matters further was the Church. They would certainly bless any decision the high court handed down. At the time Edward Guy took power, Bishop Ferdinand Willis, now *Archbishop* Willis, had been appointed as head of the Sennian Church. Their relationship was symbiotic, with each endorsing the other's decisions and edicts. Paul Teller, the former abbot, had been removed and reassigned to a small church on the southern border.

A footfall behind Mathew caught his attention.

"Any luck with our mysterious box?" Fikes asked.

"Afraid not."

"Perhaps we can take it to a locksmith when we reach Boswell. I can't imagine what's so important about it . . . probably just Church messages or that sort of thing."

"Probably," Mathew agreed. "Did you just say Boswell? I thought we were going to Nyngary. Boswell's in Mirdan."

Fikes clapped Mathew on the back. "That's why we made you navigator, Thaddeus. Very little escapes you."

Mathew gave Fikes a flat look. "I'm serious, Elton."

"The captain has decided to give the northern shipping lanes a try before we head for home, and I can't say as I disagree. This has been a dismal trip. How long do you think it will take us to get there?"

Mathew considered the question for a moment. "About a week, I should say, assuming the weather holds fair. I'll check the charts."

Fikes glanced up at the sky. "I imagine we'll be all right. It's still early in the season for hurricanes."

"They get more in the northern waters than down here. Do you think this will sit well with the crew? They've been expecting to be paid off at the end of the month, and we're already three weeks behind schedule."

"I mentioned that to the captain when we spoke earlier," said Fikes. He looked around quickly and lowered his voice. "The problem is, Edrington's stretched pretty thin at the moment. He was counting on this voyage to set him right with the banks."

"He should have stuck to being a merchant," Mathew replied. "Being a pirate doesn't suit him."

"I don't think he had much choice in the matter, at least not from what I've heard. His brother will take over the family estate when their father passes, and Edrington told me they don't get on well together. It was either make his way in the world or starve. Lord Edrington seemed only too happy to cart Fat Phil off to the navy when the opportunity came up."

"I see," said Mathew. He thought about Captain Phillipe Edrington for a moment and shook his head.

Edrington was a pompous man with small hands, who sweated profusely any time the ship went into action. It was the same thing in rough weather. If ever a man was less suited for a life at sea, it was "Fat Phil," as the crew referred to him behind his back.

Mathew had become aware of the nickname shortly after Edrington had assumed command of the ship. The captain's lack of knowledge and indecision had nearly gotten them killed twice in the last few months. The first time was when he had put the ship off a lee shore during a storm, which nearly resulted in their being pounded to pieces against Alor Satar's southern coastline. Unable to decide how to extricate themselves from the predicament, Edrington had watched the rocks loom closer and closer. Fortunately, Mathew had been on deck at the time and snapped an order for the *Daedalus* to tack, bringing the ship around. Edrington merely thanked him for his foresight in anticipating his next order.

The second incident had come three weeks earlier. Despite Elton Fikes's urgings that they take in sail during a violent squall, Edrington ignored his first officer's advice and kept them plunging ahead through the turbulent waters. His plan was to get to the southern shipping lanes before his fellow captains.

By then Mathew had determined that Phillipe Edrington knew as little about the sea as he did about the sailing qualities of the *Daedalus*. It was all he and the other officers could do to keep things together—not an easy trick to accomplish. None of them wanted to undermine the captain's authority, but neither did they want to kill everyone onboard by following him blindly, particularly when they knew his judgment was more often wrong than right.

The recent mishap could have easily dismasted the ship, but fortunately, a belaying pin falling from the mainmast had knocked the captain unconscious. This accident allowed Elton Fikes to call the watch and shorten sail with only minimal damage to two of the mizzenmast's spars. The falling pin had been Mathew's doing.

Waiting until the last moment, when no one was looking, Mathew had found the ring's echo and shook the pin loose. Neither the men nor Captain Edrington, when he recovered consciousness, were any the wiser. Thus, all interests were served, with the possible exception of the captain, who had a sizable headache and stayed in bed for two days.

Next to him, Fikes said something that Mathew only half caught.

"I say, Thaddeus, were you listening to me?"

"I'm sorry," Mathew replied, "I guess I was preoccupied."

"I said, we'll probably need to drill the gun crews harder. Hitting a stationary target is one thing, but I'd hate to be in a situation where someone's firing back at us."

"Why? Do you think the Mirdanites have cannons yet?"

"No way of knowing," Fikes said, shaking his head. "But I'd like to be prepared in case they do. In my opinion, it's just a matter of time. We've had free run of the seas now for almost two years. That won't go on forever."

"Agreed," Mathew said. "I'll attend to it in the morning."

They continued chatting until they were interrupted by Lieutenant Glyndon Pruett, the ship's third officer.

"Pardon, gentlemen," Pruett said, removing his hat and executing a theatrical bow. "The captain requests the pleasure of your company at dinner this evening."

"Ah," Fikes replied, returning the bow, "please tell his nibs that barring more pressing social matters, my companion and I may condescend to make a brief appearance."

"Naturally," Pruett answered. "And may I convey your similar sentiments, Mr. Lane?"

"You may indeed—absent the 'nibs' part, of course."

"Of course."

"What's up, Glyndon?" Mathew asked.

Pruett shrugged. "No idea. Stinson caught up with me in the companionway and asked me to pass the invitation along."

The third officer was a lean fellow with an easygoing, affable manner. Only a year or two younger than Mathew, he had recently joined the ship's company at the request of his father, a longtime friend of Edrington's. According to Pruett, his father was of the opinion that a life at sea was preferable to a career in music, where his true passions lay. He and Mathew had quickly become friends.

"Will you be joining us as well, Glyndon?" Fikes asked.

"I will. Despite my vociferous protestations to the contrary about having to stand watch, Stinson informed me that our sailing master would take my place. It seems the captain wants all senior officers present."

Mathew and Fikes exchanged glances.

"I can't imagine anything has changed since we spoke, but I'd better go check," Fikes said. He excused himself and left.

"Changed?" Pruett asked, turning to Mathew.

"Elton said the captain wants to take the ship to Boswell before we head for home."

"Really?"

"That's the word. We're also to begin exercising the gun crews harder in the morning."

"Sounds exciting, Thad. Have you ever been there?"

"No. This will be my first time."

"Me, too. Maybe we can make enough money so I can get off this tub and resume my lessons."

"Won't that cause problems with your father?"

"It doesn't matter. I've been giving it some thought. I've been a good son all my life, or at least reasonably good, and I've always done what I've been told. But it occurred to me the other day, it's *my* life, don't you see? Not his, or anyone else's for that matter. I'll be twenty-three next month and I've got to stand on my own two feet. I won't make much money playing the violin, but I'll be doing what I want."

Mathew's eyes assumed a faraway look and he stared out over the water. "I had two friends who played the violin once; so did their father. Every Sixth Day afternoon they used to play in the town square."

"Really? They gave concerts?"

"I don't think they were concerts," Mathew said. "Basically, they played because they enjoyed it. Everyone said they were quite good."

"I'm sure they were. Music is something that's in your blood. You either love it or you don't. Did you enjoy the performances?"

"They were a bit difficult to appreciate," Mathew explained. "I'm somewhat tone deaf. Can't carry a tune from here to the port side of the ship."

"You don't say?" Glyndon said. "How awful for you. If there's anything I can ever do . . ."

His friend seemed genuinely taken aback at the concept of someone not being able to appreciate music and was now looking at Mathew as if he'd just learned he had a wooden leg.

Mathew put a hand on Pruett's shoulder and kept his expression somber. "Thank you, Glyndon. That's very decent of you. Now, if you'll excuse me, I'm going to take a turn around the ship and see that everything is in order before we weigh anchor. See you at dinner."

# 4

## Camden Keep, Sennia

GAWL D'ATHERNY WATCHED THE COACH PULL IN through the main gate of the castle from his window. Despite the warmth of the autumn day, the walls of Camden Keep Tower were decidedly cool. The room had been his cell for the last four years. It was circular rather than square and sparsely furnished. A bed, a chest of drawers with a mirror over it, and a writing desk were the only pieces of furniture. The floors were bare.

A sheer drop of over a hundred feet to the cobblestones made window bars unnecessary. Camden Keep was not a place one escaped from, unless it was to the afterlife. Unlike the window, a set of heavy iron bars had been installed between the living area and a small vestibule where the room's entrance was located. They ran from floor to ceiling and were anchored with cement. A rectangle opening at the base was just large enough for his jailers to pass food through. They'd been placed there after Gawl had broken down the door for a second time.

Gawl cocked one eyebrow and folded his arms across his chest as the coach came to a halt. The door bore the emblem of the Archbishop. Two men stepped out. From his purple robes, he recognized one of them as Ferdinand Willis. The other was Edward Guy. Both of them looked up at the same time and saw him watching them. Gawl took a seat and waited.

Five minutes later the door to his cell opened and the Archbishop of Sennia and the country's Regent stepped into the vestibule. They were accompanied by a guard, who gave the king a nervous glance. The man set the two chairs he was carrying down and faced them into the room. He then bowed to the king and withdrew, closing the door after him. There was an audible click as the lock snapped shut. Ferdinand Willis and Edward Guy both seated themselves.

"Your majesty," Archbishop Willis said, inclining his head, "I trust you are well."

"Come a little closer and I'll whisper the answer in your ear."

Some of the color drained out of Ferdinand Willis's face and he gave the bars a quick glance. "Very amusing, your highness, but I believe I will stay where I am. Edward and I have come to talk with you."

"I'm not in the habit of speaking with traitors."

The archbishop shut his eyes, took a long-suffering breath, then folded his hands on his lap. "We've been through all this before, your highness. I recognize that you still harbor ill feelings, but what was done was done for the good of the country. If you would only—"

"Save your breath, Willis. You can get out, and take that vermin seated next to you with you."

A brief look that might have been annoyance flashed across Edward Guy's features, replaced shortly by a faint smile. "As you say, we have discussed all this before," the Regent replied. "We are here to offer you your freedom."

Gawl stuck out his lower lip. "Really?"

"Provided certain conditions are met." Guy did not meet Gawl's eyes, looking at him in the mirror instead.

Gawl leaned back in his chair, stretched his legs out in front of him and crossed his ankles. "I can hardly wait."

Lord Guy continued to stare at the mirror for several seconds, then took a roll of parchment from inside his doublet and slid it under the bars. Gawl glanced at it but made no move to pick it up. For a period of time, no one spoke and the silence in the room grew heavier, broken only by the ticking of a clock on Gawl's desk. The king regarded his visitors, unblinking. When it became obvious he had no intention of examining the document, Ferdinand Willis began speaking again.

"The conditions Edward was referring to are not onerous, I assure you. Indeed, they are minimal at best. You need only acknowledge that your actions were influenced by Mathew Lewin and that you now see the error of those decisions. You must also state that you are willing to voluntarily abdicate the throne. As soon as you do so, we will see to it that you are furnished with a suitable home and an income for the rest of your life. You can return to your sculpting or whatever pleases you. You'll be free, your majesty. Do you understand?"

"Provided I acknowledge Edward's right to hold the regency, leave Sennia, and never return, correct?"

"Well . . . ah, that would be part of it," the Archbishop responded, "but you'd have your freedom—immediately."

"Immediately," Gawl repeated, to himself.

"Yes . . . yes, indeed, your highness. All you need do is sign this paper. Lewin is dead, so it will hardly make a difference to him," the Archbishop said.

"And the others?"

"Amnesty will also be granted to any who supported you," Lord Guy said. "*Provided* they swear an oath of loyalty."

"Convenient," said Gawl. "And what of Siward Thomas? How does amnesty apply to a priest, particularly since he's not a Sennian?"

"Father Thomas has already accepted our terms," Ferdinand Willis said, a little too quickly.

*Only in your dreams, traitor,* Gawl said to himself. "I see. And his signature appears on that paper?"

The Archbishop glanced at Lord Guy, but the Regent's face was impossible to read.

"Ah . . . no, your majesty. Father Thomas's signature is not on this particular document, but we can certainly get it for you if you wish to see it," Willis said.

"Willis, you're even stupider than I thought. Either that or you're by far the worst liar I've ever come across. Let me save us all some time. In the first place, there's nothing you can say to convince me that Siward Thomas has signed anything remotely resembling this piece of trash. And in the second place, if you *do* have something that bears his signature, it's either a forgery or he's no longer available to refute it because he's dead. The result is the same in either case."

"Enough of this," said Lord Guy, still looking in the mirror. "We're here to offer you a way out. Be reasonable, Gawl. Your abdication is in the best interest of the country. No one wants to go through another trial."

Gawl raised his eyebrows. "Another trial?"

Guy smiled, but the smile was confined to his mouth only. "Certain *information* has recently come into our possession about taxes that were misused while you were on the throne, and a secret pact made with Mirdan to sell off the northern provinces to them for your personal gain."

Guy brushed some lint from sleeve. "This is truly distressing. If the high court finds such charges are true, it would be grounds to invoke the death penalty, as I'm sure you know. It's better for all concerned if we did not have to deal with this now."

Gawl slowly uncrossed his feet and leaned forward in his seat, his elbows resting on his thighs. "Particularly since neither the people nor the southern families are going to believe the lies you and this worm sitting next to you have dreamed up.

"No, Edward, I'm not going to make it easy on you. You are a traitor, and there is only one way to deal with traitors. I'm going to kill you. You have my word on that. And afterward, eminence, I'm going to pay you a visit."

The Archbishop swallowed and sat up straighter in his chair. Lord Guy however did not react.

"Indeed, your majesty?" Guy replied. "You may find that exceedingly hard to do without your head. You'll also find that people have short memories."

# 5

# Monastery of Saint Anne, Sennia

FATHER SIWARD THOMAS LAY ON HIS SIDE ON HIS SLEEPING pallet. The cell where he was being kept was a day's ride away from Camden Keep. During the last three years, he had only seen Gawl once since the battle of Fanshaw Castle, and that was at their trial. Neither had been allowed to speak with the other. The trial was a dismal and depressing experience, though not quite the victory Edward Guy had been hoping for.

To the Regent's chagrin, the high court did not impose the death penalty, as he was urging. Instead they convicted him of acting against the interests of the Sennian people and remanded him to the custody of the Church to administer such discipline as they saw fit. It seemed the lies that Ferdinand Willis and Edward Guy had concocted had managed to backfire on them. The basis for Guy's assumption of the regency had been that Gawl was supposedly under the influence of Mathew Lewin and his ring. Of course, wine profits were at the bottom of it, but the sword cut in both directions. If Mathew had truly influenced him, the court reasoned, then neither Gawl nor he could be held fully responsible. At the time, Edward Guy's political base was not nearly as strong as it now was, and he had to abide by the high court's decision.

That turn of events, however fortuitous, had saved them from the headsman's axe. It was a situation, Father Thomas knew, that would not remain static forever, and the proof was lying on the floor next to him.

Earlier that day Josiah Selmo, the monk in charge of his "rehabilitation," had brought him a slightly different version of the parchment Gawl had been presented with. His also required a confession. They wanted him to say that his actions had been controlled by Mathew Lewin, that he now prayed for forgiveness, and that he acknowledged that Ferdinand Wills was the Church's rightful head.

*A separate agenda for everyone,* thought Father Thomas as he read through it.

After delivering the document, Selmo withdrew to give him time to contemplate and consider his response. The parchment was still where Father Thomas had dropped it.

A key turning in the lock caused the priest to look up. They were back sooner than he expected. He got to his feet as Selmo and two monks, both armed with swords, entered the cell. All three were fundamentalists and loyal to the Archbishop. The monks wearing the swords moved to either side of the door and waited for Selmo to proceed.

He glanced at the parchment on the floor, then at Father Thomas. Like his companions, he was a large man, with eyes were so dark they could almost be said to be black. He was also someone who enjoyed inflicting pain. One glance at Selmo's face was enough to convince Father Thomas that Edward Guy was now prepared to finish the job he had begun three years ago.

Selmo picked up the parchment and saw that there was no signature on it. "I thought as much," he said. "You are not going to sign, are you, Father?"

Father Thomas met the monk's eyes and shook his head.

Selmo sighed. "Your actions betray you. We can well suppose what you are thinking."

"You can only suppose that I will not sign. You haven't the slightest idea as to what I am thinking . . . *brother*."

Selmo took a step forward and stopped himself, though apparently with some effort. "I had hoped that you would be making better progress by now. His eminence will be distressed to hear this is not the case. It appears that we must resume our lessons in humility."

"Humility is an admirable virtue," said Father Thomas.

Selmo gestured to the guards.

They seized Father Thomas by the arms and forced him to his knees. One of them yanked the cassock away from the priest's back. Despite the dim light, the scars that crisscrossed his flesh from his previous beatings were obvious. Selmo slowly removed the cat-o'-nine-tails from the pocket of his robe.

"Tell me, brother," Father Thomas said, wincing as the lash bit into his skin, "why do you suppose it took Edward Guy four years to reconstitute the court?"

"I do not concern myself with secular matters, as you should not. The pain is your friend. Give in to it and let it cleanse you of the corruption that has seized your soul."

"At least I can be confident that I have a soul."

After five minutes even the guards began to grimace as the blows cut into the priest's back. First, angry red welts appeared, then blood. Beads of perspiration broke out on Selmo's forehead as he continued to administer the beating. When it was over, the guards released Father Thomas and the priest slumped, his head bowed. In captivity his hair had grown long, and now hung down, covering his face.

Normally, Selmo kept his distance from Father Thomas, but this time he made a mistake. He reached forward and seized him by the chin, pulling his head up.

"Contemplation is the ticket, Father. Lewin's evil is deeply rooted in your soul. We must redouble our efforts—*redouble* them, I say. You must contemplate and pray for—"

The monk did not have a chance to finish his sentence, as Father Thomas's forearm flew upward, striking him between the legs. Selmo's eyes bulged and he let out a gasp, doubling over in the process. A second blow caught him under the chin, snapping the monk's head backward. Before the first guard had time to react, Father Thomas was on his feet. The priest grasped the only chair in the room and brought it around in an arc against the side of the man's head. The guard crumpled to the ground in a heap.

The second guard threw his arms around Father Thomas in a bear hug. The priest reacted by throwing his head backward and bringing his heel down across the man's instep. The man grunted as his nose broke, but he didn't release his hold. Father Thomas thrust backward with all the strength in his legs, driving them both into the wall. The impact broke the guard's grip. As soon as it did, the priest spun around and landed a heavy blow to the man's temple. Like his companion, he went down unconscious.

Selmo was just getting to his knees when Father Thomas's punch hit him in the kidney. He screamed, arched his back, and fell over onto his side, stunned. Father Thomas bent down and retrieved the keys from the pocket of Selmo's robe. "The pain is your friend. Embrace it, brother," he whispered in his ear.

His next punch knocked Selmo unconscious.

Slowly, painfully, Father Thomas slipped his robe back over his head. The wounds stung. He closed his mind to them and spent the next few minutes cutting his blanket into strips with one of the guards' swords. The men were still out when he tied them up. Satisfied the knots would hold, he walked to the door and opened it a crack. Before stepping into the darkened corridor, Father Thomas stood at the entrance to his cell for several seconds. He waited for his breathing to slow, then slipped out and silently closed the door behind him, never looking back.

The Monastery of Saint Anne was old, having been built five hundred years earlier. The first time Father Thomas saw it was the day they'd brought him there following his trial. Apart from being allowed to walk in the courtyard for an hour each a day, a journey of 1,752 paces around, he knew little about the place except that it was farther north and to the west of Camden Keep, where his friend Gawl was being held.

Through occasional conversations with the monks, he learned that the king was still alive. Mathew was another matter. No one had heard from the boy since he disappeared from Fanshaw Castle. The world might believe him dead, but Father Thomas had never given up hope.

It was he who had come up with the story of Mathew being killed by Teanna d'Elso's fireball. Jeram Quinn's identification of the charred remains of a body near the castle helped to corroborate the lie. Possibly, the members of the court were convinced, and possibly they weren't. In the end it didn't matter. The barons were anxious to get the trial over, and without evidence to the contrary, there was little they could do. The rumor of Mathew's death spread quickly throughout the countryside.

*Just as well,* Father Thomas thought as he stood in the shadows under a portico. The main courtyard lay before him. Everything depended on Mathew's finding a way to retrieve his ring. Until he did, Teanna d'Elso and the East were invincible.

Father Thomas watched the monks hurrying to vespers. It was late in the afternoon and the tower bell was ringing. The sun was barely above the rooftops. From where he stood he could see the stables at the opposite end of the courtyard.

At best he had only a few minutes before someone recognized him and raised the alarm, but he couldn't risk moving into the open yet. Frustrated, Father Thomas remained where he was, counting the seconds. Josiah Selmo's face briefly flashed into his mind, and his fingers involuntarily closed around the hilt of the sword he had taken. He couldn't remember ever having hated anyone quite so much. It was a very unpriest-like feeling. He made an effort to push those thoughts from his mind and he studied his surroundings more carefully.

The portico ran along one side of the courtyard and

was open on both sides. Its roof was made of pink and white tiles and supported by a series of slender stone columns and arches. Father Thomas cursed under his breath. There was no cover at the end of it and the stables were perhaps two hundred feet beyond that.

*Life is a series of risks,* he thought.

Father Thomas took a deep breath and began walking. He was halfway to the end of the portico when the timbre of the vespers bell suddenly changed. Several of the monks stopped and looked up at the tower, confused. Father Thomas quickened his steps.

By the time he reached the stables he could hear shouting and the sound of people running behind him. He barely had time to get a bridle on the nearest horse before the door burst open. There was no time for a saddle.

"There he is!!" Selmo shouted.

Father Thomas swung himself up onto the horse's back and ducked as a pitchfork embedded itself in a post next to his head.

"Close the doors!" Selmo screamed. "Close the doors!"

Father Thomas dug his heels into the horse's flanks. Selmo and another man, their eyes filled with rage, attempted to grab his leg as he bolted by them. Both were knocked to the ground.

To Father Thomas, everything happened in a rush—the beads of sweat on their faces, their hands reaching for him. They were gone a second later. The former general of Elgaria's western army, pastor of the township of Devondale, and more recently prisoner of the Monastery of Saint Anne, tore through the main gate at a full gallop, riding toward freedom.

# 6

## On Board the *Daedalus*

MATHEW LEWIN PACED THE QUARTERDECK OF THE *Daedalus* immersed in his own thoughts. The captain's sudden decision to take the ship to Mirdan did not fit with his own plans. Mirdan had been one of Elgaria's strongest allies, and he had no desire to participate in any raids on Prince James's country or its commerce. After years of frustration, he was no closer to his goal than he had been the night he ran away from Fanshaw Castle.

*What did Father Thomas expect him to do?*

He was alone and had neither money nor resources at his disposal.

*You must find a way to get your ring back,* the priest had told him.

Well, he *had* tried, and he'd failed as he had failed with so many things. Teanna d'Elso had taken him in, and he fell for her act like the fool he was. Now his homeland was destroyed, Sennia was under Edward Guy's rule—little more than Alor Satar's puppet—and Mirdan, the Western Alliance's last holdout, was not far behind. The truce Prince James made had only delayed the inevitable. In one instant he had helped Teanna accomplish what Karas Duren, his father, and his grandfather were never able to do.

*One nation, one rule.*

Armand Duren and his brother Eric were perhaps less obvious than their father had been, but they were equally committed to the concept. Now there was nothing to stop them from achieving their goal. It had always been curious to Mathew why Nyngary's soldiers did not take part in the military campaign against Elgaria. Teanna herself was present at several key battles, but from what he'd heard, none of Nyngary's soldiers participated. In the end it made little difference whether their soldiers joined the fight or not. Elgaria had fallen.

The Durens had promptly renamed his country Oridan, after their grandfather.

From time to time rumors reached Mathew about the situation there, and what he heard made his skin crawl. Slowly but surely, Vargoth's provisional government was systematically removing the name of Elgaria from all books, documents, and buildings. People were forbidden to speak its name on pain of imprisonment or worse. Even the maps were being altered to rename the upper two-thirds of his homeland Oridan. The lower third was simply referred to as the Orlock Territories.

Opportunists as always, the Felizians made the best of a bad situation. The fact that their country had not already suffered the same fate as Elgaria owed principally to two things. First, it was convenient for Alor Satar to let Felize harass Western shipping interests; and second, the discovery of the cannon had made the onetime merchants all but invincible on the seas . . . that is, unless Teanna chose to enter the picture. Thus far she had not.

The ship's bell rang six times, indicating the dog watch was nearly over. Mathew's mind automatically registered it and he kept on pacing. Out of respect, the crewmen moved to the opposite side of the quarterdeck. Over the years, Mathew had become a popular and well-liked figure, and it was to him they came when problems arose. Elton Fikes was aware of this, and he seemed content to let their young navigator handle the day-to-day running of the ship.

Mathew continued to pace.

His plan made it imperative they be in Vargoth's capital, Palandol, in one month's time. Through a number of

well-placed bribes, he had learned that the old fencing
master at King Seth's court had retired and they were now
seeking a new one. A Vargothan officer he'd gone out of
his way to befriend had agreed to introduce him to the
master-at-arms. It was an important opportunity he
couldn't afford to miss. Palandol was only a day's ride
from Corrato, where he believed his ring was being held.

Considering his age, it was a long shot, but all of Siward Thomas's lessons were still clear in his mind, and so
were the fencing forms his father had taught him. He knew
it wasn't much of a plan, but at least it would bring him a
step closer to retrieving the ring. How he would accomplish that, he wasn't sure. He only knew he had to try. His
problem now was the captain's decision to take the ship to
Boswell and raid the northern shipping lanes, which
would cause him to miss meeting the master-at-arms in
Palandol.

Mathew knocked at the door of Phillipe Edrington's cabin
at precisely eight bells, and a voice from within called out,
"Come."

Elton Fikes, Glyndon Pruett, and young Fred Warrenton were already there, as was the captain himself.
Edrington's steward, Stinson, stood quietly to one side.
The others were gathered by the stern widow with drinks
in their hands. Warrenton, Mathew noted, was doing his
best to look at ease in a uniform that seemed bigger than
he was.

"Ah, Mr. Lane, there you are," the captain said. "Come
in and join us. Will you have a drink?"

Mathew saluted and stepped into the room. "Aye, sir,
thank you very much."

"Stinson, bring Mr. Lane a glass of that Verdelo. It's
high time we opened the bottle. Is that acceptable?"

"Yes, quite. Thank you, sir."

"I was just in the process of informing your fellow officers of a slight change in our plans. By the way, any luck with the mysterious lockbox?"

"I'm afraid not, captain. I haven't had a lot of time with it. Perhaps over the next few days—"

"Of course," Edrington said with a wave of his hand. "Probably just a lot of religious gibberish."

"But a man was ready to die for it," Fikes told him. "Surely there must be something of importance there."

"To the Church most likely," said Pruett. "The clergy here are a bit odd in their ways. At least that's what my father always told me. They don't think like we do."

"Quite so, quite so," Edrington agreed. "Well, keep at it, Lane. Maybe it will turn out to be a case of diamonds."

The remark produced the obligatory round of laughter.

"I will," Mathew replied with a smile.

The steward returned with a glass of wine, handed it to him, then went back to his position by the dining table.

The quarters reserved for the captain of the *Daedalus* were not overly lavish, but they were certainly well-appointed. It was obvious that Phillipe Edrington had spent a good bit of money on the decor.

The woodwork was rich and dark, and three separate rugs covered the decking, dividing the room into different sections. An oil painting of Phillipe Edrington in full uniform hung on the wall over the sideboard. Mathew thought that whoever had done it must have seen a great deal more in his captain than he did. Not only were the shoulders in the painting wider, the chest was deeper, and Edrington appeared somewhat taller than he was in real life. The artist had obviously taken some license with the jaw as well, giving it a strength and conviction that it normally lacked.

"As I was saying," Edrington went on, "our plans have changed. I was originally going to take the ship to Boswell before we returned home, but it appears this will now have to be postponed."

Mathew started to speak, but a slight shake of Fike's head stopped him.

"A communication I received before we weighed anchor has changed all that, gentlemen. We are not going to Mirdan after all. We are going to Oridan, or northern Oridan, to be more precise."

"Oridan?" Pruett said. "May I ask why, Captain?"

"You may. You'll know soon enough anyway. I intend to rendezvous with two Alor Sataran ships in eight days' time. It seems Oridan's exiled king and his supporters have been harassing the shipping in that area for the last year or so. The local government has been frustrated because they've been unable to do anything about it. They have retained our services to aid them in getting rid of Delain once and for all. If we are successful, the operation should result in a handsome profit, and . . . I say, Mr. Lane. You look as though someone's been walking on your grave."

"My apologies, Captain," Mathew said. "I was born in Elgaria. We moved to Sennia when I was young. I'm afraid I've never gotten used to the name Oridan."

"Ah . . . quite so," Edrington said. "Perfectly understandable. Though I must request, you keep your feelings private should we have contact with anyone from Alor Satar. Felize is officially neutral and we can't take sides."

"Begging your pardon, sir," Fikes said, "but wouldn't that be exactly what we are doing?"

"I don't see it that way," Edrington replied, his eyes darting briefly to Mathew and away again. "Regretful as it is, Elgaria is no more. Therefore, we cannot be taking sides, because there is only one side to take, and that is Alor Satar's. We are being employed by them to do a job."

"Like the Vargothans," Mathew observed.

Startled, Edrington turned around. "Not at all," he said. "The Vargothans are a provisional government and we are acting at their request. As I said a moment ago, if we are successful—and I certainly expect us to be—it will result in a very tidy profit for everyone here, eh? Gentlemen, I must know that I have your fullest loyalty and support. Do I make myself clear, Mr. Lane?"

"Aye, Aye, Captain. You may rely on me to do all that I can."

"Excellent, excellent," Edrington replied, clapping Mathew on the shoulder. "Your services have always been invaluable."

"Exactly what is it the Vargothans want us to do, sir?" Fikes asked.

"I don't have all the details yet. But as I understand it, the basic plan will be for us to lure Delain out. Along with two other ships, we'll be posing as a merchant convoy. Once we have him under our guns, he'll have no choice but to surrender . . . or be blown to pieces."

"Sir, do you really think it's wise to make an open enemy of Delain?" Pruett asked. "There are still a lot of people in his country who support him."

Edrington held his wineglass up to the light and examined its contents. "History tends to be written by the winners, Mr. Pruett. You would do well to remember that."

Pruett looked down at his feet. "Yes, sir, I will."

"The simple fact is that Delain has lost and Alor Satar has won. It would be far more dangerous to make an enemy of the latter. No, gentlemen, it is *we* who will win in the end, and without ever having struck a blow, eh? The Vargothan government is willing to pay a pretty price to rid themselves of this problem. A wise businessman must take his opportunities where he finds them."

Phillipe Edrington raised his glass in a toast and his officers followed suit. Mathew's wine was untouched when he put it back down.

## At Sea, On Board the *Daedalus*

THE JOURNEY TO ELGARIA LASTED SLIGHTLY LESS THAN eight days, and they arrived in Moreland Bay late in the afternoon. As soon as the *Daedalus* passed the headland, Mathew saw the two ships that were waiting for them. Both had dropped anchor about a mile offshore, using the land for camouflage and positioning themselves well into the bay to avoid being seen by any passing ships.

When Lieutenant Fikes was satisfied that they had sufficient room to maneuver, he gave the order to tack and the *Daedalus* came around and dropped anchor. At Mathew's suggestion, as a cautionary measure he ordered the gun crews to stand ready and had a guard boat put into the water. Cannons were the most valuable commodity the *Daedalus* possessed.

Phillippe Edrington came on deck, looking resplendent in his new cloak and best uniform. Despite an offshore breeze and mild temperatures, he was sweating profusely. A silver monocle dangling from a cord attached to his vest swung back and forth as he walked to the starboard rail.

"What ships do we have there, Mr. Fikes?" he asked.

"The *Revenge* and the *Maitland*, sir," Fikes replied, putting down his farsighter.

"Very good. Call away my gig, if you please."

"Aye, sir."

"You will be in command of the ship in my absence. Where is Mr. Lane?"

"Here, sir," Mathew said, coming to attention.

"Mr. Lane, you will accompany me to the *Maitland*. We are going to meet with their commander and his officers. They have a number of questions regarding the waters in this area that you will be able to answer."

"My pleasure, sir."

Five minutes later Edrington was lifted into the air on a chair attached to a hoist. With his plump legs dangling, the side crew carefully lowered him into his boat. Knowing the officers on the other ships were watching, Mathew climbed down, using the boarding nets.

Just below him the crew of Edrington's gig were doing their best to hold the boat steady alongside the hull in the tossing waters. Mathew waited for a second and leapt, but his foot caught on the gunwale and he pitched forward. Fortunately, Brown caught him.

"Good on ye, Mr. Lane," the coxswain said under his breath.

"Thank you," Mathew mumbled, taking a seat.

The seas were running at just over two feet, and it took quite a while to make the trip to the *Maitland*.

"Ship oars," Brown bellowed as they tied alongside the Vargothans.

Phillipe Edrington took the lubbers hole and emerged on deck blinking against the light, while Mathew clambered up and over the side using the nets again.

The *Maitland* was larger and heavier than the *Daedalus*, and the complement of men it carried was easily three times their own. Mathew looked around and noticed a pair of evil-looking contraptions—war catapults—one located at the bow and the other in the stern. He had seen their like before when the *Wave Dancer* was captured in the Tyraine harbor. It had been his first contact with the Vargothans. Off to his right an honor guard was welcoming Phillipe Edrington on board. Behind them a complement of crew members stood smartly at attention.

The governor and captain of the *Maitland* were already

on deck waiting for them. The captain was a man of about fifty with cold blue eyes. He was nearly a full head taller than Edrington. Mathew met his glance and nodded, but there was no acknowledgment from the other man. The snub didn't concern him. Of all the people in the world he detested for their cruelty and callousness, the Vargothans were at the top of his list, and he wanted as little to do with them as possible.

"Ah, here is Mr. Lane," Captain Edrington said. "Thaddeus Lane, may I present Andreas Holt, the governor of Sheeley Province here in Oridan."

Mathew's jaw clenched when he heard the name "Oridan," but he let nothing show on his face. He had a role to play, after all. "Your servant, sir," he replied.

The governor was a barrel-chested man whose shoulders seemed to be straining at the fabric of his coat. His hair was jet black and his eyes nearly the same color. A strong, aggressive jaw and a thick neck barely separated his head from his shoulders. He reminded Mathew of what a bull might look like if it had been transformed into a man.

Holt gave him a tight-lipped smile and shook his hand, then he introduced him to the ship's captain, Tabbert Kennard.

"A pleasure," said Mathew. "Your servant as well, sir."

Kennard and Mathew also shook hands, but instead of releasing his grip, as Mathew expected, Kennard continued to hold on. "You don't have a Sennian accent, Mr. Lane."

"You're quite right, Captain. I was born in Tyraine. My family moved to Barcora when I was nine."

"I see. No sentimental feelings about visiting the old homeland again?" the captain asked, continuing to hold Mathew's hand.

Mathew smiled and slowly disengaged his hand from Kennard's. "The only thing that makes me sentimental is money. The last time we lost a prize it positively brought tears to my eyes."

The governor responded with a short bark of a laugh and clapped Mathew on the back. "A man after my own heart."

"Exactly so," Edrington added. "Now, how can we be of help, your excellency?"

Holt looked at Edrington, then at Mathew. "We can talk in my cabin, gentlemen."

Compared to Phillipe Edrington's cabin, the great cabin of the *Maitland* was spartan. Though it was at least twice the size, the only items it contained were a bed near the window, a dining table with four chairs, a lone chest, and a small writing desk. No decorations hung on the walls, save for a detailed map of the Elgarian coast with its new name.

Holt observed Mathew's reaction and said, "I trust you'll pardon the appearance, but I've had insufficient time to do this cabin up as I might have liked. Most of Captain Wilde's personal effects were sent home to his wife."

"Perfectly understandable," said Edrington. "It's always difficult to change things over from one master to another. I know that from firsthand experience."

"Yes," said Holt.

Mathew saw the look that passed between Holt and Kennard, something his captain had failed to do. "You purchased the vessel from Captain Wilde, then?" he asked.

"Something like that," Holt responded.

"Now, gentlemen," said Edrington, "how may we be of service to you?"

"I think we should wait to discuss the particulars until Captain LaCora arrives," said Holt. "He should be here momentarily. I believe I saw his boat pushing off about the same time yours did. Perhaps you would care for glass of wine while we wait?"

"Most kind of you, sir," said Edrington. "Did you say Captain LaCora?"

"Yes. Raymond LaCora. He's the captain of the *Revenge*."

"Of course," Edrington said with a pleasant smile. "No point telling the same story twice, eh? A glass of wine would be most welcome."

The governor smiled and inclined his head, then he rapped his cane twice on the floor. "I'll send for my steward. Would you also care for some wine, Mr. Lane?"

Mathew leaned back against the bulkhead. "No. Thank you very much."

The steward appeared a moment later and stuck his head into the room.

"Bring Captain Edrington a glass of port. Will that do, Captain?"

"Admirably, sir. Admirably," Edrington said.

A minute later the steward returned carrying a glass of wine on a silver tray. Mathew noted that he was wearing a short sword.

Edrington downed his glass in a single gulp. "An excellent port, Governor. My compliments."

A feeling of growing disquiet began to form in the pit of Mathew's stomach. This was the first time he could recall seeing a captain's steward who needed a sword to carry out his duties. Edrington was typically oblivious.

"Another, Captain?" the governor asked. "Or perhaps something to eat?"

"You are too kind, your excellency."

"Not at all. A sandwich, perhaps?"

"Why, that would do quite well."

The steward looked at the governor for a moment, sketched an ungainly sort of bow, and withdrew once more. The moment he did, Mathew began to search for another way out of the room, positive now that they had walked into a trap. Not only were the governor and Kennard carrying swords, everyone he had seen on the ship had been armed.

"If you'll excuse me for a moment," he said, pushing himself off the bulkhead. "I'd like to see that my coxswain has tied our gig up properly. The seas seem to be picking up, and I wouldn't want it to break loose of the mooring."

Captain Kennard got to his feet as well. "No need, Mr. Lane, I'll have one of our men check on it."

"Please don't trouble yourself. It will only take me a moment."

Without waiting for an answer, he crossed the room, opened the door, and nearly collided with Captain Raymond LaCora, who was just coming in.

The captain was a large man at least forty pounds heavier than Mathew and a good bit taller. A prominent scar ran from his hairline to the top of his right eyebrow. Mathew stepped aside allowing him to enter the room.

"Ah, Captain LaCora, we've been expecting you," the governor said. "Kennard and I have just been entertaining our guests. This is Phillipe Edrington, captain of the *Daedalus*. And this is his navigator, Thaddeus Lane. Gentleman, I present Raymond LaCora of the *Revenge*."

"Always a pleasure to meet a fellow captain," Edrington said, coming to his feet and shaking LaCora's hand.

Mathew did the same, conscious of the strength in the other man's grip.

"Mr. Lane was just on his way to check on Captain Edrington's gig," the governor explained. "With the seas running higher, he wants to make sure it's properly secured."

"It's fine," LaCora said. "We tied alongside you a few moments ago."

"There, you see, Mr. Lane, nothing to worry about," Edrington said.

Mathew looked at his captain, then at Kennard, who smiled back at him.

"Well then, now that we're all here, perhaps we should get down to business," the governor said.

"Of course," said Edrington. "Tell us how we can help you."

"As you know, we have a problem with the former government of Oridan—King Delain and the remnants of his army, to be exact. We know that they are based in the Jarosa Mountains and for the last two years they have raided our towns and killed our soldiers without provocation."

"Horrible," said Edrington.

"Yes, it is horrible," the governor agreed. "But the problem has recently gotten worse. It seems Delain has acquired two warships and has been attacking villages all along the western coast of Oridan from Sturga to Stermark. The ships are fast and well manned. Thus far we have had no success in curtailing his activities. Our allies grow impatient with these attacks and the loss of their property and they insist that something be done about it. According to our sources, Delain has been been using a place called Half Moon Bay to operate from."

"And what allies would those be, your excellency?" Mathew asked.

"Alor Satar to name one. They've suffered the most losses."

"May I say you've come to the right place, Governor," Edrington said. "My men and I will be more than happy to assist you. If I understood your letter correctly, your plan is to draw Delain into the open by posing as a merchant vessel. Of course, I was unaware that he had two ships until this moment, but I dare say that won't be a problem. Naturally, the compensation will have to be adjusted."

"Naturally."

"By God, sir," Edrington went on, pounding his plump fist on the table for emphasis. "I believe you have the right idea. Faced with being blown out of the water or surrendering, the king will have no choice in the matter."

"*Former* king," the governor corrected.

"Yes, yes, the *former* king. My apologies, sir."

"You're quite sure you'll be able to handle Delain's ships?" LaCora asked.

"Without a doubt, Captain. Without a doubt."

"And you, navigator," LaCora said, turning to Mathew,

"the waters off the northern coast are dangerous this time of year. Do you anticipate any problems?"

"I shouldn't think so," Mathew replied, "assuming he comes to us, of course."

"Why does he need to come to us?" LaCora asked.

"If Delain is using the waterways near Sturga to hide in, going in after him would be foolish. There are thousands of bays and inlets where a ship can conceal itself. It would be highly unlikely for us to find him at all, unless we stumble on him by accident."

"You've heard the governor say that we intend to lure him out," Edrington said. "He'll throw down at the first sight of us."

"Perhaps on the open sea, or possibly if we catch him against the shore under the right conditions," Mathew said. "Meaning no disrespect, but a river action is another matter. If they get close enough to board us, I wouldn't want to wager on the outcome. Delain is no fool, or so I've heard."

"How many cannons does your ship carry?" Kennard asked.

"That would be a subject for you and Captain Edrington to discuss, Captain. It's not my place to say," Mathew replied.

"Well, I can't see anything wrong with telling our friends about our armaments," said Edrington. "We carry forty guns including two long nines; one in the stern, and one in the bow. A bow chaser, we call it."

*Fool*, thought Mathew.

"How much do these cannons of yours weigh, Captain?" asked LaCora.

"Weigh? Why, I don't think I've ever been asked that question before. I'm sure they weigh quite a lot; hundreds of pounds, probably. We generally just refer to them by the weight of the balls they fire. A twenty-four pounder would fire a twenty-four-pound ball, and so on. If you see what I mean."

"I'm sure your navigator knows how much each one

of your cannons weigh, don't you Mr. Lane?" asked the governor.

"The exact figure seems to have escaped my memory."

Edrington shot Mathew a look of pure astonishment. "I suggest you concentrate, then, Mr. Lane. Now, gentlemen, I think it would be appropriate to discuss the additional compensation since we will be dealing with two ships. Let me make some quick calculations."

"How are these cannons mounted?" LaCora asked Mathew. "Are they fixed to the decking or movable?"

Mathew didn't answer. Instead he got slowly to his feet, his hand on the hilt of his sword. Kennard and La-Cora did the same. Only the governor remained seated. Edrington completely missed what was happening.

"Two against one, boy," LaCora said, his tone suddenly dangerous. "And there's a whole crew outside the door. You'd never make it."

Mathew said nothing.

Phillipe Edrington finally looked up. "Make it . . . make what? I say, what's going on here? This is most irregular. We've come to conduct business and to help you with your problem."

The governor leaned back in his seat and smiled. "But you *are* going to help us with our problem, Captain."

"Then we need to discuss the compensation."

"Fair enough," Holt said. "What about your life for the cannons?"

# 8

# Elgaria

MATHEW STOOD THERE TRYING TO DECIDE WHAT TO DO.
He was fairly certain he could take the two men in front
of him. Three was another matter. And then what? Fight
his way to the boat and then try to row back to the ship by
himself? He couldn't count on Edrington at all. If it came
to a fight the man would be worthless, if not an outright
hindrance. To compound matters, he had no idea if the
gig's crew was still alive or dead. From past experience in
dealing with the Vargothans, he had no expectation of receiving any mercy from them.

*Better to go down fighting than be hung from a
yardarm,* he decided.

When LaCora drew his weapon, Mathew did the same.
Kennard followed suit.

"*Mr. Lane,*" Phillipe Edrington said, "put up your
weapon at once, sir."

Mathew ignored him and kept his eyes on LaCora and
Kennard.

"Your excellency, I appeal to you," Edrington said.
"Tell your men—"

Phillipe Edrington's words trailed away. He glanced
down to see the hilt of a dagger sticking out of his chest.
Confusion clouded his features, and he looked at Mathew
as a red stain appeared on his shirt and slowly began to
spread.

Edrington took a step forward and opened his mouth to

say something, but the words were forever lost. His eyes rolled back in his head and the captain of the *Daedalus* collapsed to the deck.

Mathew swung his blade around, leveling the point at the governor's throat. Kennard and LaCora both started forward but stopped when Holt raised his hand.

"Gentlemen, I believe we are dealing with a sensible man here. You *are* a sensible man, aren't you, Mr. Lane?"

"What is it you want, Vargothan?"

"Only to talk and perhaps conclude the business arrangement your late captain was discussing."

"I don't do business with murderers."

"Pity," Holt said, winching as the pressure at his throat increased. "Then I suggest you go ahead and kill me. You might even get lucky and kill all three of us, but do you really care so little about your fellow crewmen? They've already been taken prisoner, and unless I give the order, we will begin hanging them one by one. Cooperate and you can buy their lives."

"I told you earlier, I'm not a sentimental man."

"That's a problem, then . . . for both of us."

A drop of blood slowly ran down the side of the governor's neck. No one in the cabin spoke. The silence was broken only by the slap of water against the hull of the ship.

"State your terms," Mathew said.

"First, I would be grateful if you would remove your weapon from my throat. I give you my word that no one will move against you. Second, we would like to employ you to act as our navigator. I was quite serious when I said we wanted to rid ourselves of Delain."

"Your word . . . as a *gentleman*? Forgive me, but people in your employ seem to have a limited future."

Holt glanced at the clock. "You have three minutes, Mr. Lane. Believe me, I would rather not harm your crewmates. We have few enough competent sailors among us as is."

"Why do you need me?"

"I just told you, we require the services of a capable navigator. The waters off this coast are treacherous. The fact is, we are an army contingent, not a naval one. I've already lost two ships and I can't afford to lose any more."

"And . . . ?"

"And I wrote to King Seth requesting more ships so that I could deal with Delain properly. His majesty wrote back expressing his confidence in my abilities, and wishing me all good fortune. So you can see, it would be to our mutual benefit if we strike a bargain with each other."

"Like the last captain of this vessel did?"

"An unfortunate excess of zeal on the part of my officers," Holt said, glancing at Kennard.

"What do I get out of it?"

"Your life, to begin with, and the lives of your fellow crew members; and the *Daedalus* as your own ship, if you like—minus her cannons, naturally."

"Naturally."

"All you need to do is guide us to the inlet where Delain is hiding. You'll help install the cannons on the *Maitland* and Captain LaCora's *Revenge*. After that you can go where you like. I might even arrange a place with us if you wish."

"And the *Daedalus* is just supposed to haul down its colors, let you board her, and carry off her cannons? Somehow I think that's not going to happen, your excellency."

"It might if her second officer told her to."

"I see."

Mathew was confident that Elton Fikes would order any approaching craft blown out of the water. He was also certain that his boat crew would all be murdered just as Phillipe Edrington had been, unless he found a way out of the predicament. The Vargothans wanted their cannons; that much was clear. Whether Felize had cannons, of Vargoth had them, or everyone had them, made no difference to him, but the lives of his men did.

Mathew slowly lowered his weapon. As soon as he did,

the governor slid his chair backward and brought a hand up to his throat. He felt the wound with his fingertips, then removed a handkerchief from the inside pocket of his coat and pressed it against his neck.

"Put your weapons away," he told LaCora and Kennard.

The governor nodded to LaCora, who promptly left the cabin.

"That was a wise decision, Mr. Lane. I'm sure your men will be properly grateful. What I'd like you to do now is to signal your ship and tell them that all is well. You will also tell them that we will be sending two barges across to begin off-loading the cannons."

Mathew leaned back against the bulkhead and folded his arms across his chest. "And they're supposed to believe that?"

"The signal will be sent under the name of the late Captain Edrington," the governor said, glancing at Edrington's body. "You will also invite your first officer to join us here on the *Maitland* for dinner."

The expression on Mathew's face immediately changed, and Holt held up his hand. "I promise that no harm will come to him . . . provided he cooperates. If he doesn't, he can remain our guest until the transfer is completed."

"What happens to the *Daedalus* after that?"

"As I said, it goes free. Our original plan was to lure Delain into the open by dangling a merchant vessel under his nose. Your ship will be that vessel . . . minus her teeth, of course. Once we have him, you and your people can go. Rob blind men for all I care, just do it someplace else. Do we have a deal?" Holt asked, holding out his hand.

Mathew was silent for several seconds before he reached out and took the governor's hand. "Deal."

"Good. It seems you have sense as well as courage. You've made the right decision."

"Apparently, running a government is more complex than I thought."

"More than you know, Lane. Whatever you may have heard about the Vargothans, we know what we are. We're mercenaries, pure and simple. Not a bunch of slip-tongued merchants trying to be something we aren't. There's a winner and loser in every transaction. Play your cards right and you'll come out ahead."

"As long as I get the ship and what we've collected so far."

"We've made a bargain and we'll stick to it. See that you do, too. Whatever financial arrangements you make with your crew is your business. I'm looking to you to keep them in line. They are your responsibility. Do I make myself clear?"

"As crystal. You realize that it's going to take several days to get the guns across and set them up? On top of that, your men will have to be trained . . . unless you want to risk blowing yourselves out of the water in the process."

The look on the governor's face was enough to tell Mathew the Vargothans had no idea what they were dealing with, at least where the cannons were concerned.

"Then we'd better be about it, hadn't we, Mr. Lane?"

Mathew laughed once to himself and walked toward Captain Kennard, who had been watching him with a look of unconcealed contempt throughout the conversation. When their eyes met, he stopped.

"Was there something you wanted to say, Captain?" he asked.

Kennard's hand tightened on the hilt of his blade, and for a second it appeared that he was going to react, but he moved aside and let Mathew pass.

"Pity," Mathew said. "It might have been interesting to see what happens when someone doesn't have their back turned."

Kennard's face colored but he did nothing.

On deck, Mathew saw the boat crew standing by the

mainmast, guarded by a group of five Vargothans armed with crossbows. LaCora stopped at the entry port where he was preparing to disembark.

"How long do you think it will take to fit out the *Revenge*?" he asked.

"That depends."

"On what?"

Mathew looked across the bay at the other ship. "On what sort of preparations you've made to receive the cannons. To begin with, you'll have to reinforce your decking. The recoil from a twenty-four-pound gun will tear the planks apart the first time you fire it. Each cannon weighs over eight hundred pounds. I'd also have your carpenter install a series of gun ports, unless you plan on shooting holes in the side of your ship."

LaCora stared at Mathew for a moment then started to chuckle. "We have a lot to learn. These cannon are new to us. All I know about them is what I've heard and seen. Personally, I think there's no honor in it. If you're going to kill a man, it's better to see his face and look him in the eyes."

Mathew didn't respond.

"You moved quickly in there, navigator. Tell me, what's a wolf doing among these sheep?"

"Foraging."

LaCora smiled and slapped him on the back. "I'll see that preparations get underway at once. You can come across tomorrow and let us know what we're doing wrong." He gestured to the guards, dismissing them, then climbed over the side rail and down into his boat.

Mathew waited until he was gone and walked over to his men. Captain Kennard also came on deck. He and Mathew locked eyes for a moment before he went back down the companionway again.

"Is everyone all right?" Mathew asked.

"As good as can be expected, Mr. Lane," Brown told

him. "They fixed Caukins here a proper bump on the head, but he'll live."

Mathew glanced at Caukins, a tough-looking seaman with a ponytail and a deeply lined face. The man nodded in agreement and gave him a smile that was missing several teeth.

"Can you tell us what's going on?" Brown asked.

"The captain is dead. That man who came on deck a moment ago stabbed him when he wasn't looking. It seems the Vargothans would like us to turn over our cannons to them and then use our ship to lure King Delain into a trap. After that we'll be free to go."

Shock and outrage appeared on the faces of his men. Caukins was all for rushing the quarterdeck and killing as many of the Vargothans as they could. The others felt the same way. Brown, however, proved the most levelheaded of the group.

"What do you think we should do, Mr. Lane?"

"Right now the important thing is to stay alive and bide our time. There are five of us and about two hundred of them. Not encouraging odds, I'm afraid. The good news is they need our services . . . at least for the time being."

"How so?" a sailor named Jervis asked.

"Several reasons," Mathew said. "First, they want the cannons, but they don't know how to use them, or even how to set them up, for that matter. They would like us to teach them how to do both. Second, the Vargothans think they know where Delain is hiding and they seem to have a shortage of navigators to get them there. They would like me to lead their ships up the coast to Half Moon Bay. Last, our new friends want me to send a signal to Mr. Fikes and ask him to join us here so they can take the *Daedalus* with no loss of life or damage to their vessels."

Jervis spat on the deck. "Well, they can go straight to hell, the murdering bastards. We ain't never going to do that, are we, lads?"

Murmurs of assent and indignation came from all around.

"Hold it down, you lot," Brown said. "We need to hear from Mr. Lane."

"This is what we're going to do . . ."

# 9

# henderson

TEANNA D'ELSO SAT IN A SMALL OUTDOOR CAFÉ AT ONE OF the tables with colored umbrellas. Odd music played in the background, coming from two small boxes on either side of an awning made of the same material as the umbrellas. The music was not unpleasant, she decided, only different from what she was used to. The café's name, written in the archaic old tongue, was difficult to pronounce. At least, she assumed it was the café's name; it might have been the name of its owner, for all she knew.

She was the only person there, and indeed in the town.

Directly across from her was, she assumed, a theatre, given the two hundred seats arranged on either side of a center aisle. She had actually counted them one day. And yet, oddly, there was no stage. The only thing in the auditorium other than seats was a large white wall at the front.

She glanced at the other tables and a smile touched the corners of her mouth. She was sitting at the same table where she and Mathew Lewin had sat the first time they met.

In recent months Teanna had spent more time in Henderson, which was the town's name. She knew that worried her father, but it couldn't be helped. Apart from meeting the Guardian, she had other pressing reasons for being there.

Their first meeting happened when she was standing in front of a dress shop looking at the clothing the manikins wore. A reflection in the glass caught her eye and she whirled around to see a man. His sudden appearance frightened her so badly she nearly used her ring in self-defense, but there was something about the calm way he was watching her that made her pause.

The Guardian was a middle-aged man. His hair was brown with gray sprinkled throughout and he was slightly overweight. His clothes were archaic, their style recognizable as the kind her ancestors had worn. She had seen enough examples in the shop windows.

"Where did you come from?" Teanna had asked.

"Here."

"You frightened me. I never heard you approaching."

The Guardian didn't reply.

"Do you live here?"

"I did."

Teanna frowned. "Have you been here long? I've never seen you when I visited."

"Oh . . . quite a long time."

It was a frustrating conversation because he seemed to be talking in circles, and patience was not one of her virtues. Initially, she thought that he was deliberately trying to provoke her, but it soon became obvious the only thing he would respond to were questions. He offered nothing on his own. It also became apparent that he wasn't alive.

The Guardian looked like a person. He could walk and talk and answer questions, but light passed through his body when the angle was just right. During their first meeting, Teanna had learned that he was an image created by the Ancients' machine. That was four months ago.

Now, gazing out across the square, she sipped her glass of wine. The wine had a fruit taste she couldn't quite identify and warmed when it went down. It had taken only a thought on her part to create both glass and bottle.

On the opposite side of the square a large clock sat atop a brass lamp post. The time read two-fifteen. Far above, stars twinkled in the sky, except they weren't stars at all. She knew that now. She also knew it wasn't a sky, but a dome of some kind. She'd discovered that fact on her first visit to Henderson almost four years ago. At night the dome would grow dark, and when it was supposed to be daytime, it grew bright. It was the strangest place she had ever been in—totally empty, for not a soul lived there.

The Ancients were all gone. Once they had brought their machine *online*—a term the Guardian used—the thousands of men and women who once populated the town simply abandoned it. Plates and glasses could still be seen on the tables of their homes. In the three thousand years since the last person had left for the surface, nothing had changed in Henderson.

"Guardian," Teanna said.

After the barest of pauses a section of light appeared in the street near her and took on a liquid quality. Bright spots like fireflies began to move within the liquid. It was fascinating to watch them solidify into the form of a man.

"How may I help you?" the Guardian asked.

"You have a strange accent. What country are you from?"

He told her, and Teanna searched her memory, but the name was one she had never heard before.

"You've never said how you got here," she said.

"I have been here since the beginning."

"But you weren't here before the machine. Nothing was here then. You told me so yourself."

"That's true. The engineers who built this complex often had the need to access online information, so they created me."

"Online? You used that term before. I don't understand it. Do you mean you would tell them what they needed to know?"

"In a manner of speaking, Teanna."

"You're very strange."

The Guardian said nothing.

"I have another question. For the last several months

I've been having dreams about Mathew Lewin. Is it possible he is still alive?"

"I cannot tell you that," the Guardian replied.

"I suppose it's a silly thing to ask," she said. "They identified his body years ago, but every now and then I get the strangest feeling. It's not like it was when he had his ring. I could always tell it was him when he put it on. This is different. Could there be any other people with rings such as mine?"

"No other people possess the rings."

Teanna frowned. There was something in the way the Guardian answered Teanna's question that caused her to go on. "Three were destroyed," she said, counting to herself. "One is in Alor Satar and I hold two of them. That makes six. You told me there were eight."

"That is true."

"Then there are two unaccounted for."

The Guardian's gaze became unfocused for a second. "Only one ring is unaccounted for, Princess."

"That's impossible. I just added them up. There are two left."

"Your statement was flawed."

"My state . . . I don't understand. I asked if there were any other people with rings and you said *no*. If only one ring is unaccounted for, then someone has to have it."

"Correct."

Teanna took a deep breath and counted to five mentally. "All right, who is it?"

"Shakira."

Teanna's mouth dropped open. "The *Orlock* queen? That's impossible!" She got to her feet so abruptly she knocked her chair over in the process.

The Guardian simply stared back at her.

"How could the Orlocks have one of the rings?" she asked.

"They have had it in their possession for three millennia."

"But it can't work for them. They're not people."

"The Orlocks are not people as you use the word, but the ring can and does work for them."

Teanna was so taken aback by the news, she found it difficult to think clearly. "Then why haven't they used it to destroy us?"

"It is not within my program to speculate on the creatures' motives. I can only tell you the ring they possess became active a little over four years ago."

"Four years ago? I don't understand. What happened four years ago?"

"You created the opportunity for them."

# 10

## On Board the *Revenge*

WHEN MATHEW SENT HIS SIGNAL TO ELTON FIKES, Mathew's goal was only to keep his men alive. He had no doubt that the *Daedalus* was capable of sinking one or both of the Vargothan vessels. Not only did his crew know how the cannons worked, they knew how to use them. His problem was getting his men out of the trap they had sailed into.

The *Daedalus* was now at anchor in a bay with enemy ships on either side of her. Moreover, despite the superior firepower the *Daedalus* possessed, the Vargothans were far from helpless. Not only did they have four catapults that could pound a ship into submission in a matter of minutes, their people outnumbered those on the *Daedalus* three to one. In a close action, that would count for a great deal. If the *Revenge* and the *Maitland* succeeded in getting their crews under the elevation of the *Daedalus's* guns, its advantage would be nullified.

Mathew and Fikes stood near the rail on the *Revenge's* quarterdeck and watched as a barge tied alongside the ship. It was late afternoon and the sun was a red ball above the hilltops surrounding the bay. For the last two days Mathew had been supervising the transfer of cannons from the *Daedalus* to the enemy ships. It was slow work and the job was only half complete. Once Fikes had calmed down and examined their situation objectively, he understood why Mathew had agreed to the transfer.

"Another two days and we can get out of here," Fikes said.

Mathew glanced up at the sky. "The weather is picking up a bit, I think."

Fikes looked up and then back at the barge crew. "Careful there!" he bellowed. The men were in the process of securing one of the cannons to a boom. "If the seas continue running like this, it'll be hell bringing anything across tomorrow."

Mathew nodded, turned the farsighter toward the inlet and began examining the base of the hills.

Not receiving a response to his last comment, Fikes turned to him. "What are you thinking, Thaddeus?"

"We've had fog the last two nights," Mathew said. "It looks like same tonight."

"What good will that do us? If we try to make a run for it, we'll still have to fight our way past them, plus they now they have half our cannons."

Mathew swung the farsighter around and examined the *Daedalus* for a moment. "Our friends have one guard boat in the water. With four men, I could swim across and surprise them before they raise the alarm."

"What about the rest of our people?" Fikes asked. "We'd still have four men on board."

"They can go over the side, cut the rudder, and swim to shore. It doesn't look like more than a half mile. We'd pick them up on the other side of that point at the north end of the harbor."

"I don't know, Thaddeus. It's risky."

Mathew started to reply but stopped as the topsails of a sloop became visible. A ship was rounding the point near the entrance to the harbor. With his farsighter trained on the approaching sloop, he could see it was flying Vargothan colors, and from the amount of sail, it was carrying it was obvious that her commander was in a hurry.

The sloop dropped anchor about a hundred yards off

the *Revenge's* stern and immediately lowered a boat into the water. Mathew could see the men at the oars pulling over the waves. Judging from the gold braid on his cloak, their captain was seated in the stern. As soon as they were alongside, he jumped for the chains and clambered up onto the deck. He took in Mathew and Fikes with a single glance but made no effort to introduce himself.

The first officer of the *Revenge*, accompanied by a bosun's mate and an honors party, came hurrying up the port rail to meet him. The sloop captain and first officer shook hands and moved to the opposite side of the deck to speak with one another. After a few seconds the first officer signaled for the bosun's mate to join them. Mathew couldn't hear them, but he saw the mate salute and promptly disappear down the companionway. The governor appeared a moment later.

Mathew and Fikes watched the goings-on with increasing interest. When the meeting was concluded, the first officer, the governor, and the sloop captain all shook hands, then the sloop captain returned to his boat. Interestingly, he made for LaCora's *Maitland* instead of heading back to his ship.

*News to deliver,* Mathew thought.

"Here it comes," Fikes said under his breath as the governor and his first officer walked toward them.

"Well, gentlemen, it appears we've had a piece of good luck after all," Holt said. "It seems we won't have to go out and find Delain. His majesty is coming to us."

Mathew felt his stomach sink. "May I ask how you know this?"

"That man you were both trying so hard not to notice is the captain of that sloop yonder. He's just brought me news that a plan we set in motion some months ago has finally borne fruit."

"So Delain is simply going to sail in here and surrender?" Mathew said.

"Something to that effect," Holt replied. "The surrender part may come later. I'm indifferent on that point. At any rate, he won't sail out of this bay again."

"Why would he do something so foolish?" Elton Fikes asked.

"Because we've given him sufficient motivation. To begin with, Delain thinks there is only one ship here—ours. And due to certain reports we've allowed to fall into his hands, he thinks we were forced to put in here to repair damage to our mizzenmast from the storm earlier this week. The fool is rushing here under full sail."

Mathew folded his arms across his chest and leaned back against the rail, waiting for the rest of the explanation. He had met Delain before, and the king was nobody's fool.

"He also has a personal interest in me in particular," the governor went on.

"How so, excellency?" Fikes asked.

"I recently had cause to crucify the Duchess Elita and her family . . . to set an example for citizens who were slow in paying their taxes. The duchess had been spreading dissension among the good people of Sheeley Province. She and Delain were related . . . cousins or something, I was told."

"You crucified a woman?" Fikes said, taken aback.

Holt adjusted the sleeve of his shirt. "People die in wars all the time, Mr. Fikes. It made an effective example to the population."

"Elita had four children." Mathew said.

The governor took a deep breath. "Yes, that was most unfortunate . . . they took an unconscionably long time to die."

It took every bit of control Mathew possessed to keep him from putting a sword through the governor's heart. The situation had just changed—markedly. It was no longer a matter of escape. Unless he did something, Delain and his men would be blown to pieces once they entered the bay.

"This doesn't change our deal, Holt," Mathew said. "Frankly, I don't care if you destroy Delain here or there. It's no concern of mine. After we get this last gun set up, I'd like to exercise your crews again. They haven't had much time to practice, and I don't think you'd want to put a shot through your own hull in the middle of a battle."

The governor smiled. "Very generous of you, Lane. I'd like you to stay on board and take personal charge of the situation. Mr. Fikes can go across to the *Maitland* and help Captain LaCora."

Mathew shrugged. "Just so long as I get the *Daedalus* when this is over."

Fikes waited until they were alone again then turned to Mathew, his face white. "Making war is one thing, but crucifying women and children . . . and he stands there talking about it like he was discussing the weather."

"There are all kinds of monsters in the world, Elton," Mathew replied quietly.

"Were you serious about what you said a moment ago?"

"If we can get underway quickly enough, we'll try to intercept Delain and warn him."

"Good man," Fikes said. He shook his head and looked down at the water. "I'll take four men and head over to the *Maitland*. I'd appreciate it if you'd remember to pick us up when this is over."

Mathew put his hand on Fikes's shoulder. "Just be off that ship by first light."

"This won't be easy," Fikes said. "The Vargothans aren't going to sit by while you rake them."

"I know," Mathew said. "Perhaps it's a good thing I forgot to teach them the finer points of hitting a moving target in rough seas."

Fikes blinked and stared at his friend for a second. "Such as shooting on the up roll?"

"Or about recoil, and swabbing out. There may have been one or two other things I neglected to mention. Memory fails me."

The expression on Fikes's face was one of astonishment. "You've been planning this?"

"It may have crossed my mind. As I say—"

Fikes laughed. "Memory fails you; yes, I know."

At approximately four o'clock in the morning, as the middle watch was ending, Mathew pushed himself out of his bunk. Andreas Holt had been kind enough to assign him a cabin near the bow of the ship. When he got on deck, he saw that the harbor was shrouded in fog. The air felt damp and cool on his skin. Across the water he could hear the ship's bell on the *Maitland* ring out eight times. Her rigging was little more than a ghostly gray outline. Brown and Caukins were waiting for him amidships with two other crewmen from the *Daedalus*. The men were smoking pipes and talking quietly.

Since the *Revenge* was riding at anchor, there was no one manning the wheel. The only person on watch was a master's mate. Mathew waved and walked over to join him.

"Lucky to draw the morning watch, or do you have friends in high places?"

The man laughed. "Friends in high places," he said. "It ain't so bad."

Brown and Caukins sauntered over to join them.

"Couldn't sleep, Mr. Lane?" Brown asked.

Mathew shrugged. "I thought I'd take a turn around and deck and make sure everything is in order."

"I hear we're going into battle this mornin'," the master's mate said. "We're finally gonna try these cannon you've given us. They sure do make a racket."

"And a bigger hole," Caukins observed.

The master's mate chuckled. "All you Felizians must be light sleepers. Here come two more of your men. Got a regular church social today."

The master's mate never got a chance to say another word. Caukins's dagger plunged into his back, the blow traveling upward and puncturing his lung. He opened his mouth to scream but no sound escaped his lips. Caukins clamped a hand over the man's mouth and held it there until the sailor's knees gave way. After several seconds he died. Brown and Caukins carried him to the starboard rail and dropped him over the side. In the stillness of the early morning the splash seemed unnaturally loud. Mathew and the rest of the men joined them, and using the boarding nets, they climbed silently down into the waters of the North Sea.

With the position of the *Daedalus* fixed in his mind, Mathew started swimming. During the night the seas had picked up again and were running at better than four feet. It took less then five minutes for his breathing to become labored. Blowing salt spray stung his eyes and made it difficult to see clearly. To his annoyance, Brown didn't appear to be struggling at all. The big coxswain flashed him a smile and kept swimming.

Mathew heard the splash of the guard boat's oars before he saw it. Disembodied voices from its crew reached him across the water. The Vargothans might not be sailors, but they had taken the right step in putting a boat into the water. As an added precaution, they had separated the *Daedalus's* senior officers from the crew. The only one left on board was Glyndon Pruett, who had almost no experience in battle.

Mathew signaled for his men to stop. He had made a point of observing the guard boat the previous day and knew it contained only four men. His people would have to be especially careful. One false move would raise the alarm to the other ships. He motioned everyone closer.

"There are four of them," he said, keeping his voice low. "It will take about two minutes for them to complete their pass around the ship . . . perhaps a little more with the seas picking up. Brown, you and Caukins wait until they've gone around the bowsprit, then move to the inside of the *Daedalus*. Go for the two in the stern as they pass.

Bowling, Maddox, and I will be on the outside of the boat and we'll take the men at the bow. Is everyone clear?"

All the sailors nodded.

"Move quietly, men."

"What about the anchor, Mr. Lane?" asked Brown.

"Too risky. Sound will travel in this fog. As soon as we're on board we'll cut the cable and get underway as quickly as possible."

"Beggin' your pardon, sir," Bowling said, wiping spray from his face, "but if that land breeze continues to blow like this, the fog's gonna start breakin' up by first light. I come from a town just north of here."

"Do you?" Mathew said, surprised. He had no idea there were other Elgarians beside himself among the crew.

"Aye, sir. And Maddox here's from Sturga."

Mathew looked at Maddox, who responded with a toothless grin.

"I've been there," Mathew said.

Maddox's grin got even wider.

"All right, lads, let's go."

They all started forward, then froze in place as a spill of yellow light from a lantern in the guard boat's bow briefly lit the water. It disappeared around the ship and the oars' splash receded in the distance. Having a light would make surprising them more difficult. Not daring to risk the sound of his own voice, Mathew motioned for Bowling and Maddox to move away from him, then used hand signals to indicate that he wanted them to go under the surface once the boat came back around. They nodded. The wait seemed interminable.

Mathew removed the knife from his belt, put it between his teeth, and continued to tread water. A strong undertow was trying to pull him away from the ship and he had to fight against it. Chill and damp, the fog floated just above the surface of the water. Occasional breaks appeared and were gone again moments later.

For the tenth time in as many minutes, he reviewed the plan in his mind. Given the circumstances and the need for silence, he knew there was no way to coordinate their timing. But Brown had a good head on his shoulders, and from what he'd seen of Caukins, he would do well, too. Bowling and Maddox were another matter. Both were topmen, and he had no idea how they would react once things started to heat up. Topmen had their own way of doing things.

The sound of someone laughing in the guard boat interrupted his thoughts. A watery light followed as the Vargothans pulled around the *Daedalus's* stern.

He waited several seconds, took three deep breaths, and ducked under the surface. His own buoyancy tried to push him back up and the salt made his eyes burn. Just when he thought his lungs were ready to burst, a dark shape slid past his head. Mathew kicked his legs and broke the surface of the water, only to be thumped on the head by one of the oars. Colored lights exploded in front of his eyes and a startled exclamation came from inside the boat.

Mathew grabbed hold of the oar with his left hand, thrust himself partially out of the water, and threw his knife with the other. The surprised sailor fell over sideways, dead. He felt the boat lurch as Brown and Caukins came over the top of the gunwale from the opposite side. Caukins seized the nearest sailor by his hair, yanked backward and cut his throat. The second man died of a broken neck courtesy of Brown. Bowling and Maddox dragged the last sailor out of the boat and held him underwater until he stopped kicking. It was over as quickly as it had begun.

Mathew took a few seconds to clear his head and looked at the eastern horizon. The fog made it difficult to tell, but the sky looked lighter to the east. He motioned for Brown and Caukins to go up into the ship. Maddox slid over the side and swam toward the anchor cable, while Bowling went for the stern. Thus far everyone was acquitting themselves well. Mathew used the boarding nets to climb up.

The moment he set foot on deck of the *Daedalus*, he knew something was wrong. There was no sign of anyone. When he'd left a day ago, there were sixty-five men there. On the opposite side of the deck, Brown faced him and turned his palms up. Mathew looked at Caukins, who shook his head, equally puzzled. At that hour of the morning a number of people should have been up and about. Many would have slung hammocks on deck because of the milder conditions.

*"Oh, God,"* came Bowling's voice from the stern. *"Oh, God."* The sound came from belowdecks.

Mathew dashed for the companionway and the others followed. They located Bowling, slumped against the bulkhead near the entrance to the stern hold, his face the color of chalk.

"Dead," Bowling whispered. "They're all dead, Mr. Lane."

Mathew pushed past him and stared into the hold. The bodies of his crewmates were everywhere, stacked on top of one another. Their throats had been cut. Unseeing eyes stared back at him in silent accusation. It was the most horrible thing he had ever seen. At first his mind refused to accept it. A moment later his stomach revolted and he threw up. Brown, Caukins, and Maddox were equally stunned.

Mathew forced himself to drag a deep breath into his lungs and staggered to the side of the passageway. He had to think.

"Check the rest of the ship," he told Brown and Caukins. "Do it quickly and quietly. I want no noise. Maddox, take Bowling and start working on the anchor cable. Send word to me as soon as it's ready to go."

"What about the men, Mr. Lane?" asked Maddox. "We can't just leave 'em here like that."

"We don't have time to bury our friends now."

"But—"

"Listen to me, Maddox: I can't help those men, but I can help our crewmates who are still alive on the *Maitland*. They and the king are our first concern. Delain will be here soon, and he's sailing straight into a trap. I don't intend to let that happen."

"All right, lads," said Brown. "You heard what Mr. Lane said. Let's jump to it."

Mathew's hands were shaking. Whether it was from anger or shock, he didn't know. He squared his shoulders and forced his legs to start moving toward the companionway. The rest of the men dispersed to carry out his orders as he stood alone at the bottom of the stairs, still trying to compose himself.

He knew that the survival of his men depended on his keeping a clear head. Equally important was their confidence in him. It had to remain unshaken. He was sick to his stomach, but if he had to convey the impression of being calm, then by God he would. Slowly, methodically, he started up the steps.

Back on the deck, Caukins hurried toward him. "We found four alive in the forward hold, Mr. Lane. They ain't hurt."

"Thank God. Who do we have?"

"Mr. Pruett, Mr. Warrenton, Grady, and Harkins, sir."

Glyndon Pruett and the others looked haggard but appeared unharmed. It felt like a weight had been lifted off his shoulders.

"They fell on us last night, Thad," Pruett explained. "I was supervising off-loading the one of the cannons when they came over the side. There was nothing I could do. They killed Stinson right in front of me. The rest of us were rounded up and locked in the forward hold. We heard the screams coming from the stern. We—"

"All right, all right," Mathew said, putting a hand on his shoulder. "Are the rest of you men in one piece?"

"Yes, sir . . . I mean, aye, sir," Warrenton stammered, white-faced.

Grady and Harkins both nodded.

A dull thud from the stern turned everyone's head at the same time.

"That's Bowling," Mathew told them. "We're going to slip the cable and make a run for it. Mr. Grady, how long will it take us to get the ship underway?"

"Caukins said everyone on the crew's been murdered. Is that true, Mr. Lane?"

Mathew took a breath. "It's true. Listen men, I know how you all feel, and I feel the same way, but right now we need to move. We have very little time. The second they know we're missing, they'll fall on us from all sides, so we cannot waste another second. I ask again, how long will it take us to get the ship ready to sail?"

Grady stared at Mathew and slowly shook his head. "We can't."

"What do you mean, we can't?"

"They cut our rudder, Mr. Lane. We tried to stop 'em. That's how I got this knot on my head."

That news only momentarily surprised Mathew. Of course the Vargothans had cut the rudder. He and Fikes had thought of it—why shouldn't they? What better way to ensure that the *Daedalus* wouldn't make a dash for the open sea? He could have kicked himself for his own stupidity.

"All right, we'll have to splice it," he told Grady.

"In the dark, sir? I don't see how we can."

Mathew grabbed him by the front of his shirt and yanked him closer. "Unless you feel like hanging from a cross or having your throat cut like the rest of your crewmates, you'll find a way to get it done. Jury-rig the damn thing or weave a new cable if you have to, but I want that rudder fixed within the hour."

"Aye, sir," Grady said. "I'll need some help."

"Take whoever you have to," Mathew said. He turned

him by the shoulders and gave him a push. Next he addressed Pruett.

"Glyndon, gather the rest of the men and see that we're ready to move the moment that cable is repaired. Mr. Harkins, I require your assistance."

Pruett nodded, tight-lipped, and started off toward the stern. Mathew and Harkins went the opposite way. He spared another glance at the horizon as they walked down the deck. If an hour remained before daylight, it would be a miracle. He prayed the fog would hold until then. For the next fifty minutes he and Harkins moved along the deck working feverishly, loading each of *Daedalus's* remaining twenty guns.

The false predawn light gave way to a red glow on the horizon that gradually turned into morning as Glyndon Pruett trotted toward him. Mathew was already sweating profusely.

"Bowling says the anchor cable is ready to go."

"How's Grady doing?"

"Better now that he and Warrenton can see a bit. Another five or ten minutes and we should have it."

Mathew was about to reply when he heard a horn blowing across the water from the direction of the *Revenge*. A minute later there was an answering trumpet from the *Maitland* and another from where the sloop was anchored. He could just make out the shape of the nearest ships. Maddeningly, the fog was beginning to burn off, just as Caukins predicted it would.

*"Damn,"* Mathew said under his breath. "Well, I imagine they know we're gone."

The rapid rat-tat-tat of a drum and of men shouting on the *Maitland* drifted across the water. It was followed by the recognizable sound of the ship's anchor being hoisted.

"Tell Mr. Grady I would appreciate his haste," said Mathew.

Pruett nodded once and sprinted toward the stern.

The next five minutes were the longest of Mathew's life. While he waited, the land breeze continued to freshen, all but blowing the fog out of the bay as the sun climbed higher in the sky. Across the water he could see that the sloop was already moving; so was the *Revenge*. He stood there transfixed, watching the enemy ships draw nearer.

"Rudder's repaired, sir." Brown's cry made him jump. Apparently, the coxswain had concluded there was no longer any need for secrecy.

"Get the men on board and cut the cable!" Mathew shouted. "Top gallants and royals. Caukins, put the wheel over and bring her into the wind."

"Hard over it is, sir," Caukins answered, repeating Mathew's last order.

"Mr. Pruett, would you be kind enough to take a slow match and stand ready at the bow chaser, please? You are not to fire except on my command."

"Aye, sir."

Slowly, inexorably, the *Daedalus* began to turn as the wind filled her sails. Mathew hurried along the deck to help Brown and Caukins secure the main brace. Grady and Warrenton scrambled over the side and waved to him. On the opposite side of the deck Pruett and Bowling quickly descended down the lines at a frightening speed, having just loosed the mainsail. With as few men as they had, it would be all they could do to get the ship to maneuver.

A loud boom and a puff of smoke came from the bow of the *Revenge*, and a hole appeared in the *Daedalus* mainsail.

"It appears our friends are fast learners," Pruett said, coming to join him.

Two more booms followed and a cannonball streaked overhead, causing them both to duck.

"So it appears," Mathew said.

"The sloop's making for the harbor entrance," Pruett said.

"Man the long nine at the stern, Glyndon. We'll be in position in another minute. You'll only have time for one or two shots. Make them count."

Everything about the situation urged him to race down the deck, but he forced himself to walk. Grady was already waiting at the bow chaser.

Mathew watched the progress of the *Daedalus* for a moment then turned back and yelled, "Let her fall off another point, Mr. Caukins."

"One point it is, Mr. Lane."

"Are we sighted in, Mr. Grady?"

"Aye, sir."

"On the up roll then . . . ready, steady, *fire!*"

The bow chaser roared out and Mathew felt the deck move under his feet. He watched intently as the ball struck home on the *Revenge*'s forward quarter. On the starboard side four shots fired by the *Maitland* flew overhead and well wide of the ship.

"They needs a bit more practice, I'd say," observed Grady.

"Yes," Mathew replied. "It seems that I forgot to teach them about adjusting the aim when the deck is moving—"

A loud bang from the *Daedalus*'s stern gun stopped him in mid-sentence. He saw the shot strike *Maitland*'s waterline. A cheer went up from the men on his ship.

"That's holed her for sure, Mr. Pruett!" Bowling yelled out.

Seconds later he and Pruett were dead as three shots fired by the *Revenge* struck the quarterdeck in rapid succession. Blood and bone were everywhere.

Mathew pulled his attention away and yelled to Caukins, "Hard over. Keep her coming around."

The *Daedalus* continued to swing, presenting its broadside to the *Revenge*. Two more cannonballs streaked overhead; one punctured another hole in the mainsail, the other fell short of the bow. Mathew and Grady moved along the starboard rail, sighting and firing each of their guns.

"There goes her foremast!" Warrenton screamed.

"And the top gallant mast," Caukins added, grabbing Mathew's arm.

Mathew turned in time to see the mast on the *Revenge* slowly topple like a felled tree. He grabbed his farsighter and trained it on the enemy ship. Men were running back and forth on her decks carrying axes, trying to clear away the wreckage.

He rapidly calculated the distance between the ships, knew it would be close, but estimated they had sufficient headway to cross the *Revenge*'s bow and head out to sea. The *Daedalus* was the lighter and handier of the two ships, and the *Revenge* lacked any long range guns to damage them. The *Maitland* was simply too ungainly to sail them down once they reached open water. The problem was getting out of the bay in one piece.

As he considered the problem, the deck lurched violently and the rear section of the *Daedalus* burst into flames. Projectiles fired by the catapults on both the sloop and the *Maitland* found their marks at the same time.

Brown, Maddox, and young Warrenton came sprinting down the deck toward him.

"We're on fire, Mr. Lane!" Maddox shouted.

"I can see that. Mr. Warrenton, get one of the pumps out of the bilge, if you please, and see if you can slow it down."

"Aye aye, sir," Warrenton answered, and sped off.

"Mr. Lane, there's a ship just over the horizon to the northeast," Brown told him.

Mathew looked in the direction Brown was indicating. "Damn," he said under his breath. "That has to be Delain."

Another shot from the *Revenge* crashed into the deck and blew a hatch cover skyward. They all ducked out of reflex.

"Where the devil is Warrenton with that pump?" Mathew snapped.

"Here, sir!" Warrenton yelled, emerging from the forward companionway.

Maddox ran to help him, and together they got the pump started. With the ship's dry timbers, the fire was spreading rapidly. Another fireball from the sloop fell short, sending up a plume of steam from the water.

"Brown, you and Grady reload the guns and see if we can give our friends something to think about. Concentrate on their masts and sails."

Mathew clasped his hands behind his back and turned back to the ships pursuing them.

It would take another two minutes for the *Daedalus* to complete its turn. The *Maitland* had finally begun to move and was now coming around. As a result of the damage they had inflicted, the *Revenge* was falling away. But at the last moment it swung wide to port, presenting their broadside to them. A series of smoke puffs came from the decks, and the sound of its guns reached him a moment later. One cannonball managed to strike their stern quarter, while the others scattered wildly with no discernable pattern. Without warning another puff of smoke came from the *Revenge*. It was followed by two loud explosions and an orange tongue of flame that leaped up from her deck.

A cheer went up from the men on the *Daedalus* as they realized that two of the *Revenge's* cannon had just exploded.

"*The value of swabbing out a gun's muzzle,*" Mathew said to himself.

He grabbed the farsighter and trained it on the horizon. The topsails of Delain's ship were much closer now. If he entered the bay, Delain would have three ships to contend with instead of the one he was expecting. Injured as she was, the *Revenge* was still dangerous, and the *Maitland* and the sloop were still largely unharmed. They were the main problem.

Farther down the deck he heard the *Daedalus's* guns roar out one after the other. Most of the shots struck home, dismasting the *Revenge* and holing her badly. She continued to fall farther away.

"Shall I make for the ocean, Mr. Lane?" Caukins yelled.

Mathew didn't answer.

"Mr. Lane?"

"No," he said, "we're coming about."

# 11

## On Board the *Daedalus*

CAUKINS LOOKED AT HIM AS IF HE HAD LOST HIS MIND.

"The king is doomed if he enters this bay," Mathew told him. "The moment he does, the sloop will seal the entrance and the *Maitland* will pound him to pieces."

"But—"

"All hands to the braces!" Mathew bellowed. "Wear ship. We're coming around."

Brown and Grady exchanged glances and returned to the ship's wheel. Maddox and Warrenton came trotting up as well. Mathew quickly explained the situation to them.

"Gentlemen, once we come about, we will hold the weather gauge on the *Maitland*. I intend to cross her bows and rake her. She cannot be waiting for Delain when he clears that point."

There was a pause.

"All right, lads," Brown said. "Let's jump to it. All hands to the braces. Mr. Lane, a bit of help would be appreciated, sir. We're a little short on crew at the moment."

Mathew smiled, clapped Brown on the back, and took up a position at the main brace along with Maddox. Brown and Warrenton took the opposite side.

"Ready, men? *Now!*" Mathew yelled. "Hard over the wheel, Caukins."

Mathew stood on the charred planks of the quarterdeck watching as the distance between the *Daedalus* and the *Maitland* closed. As he expected, the moment he began his turn, LaCora turned with him, not wanting to let him cross his bow.

"Fire as you bear!" Mathew called out.

In less than thirty seconds all twenty guns along the *Daedalus*'s starboard side had fired. Brown and the rest of the men were now working frantically to reload them. The *Maitland*'s reply was a single broadside that blasted the forecastle of the *Daedalus* and much of the ship's bow to pieces. Grady went down with a splinter sticking out of his shoulder. A second volley hit the ship moments later, rocking it. Mathew ducked as more parts of the forward deck and railings were blown away. Other balls slammed into the hull. Black smoke began drifting up from the forward hatches.

"Concentrate everything we have amidships, men."

For the next four minutes Brown, Maddox, Mathew, and Warrenton pounded shot after shot into the *Maitland*'s midsection. The last salvo produced the result Mathew had been praying for.

The explosion was an awesome and spectacular thing to see.

He had no idea which of their shots had struck the *Maitland's* powder magazine, but when it did there was a terrific bang and a white-orange flash. One moment the ship was there and the next it was gone. He felt the concussion seventy-five yards away. A blast of hot air followed, and all that remained of the *Maitland* was a burning hulk on the water. There was a metallic taste in his mouth.

"Fire in the forward hold!" Maddox yelled, pointing at the hatch.

Mathew spun around and saw a tongue of orange flame leap from the hatchway. Smoke was now coming from the sides of the ship. In the heat of battle he had completely forgotten that they were burning. And as if things weren't bad enough, the *Revenge* was now coming round again, having cleared away her wreckage.

Brown dashed to the forward companionway to investigate, but barely got a foot on the first step before the fire forced him to retreat. He looked at Mathew and shook his head. It was clear the *Daedalus* was lost.

Mathew signaled for Warrenton to join him.

"Mr. Warrenton, my cabin is just below us. Would you be good enough to retrieve that lockbox we picked up in Coribar? The fire is confined mostly to the forward area so you should have no difficulty."

"Aye, sir," Warrenton said with a salute.

As soon as he returned, Mathew called the remainder of his crew together.

"Gentlemen, as soon as we wear ship, you will abandon it and swim for shore. Mr. Fikes and the rest of our people will be waiting for you on the other side of that point. I regret that our voyage has not been a more profitable one, but it has been my privilege to serve with you. Your best chance will be to make your way north toward Anderon and then cross the border into Alor Satar. You should be able to pick up a ship in Sturga that will get you home again."

"What about you, Mr. Lane?" asked Warrenton.

"I will stay aboard as long as I'm able. If Brown and Maddox will linger with me for a few more minutes, I'd like to see if we can reposition the bow chaser so we can fire it down into the forward hold."

Warrenton's mouth dropped open. "You're going to sink the ship?"

"I am. The mouth of this bay shallows rapidly and only one ship at a time will able to get through. I intend to slam the door shut on our friends as permanently as I'm able. The *Revenge* can rot here until the wreckage is cleared away."

Protests came from everyone at the same time, but Mathew was having none of it. Beneath his feet the pitch that sealed the deck seams was already beginning to ooze, and several planks were buckling in spots. They had very little time left.

The *Daedalus* was moving sluggishly, but she came around and began her run toward the mouth of the bay. All the while, Mathew, Brown, and Maddox worked feverishly to reposition the gun. When he was satisfied, he shook hands with both men and ordered them over the sides. Warrenton and Caukins had already gone.

Through the billowing smoke near the entrance to the harbor, Mathew saw that the commander of the sloop had positioned his ship to block their escape. He watched the flames run up the mizzenmast and consume the sails. In a matter of seconds they spread to the yardarms, climbing higher still. The smoke billowing from the hatches was making it harder and harder to see.

The box Warrenton had gotten for him was sitting on the coil of rope where he had placed it. Mathew stared at the lock for a second and closed his eyes. Four distinct clicks followed in succession as the locks sprang open. He had not wanted to use the rose gold ring's echo again because it was dangerous to do so. Shortly after he had first put on his ring, he had learned that an affinity existed between anyone who wore them—it was possible to feel their minds. To the world, Mathew Lewin was dead, and each time he accessed the echo, he had no idea whether it reached Teanna. He doubted it, because it was so weak, but better not to take any chances. Under other circumstances he might have let the box go, but a man had died trying to protect its contents, and his instincts told him it might be important.

He found a sheet of parchment wrapped in oilskin, opened it and noted the writing in surprise. It didn't look like any language he had ever seen before. After a few more seconds of study he concluded that he was looking at a code of some sort, but this was not the time or place to try and break it. A burning spar crashing to the deck jerked his attention away from the parchment. He quickly wrapped it back in the oilskin and tucked it into his breeches.

Barely a hundred yards separated the two ships now. Flames were leaping from the hatches of the *Daedalus* and smoke was pouring from its gun ports. Behind him, fire was gradually inching its way from the bow in his direction, devouring anything capable of burning. It was then that Mathew realized there was no way he could reach the bow chaser and scuttle the ship. The heat on his neck and back was already too intense.

*"Marvelous,"* he said under his breath.

He looked at the sloop again and quickly reached his decision. Through the smoke he could see men running back and forth on her deck, pointing at him. If what he intended was going to work, his timing would have to be perfect. Their commander had made a fatal mistake. He had succeeded in trapping the *Daedalus* inside the bay, but now he had a fire ship bearing down on him at full speed and precious little room to maneuver. Behind him the *Revenge* had put on more canvas and was closing fast.

*Let them come.*

Mathew let the ship fall another point then secured the wheel in place with a rope.

*Fifty yards,* he said to himself.

When he turned to check on the *Revenge* again, he was forced to shield his face from the heat, so close were the flames. He shrugged out of his coat and tossed it aside.

*Twenty yards.*

At the mouth of the bay he saw Delain's ship move past the point.

*Close enough.*

Mathew ran to the starboard rail and dove over the side. The last thing he heard before he hit the water were the sounds of men screaming, lumber breaking away, and the awful crash of two ships colliding with one another.

# 12

## Corrato, Nyngary

TEANNA D'ELSO KNEW THE INSTANT MATHEW ACCESSED the Ancients' machine. The contact had only been momentary and exceedingly weak, but there was no doubt it was him. Impressions of fire and a ship flashed into her mind but disappeared so quickly she questioned whether they were real. The Guardian's refusal to answer her questions about whether Mathew was still alive was further confirmation. She'd had enough experience with politics and politicians to know when someone was avoiding her questions. She transported out of the cavern and returned to her apartments.

To her surprise, there were two notes waiting for her. One was from her cousin Eric, asking her to join him on the veranda in an hour. The other was from their spy in Garivele. She read the second note quickly and tucked it away in her book safe. She would deal with it later.

Her father had made no mention of Eric's arrival. It was an annoying interruption; nevertheless, she composed herself and went to meet him. Showing emotions in public was something her mother would never have done—and neither would she.

*Typical of Eric,* she thought.

He had a tendency to pop in unannounced. He was the younger of her two cousins, and far more cunning than his brother Armand, who had assumed Alor Satar's throne following their father's death. A brilliant general by all accounts, Armand now devoted the majority of his time to strengthening the country's military forces. He was apparently content to leave running it to his younger brother, as Regent. Where the complexities of politics bored Armand, Eric excelled at them.

Teanna was still angry with Eric for invading Sennia without her knowledge. Despite the fact that it was her fireball that killed—or was supposed to have killed—Mathew Lewin, in her mind Eric bore the lion's share of responsibility by forcing her into such a position. At least that was the way she had rationalized it. But Mathew was alive, she just knew it. Family would always come first—it had to. When time permitted, she would find him. She would explain to Mathew why she had acted as she had. It was desperately important to her that he understand.

The veranda was lit at both ends by flickering gas lamps. It was not quite dark yet, and there was a mist in the air that created haloes around the lamps. The recently rediscovered electric lights were certainly more efficient and less costly than gas, but the illumination they provided was hard on the eyes and Teanna preferred to remain with what she knew. She supposed she would give in eventually.

Eric was seated at a table, waiting for her. He got up as soon as she entered the room and embraced her. When the hug lasted longer than it should have, Teanna gently disengaged herself and sat down. Eric did the same.

"It's good to see you again, cousin," he said.

"And you. What brings you all the way to Corrato?"

"Do I need a reason to visit my family?"

Teanna smiled at him with her lips together.

"At any rate," Eric continued, "I was in Umera and thought I would stop by to see how you're getting on."

"I'm fine. Why the concern?"

Eric took her hand. "I've always been concerned about you, Teanna," he said. "Is that so unusual?"

Teanna took a deep breath and met his eyes.

Eric made a dismissive gesture and sat back. "All right. A month ago I visited the Lirquan royal court. You know that Humphrey's wife passed away a little over a year ago."

"And . . . ?"

"Humphrey has always been fond of you, and I thought the two of you might hit it off."

"He's five years younger than I am *and* he has pimples."

"He's only seventeen, for God's sake," Eric protested.

"So?"

"He won't have pimples forever."

"Humphrey is a pimple," said Teanna, "and he doesn't bathe, at least not as far as I could tell."

Eric took a deep breath and looked over the railing at the fountain below them. Three magnificently carved horses rose out of the water while men struggled to hold them back. Around the perimeter of the sculpture were a host of small cherubim with water spouting from their mouths. A bearded pagan god stood in the middle of the pond holding a trident.

"Don't we have one like that in Rocoi?"

"I believe so," Teanna said. "I saw it when mother and I came for Uncle Kyne's funeral."

"Really?"

"I asked Father to have the sculptor come here and make one for us."

"Hmph," Eric said, his eyebrows going up. "Honestly, Teanna, you've not shown the slightest interest in anyone who's called on you. What's the problem?"

"There *is* no problem. I'll marry one day, but it will be someone I choose. Why is it so important for us to form an alliance with Lirquan?"

"You make it sound so venial."

"Isn't it?"

"*No,* it isn't. It's the way things have been done for thousands of years, and I see no reason to change."

"I'm not a piece of baggage you can simply ship off to the other side of the world because it's convenient," Teanna told him.

"No, no, of course you're not. But an alliance with Lirquan would go a long way to strengthening our position in that part of the world."

"Leave me out of your plans, if you don't mind. I have enough to do right here."

"Such as?"

"Such as running a country. In case you hadn't noticed, Father leaves most of that up to me. He's done so ever since I turned twenty."

"I see."

"We are putting in a new road from Danover to Cirella, and a delegation from Bajan will be here next week to discuss the new trade agreements. There are also a number of schools and universities that need to be completed this year."

"Obviously, you've been very busy. Wouldn't it help to share these burdens with a partner?"

Teanna sighed mentally and looked out the door, wishing that Eric would get to the point. All the verbal fencing was tiring. "It would," she said. "We've been at war in one form or another since I was a child. I thought our people might enjoy a change. I'd like to do something to make their lives better."

Eric considered the concept for a moment, or appeared to, then abruptly changed the subject. "Did you know that Siward Thomas escaped three weeks ago?" he asked.

Teanna swung around to face her cousin. "Are you serious?"

"It seems he killed one man in the process and severely injured two others. We think he's headed back to Oridan to find Delain and his people."

"What difference will it make if he does?"

Eric shrugged. "Perhaps some, perhaps none. The fact is, Thomas is a dangerous man, not to mention an extremely competent general, priest or not."

"A general without an army."

"Delain not only has an army, but the beginnings of a

navy. The Vargothans have been hunting him for two years without success. Unfortunately for us, Delain is getting stronger rather than weaker. We need to put an end to him once and for all. If the reports Vargoth has been sending back are accurate, he has better than forty thousand men at his command."

Teanna's eyes opened wider. "Forty thousand. The last I heard he had five thousand men."

"That was two years ago, dear. We have every reason to believe there are other parts of his army hiding in the mountains over the western border in Mirdan."

"But—"

"That's not the worst of it. That fool Edward Guy has been so nervous about an uprising by Gawl's supporters, he took it on himself to announce another trial—this time for treason. Two days after the news became public, the country erupted in civil riots. Fourteen commanders from Sennia's Southern and border armies promptly defected along with their troops and crossed the border into Elgaria."

"That's insanity," Teanna said. "The Orlocks control the lower third of the country."

"Apparently, their general, Arteus Ballenger, is not unduly worried about the Orlocks. He took upward of ten thousand men with him when he left."

"I begin to understand," Teanna said. "Marry me off to Humphrey and you cement relations with Lirquan and gain an ally in the south."

Eric smiled at her. "You should have been a man, cousin."

"If I were, we'd probably have a bigger mess than the one you've created. How did you let things get so out of hand?"

Eric made an annoyed gesture. "I can't be everywhere. That's why I need to know my back is being defended. Three weeks ago I made contact with Shakira. I believe it will be possible to forge an alliance with the Orlocks."

Teanna's mouth dropped open. "You want to form an alliance with the creatures?"

"Why not? My father did, and I honored the bargain he made. They've fought with us before. I don't see why they wouldn't do so again. War is looming, cousin. We need to act now."

Eric's news about wanting to form an alliance with the Orlocks caused a knot to form in Teanna's stomach. She forced herself to consider the possibilities one at a time. "Have you ever asked yourself why the Orlocks went along with your father in the first place?"

"Obviously, because they wanted a country of their own," Eric answered. "As long as we keep them confined, they're controllable. It's better to dance with the devil you know than the one you don't."

Teanna looked at her cousin for a moment before responding. It was probably as good a time as any to tell him what she had learned in Henderson and about the note her spy had sent back. "Well, here's something you don't know, cousin: Your friend Shakira has one of the rings."

The pleasant smile evaporated from Eric's face.

"How do you know?" he asked, his tone suddenly cold.

"Let's just say I know and leave it at that. We have a man close to Seth. I also received a message from him just a little while ago. It seems King Seth and Shakira recently met in Garivele."

"Seth and Shakira? Why? To what purpose?"

"I don't know. Let me ask you this . . . If Shakira wanted to raise an army, do we know how many Orlocks she would have?"

Eric thought about it and shook his head. "No, not really. I was only an infant when they fought in the Sibuyan War, but my father told me there were upward of six thousand of the creatures present during the final battle. I imagine it would be somewhere around the same number; perhaps a little more."

"And the size of Seth's army?"

"Vargoth has between fifty and seventy thousand," Eric answered, "but thirty thousand of them are in Oridan at the moment. You won't believe the cost. Are you thinking that Vargoth and the Orlocks are trying to develop a pact with each other?"

"I have no idea what their plans are," Teanna said. "I only know they met. My source is a reliable one. Interestingly, our man didn't know about the meeting until the last moment, which is also strange. More interesting still is that according to him Seth and Shakira met by themselves. When it was over, Seth sailed straight back to Palandol."

"This is disturbing," Eric said. "I need some time to digest it."

"Good," Teanna said, getting up. "We can talk about it over dinner. Father often has good insight into these things."

During their conversation, Teanna had considered telling her cousin that Mathew Lewin was still alive, but she decided against it. Thinking about it later while she lay in her bath, she was uncertain why she'd chosen to keep the information to herself.

# 13

## North Sea

MATHEW WAS DIMLY AWARE THAT HANDS WERE PULLING him from the water. The last thing he remembered was a blow to the back of his head when the *Daedalus* blew up. Seconds after he broke the surface, he found himself in the grip of a strong undertow, being pulled out to sea. Dazed, he struggled against the powerful currents until he was nearly blind with fatigue. Even so, he watched the land moving farther and farther away. He tried to swim and hold his sword at the same time. His father had given it to him, and he was not about to lose it.

Minutes turned into an hour and he lost track of time. Images of his father came and went in his mind, and of Collin, Lara, and his other friends. It was funny how his mind worked, he thought. Eventually his arms grew heavy and his breaths came in ragged gasps. It was all he could do to avoid swallowing the saltwater.

He was more than a half mile offshore. In the mouth of the bay the *Daedalus* and the sloop were still burning. Through the billowing smoke he could make out the shape of the *Revenge,* trapped in the bay. At least he could derive satisfaction that his men had gotten away.

Despite his efforts, he was aware that he was making no headway against the undertow. Somewhere in the back of his mind he recalled seeing a notation about it on one of his charts. *Of course, that was why the Vargothans wanted him.* He was such a fool—a navigator who forgot about northern Elgaria's treacherous offshore current. It would have been laughable if it wasn't so pathetic. The only reason he didn't drown was because he grabbed part of a spar that had broken from the sloop and was floating nearby. For another hour he tried swimming toward land, until his arms and legs wouldn't work any longer. He wanted to rest, needed to rest, but that would only let the current pull him farther out to sea.

Suddenly, hands grasped him under the arms and were pulling him into a boat. He was still clutching his sword when someone took it from him. He was too weak to stop them. There were voices, muffled and indistinct, and he was having trouble making out the words properly. Desperately he clung to consciousness.

A shape loomed over him and Mathew tried opening his eyes. The moment he did, sunlight blinded him. Instinctively, he raised his arm to shield them and tried to sit up. Strong hands restrained him. The voices were clearer now. He heard the words *fire* and *explosion*. Then his right hand brushed against the dagger in his belt and his heart leapt. They hadn't taken it. The shape was still in front of him. Mathew's fingers closed around the hilt and with all the strength remaining he pulled it free and struck, shouting as he did.

The man easily blocked the blow and pushed him back down again.

"Rest easy, Mathew. You're among friends."

Those were the last words he remembered before darkness settled over his eyes and he passed out. He awoke an hour later and looked around.

*Still alive,* he thought.

He was lying on a cot in the cabin of a ship, and from the gentle rocking motion he could tell they were at sea. Incredibly, seated at a table across from him were Father Thomas and Delain, talking in low tones.

"Father?" Mathew said uncertainly.

Both men got up and came to him. The priest brought him a cup of water and supported the back of his head while he sipped it. Delain smiled and gripped his shoulder.

"It's good to see you again, Mathew," the king said.

"Thank God, thank God," Father Thomas whispered.

"Your majesty," Mathew said, pushing himself up onto one elbow. "I thought—"

"When we saw the smoke and heard the first explosion, we realized something was wrong," Delain told him. "I ordered the helmsman to steer away from the bay, fearing a trap had been set for us. To our surprise, we saw two more ships in the harbor than we expected. One was burning and another was bearing down on a sloop that was blocking the entrance. A third ship is still trapped in the bay. I must confess, you're the last person in the world I expected to meet under these circumstances. Nevertheless, I'm delighted to find that you're alive. My intention was to seize Andreas Holt and hang him."

"It *was* a trap. I met with Holt and his captain, a fellow named Kennard, on board the *Revenge*. He was crowing about how they'd let information leak out. They knew you would come after him."

"He was right. But what in the world were you doing there?" asked Delain.

"One of the ships you saw burning was the *Daedalus*, a Felizian merchantman. I've been her navigator for the past four years. Just over a week ago the Vargothans sent a message to our captain asking that he meet with them. They wanted to use the *Daedalus* to draw you out into the open and then destroy you with her cannons. Unfortunately, it was as much a trap for us as it was for you."

"Explain."

"The Vargothans had two goals in mind. They wanted Felize's cannons and their black powder—and they wanted you. Our captain was a man named Phillipe Edrington."

"Was?" Delain said.

"He's dead, your majesty. He was killed by Kennard.

Andreas Holt was there at the time. By the way, he told me that he was the governor of Sheeley Province. I've never heard of Sheeley Province."

"That's what the Vargothans have renamed it. What else did Holt tell you?"

"That he wanted to enlist my aid as a navigator. Apparently, he's been under some pressure to get rid of you. He said he had asked his king for reinforcements, but was refused."

Delain smiled. "Good."

"Not really," Mathew said. "They succeeded in getting twenty of our cannons."

Father Thomas and the king exchanged glances.

Mathew quickly explained what happened after the *Daedalus* sailed into the bay, and about his attempts over the last four years to try and retrieve the ring. He told the story without embellishment, but his bitterness at his failure was apparent. Father Thomas and Delain listened without interruption. When he was through, the priest gently touched him on the head.

"I set an impossible task for you, my son, but I'm proud of what you tried to do. Your father would be, too."

Mathew felt a lump forming in his throat and he looked out the window.

"So your plan was to go to Palandol, take up employment as a fencing instructor in Seth's court, then sneak across the border to Nyngary and steal the ring back?" Delain asked.

"Yes."

Delain shook his head. "A bold plan, my friend. Did you consider what would happen if you met Teanna again?"

"I didn't see that I . . . that we have any other choice, your majesty. I believe the ring is in Corrato, though I don't know exactly where. Unless I can find a way to retrieve it, the end is a foregone conclusion, more so now that Vargoth has our cannons."

"Indeed," said Delain. "We've been trying to get them

ourselves for some time now. Perhaps you could tell us how they work and how we could make one?"

"Of course," Mathew said. "But they're useless without the black powder. That's what makes the guns function. The Felizians discovered it two years ago, and you know what they've been able to accomplish since."

"I hardly consider anything the Felizians have done as accomplishments. Black powder, you say?"

"Yes, your majesty. It's a mixture of sulfur, charcoal, and saltpeter. In the right proportions, it causes an explosion within the muzzle of the gun that propels a ball forward. They mine the chemicals in the southern part of Felize."

"Could you reconstruct such a mixture? The substances seem common enough."

"I think so. I could also draw a picture of what a cannon looks like and how it works."

"Excellent. That should help us even the odds a bit. But we still have the problem of the ring. A hundred cannons are no match for Teanna, but I may be able to help a bit with that.

"Until a few days ago we believed you dead. One of the lessons I've had to learn as a king is the value of gathering intelligence on what the enemy is up to. Some time ago James of Mirdan and I managed to place a man in Nyngary's palace guard. The details aren't important. Suffice to say that he's there.

"I recently received a report from him that says he believes the ring is hidden in Teanna's personal apartment. I'll give you the details after you've had something to eat and a chance to recover."

"That would be wonderful," said Mathew.

"It still leaves us with the problem of getting you into her palace and getting you out again in one piece. I agree that we cannot win without your ring. Of course, there is another alternative, but I'll discuss that later."

Mathew wasn't sure what the king was referring to, but decided it would be best to wait and see what Delain had in mind. "I'm willing to try," he said.

"Man for man our people are a match for anyone. I've recently been in contact with Bajan, and I believe they will join us when the time is right. James will, too. Much will depend on what you can or can't accomplish in Corrato. Bajan and Mirdan look at Alor Satar and can see it's only a matter of time before the Durens turn their attention to them. Unfortunately, fighting against the Ancients' magic is another matter. We'll have to figure out a way to get you to Nyngary, since we can't simply sail into Corrato and drop you off."

"If we travel south and use Cole's Pass, we could cut across the lower portion of Cincar and be in Nyngary in less than two weeks," Father Thomas pointed out.

Delain thought for a moment. "Yes, that would work."

"If Father Thomas can accompany me, I'm willing to try," Mathew said. "I've never been to Cincar, or Nyngary, for that matter. After that I'd like to see what can be done about freeing Gawl from his prison."

"It's being taken care of," Delain told him. "When Father Thomas returned to us, he brought news about what Lord Guy is up to. Quite a number of people in Sennia were already upset by what he did, and the country is now in a state of civil war. If all goes well, we should have him out within a week. Jeram Quinn is there now seeing to the details."

"Quinn?" Mathew said. "In Sennia? I haven't thought of him in years. He certainly gets around, doesn't he?"

"Generally, at least where you are concerned," Delain observed mildly.

"I suppose I should be glad he's not here to arrest me," Mathew said.

Delain and Father Thomas both smiled. "Jeram tends to be somewhat single-minded in his views," said Delain.

"I suppose this is as good a time to talk about it as any. Siward has told me what happened in Devondale, but I would like to hear it from you. Is it true you . . . ah—"

"Strangled Berke Ramsey? Yes, your highness . . . after he murdered my father."

Delain leaned back in his chair and considered the young man in front of him. There was no anger in Mathew's voice, and whatever emotions were going through his mind were impossible to read on his face. The law was something important to the king and he held it in high regard.

"What if Ramsey's act was an accident?" Delain asked.

Mathew swung his feet over the edge of the cot and stood up. "He was in the process of trying to load another bolt into his crossbow when I reached him. I understand that it was wrong to take matters into my own hands, but I don't regret what I did. I've had a chance to think about it over the last four years, and in retrospect I would not have altered my conduct even now. What would you do if someone murdered your father?"

"Probably the same thing you did, but then, Jeram Quinn works for me. Tell me, Mathew, did you hear Quinn yell for you to let Ramsey go?"

"I don't recall. He may have. I do remember one of his deputies trying to pull me off Ramsey, but it was too late by then."

"You were beside yourself?" Delain suggested.

Mathew took a deep breath and let it out. "No . . . I was angrier than I've ever been in my life and angrier than I can ever remember being since, but I would be less than honest if I told you I didn't know what I was doing."

"But you *were* beside yourself with rage, correct?"

"Uh . . . correct, your highness."

"Excellent. That is exactly what I, your king, had thought. Given the strained circumstances of seeing your father murdered, and the fact that the man who murdered him might have done the same to you or your friends, it is

the crown's judgment that the circumstances were beyond
what any reasonable man could be expected to bear. I pardon you for the crime. Now where the hell is my drink?"
Delain asked, looking around the room.

Father Thomas, who had retreated to the table during
the conversation, picked it up from the table and handed it
to Delain. Save for the barest hint of a smile at the corners
of his mouth, his expression was serious. Delain downed
the glass in a single gulp.

Mathew blinked. "Thank you, your highness. Perhaps
you could mention it to Jeram Quinn when you see him."

"I'll do that," Delain said. "And I assure you he won't
be displeased by the news."

"That's wonderful. There are two more things I need to
tell you."

The first was about the crew of the *Daedalus*, who were
waiting for him, and where they could be picked up.

"Of course," said Delain. "I'll give the orders at once.
And the second?"

Mathew took the oilskin envelope from the pocket of
his breeches and showed it to them. He explained about
the strange lockbox they had recovered on Coribar and the
priest who died trying to protect it. They both examined
the letter for several minutes, but neither could make anything of it. Delain eventually gave up and tossed it on the
dresser, telling Mathew he would see him at dinner. Then
he and Father Thomas went on deck.

In truth, Mathew was still weak from his ordeal and
more than happy to rest. The cabin steward knocked on
the door a few minutes later. He was carrying a tray with
a bowl of broth and a sandwich, courtesy of the king.
He also brought a razor and some shaving soap. Until
Mathew took the first bite, he didn't realize how hungry
he was. He finished the food in no time at all. He was too
wide awake to sleep by then, so he decided to make use of
the razor. The beard definitely had to go.

While spreading the shaving soap over his face, his eye

happened to fall on the parchment's reflection in his mirror. It was still lying where Delain had left it. Mathew blinked and looked more closely. The words suddenly made sense. A code it might be, but it was no longer just gibberish. The words had been written backward.

He called for the cabin steward and asked him for paper and a pen. The man brought them a few minutes later. It took Mathew a little over a half hour to rewrite the message. Even after he did, most of the references and numbers were meaningless, but one thing caught his eye. Part of the letter talked about a meeting a week earlier between someone named Htes—he figured out that meant Seth— and two people named Keram and Arikahs. It was supposed to have taken place at a town called Elevirag. Keram, of course, would have been Marek, and Arikahs Shakira. He'd never heard of either of them. Elevirag was Garivele, a seaside town in the western part of Vargoth.

Excited, he went on deck to tell Delain what he had found. Father Thomas and the king were talking on the quarterdeck.

"Mat," Father Thomas said, surprised to see him up and about already.

"I think I know what the message on the parchment says. Well, at least part of it."

"Let's go back to the cabin," Delain suggested.

Once there, Mathew demonstrated how the words had been written by holding the parchment up to the mirror. He went on to explain about the parts of the document that he had been able to decipher. As soon as he got to the name Shakira, Delain and Father Thomas looked at one another.

"What did I say?" Mathew asked.

"Shakira is the Orlock queen," Father Thomas explained. "Her name is only known to a few people."

"The Orlocks have a queen?"

"They do," Father Thomas replied. "It was she who struck the bargain with Karas Duren to take the lower third of Elgaria in return for her people's help. You look surprised."

"I am."

That the Orlocks had a queen puzzled Mathew since the only Orlocks he had ever encountered were males. But of course, if there were males, there had to be females. It also followed that they had some form of government, particularly after the buildings he'd seen in the Emerald Cavern.

"This is very strange," said Delain. "Coribar is not exactly in the next province. To get there, Shakira would have had to travel by ship, and I've never heard of any Orlock setting foot on a ship . . . any kind of ship. But she obviously met with Seth and Marek. The question is, why?"

"Because it's well-situated for all three," said Father Thomas. "Do you have any idea what they would want to meet about?"

"I'm not sure," the king answered, "but this is most disturbing. I want both of you to remain alert if any more information about this meeting comes to light. It makes me very uneasy."

"Why?" asked Mathew.

Delain walked to the window and looked out at the foaming trail the ship left on the water. "Because I can see no reason for it. The world is changing before our eyes. Orlocks have left their caves and now live on the land— our land. Coribar has remained largely apart from the wars and conflicts of the past three centuries, and now suddenly seeks to open a dialogue with creatures who detest mankind. And last, Vargothan mercenaries who are *supposedly* allied with Alor Satar may now also be involved with Coribar. It is not only strange, it is bizarre . . . So I say again to you, should any more information come your way, you are to communicate it to me with all haste."

# 14

## Camden Keep, Sennia

THE LAST THING GAWL EXPECTED TO SEE THROUGH THE
bars of his cell door was Jeram Quinn's face. He was so
surprised, he stood up, spilling his drink.

"Quinn?"

"Yes, your majesty. Please keep your voice down."

Gawl crossed the room in three strides. "What the devil
are you doing here?"

"Rescuing you."

"Rescuing me? How? I assume you didn't just walk
past the guards?"

Quinn opened the outer door a little wider and motioned with his head. A heavyset man with him came into
the room. The man bowed to the king and promptly
dropped down to one knee to examine the lock on the cell
door.

"This is Master Samuel Parrish of Blekley Province,"
Quinn explained. "He's a locksmith of some talent. We'll
have you out in just a moment."

Parrish unrolled a leather pouch he was carrying and
spread it open on the floor. It contained a variety of tools.

"Quinn, how the hell did you get in here?"

"By order of the Council of Bishops. Paul Teller has se-
cretly been meeting with them for the past two weeks, ever
since Guy announced that he would try you for treason."

Jeram Quinn slid a piece of paper through the bars for
Gawl to see. It bore the seal of the council.

"So you were in the neighborhood and decided to stroll into Edward Guy's stronghold with that piece of paper and wave it around?"

"The garrison commander here seemed suitably impressed by it," Quinn said. "Of course, the hundred thousand gold crowns that Delain raised went a long way toward easing the man's conscience. Fortunately, Lord Guy is in Barcora at the moment, but I think you'll find that the garrison is now loyal to you. The bribe was Siward Thomas's idea, by the way."

"He's still alive, then," Gawl said. "Excellent. I'm going to kill him when I see him. He's responsible for my spending four years in this hole."

"He's responsible for your being alive," Quinn said without looking up, as he concentrated on what the locksmith was doing.

Gawl leaned closer and watched as well. He was about to reply when a distinct click of the lock stopped him. The door swung open an inch. Tentatively, Gawl pushed it a little farther, as if he didn't believe it would move. Quinn smiled up at the king, then took a step back along with the locksmith, who seemed quite pleased with himself. Gawl pushed the door open the rest of the way and stepped through.

The first thing he did was to embrace Quinn, who all but disappeared from view for several seconds. He then turned to the locksmith and gripped him by the shoulder.

"My thanks, Master Parrish."

Quinn put a hand on his chest and sucked in a deep breath as he tried to recover from Gawl's hug. "I would like to be gone from here as quickly as possible, your majesty. However effective money is as an inducement, it does not guarantee loyalty."

"Good point. Did you happen to see Rowena on the way in?"

"No. She's at Tenley Palace with her father. I have fifty

soldiers with me. They should be more than enough to get us to Marigan. A ship is waiting there to take us to Mirdan."

"Mirdan?"

"I don't know how much of the recent developments have reached you," Quinn told him. "But Arteus Ballenger and a substantial portion of the Southern Army defected the day after Guy announced your trial. Riots have broken out all across Sennia, in spite of the Church's endorsement. The country in now in state of civil war."

"No, I didn't know that," Gawl said, his face going serious.

As they made their way down the narrow staircase, Gawl let Quinn do most of the talking.

"There has also been a schism of sorts within the Church," Quinn explained. "When the riots started, Ferdinand Willis fled to the Abbey of Barcora and ordered that the gates be locked. All foreigners were expelled and the schools were closed. He has posted armed guards within the complex and along the walls."

"Priests should stick to what they do best," said Gawl.

At the bottom of the staircase was the great hall of the castle, and they came to a halt. Gawl stopped and looked around the room. Hanging above a limestone fireplace against the wall was a coat of arms with two crossed swords. He strode over to it, reached up and yanked the crest down, then removed one of the swords. He hefted it in his hand a few times, testing the balance. Satisfied, he glanced at Quinn and the locksmith and flashed them one of his smiles. The sword looked like a child's toy in his massive hand.

"I'm not going back to that cage again. Are you sure Rowena isn't here?"

"Positive. I know how you feel, but we need to get you to safety."

A significant look passed between the two men.

"At the risk of offending you, Jeram," Gawl said, "you haven't the first idea how I feel."

"It may surprise you, your majesty, but I think I do. You have every right to seek vengeance against the traitors, and there will be a time and place for that. This is not it. Siward Thomas once said something very similar to me. I believe that's what got me started in this whole affair."

Gawl looked from Quinn to the locksmith, who gave him a weak smile and looked very much like he wanted to be anyplace other than where he was at the moment.

"All right," Gawl said. "When the time comes."

One of the first people Gawl saw when he entered the courtyard was Shelby Haynes, the gray-haired colonel who had been in charge of his personal bodyguard before he was imprisoned. The moment Haynes caught sight of the king, he fell to his knees and bowed his head.

"Forgive me, your majesty. I failed you."

Gawl shook his head. "Get up, man. You didn't fail anybody. There was nothing you could have done. Fighting against men is one thing. Fighting against the Ancients' magic is quite another. I assign no blame to you."

Gawl put his hand under Haynes's elbow, helped him to his feet, and the two men embraced.

"Who are these others?" Gawl asked.

"These are men I've been in contact with for the last three years. Some come from units of the Southern Army and some from the Northern Battalions. Many were at the battle of Fanshaw Castle. Others came to me in ones and twos. The men of your bodyguard who remained loyal to you and refused to pledge their loyalty to Lord Guy were all executed on the main square in Barcora."

"And what about you?" Gawl asked. "You were their commander."

"I was made a particular example of Guy had my legs and arms broken and I was thrown from the cliffs into the sea and left to drown. I didn't."

"Dear Lord," Gawl whispered. He looked at Colonel Haynes and then at the other assembled soldiers. Most

stood quietly beside their horses and smiled back at him.
A few nodded in his direction. Gawl opened his mouth to
speak, closed it again, and turned his head away. He stared
out of the front gate of the castle for a space of time. There
were tears in his eyes when he turned back.

"I have always taken my responsibilities as king seriously," he said, his voice rising. "Rulers are often said to
be the seeds of war, but they can also be the seeds of
peace. I want to thank all of you for the risk you have un-
dertaken in coming here. I'm told that our country is at
war now. I intend to remedy that.

"A moment ago I said no one could stand against the
Ancients' magic. I was wrong. Together we can do anything. Let them throw what they will against us. You have
held true to me, and as your king, I pledge my solemn oath
to do no less for you and for our people. I will do this or
die trying."

The seaside village of Marigan was no different from ten
other small towns along the Sennian coast. It spread out
along a small horseshoe-shaped bay, and above it rose a series of green tree-covered hills. Those hills eventually
merged into the Camenon mountain range. Apart from a
lively merchant trade made possible by a deep harbor, most
of the people in Marigan made their living from the sea and
produced some of the region's best wines. As a rule, they
had no more to do with the country's politics than was
strictly necessary. Quayside shops sold everything from
silks and perfumes to furniture and fruits from such faraway
neighbors as Coribar and Senecal.

The largest and most dominating building in Marigan
was the church. It sat on a hillside overlooking the town,
like a watchful mother guarding her children.

The Falcon's Nest, located alongside the harbor, was
one of the town's two taverns. It was a low one-story stone
structure with rough-cut wooden beams in the facade. Inside, the building was about what Gawl expected. There

was a long bar of dark polished wood and a number of tables. At ten o'clock in the morning he, Quinn, and Haynes were the only customers there. In order to avoid attracting attention, they left their escort on the outskirts of town. Despite some grumbling on his part, Gawl agreed to wear a cloak Quinn had brought with him, though it did little to disguise the king's giant form.

The landlord appeared and took their orders. He returned fifteen minutes later with two plates of eggs and sausages for Gawl, a sandwich for Haynes, and some toast and jam for Quinn. A serving girl followed him out, carrying a pitcher of orange juice and a pot of hot tea. After she set them down on the table, her gaze lingered on Gawl for a moment and she smiled at him with parted lips. There was a touch more sway in her hips when she returned to the kitchen.

"Shrink down a bit, Gawl," Quinn said under his breath.

"This *is* down."

Quinn drew a long-suffering breath and sipped his tea. "If all goes well, our ship should be here at midday."

"And if it doesn't go well?"

"It will," Quinn assured him.

"I don't see why you didn't just have it wait in the harbor for us."

"Too risky," Colonel Haynes replied.

"Why is that?"

"The Archbishop's guards, your majesty."

"What are you talking about? When did Willis get guards?"

"A little over two years ago. It was one of his first edicts after he was elected archbishop, and I use the term 'elected' advisedly. There are probably a thousand of them throughout the country."

Incredulous, Gawl put his drink down. "You're not serious?"

"I wish I wasn't," Haynes said. "They have the right to

arrest anyone charged with the crime of heresy, or who engages in the practice of magic."

*"What?"*

"Or who worships the devil," Haynes added

"Worships the devil?" Gawl repeated.

"Oh, there's an entire list of what constitutes heresy and devil worship," Haynes told him. "Offenders are hauled before an ecclesiastic court and given the opportunity to repent and atone for their sins. Usually that means jail or working in his eminence's vineyards. Those who don't are tortured . . . or disappear."

Gawl's mouth dropped open in disbelief. "I'll hang that lying bastard myself."

"Willis generally targets foreigners or anyone who has the audacity to speak out against him," Quinn explained. "The amount of foreign trade visiting Barcora these days is less than one-tenth of what it was four years ago."

"The result," Haynes said, "is that the price of wine has reached almost twenty dollars a barrel for the red and nearly thirty dollars for the yellow."

Gawl picked up a tangerine and slowly began to peel it. "It took me five years to ease our tariffs and open the ports to the outside world, and they slam them shut with this rubbish. It all comes down to lining the pockets of a few at the expense of the many. I won't have it, I tell you."

Two other patrons who had entered the inn turned in their direction.

"Keep your voice down," Quinn whispered.

Gawl glowered at the constable for a second then popped a section of the tangerine in his mouth and began chewing. His chest rose and fell slowly as he looked out the window at the bay. Nearly a minute passed before he spoke again. "I remember the water being bluer," Gawl said quietly.

Quinn and Haynes both exchanged glances, and the rest of the meal passed in silence.

When they were finished, they called for the bill. Quinn

handed the innkeeper a gold sovereign and waited while he went to get their change. But instead of giving the money to Quinn when he returned, the innkeeper walked past him and directly up to Gawl. The king was still staring out the window, his hands clasped behind his back.

"My name is Tom Dunn, your majesty. There are three Archbishop's men outside."

Gawl turned around and looked down at Dunn. He was a man of medium build with gray hair and a broad, honest face.

"My disguise must not be as effective as I had hoped," Gawl said.

Haynes and Quinn moved to the door and looked out.

"How did you know?" Quinn asked the landlord.

Dunn opened his hand to reveal three silver half-crowns bearing Gawl's profile.

Gawl glanced at them and then at Tom Dunn. "It never was my best angle."

"I guess you're every bit as big as they say you are," said Dunn. "Never thought to meet you in person, sire."

"Why tell me about the Archbishop's men, Master Dunn?"

"I'm guessing that Lord Guy didn't let you out of the keep just so you could enjoy breakfast here."

"And . . . ?"

"And a lot of people don't hold with what they did to you, your majesty."

"Are you one of those people?"

"Me? I stay as far from lords and ladies as I can. The fact is, things were going along pretty well before they locked you up."

"I see."

"Now, if I did have a mind to get involved with politics, which I don't, I'd say it's for the people to decide when they don't want a king anymore, and not a few who are out to make themselves rich. If you know what I mean."

The smaller man stared up at Gawl, and after a few seconds the king started to chuckle. "Well said, Master Innkeeper. I shall remember your words."

"There's a back door you and your people can use, sire. It will be more convenient. The three outside generally meet their two friends every Sixth Day for drinks. I imagine the others will be here soon. If you follow the alleyway to the street and turn right, it will take you down to the docks."

"What makes you think we're going to the docks?" Quinn asked.

"Just a guess," Tom Dunn said, "but there's a big ship from Mirdan that dropped anchor a while ago. We don't get a lot of Mirdanite's here."

"They're headed this way," Haynes said.

"Thank you, my friend. I'm in your debt," Gawl said.

"Just see you clean house when you're back at the palace. There's been a nasty collection of wharf rats around lately."

Gawl and the others made their way down the alley. Standing out in the middle of the harbor was the Mirdanite ship the innkeeper had told them about. A longboat was moored at the second pier, with the crew and its officer waiting nearby, watchful. Haynes quickened his pace and went ahead to speak with the officer, while Gawl and Quinn pretended to look in the window of a leather shop. After a minute Haynes motioned to them, and they began walking. They had only gone a few steps, however, when someone called out, "Halt, citizens."

Gawl turned to see two men wearing blue and white cloaks. Both were armed and wore the insignia of the Archbishop on the left shoulder of their vests.

Quinn went to speak with them. "What can I do for you, gentlemen?" he asked.

"You are not from this town, are you?" one of soldiers asked.

"No," Quinn replied, "I am here visiting with my companion. And who might you be?"

"I'm Sergeant Jacks of his eminence's guard, and this is Corporal Cray. Your passes, please."

"Passes?"

"It's required that all foreigners traveling within the country carry a pass signed by either the council, the Archbishop, or with the seal of Tenley Palace. The same applies to citizens who are visiting other provinces."

Colonel Haynes started back toward them, but a shake of Gawl's head stopped him.

"I was unaware of such a law," Quinn said. "My friend and I are from Elgaria."

"Is that right?" Sergeant Jacks asked, addressing Gawl.

"My companion cannot speak," Quinn explained. "He's deaf and dumb—an unfortunate accident at birth."

The sergeant shook his head. "Sad," he said. "The law is still relatively new. Normally, you could be arrested for traveling without passes. You and your large friend will need to present yourselves at the church up on the hill and make an application. I'd take you there myself, but we're late for an appointment. Ask for Lieutenant Fredricks and tell him I sent you. If you'll bring the passes back to me, I'll countersign 'em for you."

"You may have to bring two for your friend," his companion joked, looking up at Gawl. He was met with a baleful stare and turned back to Quinn. "How are things in your homeland? We've only heard rumors about what's happening there, but they sounded bad."

Quinn shrugged. "It gets worse by the day. We're on our way to Mirdan. Prince James is building a cathedral in Stermark and needs craftsmen. My brother-in-law sent word to me last week."

"Ah, is that what you do?" the sergeant asked.

Quinn saw the men glance at his hands and nodded. "I work in stained glass, and Jonah here is a stonemason."

"Is the pay any good?" the corporal asked him.

Quinn turned his palms up. "Work is work."

"We'll be at the Falcon's Nest," the sergeant said. "It's

that stone building at the end of the next block. The whole business shouldn't take long. You can pick up your swords when you return."

"Excuse me?"

The sergeant took a deep breath and held out his hand. "I don't make the rules, friend." He motioned for their swords with his fingers. "The lieutenant will give you a permit with no problem, but it'll cost you a half-crown each."

"A man needs a permit to carry a sword in this country?" Quinn asked, taken aback.

"Like I said, I don't make the rules, but you being foreigners and all, I can see as how you might not be up on our local customs. That's why I'm not arresting you. And since you're leaving anyway, it would just be more paperwork for me. Just get your passes and bring them back, then you can be on your way."

The sergeant continued to hold his hand out to Quinn while his companion took a hesitant step toward Gawl and pointed at his sword. The feral smile that slowly spread across Gawl's face stopped him in his tracks. He looked up at the king's bearded face and gave a nervous swallow.

"Uh . . . could you ask your friend to give me his sword, please?"

Quinn sighed and tapped Gawl on the chest to get his attention, enunciating his words loudly. "This gentleman," he said, gesturing to the corporal, "would like your sword, Jonah."

The corporal nodded in agreement and supplemented it with a friendly smile.

"Over my dead body," Gawl rumbled.

Quinn rolled his eyes to heaven and put a hand over his face.

The sergeant's mouth dropped open. "I thought you said he couldn't—"

The man never got a chance to finish his sentence. A crashing blow from the bottom of Gawl's fist buckled his knees, knocking him unconscious. His companion, slower to react, found himself lifted off the ground by the front of his vest, his face suddenly inches from Gawl's.

"A word of advice, *citizen*. When you see that lying, backstabbing maggot you call the Archbishop, tell him that I'm coming for him."

With one heave, Gawl tossed the corporal over the edge of the quay and into the harbor. He hit the water with a loud splash.

Quinn walked to the edge, looked down, and turned back to Gawl. "Subtle," he said.

# 15

## Outside Gravenhage

THE NORTH ROAD LOOKED THE SAME AS MATHEW RE-
membered it. Much of it passed through Elgaria's dense
forests and small towns. As a boy, he'd made the trip a
number of times while visiting Anderon with his family.
Eventually, the road would take them to Gravenhage,
where they would stop for the night before heading on to
Devondale. It would have been possible to skirt it, but for
Mathew the pull of home was just too great.

Delain had provided them with horses, money, and
provisions, along with the information his spy had sent
back about where the ring was kept. They bade the king
goodbye and agreed to meet in the town of Mechlen in a
month's time. By then Mathew knew he would either have
his ring or he wouldn't. Either way, the war for Elgaria's
independence was coming.

A light rain was falling by the time Gravenhage came
into view. Mathew had always thought of it as a city.
Though nowhere near as big as Anderon, it was many times
larger than Devondale, with its own stadium and the largest
watchtower in the province. Now, seeing the skyline, he
frowned. In the years since he had left Elgaria, he'd visited
places like. Tyraine, Barcora, and Senecal. Gravenhage
seemed small in comparison.

"Everything is large in the eyes of a child," Father
Thomas said, reading his thoughts.

Mathew nodded absently. "I wonder if Jerrel Rozon
still lives here."

"Delain told me that Jerrel was killed two years ago at the battle of Broken Hill."

Mathew shook his head sadly. "I liked him. He was a good man."

"And a good general," Father Thomas added. "I was shocked to hear of his passing. Jerrel led Elgaria's last cavalry charge against the Vargothans. It's a terrible . . ."

Mathew looked at the priest when his words trailed away. "What is it?"

"You've just reminded me of something. Jerrel taught fencing to the young men of this town, as I did in Devondale. If any of them recognize you . . ."

"I see what you mean. Perhaps it would be best if we continue on to Devondale and—"

Mathew stopped talking as a Vargothan patrol emerged around a bend in the road a hundred yards from them. There were seven soldiers, and they carried a man on a litter. The leader raised his hand, then pointed at Mathew and Father Thomas.

"Father—"

"I see them, Mathew. And they have seen us. Do nothing until I tell you to. Let's go meet our new friends."

When they were within range, Father Thomas called out, "Good day to you. Is there a problem?"

The leader studied them for a few seconds and nudged his horse forward. "Good day, yourself. One of our men was gored by a boar last night. We're taking him to Graven-hage—there's supposed to be a doctor there. And who might you be?"

"I'm Father Laurent Silver and this is William d'Arp, a young man on his way to Palandol in Vargoth. We met a while back and have been traveling together."

"You're not dressed like a priest."

Father Thomas smiled. "It doesn't do to travel in one's robes, my son."

The soldier thought about it for a second and nodded. "I guess that makes sense. Where are you bound, Father?"

"I'm on my way to take up a post in a small town called Devondale. Can you tell me if this road will take me there, Sergeant?"

"It's *Corporal*, and Devondale's about a half-day ride from here. I hope you brought some books to read because it's in the middle of nowhere."

"All the more need for a priest, then. I'm told they have a lovely church. Perhaps you've seen it?"

The soldier shrugged. "It's all right. Why are you going to Vargoth?" he asked Mathew.

"The royal garrison at Palandol has need of a fencing instructor. A good friend of mine is going to introduce me to the master at arms."

"So you're a fencing instructor?"

"I will be if I get the job."

The corporal laughed. Mathew noticed that the soldiers were unshaven and looked weary. Their clothes were dirty and rumpled, as if they'd been out on patrol for quite some time.

"Do you have anything that proves you're a priest, or says that you're taking over the church?" the leader asked Father Thomas.

"Lying is a sin, my son. I have my vestments in the saddlebag. If you wish to see them, I will not be offended. I understand you are just doing your job."

"No papers . . . nothing?"

"I'm afraid not," said Father Thomas.

The soldier looked at Mathew, who responded with a shrug.

"I'm sorry, Father," the corporal said, "but you're going to have to come with us into Gravenhage. If my captain says it's all right, you'll be free to go."

Mathew's hand drifted closer to the hilt of his sword, uncertain what was going to happen next. He half expected that he and Father Thomas would have to fight their way out of the situation until a groan from the man on the litter turned everyone's head in his direction.

Curious, Mathew dismounted, walked over to him, and felt the soldier's forehead. The others watched but did nothing to stop him. Mathew lifted up the edge of the blanket and stared at the man's leg. It was swollen to almost twice its normal size and hot to the touch.

"We're taking him to Gravenhage," the leader said again.

"This man won't make it, that far," Mathew replied. "He's burning with fever and the leg is infected."

"Gravenhage is only ten miles. You can see it—"

"*You*, priest," Mathew snapped. "Can you get a fire going?"

"Why, yes. I'm sure I could," said Father Thomas, dismounting.

"I'm going to need some water and a pot to boil it. You," Mathew said, pointing at one of the soldiers. "Do you know what redwort looks like?"

The soldier responded to the tone of command in his voice and answered, "Yes, sir."

"Move, then. I'm going to need about three handfuls. There's a white shirt in my saddlebag," he continued, speaking to the corporal. "Get it out and cut it into strips about this wide." Mathew spread his thumb and forefinger apart to indicate the size he wanted. "You others, unhitch that litter and get it on the ground."

A short while later the soldier Mathew had sent for the redwort returned. Father Thomas already had a fire going. A nearby stream provided the water he needed. One of the soldiers got out a cooking pot and suspended it above the fire. The injured man on the litter turned one way then the other, his face bathed in sweat. One of the men at his side tried to keep him still. Mathew waited until the water had reached a rapid boil, removed the dagger from his belt, and stuck the blade in the water.

"We need to sterilize this first," he explained to the leader. "Put half the bandages in along with the redwort and boil them as well. Make sure you don't get the others dirty."

"Right."

"I'm going to lance his leg to relieve some of the pressure. Then we'll clean the wound to clear away as much of the infection as I can get at. Hopefully, it hasn't gotten into his blood yet. I'll need two of your men to hold him."

The corporal turned to his men. "Charley, you get Ted's shoulders. Micah, make sure you keep his hands still."

"I've seen this sort of thing before," Mathew said. "What did you say his name was?"

"Ted . . . Ted Wilkes."

Mathew removed the knife from the boiling water and went to Wilkes. He nodded to the other soldiers, and they grasped a hold of Wilkes by his shoulders and arms.

"Ready?"

Both men nodded.

Quickly, Mathew made a small incision where the boar's tusk had gone in. A mixture of green puss and blood immediately oozed out of the wound. Wilkes screamed and tried to sit up, but the soldier named Charley forced him back down again. The stench from the wound caused Mathew to turn his head away. He took a gulp of air and made the second incision. Wilkes screamed again and tried to hit him. His companions stopped him from doing so.

"Hold him tight now," Mathew said. "I've got to remove this infection. The bite marks already have scabs on them."

The men watched as Mathew continued his ministrations. When it was over, the injured man lay there limp. Mathew took the remainder of the bandages and wrapped them around the wound, aware that Father Thomas and the others were watching him.

"Get him to a doctor as soon as you reach town," he told the leader. "It's important that he gets plenty of rest and a lot of water to drink. You'll need to keep a close watch on his leg over the next few days to make sure the infection doesn't come back. I'm pretty sure I got most of it."

"Thanks, friend," the corporal said, shaking Mathew's

hand. "These are difficult times, and there's not many of your countrymen that hold us in high regard—I know that. In fact, I can't think of anyone in these parts that would lift a finger to save one of us like you just did."

"You're welcome. Kings and princes make the law. Life's tough enough without the rest of us being at each other's throats. Do you think we'll have to spend a great deal of time in Gravenhage? Getting to Palandol is already going to be close for me."

The leader took a deep breath and looked at his men. An unspoken communication passed between them.

"I think you and Father Silver here can go on," he said. "I'll square it with the captain. It's the least we can do for your help. You'll want to keep to the main road. A good swordsman you may be, but there are all manner of brigands and cutpurses about these days, and they won't just ride off because there's a priest around."

"That's very decent of you," said Mathew. "You have my gratitude. If you're ever in Palandol, look me up. The fencing lesson will be free."

Mathew and Father Thomas bade the others goodbye, mounted, and continued on their way. They rode in silence for a space of time.

"That was quick thinking back there, Mat," said Father Thomas. "I was afraid we were going to be the Vargothans' guests for the night."

"I'm sorry, Father. I know you told me to wait until you acted."

"Not at all. What you did was exactly correct."

"Thank you," Mathew said. "I've been wondering," he continued. "Do you think we should skip Devondale?"

Father Thomas raised his eyebrows. "Why? Our friends there are not likely to reveal who you are, even if any of them do recognize you."

"It's been a long time since either of us have been home, and things may have changed."

"That is true," said Father Thomas.

"What if we run into more of the Vargothans?"

"I suppose we'll deal with them as best we can. Is that what's really bothering you?"

"No," Mathew answered glumly.

"Would you like to talk about it?"

"No."

Father Thomas already had a good idea what was bothering his young friend, but kept riding, knowing there was more to follow.

"I haven't seen Lara in almost four years," Mathew suddenly blurted. "What do you think she's going to say if I just pop into her life again? As far as she knows, I'm dead."

"*That* is a difficult question, and unfortunately I don't have an answer to it. You and she were in love with each other, so I hope she would be happy to have you back."

"You really think so?"

"I'm sure of it. Lara is a fine girl . . . though I suppose I should call her a woman now. I haven't seen her myself since that night at Fanshaw Castle."

Mathew nodded. "What about Ceta, Father? Does she know you escaped? Don't you want to see her?"

Father Thomas took a deep breath. "I would love nothing more, but unfortunately I don't know if Ceta is alive or dead. After our trial, she came to visit me in the prison. We spoke for a long time. As you know, my prospects for being released in the near future were not good then. She wanted to stay, but Sennia was no longer safe, and it was far too dangerous for her to remain in the country. I made her promise to return to Elberton with Collin, Quinn, and Lara. In retrospect it was a terrible mistake, and one which may have cost her her life."

"You mean because of the Orlocks?"

"Precisely. The creatures control everything from Ritiba to Tyraine. During the first year I was imprisoned, Ceta's letters came to me on a regular basis. They stopped about the time Alor Satar turned the land over to the creatures. I have spent the last two years praying for her."

"I'm sorry, Father. I guess I was just thinking of myself."

Father Thomas reached over and squeezed Mathew's forearm. "We both have a lot to deal with. These are difficult times. Thousands have died and I fear more will do so in the future. A long time ago I told you that you are the last best hope of our people. Eric Duren and his brother would like to eliminate not just our country, but its very soul. You and your ring are the fulcrum on which the future rests. That is why we must recover it at any cost. We can skip Devondale if you like."

Mathew thought about it for a moment. "No," he said. "Let's go on."

# 16

## Stermark, Mirdan

THE SUMMER RESIDENCE OF PRINCE JAMES WAS SMALLER than Tenley Palace. Composed mostly of rust-colored granite and four separate watchtowers, it sat high on a hill above the city, overlooking the harbor.

The harbor was nowhere as large as the one in Barcora, but it was still a lively center of commerce capable of supporting more than thirty good-sized ships. With the recent shift in the political and economic climate of the world, Stermark's fortunes had also changed. Originally a secondary port of call, it was now home to a dozen guilds and industries.

Gawl rested his forearms on the battlements and looked down. It was a beautiful view, he thought. James was fortunate. Of course, getting there a thousand years before anyone else with your own army had a lot to do with it.

Mirdan had been a stanch ally of Sennia since he had taken the throne. The last of the free Western countries, it had not yet come under attack because Eric and Armand Duren were still busy consolidating their positions in Elgaria.

In the past, Mirdan had fought bravely alongside both Elgaria and Sennia at Ardon Field. James made a forced march in order to get there in time. Looking back on those events, Gawl conceded their breaking through Alor Satar's rear line had been a major turning point in that battle. The other, of course, was Mathew Lewin.

Through negotiation, compromise, and treaty, James Genet had so far managed to keep his country out of the seething cauldron of troubles that had plagued the other Western nations. He was a shrewd young man with uncommon political sense.

Their present situation was dismal, though. The hopes of their world rested on the shoulders of a farm boy from Devondale, assuming he was still alive. During the brief time he and Siward Thomas had together before their trial, the priest had shared his plan with him. How much James actually knew of those events, he was about to find out.

James was not much older than Mathew. Gawl had met the prince only four times since he had taken the throne, and he liked him from the start. He was slender and just above middle height, with intelligent eyes that were more gray than blue. Due to a riding accident when he was eight years old, James walked with a pronounced limp. In all their time together, Gawl found him to be plain-spoken and direct, qualities he admired.

The young man was also an amiable companion. During his visit to Barcora, despite the injury to his leg, he and Gawl had hunted deer together in Bryant Forest and spent the night drinking. James bested him twice.

That morning, instead of meeting in the palace, James suggested they go trout fishing together so they could speak in private. He claimed to know of two wonderful streams that were less than a day's ride away. In truth, fishing was the last thing Gawl wanted to do, but he agreed. He had been a respectable fisherman as a boy himself, and so long as the trip ended with a commitment of soldiers and arms from Mirdan, he would stand on his head if he had to. It might also give him a chance to pull even with James for the deer hunting.

Gawl mentioned the idea of a fishing trip to Jeram Quinn and got the response he expected. The former constable raised his eyebrows and wished him success but declined the invitation. It was the same with Colonel Haynes. Some frantic last minute work by the palace tailor and their boot maker produced a suitable outfit in his size.

Even after Gawl had taken the throne, he had continued to dress in clothes more suited to a commoner than a king. Wearing a crown gave him a headache, and he had never been able to look at himself in flowing ermine robes without feeling somewhat ridiculous.

From the parapet, he saw James emerge from the stables dressed as plainly as he himself was. They waved to each other.

"Be right down," he called out.

Their ride to the upper Taylor River was as pleasant as any Gawl could remember. To his surprise, James suggested they spend the night in the woods and get up early in the morning to try their luck on the streams. Both were fast moving and so full of fish, James told him, even a Sennian could catch them.

For the better part of the day they climbed through hazy green mountains, eventually descending into a broad valley where the Taylor River flowed swiftly. They passed through several towns along the way, and a number of people recognized the prince and came by to visit. All of them inquired after his father's health.

King William, Gawl knew, had been unable to manage his daily affairs since James was sixteen. He suffered from a disease of the mind that grew progressively worse each year. The illness eventually robbed the old man of even the simplest of life's pleasures. Though William still knew his wife, his own children had become strangers to him. With each passing day he had grown increasingly mistrustful of others. Gawl had seen such problems before, and his heart went out to James, who explained that William's sickness had become so bad in the last year, he could often not recognize his own image in the mirror.

Gawl heard the pain in the young man's voice and admired the way he was handling the situation. Nine years earlier, James had met with the barons and lords of Mirdan and shared his father's problem with them. Instead of summarily informing them that he was taking the king's place by right of succession, he asked the elder nobles for their advice. To a man, they all pledged their loyalty and suggested that his mother appoint him Regent. She did so, and the transition of power from one generation to the next was conducted so smoothly it was barely noticeable.

James Genet had not changed much. He was still open and affable and stopped to chat with everyone who engaged them. He introduced them to Gawl, making no secret of who he was. The people were properly respectful and offered their welcome. Most wished them good fortune and a few joked that one look at Gawl would probably scare the fish out of the water.

They arrived at the first stream about an hour before sunset. The underbrush was so thick they were forced to make camp, leave their horses, and hike a little over a mile to the spot James wanted. The water was alive with insects hatching, and trout could be seen rising in the pools along the banks, out of the fast moving current. Both men studied the hatch for a few minutes and selected the proper flies. Slowly, the sun descended lower in the sky until it was just above the treeline.

Gawl caught six, and let two small ones go. The rest he put in his creel. James caught eight and released four. Altogether, it was a marvelous day. They returned to camp thoroughly exhausted. After dinner, Gawl stretched out by the fire, his belly full. He lay back, put his arms behind his head and looked up at a sky alive with stars. Night birds and crickets called to one another in the darkness. On the other side of the fire, James unlaced his boots, kicked them off, and sat with his back against a tree.

"This was more fun than I've had in a long time," he said.

"It was indeed fun," Gawl agreed.

"I wish we could do this all the time. I love being out here."

"A wonderful night," Gawl said. "Do we have any more of that wine left?"

"I hung it on a branch by the horses."

Gawl lifted up his head and looked at the wineskin. "I'll get it later," he said, and lay back down again, staring up at the stars. His ancestors must have had vivid imaginations to see pictures and shapes up there, he thought. "There are eighty-eight constellations I'm told, but I can only recognize a few. The rest just look like stars to me."

"Don't you wish you could stay out here forever?"

"A little. But that wouldn't be a good thing. People are being hurt, James."

"I know, but it would be nice to forget about all that, wouldn't it?"

"It would be nice," Gawl agreed. "Do you not wish to talk tonight?"

"I suppose we can," said James, though he didn't sound convincing. "This whole business makes me ill. What I'd really like is for them to leave us alone. Do you think there's any chance they might?"

Gawl listened to the sound of a bullfrog calling to another for several seconds. "No . . . I don't . . . and neither do you."

James rolled over onto his side and propped himself up on one elbow. "What is it you want from me?"

"Supplies and men, for a start—as many as you can afford. Sennia is in a state of civil war right now. Guy's forces are spread out across the country trying to quell things, but from what Haynes tells me, the situation is getting worse, at least from their standpoint. With twenty thousand men—"

"Impossible. The Vargothans have recently moved eight divisions to Elgaria's northern territories. They sent us word they're only conducting military exercises, but of course that's a lie."

"How many can you give me?"

James shook his head. "The most . . . five thousand,

maybe six, provided we can move some people from the western border. I'll be stretching myself thin at that. Supplies are another matter; they're no problem. The bulk of your Southern Army are now our guests in southern Mirdan. Edward Guy sent me a letter demanding that we expel them. He said that he will consider anyone who aids his enemy as an enemy. That was our first communication."

"The first?"

"A second letter followed a week later, delivered in person by his ambassador. It seems Arteus Ballenger has been declared a traitor and sentenced to death as . . . have you."

"Really?"

"They're offering amnesty to all who voluntarily return and pledge their loyalty."

"Interesting."

"Why so?"

"Well . . . one would think a soldier's loyalty should be to his country rather than its Regent."

"Good point," James said.

"I know."

"If I agree to give you the men you are asking for, what are your plans?"

The question caught Gawl by surprise. "Why, to take back my throne, of course."

"Just like that?"

"What do you mean?" Gawl asked.

"I'm not trying to raise a sore subject, but you were overthrown once before."

"I understand that, but circumstances have changed. To begin with, Guy had the full support of the Church before. He doesn't now. They're very much fragmented on this point, and his power base has been eroding rapidly. I've received a number of communications from various Church officials in the last week, saying they'll support my efforts to oust him."

"Excellent. And assuming you're successful, how long do you think you'll be able to hold the throne?"

Gawl's brows came together and he looked at the prince across the fire. "Excuse me?"

"How will this time be any different from the last?"

"Are you serious?" Gawl asked. "We'll have almost fifteen thousand men at our command and twice that many from our supporters throughout the country. We had less than twenty-five hundred at Fanshaw Castle."

"Twenty-five hundred or twenty-five thousand, there is still the problem of Teanna d'Elso. She could wipe you off the map in the blink of an eye."

"She's only one woman."

"Who controls the combined science and power of the Ancients." James suddenly sat up and leaned forward. "Mirdan is pledged to you as an ally, Gawl, and we'll behave as such, but I'm not about to throw my people away in a hopeless battle."

"Just say it plain," Gawl told him.

"All right, I will. As long as Teanna d'Elso lives, there's no hope of prevailing against the East. She must die; it's as simple as that. Delain thinks war is coming, and you've told me as much yourself. The dispatches we've received from him say that he'll be ready to move in less than two months' time, so I ask you again, how will it be any different?"

Gawl considered the question. He had always thought of the young prince as intelligent, but his words conveyed a maturity and sophistication beyond his years. James was right. Even if he was successful in removing Edward Guy from the throne, how long would it take for Teanna to destroy them? Guy had made a pact with Alor Satar, and there was little question that Teanna would support her cousins.

"Much of it depends on whether Mathew Lewin will be successful," Gawl finally answered. "Unfortunately, I don't know whether he's alive or dead. There's been no word for over four years now. You may be right. Throwing good men away in a meaningless battle would be folly."

"Lewin is alive," James said. "I received a dispatch from Delain the day before you arrived. He and Siward Thomas have left for Palandol. They're going to make an attempt on the ring."

"Alive," Gawl repeated softly. "This is wonderful news."

"Wonderful as long as they succeed. If they should fail, we're back in the same position, or worse."

"I see what you mean."

"That's why Delain and I have made an alternative set of arrangements."

One of Gawl's eyebrows went up. "Explain."

"We have a man in Nyngary who's been able to maneuver himself close to the royal family. His original instructions were to get Mathew Lewin's ring out, or to make sure that Teanna won't be able to use hers. He recently reported that he knows where it's hidden. If he can't get it within the next month, he'll receive word that the time has come for him to act."

The crease on Gawl's brow deepened as the meaning behind James's words became clear. "You mean assassinate her?"

"I do."

"And Delain is part of this?"

"He is."

At first Gawl didn't know what to say. The idea of sending someone to assassinate a woman was repugnant, and he said as much.

"I don't like it any more than you do, but I don't see another way," James replied. "Personally, I'd rather meet Alor Satar and Vargoth across a battlefield. Having to deal with these other things makes me want to take a bath."

"How can you be sure your man will do what you ask?"

The prince shrugged. "I can't, but he seems to be strongly attached to the money we're paying."

"You're an interesting fellow, James. I'll need some time to think about this."

The two men talked awhile longer, before the warmth of the fire made their eyes heavy and they lay down to sleep. The last thing James mentioned before he drifted off was about the mysterious letter Mathew had recovered. He said it largely as an aside, and Gawl listened without commenting and filed it away.

When Gawl awoke before dawn, however, it was the first thing on his mind.

# 17

## Garívele, Vargoth

IT HAD TAKEN TEANNA D'ELSO TWO DAYS TO TRAVEL FROM
Corrato to Garívele, a port city twenty miles from Seth's
capital, Palandol. Heavy rains had flooded the roads and
made the going slow. During the best of times, Vargothan
roads tended to be poor. Whatever Seth did with the
money other nations paid him for his mercenaries, it was
obvious very little of it found its way into public improvements.

As a country, Vargoth had few natural resources and
was forced to rely on importing goods from other nations.
In order to balance things out, they had turned to the one
resource they had plenty of—manpower. For more than a
century Vargoth prided itself on exporting soldiers for
hire. There were other professions a young man could
go into, but the fastest road to wealth meant becoming a
soldier.

Though she was still a child at the time, Teanna could
remember when her father hired Vargothans to patrol
Nyngary's eastern border with Cincar. It was a complete
fiasco that nearly caused a war between the two countries.
All the mercenaries had to do was stop two local warlords
who had been harassing the textile guild in Lipari. Without bothering to consult the king, they took it on themselves to capture both men. Afterward, they burned their
villages, beheaded one, and drew and quartered the other.
It took nearly five years before relations were restored,
permitting travel between Cincar and Nyngary once

again. Her mother was so annoyed at the waste of money, she swore they would never use Vargoth again.

The man sitting across from Teanna now, Treton Baker, was dressed in civilian clothes. Usually, he wore a cloak that marked him as the captain of King Seth's bodyguard. Her guess was that Baker was somewhere between thirty-five and forty years of age. His face was all planes and angles, which made it difficult to tell. The skin was drawn tightly across his forehead and cheekbones, and his clear brown eyes seemed never to be at rest. They were at odds with the rest of the man, because all of his other movements were methodical, as if planned.

At one time, Baker had been a major in Vargoth's Northern Legions, but after a falling out with his commander, he was demoted and assigned to duties at Seth's palace. It was an insult he never forgot—or forgave— making him an easy and logical recruit to head Teanna's spy network. A man motivated by revenge was inherently more reliable than one whose goal was money alone. Her mother had taught her that lesson before she was ten years old, and it was proving apt now.

It was raining that afternoon. It had been raining all day. Baker, who was waiting when she arrived, sat at a table in the corner of a small café situated at the edge of the tanning district. She was there to learn more about the meeting between Shakira and Seth. That they had met at all was highly unusual, if not frightening. During the best of times, the balance of power in the East was never stable. Alliances were formed and pacts made between the nations almost as frequently as they were broken. Unwilling to trust others to communicate the information accurately, she had elected to endure the two day trip herself. Normally, she could have done so in an instant, but since learning that Shakira also had a ring, she decided against using hers until she had a better idea of what the Orlock queen was capable of. Caution was something else she had learned from her mother.

Teanna felt a twinge of guilt at not missing Marsa more. It had been nearly four years since she had died. During that time, Teanna had tried to recall a single spontaneous act of affection, and couldn't. She wasn't sure how that made her feel—sad, mostly. By the time she had reached her eighteenth birthday, people remarked on how difficult it was to tell them apart. That was all well and good, but physical similarities weren't internal ones. Certainly, she knew she emulated her mother in many things. What other model did she have? She knew she didn't possess Marsa's level of detachment, or her patience, but she had inherited her intellect. Sitting there in the café, she wondered how much mothers live on in their daughters. She supposed the answer would reveal itself one day.

The café was nondescript and grimy. It had one large window that looked out into the harbor. From where she sat, she could watch people pass by on the street. Teanna kept her hood up even after she was seated and pretended to sip a glass of wine the serving girl had brought. It was an inexpensive yellow from Cincar, and a slightly sour taste. Usually, she would have ordered one of the reds from her own country, but lately prices had been running so high it would have only have drawn unnecessary attention.

"How can I help you, your highness?" Baker asked.

"I'd like to know more about the meeting between Seth and Shakira."

"Such as?"

"Tell me how Seth was dressed, for a start."

The question seemed to surprise Baker, and he paused to consider it. "Plainly," he said after a moment, "no cloak, no crown, just breeches, a shirt, and his sword."

"Was Shakira also armed?"

Baker shook his head. "The only thing she had was a belt dagger. I wasn't able to get very close, though."

"And her clothes?"

"Also plain. She kept the hood of her cloak up, but you could see the yellow hair clear enough, and her white face—no mistaking that." He gave an involuntary shudder. "The rest of the clothes were nothing special, just a light-colored dress."

"Any jewelry or rings?"

"Not that I saw, Princess."

Teanna brought the wineglass up to her lips and feigned taking a sip. "I was told that they met by themselves in an old house. Is that true?"

"You were told correctly."

"How long did the meeting last?"

"About two hours. I waited outside with her guards and the priest."

Teanna's eyes came up sharply. "What priest?" she asked, putting the glass down.

"I never heard his name, highness, but he was definitely from Coribar, and he was definitely a priest. He wasn't wearing their white robes, but I saw his hand as plain as day." Baker smiled and held up his own hand to illustrate, folding back the top half of his fourth finger. "It's the same with all of them," he added.

"Put your hand down," Teanna hissed. "Why wasn't I told this?"

"Don't you people read the reports I sent? I mentioned it to your man, but he seemed much more interested in the Orlock. Not that I can't blame him; they're not something you see every day. Your blood goes cold just looking at them."

"Did you speak with this priest?"

Baker shook his head. "The only time I saw him speak to anyone, it was with the Orlocks. I couldn't hear what they said, and to be honest, I was happy not to get any closer than I had to. He stayed apart on the return voyage."

"He went back with your ship?" Teanna asked.

"Not all the way to Palandol. We dropped him in Bokras. For what it's worth, I know that he arrived with Shakira on a Vargothan galley."

Teanna felt her heart thumping in her chest. "He was

traveling with the Orlocks," she repeated half aloud. "Can you describe what he looked like?"

"Certainly. He was small, maybe five-foot-six, no more . . . clean shaven, and his hair was mostly gray. It may have been red once. My guess is that he was about sixty years old. And his eyes were hazel."

The description didn't fit anyone Teanna knew. Perhaps her father would know him. "What happened after the meeting?" she asked.

"Like I said, we left, and they left. I was glad to put the distance between us. I don't particularly relish being around Orlocks, and the stench from those galleys is something awful."

"Did Seth and this priest ever speak in private?"

"I didn't specifically see them, but one of the men in my unit told me they had dinner together. We landed at Bokras the following morning then continued on to Palandol."

Teanna questioned Baker for the next five minutes but failed to learn anything else of significance. The only other thing of interest he had to say involved a rumor that Seth was conducting war games in Vargoth's western territories.

After they separated, she decided to walk back to the tavern where she and Bryan Oakes had taken rooms. It would give her time to think. Fortunately, the rain had let up, though a watery mist hung in the air, making it heavy with the taste of salt. Wet cobblestones reflected light from gas lamps, and produced false rainbows on the ground. Teanna took a deep breath, filled her lungs, and looked up and down the street. At one end was the tannery with its potent odors, and at the opposite end, the merchant shops and the town's center. It was early in the evening and a few businesses were still open.

Garivele was reasonably close to the Vargoth capital, and in recent years it had gained popularity as a resort town. A few ships were moored in the harbor, their masts black silhouettes against the sky. On the next block Teanna saw a shop with all manner of flowers outside. She slowed as she walked by, trying to decide whether to buy any of them. Then something caught her eye. In the midst of a cluster of deep red roses were a bunch of blue ones. The only other time she had seen blue roses was at Tenley Palace in Sennia. A flood of memories went through her mind as she stared at them, then she continued walking.

Three doors away from the flower shop she again stopped, in front of a store bearing the name Hidden Treasures, and looked in the window. A variety of jeweled pins and artifacts were on display. Some were whole and in good condition and some were broken. They ranged from hand mirrors to cups and empty perfume bottles. Curious, she went in.

A diminutive woman seated behind one of the counters got up when she saw her. "Good evening, my dear," she said. "Are you looking for anything special?"

Teanna pushed her hood back. "No, just looking."

"Take your time. We have a lot of nice things to see. I'm Verna Talbot."

"Lisa Melroy," Teanna replied, shaking hands.

*This is fun,* she thought. She couldn't remember the last time she had gone shopping alone. It might be interesting not to be a princess for a while . . . just a normal girl.

"You have such pretty hair," Verna said. "I have some combs in this case that would be perfect for you. Let me see your eyes, dear."

Amused, Teanna opened her eyes a little wider and leaned down. She was quite tall and towered over the smaller woman. "Is this your shop?"

"Yes, it is. My husband and I run it, but he's away for the week, so I'm in charge."

"Women should always be in charge," Teanna said with a smile. "It's a lovely shop."

"Thank you. That's what I tell my granddaughters. If more women were in charge, things would get done a lot quicker."

Verna took Teanna by the arm and guided her to a

case on the opposite side of the room. "Are you here for the festivities?"

"Festivities?"

"The Feast of Saint Gavrila," Verna said. "Goodness, I thought everyone knew about it. That's what all the people are in town for. You're just visiting, then?"

"Yes, we stopped here for the night. I'm actually from Calisto. It's a small town in Nyngary."

Verna frowned as she tried to place the name. "Hmm, I seem to recall it, but it's been years since Roger and I were there. He's my husband, by the way. We used to sing with a group of traveling musicians. Is that the one with the gray watchtower? It has a big clock that shows the sun and the moon."

"Yes," Teanna said, surprised. "You were a singer? How interesting."

"It was a long time ago—thirty years at least. We bought this shop when we retired."

"Thirty years," Teanna exclaimed. "You must have retired at a very young age."

"Thank you, dear. Actually, I'm eighty-two," Verna said with a wink.

Teanna spent the next few minutes looking at various objects and talking with Verna. She found herself liking the older woman, and it was enjoyable passing the time that way. Having grown up in a palace as an only child, she had never made many friends. A few of the local nobles brought their daughters to visit from time to time, something her father arranged, but the differences in their positions made getting close to anyone difficult. Her mother had drilled the fact that she was a princess into her head from the time that she was little.

"You certainly don't look eight-two," Teanna said.

"I used to be a lot taller . . . not as tall as you, but about two inches, I should say. I've been shrinking as I get older. I suppose if I keep on going, I'll just disappear one day."

Teanna giggled and made a dismissive gesture. "Oh . . .

what's this?" she asked, noticing something in one of the cases.

"That's one of the combs I was telling you about. There's a brush and hand mirror to go with it. Roger brought them back from Tadero a few months ago. Aren't they lovely?" Verna took the items out of the glass case. "Sit here," she told Teanna. "There's a mirror on the counter you can use."

Teanna sat and watched as the old woman rearranged a few strands of her hair, then held them in place with the comb. It was decorated with amber and brown stones.

"I love it," Teanna said. "How much for all three?"

The price Verna quoted was a little steep, but Teanna paid it anyway. Her mother would have probably driven a harder bargain, she thought.

"Are you married?" Verna asked.

"No."

"Then you really should consider staying for the feast. It's great fun, and a pretty young girl like you might even be able to find yourself a husband."

"I'm afraid I don't know much about it," Teanna admitted.

"All you have to do is prepare a picnic basket then go to the gazebo in the town square. All the single girls will be there, and many from all over the province, too. We do it every year. The boys make bids and the money goes to charity. The highest bidder gets the girl and the basket. Afterward there's a dance. Both my granddaughters will be there."

"It does sound like fun. I'll certainly think about it."

Teanna was still smiling when she left the shop. She began strolling back in the direction of the tavern, thinking about what it would be like to live in a little town where everyone knew everyone. There would be none of the complications of palace life; no plots, no intrigues, no battles to fight or countries to run—a life without consequences. She breathed a sigh and imagined herself standing on a stage while handsome young men made bids to have a picnic with her.

Her mind wandered then to the soldier who was waiting for her at the tavern. Bryan Oakes was a lieutenant in the palace guard, a serious man with a fine, handsome face. She had already taken more time than she should have, and knew he would probably be worrying. Although he concealed it well, her decision to meet with Baker had upset him. It might have been a trifle petty on her part, but the thought of having a man worrying about her was . . . well . . . nice. Teanna wondered how much money her father paid a lieutenant in the Royal Guard. Picnic baskets were sometimes expensive.

"Bit dark out to be walking by yourself, missy," a voice from the alley said, startling her.

She turned to see two men dressed as sailors step out of the darkness. Both were large, rough-looking, and in need of a bath. The man on the right had a scar across his cheek.

"I'm on my way back to the Stone Bench to meet my friend," Teanna told them.

"Whatcha carryin' there, little lady?" the one without the scar asked.

"Something I bought a little while ago, if it's any of your business. Nothing you'd want."

"Now how would you knows what we want?" the man asked.

"I don't have time for this," Teanna said. "I don't want to hurt you, so I suggest that you and your friend—"

Her words were cut off when a callused hand was clamped over her mouth. She found herself being lifted off the ground by a third man, who had come up silently behind her. The assailant put his other hand around her waist and carried her into the alley. Teanna was so shocked by the attack, she had no time to react. Once they were off the street, the scar-faced man took the package from her while his companion held a knife at her throat. She felt the breath of the man holding her on her neck, as she watched Scar Face pull the wrappings apart. He tossed them on the ground, looked at the jeweled comb for a moment, then at the brush and mirror.

"Nothin' but junk," he said to the second man. "What else you carryin', missy?"

Teanna didn't answer.

The man holding her pulled her head back sharply and increased the pressure of the knife at her throat. "My friend just asked you a question," he said in her ear. "Didn't your mother teach you any manners?"

*My mother taught me a lot of things. One of them was not to show fear to your enemies.* "I'm not carrying anything of value," Teanna said through clenched teeth.

"If you ask me, she might have something concealed under this skirt," the man holding her said. He released her chin and laid his hand flat on Teanna's stomach. "Hmm, nothing here."

The other man seemed to think it was very funny and moved closer.

The man holding her let his hand drift lower until it reached Teanna's thigh. He began to bunch up her skirt. It took every ounce of willpower she possessed not to draw on the ring. The knife was still poised at her throat, too close. If she could get him to move it, just a little, she could use it.

"You have such strong hands," she whispered, pressing herself backward a little. "No need to be so rough."

The man chuckled and pulled her skirt higher. "I told you she was a hot one," he said to his two companions.

Both of his friends had their eyes glued to her legs, which were gradually being exposed inch by inch. Teanna thought rapidly. Making a little noise, she rubbed her shoulders against his chest, something her mother told her men liked.

Scar Face's tongue darted out and he licked his lips. The man nearest him gave a nervous laugh and he took a step nearer as Scar Face put his hands on Teanna's hips.

"D'ya know, Deacon, I might have been wrong," the man holding her said. "I think she is hiding something. I was just a little low on the chart, is all."

The pressure from the knife's point finally slackened and he moved the blade lower, trailing it between Teanna's breasts until it was just under the top button of her blouse. With a quick flick of the wrist he popped the button free.

Teanna smiled and looked back over her shoulder into his eyes. A second later, it was her turn.

The man holding her let out a startled cry as the knife vanished from his hand. At the same time, both his companions were lifted off the ground and slammed backward into a brick wall at the end of the alley. One of them fell to the ground in an unconscious heap. The other lay there stunned. Teanna twisted around to face her assailant, whose mouth had dropped open.

"You're a witch," he hissed, taking a step backward.

It was the last thing he ever said. In the next second his eyes filled with blood and he let out a strangled sound as his chest and shoulders caved inward, crushing his heart and internal organs. He collapsed like a marionette whose strings had been cut. Teanna spun around in time to see Scar Face getting to his feet. With a dagger raised above his head, he started to run at her.

After four steps he burst into flame.

A horrible scream tore the night air. Waving his arms in blind panic, he crashed into a wall, shrieking in agony. He was dead a moment later.

The third man was just regaining consciousness when he looked up to see Teanna walking toward him. He scrambled backward until he bumped into the wall.

"Have mercy, mistress," he begged. "I didn't lay hands upon you. Spare me. I swear to God Almighty, I'll never tell anyone what happened."

One of Teanna's eyebrows arched. "I know," she said softly.

A column of white light appeared out of nowhere and

enveloped the man. It moved inward, compressing itself into a thin line that consolidated itself into a single dot and then winked out of existence. Somewhere, far away, the sound of a chime echoed.

The only living occupant in the alley was now Teanna d'Elso.

The man who had been there a moment ago materialized two hundred miles out at sea. He fought to stay afloat as a large swell nearly engulfed him. He turned himself in a full circle to see where he was and treaded water because it was the only thing he could do. All he saw was a limitless white sky that merged into the horizon until the two became indistinguishable. There was nothing anywhere. Nothing. He began to scream.

Back in the alley, Teanna picked up the hand mirror and saw that it was cracked. Absently, she tucked a strand of hair behind one ear and waited until her breathing returned to normal. She stared at her reflection in the broken glass for a long time.

*Every enemy you leave alive is one more person who can harm you.* That was something else her mother had taught her.

# 18

## Devondale

IT WAS MID-MORNING BY THE TIME THEY REACHED DE-
vondale. The little church stood at the north end of the
town near the loop road. Silas Alman's home was next to
it. Mathew and Father Thomas slowed their horses and
came to a halt. Neither spoke. Father Thomas looked up at
the stained-glass window above the double doors and
shook his head at some distant memory. Mathew wanted
to say something to his friend, but his tongue seemed to
have deserted him. A variety of thoughts and emotions
were going through his head, more than he had been prepared for. How many Sixth Day services had he attended
with his father and mother there? He couldn't begin to
count them. The stones of the building bore the same gray
patina he had pictured in his mind's eye, though the steps
looked as if they had been newly painted. He wondered if
Father Thomas would notice.

*Probably.* The priest noticed everything.

The memory of the last time he had set foot in Devondale's church abruptly surfaced in his memory. For the last
several hours he'd been doing his best to think of other
things because that had been the day his father was buried.
They'd laid Bran Lewin to rest in the cemetery behind the
church.

A sudden pang gripped Mathew's heart and he got
down off his horse. His father's face, always so strong and
confident in all that he did, came to him. Circumstances
had prevented him from getting a proper marker for the

grave. He'd left to save himself without seeing to his father's memorial.

In his eyes it was a cowardly act, and self-loathing caused his hands to clench.

Mathew took a deep breath and walked to the cemetery at the side of the church. Ben Fenton's name he expected . . . Silas Alman's came as a shock, as did Truemen Palmer. Truemen had been the town's mayor and Lara's uncle. Thad Layton was there alongside his wife Stel.

The memories were coming so fast, he was finding it difficult to breathe, and to his surprise he found his eyes brimming with tears. He had been prepared and not prepared for this, and it felt like an old wound was being opened. He'd grown up with these people. He tried to look anywhere other than at the headstones, but his eyes were continually drawn to them.

*"Four years,"* he whispered to himself.

The sight of Lucas Emson's grave in the next row caused him to draw in his breath sharply and he put a hand up to his mouth. Fergus Gibb's grave was only a short distance away. He felt Father Thomas beside him and the priest's hand on his shoulder.

Half blinded by tears, Mathew looked around the cemetery. There were more graves than he remembered . . . so many more. He didn't want to go on. It took considerable effort to make his feet start moving, and he forced himself to walk up and down the rows. He whispered the names to himself, praying the next grave wouldn't contain someone he had been close to. He was wrong . . . they all did. Every one of them was familiar. When he looked back on that day in later years, and he did many times, he would recall it as being one of the most painful moments of his life.

He didn't remember making his way to the old chestnut tree in the corner of the cemetery. Both his father and mother were buried there. She had died when he was quite young, and her loss had retreated to a dull ache over the years. Bran was another matter. They had been as much friends as a father and son could be.

Mathew stared at the grave in shock, for it now contained a granite tombstone that read:

BRAN LEWIN, SOLDIER,
BELOVED HUSBAND AND FATHER

Confused, he turned to Father Thomas for an explanation, but the priest shook his head and turned his palms up. Mathew looked back at the two graves in front of him and knelt down. He reached out and ran his fingertips over the top of the stone and across the letters.

Father Thomas closed his eyes and said a silent prayer for Bran and Janel, then moved away to give Mathew time alone. A mild breeze rustled through the leaves in the chestnut tree, and the sun shone warm on his shoulders. His old friend had been murdered by Berke Ramsey a few hundred yards from where he was now standing. It seemed a hundred years ago. He watched when Mathew looked up into the branches of the tree and his heart went out to the quiet young man.

Several minutes passed before Mathew got up. Father Thomas guessed at the kaleidoscope of emotions that must have been assailing him, because he was experiencing much the same thing.

"All right?" he asked.

Mathew took a deep breath. "All right."

The priest put his arm around Mathew's shoulders and they walked back along the path together to the church.

Father Thomas's house was located to the right of the church. When they reached the point where the brick path split, Mathew thought his friend would go there next, but he was wrong. Father Thomas hesitated for a moment,

then headed for the back door of the church. It was un-
locked, and they let themselves in and came out behind
the altar. Father Thomas walked around it.

He stood in the middle of the room between two rows
of oak pews.

It was not an especially large church, at least by the
standards of most churches in Werth Province. Nevertheless, it was capable of holding three-quarters of the town's
population at any one time. As a boy, Mathew could remember sitting through some of old Father Halloran's services and trying not to fidget or make eye contact with his
mother, who darted warning glances in his direction. The
year Father Thomas came to the village to take Father
Halloran's place was the first time Mathew recalled actually listening to what was being said from the pulpit. His
friend's sermons always seemed to deal with things that
made sense.

He watched Father Thomas standing there. The priest
slowly turned in a full circle then stopped and gazed up at
the stained-glass window. The excitement that ran through
the town the day they had put it in was still a vivid memory. Morning sunlight streamed in and cast a dozen colors
onto the floor.

Father Thomas walked to the nearest bench and sat
down. "This is harder than I thought it would be," he said.

Mathew gave him a smile.

"So many things have changed and yet nothing has
changed," the priest said. "For the last four years, I have
agonized over the choice I made, Mathew."

"Father—"

"No, I took you away from your home and your friends,
my son. At the time I believed I was doing the right thing,
but now, I don't know," he said, shaking his head.

"I could have said no and gone with Jeram Quinn,"
Mathew answered. "It was *my* choice."

"But you were so young at the time."

"I've thought about it . . . many times. I don't regret

killing Ramsey, nor do I regret going with you when we did. I've never blamed you for anything that happened."

The priest appeared unconvinced. "Our country is in ruins, your father is dead, and your ring is gone. These are sad, terrible times, my son. You could have been living here happy and safe."

Mathew pondered the last statement before replying. "Not safe, Father. Karas Duren sent the Orlocks for the ring. It would only have been a matter of time before he got what he wanted."

"But—"

"I didn't know what it was then. I didn't know about the machine the Ancients had created or what the ring was capable of. It's up to us now to get it back and set things right. Alor Satar wants everyone and everything to be the same as they are. No one has a right to do that. Not Karas Duren, or Teanna, or her cousins, or even God. I'm not being rude, but we make our own lives and our own choices about how we live. You taught me that. I made my choice and I don't regret it . . . honestly I don't."

The priest smiled at him and stood up. Both men hugged.

When they separated, Father Thomas told him, "I haven't been very diligent about my prayers lately, and I know you have people you want to say hello to. Why don't you attend to that now? We can meet at the tavern in an hour."

Mathew understood why Father Thomas was sending him off. Part of him wished the priest wouldn't. Seeing Lara again was not going to be easy, and while he appreciated the offer of privacy, he wasn't sure how to handle the situation. It had cost him a great deal of lost sleep over the last few days. What does a dead man say to the woman he was in love with? Every scenario he had rehearsed in his mind sounded more idiotic than the one before. There were a hundred questions sailing around in his brain. How much had she changed? How would she feel about seeing

him again? And then there were Collin, Daniel, and his
other friends.

*Just pop back into their lives and leave again? He'd be
lucky if they didn't throw him down a well.*

A little voice in the back of his head urged him to get
on his horse and ride out of town, but it was already too
late for that.

*This day had to come sooner or later,* he said to himself.

When Mathew looked up, he saw Father Thomas
watching him.

"What's so damn funny?" he asked, seeing his expression.

Father Thomas held his hands up defensively. "I was
just imagining if I can avoid looking like that when I see
Ceta. Lara will understand, Mat."

Mathew let his shoulders slump. "You don't know
Lara," he answered morosely.

"Yes, I do. And I know you as well, Mathew. The circumstances that forced you to leave were not of your
making. She's a fine girl—and I promise she'll be overjoyed to see you."

Somehow, the priest's words seemed less convincing
than usual. Mathew opened his mouth to say something
but changed his mind. "I wish I knew more about women,"
he blurted out.

The corners of Father Thomas's mouth moved slightly
and he took Mathew by the shoulders and turned him
around. "So do I, my son. And if I ever gain any insight into
that subject, you will be the first person I pass the knowledge along to."

"Wonderful."

There had been changes in Devondale since he'd left.
For one thing, few homes had thatch roofs anymore. Most
of the roofs had been replaced with wood shakes or slate.
For another, the main street had been paved with cobblestones and sidewalks had been added, complete with gas
lamp posts. It took Mathew by surprise. He stared at the

new improvements trying to decide how he felt about them and couldn't make up his mind.

It was late in the morning and a number of people were out. Surprisingly, most of them were unfamiliar to him, which was more disturbing than the new sidewalks. A few glanced at him as he passed by, but no one said anything, perhaps because he was avoiding eye contact and his hair was now black. The beard was gone of course. He'd shaved that off two nights ago—because he was afraid of scaring Lara, he'd told himself, but he knew that wasn't the truth. He wanted to look as much like his old self as he could. He glanced at his reflection in a window and rubbed his jaw. The face was the same, if older and more mature, but it was still him. Regardless, he half expected someone to stop and say "Hello," or at least "Good morning," and when no one did, it seemed out of character for the town he thought he knew.

When he left Devondale, he had known just about everyone there and exchanging pleasantries was something that was more or less expected. It was one of those unwritten rules that people followed. Sometimes it was a hindrance, particularly if you were in a hurry to get someplace, but in his mind it had made Devondale a better place to live. Such things happened in larger cities like Tyraine and Barcora, but he never thought it would occur in his hometown, and it made him angry.

The farther down the street he went, the more he became cognizant of how many new faces and shops there were in town. To his shock, two more side streets had been added since he left. Essentially, it was the same place, and yet it wasn't. By the time he reached the main square, most of his surprise had worn off and he unconsciously began to catalog the changes.

"At least the gazebo is still here," he grumbled to himself.

On the opposite side of the square, a small silver shop bore the name GIBB & SONS. Akin and Fergus had never bothered to change it after their father died. Mathew remembered Akin as a tall blond man with slender fingers. Fergus, the older of the two sons, was dead. Seeing his name in the cemetery had come as a blow, much like the others he had been close with. Because so many of the graves bore the same date of death, he assumed that a battle must have taken place after the invasion. A good number of the tombstones were inscribed with women's names. It was a morbid piece of conjecture, because he knew the people of Devondale would not have given their town up without a fight. Elgarian women had never shown any hesitation in fighting alongside their men. Whatever the tragedy, it drove home once again how important it was to recover his ring.

*These people must not have died in vain*, he thought. He would explain that to Lara and the others and make them understand. Father Thomas's words about him being Elgaria's last hope took on renewed meaning.

Mathew looked at the old oak tree where Akin and Fergus used to play their violins on Sixth Day afternoons. He thought of his friends, so much alike in their appearance and mannerisms, and wondered whether Akin had continued to play after his brother's death. Once he saw Lara, he would go to see his old friend.

Thankfully, the square still looked very much the same. There were no flowers in the beds the day he left, and there was the lawn near the town council building where he had fenced the last bout with Giles Naismith.

"*Giles*." Mathew said the name aloud. The fencing strips were all gone, as were the tables where they had eaten dinner after the competition was over. He could almost hear the music and see his friends dancing. That night had ended badly when Thad Layton stumbled into the dance carrying the body of his dead child. The boy had been mutilated by the Orlocks. Mathew shut his eyes, willing away the gruesome image. An odyssey of nearly four years had now brought him full circle.

At the end of one street several new buildings had been

erected. Mathew continued walking toward them. On the next block, at the corner of a building, a sign read BLAKLEY'S METAL PRODUCTS. It was just above where Randal Wain's shop should have been. He didn't remember seeing Randal's name in the cemetery, and wondered what could have happened to him. Memories of trying not to listen while his father negotiated a price for his first sword with Randal brought a smile to his face.

Mathew reached down and touched the weapon's pommel. The Kaseri steel had never lost its edge over the years, and its balance was the best he had ever found. In two weeks he and Father Thomas would be in Vargoth. It was comforting to have the priest with him, though the job of fencing master might be moot in light of what Delain had told them. All he had to do was break into Teanna's palace, find the ring, and get out alive. He had no clear idea how they would accomplish that, but they would find a way—they had to.

Lara's father's shop was on the next street. The closer he got, the more Mathew felt his pulse racing, so he decided to stop and rehearse what he was going to say one more time. But then he saw two people who were familiar to him coming down the street. Fortunately, neither had seen him yet. He ducked into an alley and waited for them to pass. Alone again, his tried the words in his mind until he felt foolish. It was just delay, and he knew it.

Mathew stepped out of the alley and crossed the street. Daniel's house was on the next block. Collin probably had his own farm by now. Either that or he was living with his brother or his parents, assuming he was still in Devondale at all. Collin had always wanted to see the world. Mathew guessed it was a fifty-fifty chance that he'd be gone. The prospect of missing him hurt, because he very much wanted to see him again. None of Delain's people had known anything about Collin Miller, or anyone else in Devondale for that matter. If they had, the names of his dead friends in the cemetery might not have come as such a shock.

The dye shop was a nondescript affair. As Mathew got closer he saw several people inside. A horse and wagon were tied up out front. He slowed down and walked past it, glancing in the window and trying not to be obvious. Lara's father was standing on a ladder talking to a man Mathew had never seen before. Amanda Palmer was behind the counter. The heavyset lady she was waiting on was Ella Emson, wife of the town blacksmith. Having seen Lucas's grave only a short while ago, Mathew's first instinct was to go in and tell her how sorry he was, but that would involve complications he couldn't afford. He watched Martin Palmer get down off the ladder and hand the man a small parcel. The man paid him, came outside, got on his wagon, and proceeded down the street.

He decided to wait until Ella was gone, hoping she wouldn't be in one of her talkative moods. The longer he waited, however, the more doubts crept into his mind. He tried convincing himself that everyone would be better off without his showing up and disrupting their lives again.

"This is impossible," he said finally.

Ella finally emerged from the shop and headed toward the square, clutching a bundle under her arm. A big, solid figure from his past, she had always been pleasant and well-meaning, particularly after his mother had died.

*How bad would it have been to have said a few words to her?*

*Bad,* he decided. The answer presented itself almost as soon as he had thought of it.

The fewer people who knew that Mathew Lewin was alive, the greater his chances for success would be. One word to Teanna or Alor Satar and the mercenaries would be scouring the countryside for him.

Mathew walked back to the shop, opened the door and stepped in.

# 19

## Devondale

LARA'S FATHER WAS SEATED AT AN OLD ROLLTOP DESK
making an entry in his ledger. He was a man of medium
build, fifty-two years old, with salt and pepper brown hair.
He glanced up when he heard the door open and half
turned in his seat. "Good morning, young fella," he said
over his shoulder. "Give me a moment and I'll be right
with you."

"Hello, Master Palmer."

Martin Palmer's pencil paused and he turned around,
staring at the newcomer. Several seconds passed and he
said nothing, then a small crease appeared in the middle
of his forehead and he slowly got to his feet.

"Martin," he said absently. The frown deepened and he
took a step forward. "My God . . . Mathew?"

"Yes, sir."

Lara's father recovered himself, crossed the room in
three strides, and seized Mathew in an embrace. "My
God, my God. Let's have a look at you, boy." He held
Mathew at arm's length. "We thought you were dead."

"I'm sorry, sir. I know what a shock this must be, but
the deception was necessary. I'll tell you all about—"

A sharp intake of breath followed by a loud crash
stopped Mathew in mid-sentence. Amanda Palmer stood
there in the doorway with her hands over her mouth. A
glass bowl lay in pieces at her feet. Mathew immediately
went to her and they hugged. She was as much in shock as
her husband had been and her green eyes were filled with

tears. They were almond-shaped, like Lara's. She took Mathew's face in her hands and kissed him, stepped back and then pulled him back to her again and kissed him once more. Mathew smiled and returned the embrace.

Martin turned the sign hanging from the knob over, indicating the shop was closed.

It took Mathew fifteen minutes to recount what had happened after Fanshaw Castle, and the Palmers had a hundred questions. He answered them as honestly as he could. They were clearly happy to see him and overjoyed when he told them that Father Thomas was also back.

"But why didn't he come with you?" Martin asked.

"I think he wanted to give me some time to see Lara alone."

Martin cleared his throat. "Oh, yes. Quite right. Unfortunately, she's not here now. She's gone to Becky Enders's house to deliver a package. She should be back shortly."

Mathew sighed. "I've been trying to figure out what to say to her. Is she all right?"

"Lara? Yes, yes. She and—"

Martin abruptly broke off the rest of his sentence when his wife stepped on his foot. A look passed between them.

"Is something wrong?" Mathew asked.

"Nothing at all," Amanda said. "Will you stay to dinner with us, Mathew?"

"Yes, indeed," Martin added. "That's a wonderful idea. I'm going to break out that bottle of that Nyngary Red we've been saving. I put it around here somewhere. Mother, do you know where it is?"

"It's upstairs in the cupboard," she said patiently.

"The cupboard? Well, of course it is. I'll just pop up and get it. You wait right here, Mat. It won't take me a second."

Amanda watched her husband disappear through the back door of the shop and shook her head.

"He's very happy to see you, Mathew. We both are."

She reached up, brushed the rebellious lock of hair off

his forehead, and gave him a warm smile. "Lara will be as well."

Mathew opened his mouth to say something and closed it again. When Amanda didn't say anything else, the silence closed in.

"Is . . . uh, Lara still living upstairs with you?" he asked, glancing up at the ceiling where Martin could be heard walking.

"No, Mathew. She has her own home now. It's on the outskirts of town. I'm sure there's a lot you'll both want to talk about. She shouldn't be long. By the way, where is Father Thomas now?"

Mathew felt his stomach turn over. It wasn't so much Amanda's words as the way she had said them. Until that moment it had never occurred to him that Lara might have found someone else and settled down to a life of her own. *What a fool he was.* He was dead, and dead men didn't have any claims on the living. He felt face go red at his own stupidity.

"I think he went to see if his house was still in one piece," he answered, averting his eyes.

Part of his brain registered Martin coming down the steps and reentering the room, and part caught the look of sympathy on Amanda's face. Suddenly, he didn't want to be there anymore. Coming back to Devondale had been a mistake. He knew that now.

"Here we are," Martin said, holding up the bottle of wine. "I think we should . . ."

His voice dropped off when he saw Mathew's expression, and he turned to Amanda. She responded with a slight shake of her head.

"Where did you say Lara's house was?" Mathew asked.

"It's on the South Road a little over a mile past Westrey Bridge," Amanda answered.

Mathew thought for a second. "But that's Askel Miller's farm."

"Yes, it is, Mathew."

Another silence followed. Martin Palmer went to stand next to his wife and he put an arm around her shoulders. Both of their faces were somber. Mathew could feel his stomach tightening as he fought to gain control of his emotions.

"Perhaps it would be best if I come back a little later," he said. His own voice sounded strange to him. "Does Collin still live in town? I'd like to see him before we leave."

Martin nodded. "Mm-hmm."

Beyond that he didn't elaborate, nor did he need to. The unspoken message struck Mathew like a blow.

*Lara and Collin were married!*

He looked from Martin to Amanda, who had a hand over her mouth.

"I see," Mathew said.

"You see *nothing*," Martin said. "And I need something stronger than this wine. Amanda, why don't you run up and fix dinner? Mat and I need to have a little talk."

Martin reached under the counter, and retrieved a bottle of brandy. A little more rummaging produced two glasses and an arch look from his wife. Once again something passed between them, which was more or less unique to people who were married. Mathew didn't care; it suddenly felt like his ears were on fire, and he very much wanted to be gone.

*Collin and Lara,* he thought.

It was Martin who broke the silence "Mat, if you'll excuse us for a minute, I need to speak with my wife— in private."

"That's fine, sir. But I really do need to be running along and—"

"*Martin,*" he corrected. "We've known each other long enough to be on a first name basis by now. Will you do me a favor?"

"If I can."

"You can. I'd like you to promise you'll be here when I return."

"Well, it's just that—"

"I'd like your word on it, Mat. I've never asked you for anything before, and I'm going to take it real bad if I come down and you're gone."

Mathew's eyes locked with Lara's father's. Martin's face was as serious as he had ever seen it. It was also a small enough thing for one friend to ask another.

"All right."

Five minutes turned into ten as Mathew waited. Below in the shop, he could hear the raised voices coming from the floor above. He couldn't make out the words, but what they were talking about was obvious. Had he not given his word, he *would* have left as soon as they were gone. Now he had no choice but to wait.

*Collin and Lara.*

It cut like a knife. He took a deep breath and hoped the Palmers would hurry. The last time he saw them had been the day of his father's funeral. It seemed so very long ago. He didn't remember much about that day except sitting in Lara's room with her and talking until he fell asleep from exhaustion. The Palmers' house was actually behind their place of business, at the end of an alley. They'd given Lara her own room above the shop for her sixteenth birthday.

Mathew fidgeted and waited and fidgeted some more and still neither Martin or Amanda had reappeared. The loud conversation going on above him gradually subsided. But he could still hear them talking and wished that they would hurry so he could leave. Strangely, every once in a while he thought heard the sound of a child's voice.

He remembered that Harry, one of Lara's brothers, lived in Mechlen, a town not far from Devondale, and ran a dry goods business. Garrick, her other brother, owned a farm to the west of town. Neither had had any children when he left. He supposed that was no longer the case.

If the Palmers didn't finish their discussion in the next few minutes, he decided, he would call up to them and tell them that he had to go. He still needed to see Akin and Daniel before he left town.

Mathew was reiterating what a bad idea coming back had been when the door at the front of the shop opened.

"Why are we closed at this time of day?" a familiar voice asked.

He turned to see Lara standing in the doorway, and all of the words he had so carefully rehearsed promptly deserted him. She saw him at the same time and froze. Neither of them moved for several seconds.

Lara's lips parted slightly. "Mathew," she whispered.

Somehow he managed to take a step toward her, and then another. The mass of chestnut-colored hair was immediately familiar, as were the contours of her face and figure. She had the slightest cleft in her chin.

*Say something, you fool*, his mind shouted.

"I've come back. I wanted—"

The rest of Mathew's sentence was interrupted by a perfectly thrown right cross that landed flush on his jaw and knocked him backward.

"You son of a bitch!" she shouted. *"Four years and not a word!"*

Mathew shook his head and felt his jaw. "I couldn't," he said. "It was too dangerous."

*"Four years,"* she repeated, taking a step toward him.

Mathew took a half step back and raised his hands defensively. "I'm sorry."

*"Sorry? Sorry?"* she shouted. "I thought . . . you let me think that you were dead and all you can say is *you're sorry*? It's been four years since I've seen you and you come waltzing in here with not so much as a letter in all that time. You—You—"

"I didn't mean to hurt you," Mathew said, rubbing his jaw.

Lara stamped her foot in frustration. "Oh, Mathew."

This was not exactly going the way he had planned, and saying he was sorry again would probably just get her more upset. The footfalls coming down the steps told him that Lara's parents were returning. At the moment, the last thing he wanted was a public scene.

"Look, I didn't ask for any of this," he said. "I know you didn't, either. It was a mistake my coming back. I see that now, but I thought . . ."

Mathew paused while Amanda and Martin Palmer entered the room. Amanda was carrying a young child in her arms, a little boy. Mathew paused and smiled at him, and the child gave him a shy smile in return.

"At any rate," he continued, pulling his eyes away from the boy, "I can see what a shock this has been. I don't know what I was thinking. I suppose that sounds stupid, but I want you to know that I wish you all happiness."

As he was speaking, Lara's expression softened and she moved closer to him. Mathew's jaw was beginning to throb from where she had punched him, and he half expected to have to duck. To his surprise she reached up and brushed the lock of hair off his forehead, as her mother had done.

"You are *such* an idiot," she said, throwing her arms around him and pulling him to her.

Confused, Mathew returned the embrace and looked over his shoulder at her parents. Martin tapped the side of his head and Amanda gave him a warm smile. She was becoming teary-eyed again. The intensity with which Lara held him communicated itself through his body, and images of the last time they had been together surfaced in his mind.

His next thought was of Collin.

Loyalty to one's friends wasn't something that came and went with the seasons. If Lara was married to Collin now, there was nothing he could do, or ever would do, about it. Feelings of loss and anger at missed opportunities threatened to overwhelm him and it took all his willpower not to let them show.

"Well," Mathew said, drawing away from her. "It has certainly been an education seeing you all again." He tentatively moved his jaw from side to side. "Thank you for your kind invitation, Amanda, but I'm afraid I'll have to decline. I'll be leaving town shortly and I have a number of other calls to make." He turned to Lara and added, "Would you tell Collin that I said hello?"

Her mouth dropped open. "You're leaving?"

Mathew smiled. "I think it's for the best. You're all quite busy and I see there's been a new addition to your family since I've been gone. What's his name?"

"Bran," Lara replied softly.

The mild expression Mathew had assumed promptly dissolved. "Bran?"

"Yes, Mathew."

The two of them held each other's gaze for several seconds until Mathew broke it off. He looked down at the floor and smiled. "That's a good name."

"I know."

"Well, Master Bran," he said, turning back to the boy and dropping down to one knee. "It has been a pleasure meeting you." He held out his hand, and to his surprise, Bran took it. "You have a wonderful mother and a wonderful family. I'm envious.

"Harry's?" he asked Martin.

Martin Palmer gave him a tight-lipped smile and shook his head.

Mathew frowned and turned to Amanda. "This is Garrick and Nell's son?"

Her eyes flicked first to Lara then back to his, and she also shook her head.

He didn't think it was possible to feel any stupider than he had for the last few minutes, but there it was. *Bran was Lara's child!*

Astonished, Mathew twisted around and looked over his shoulder. His mouth fell open. "Lara, you're a mother?"

An expression he'd never seen before crossed Lara's face and she nodded. A faint smile played at the corners of her mouth. Mathew's laugh was rueful and he turned back to the boy, studying him more closely. He should have seen the resemblance earlier.

"He has the most beautiful blue eyes," he said, trying to buy himself time.

"Just like his father's," Lara whispered.

The fact that Collin had brown eyes didn't occur to Mathew for several seconds.

# 20

## Devondale

FATHER THOMAS SAT IN THE PARLOR OF HIS HOME, FRET-ting about his young friend. He would have gone with him to see Lara and her family, but a man had to do some things alone. This was one of them. Mathew and Lara had been in love almost since they were children, and they deserved a little time to themselves. On top of that, he was privy to certain things that Mathew was not. The first was apparent, the second less so.

From the letters he'd received from Lara over the years, he knew that Mathew now had a son. Over the past few days he had wanted to tell Mathew about it, but the timing was never right. Delain was also aware of it and urged him to avoid Devondale completely, but he had not the heart to do so. A dozen times he had debated the wisdom of coming here. Perhaps, he thought, his hesitation about telling Mathew the truth was because he was the one who had set him on his course four years ago.

What other choice did he have? Two things had been clear to the priest at the time. The battle at Fanshaw Castle was lost the moment Teanna d'Elso had entered it, and unless Mathew found a way to recover his ring, the downfall of the West was just as inevitable. To his chagrin, both predictions had come to pass in varying degrees.

In a short while Mathew Lewin would learn that he had a son, if he had not already done so. He would probably be furious at not being told the truth. That was to be expected, but it was something that couldn't be helped.

The problem now would to be to get the boy to finish what they'd started, and that promised to be no easy task. Delain needed his military skills, and Mathew needed him to make sure he got to Nyngary.

Father Thomas knew how strong Mathew's sense of responsibility was. He only hoped it was strong enough to pull him away from his newly discovered family. He had heard Karas Duren's tired refrain about "one country, one rule" many times. It was pure artifice, nothing more than a clever way to hide the real reason behind their invasion in the first place—power. That's what it always came down to. Revenge for their father's defeats might have been a factor in Eric and Armand Duren's thinking, but *power* lay at the core of it.

Once people had tasted freedom and learned what it was like to lead their own lives, to be able to travel from province to province without a pass, to live where and how they pleased, their decisions were dangerous for those who would deny them those rights.

And then there was Lara.

Having just gotten him back, would she let him go again? Certainly the child deserved a father. What child didn't? As Siward Thomas sat there in the dark, a conversation he and Mathew had a long time ago came back to him. He had told the boy that there were times when the needs of the many outweighed the needs of the few. As cynical as it was, nothing had changed in that respect.

Father Thomas wasn't proud of himself for withholding information about Mathew's son, but he was convinced that he had made the right decision. Many pieces of a carefully laid puzzle were just now falling into place.

From the messages Paul Teller had been able to smuggle in to him over the years, he knew that Sennia's Ecumenical Council was aware of their mistake in supporting Edward Guy and Ferdinand Willis almost from the beginning. Slowly but surely priests throughout the country had begun a campaign to rectify the situation. Because they couldn't preach rebellion or engage in open acts of sedition, sermons were written to get the message out to the people. Curriculums in school classes and at the university were adjusted to teach what happens when the law was bent to serve the purposes of a few. Poems and songs began to circulate throughout Sennia on that very subject, and the same thing had happened in Elgaria. The Vargothans, of course, did their best to censor them, but had met with little success.

It had taken his brethren almost four years to motivate the people of Sennia to act. Guy's announcement of a new trial for Gawl was the spark that ignited the blaze. Riots broke out all across the country, and Guy was now fighting to retain his position. That fire would soon spread to Elgaria, no matter what the Durens now called it.

Four years of planning had thrown Sennia into a civil war. Once Gawl was back in power, he and Delain would launch their attack on the mercenaries, with Mirdan supporting them from the west. The war was coming.

And at the heart of it was Mathew Lewin, an awkward young man he had sworn to protect. Without him to nullify the Nyngary princess, they would be back where they started.

*Yes, Mathew will be angry. He has every right to be, but the needs of the many—*

A creak on the steps outside brought his head around, and he saw the silhouette of a man standing at the front door.

"Hello the house. Is there anyone in there?"

He knew that voice. "I'm in here, Akin."

The figure outside froze and then the door opened slightly and a blond head poked itself in. "Father Thomas?"

"It's me. Come in."

The door opened the rest of the way and an open-mouthed Akin Gibb stood there on the porch staring at Father Thomas in disbelief. The priest, chuckling, got up and went to him, and both men embraced. When they separated, Akin closed the door behind him and pulled the shade down. He did the same with the windows. It was a curious thing to do and Father Thomas looked to his old friend for an explanation.

"I saw the horses tied up in front of the church and came by to see who was here," Akin said. "I'm sorry, Father, but Devondale may not be safe for you."

Father Thomas's eyebrows went up. "Indeed? Have they filled the job?"

"No, no. Nothing like that," Akin said. "I've been doing the Sixth Day services since you've been gone. Actually, I'm getting pretty good at it, if I do say so myself. Give me a moment. I want to put the horses around back. Was there someone else with you?"

Father Thomas considered his friend briefly. "I'll tell you when you return. Go take care of the horses."

Akin looked like he wanted to say something more, then changed his mind and slipped out the back door of the cottage. He returned three minutes later. "You are the last person I expected to see."

"Not the last," Father Thomas said. "Mathew is with me."

If Akin Gibb appeared shocked before, it was nothing compared to his reaction now. He took a step back. "Dear Lord. We thought he was dead. We were told—"

"I know," Father Thomas said. He took Akin by the elbow and led him over to the kitchen table. The priest hooked his leg around a chair and pulled it out. Once Akin sat down, he went to the pantry found a bottle of wine and two glasses and came back to join him.

"Mathew is alive?" Akin asked.

"Mathew is alive." He worked the cork out and sniffed the contents of the bottle. "Hmm, still good, I think." He poured each of them a glass. "Supposing you tell me what's going on."

Akin took a second to collect himself. "Seeing you was shock enough, but this . . . I mean it's wonderful, Father."

"But . . . ?"

"But there have been changes since you've been gone. I don't know how much you know, but there have definitely been changes—few of them for the better."

Father Thomas laced his fingers together and rested his chin on the back of his hands. "All right. Tell me."

"When I said it wasn't safe, I meant it. There are informants in town now who work with the Vargothans."

The priest blinked and sat back in his chair.

"I'm quite serious. Devondale is not the same place it was four years ago. Everything has changed."

"Go on."

"To begin with, there are a lot more people living here than we ever had before. We have people from Bremen, Broken Hill, Tyraine, Elberton—you name it. It all started after the invasion. The whole lower third of the country has had to move north, Father. Our population is probably three times what it was."

"You mentioned something about informants."

Akin nodded. "We don't know all of them for certain, but it's a safe bet the Vargothans are using them. People who have spoken out against the government have been either arrested or they simply disappear in the night—and that includes women. If any of them own a business, the Vargothans confiscate it and give to another. They come up with a new law or a new tax every other week."

Father Thomas's face was somber. "I hadn't expected this. I suppose we'd better get Mathew back here as soon as possible."

"He's gone to see Lara, hasn't he?"

"Correct."

"He should be safe. Martin and Amanda know what to do. I imagine he went to the store and not her home."

"I didn't know Lara had a home," said Father Thomas, "but then the last correspondence I had from her was nearly three years ago."

"She and Collin have been living together. They're pretending to be married."

"What?" Father Thomas said. "Why in the world would they do that?"

"Because single men and women under the age of thirty-five are subject to conscription. The men are sent to serve in the military for a period of two years. The women serve the Vargothan officers in other ways."

Akin saw the muscles in the priest's jaw clench and he put his hand over Father Thomas's.

"I'm sorry to have to tell you this, but you'd have found out eventually."

It took Father Thomas time to recover. He had been back less than two weeks, and if Delain was aware of the changes, he'd deliberately chosen not to mention them.

*An interesting world we're creating. Everybody uses everybody.*

Father Thomas shook his head. "This is wrong," he said softly. The words were spoken more to himself than to Akin.

"I know, but what can we do about it?"

"Hopefully, a great deal. That's why I've come back. By the way, I saw Fergus's grave near the maple tree, Akin. I'm very sorry. He was a good man. How did it happen?"

"The second month after Vargoth invaded they sent a column against us and there was a fight at Westrey Bridge. We held them off for two days, but there were too many. We lost half our people . . . Lucas Emson, Silas Alman, my brother Fergus, Truemen Palmer, Randal Wain, Carly Coombs and his father Bertram White . . ."

As Akin recited the names his gaze grew unfocused and he stared at a point over Father Thomas's shoulder. By the time he finished his voice was barely audible.

"I did the best I could," he said, "but in the end the only option was to surrender. It was the only way I could save what was left of our people. To make sure the lesson stuck, the Vargothans lined everyone up in the street and selected each tenth person. It didn't matter if it was a woman or a child. They hung them."

Father Thomas shut his eyes tightly and he murmured a prayer for the souls of the departed. He would do so again every day for the next year. Each name Akin had said struck him like a hammer. These were more than just members of his congregation; these were his friends, people he had lived with for many years. Something had to be done, and the sooner the better.

"We had better go and find Mathew," said the priest.

"There is something else you should know—"

"It will have to wait," the priest replied.

## 21

## Devondale

MATHEW DIDN'T REMEMBER MARTIN OR HIS WIFE LEAV-
ing the room. At some point he must have gotten to his
feet because he found himself standing in front of Lara
and looking into her eyes.

*Such beautiful eyes,* he thought.

He had always loved her eyes; they were green like her
mother's and slightly almond shaped. Eventually, Bran
toddled over and looked up, first at her and then at him.
The boy took hold of Lara's skirt and she bent down to
pick him up. He had her coloring, but his hair was dark
brown, like his had been before he'd dyed it. Bran didn't
appear shy or fearful, Mathew noted, only curious.

"Bran, this is your father," Lara said softly.

Mathew smiled at him at reached out to touch his face.
"Hello, Bran."

Again Bran didn't pull away. Instead he reached out
and touched Mathew's face in return. "Hello."

Mathew blinked. "He talks," he said to Lara.

"Well, of course he talks. He was three last month."

Bran held up three fingers to illustrate, which caused
Mathew and Lara to start laughing.

"Can I hold him?"

Lara nodded and handed Bran to Mathew.

"Gosh, he's heavy," Mathew said, hefting the child
higher.

For the next few minutes he and Bran got to know each
other while Lara tactfully moved off to one side. Eventu-

ally, Bran wanted to be put down. Mathew rubbed his arm and mouthed the word *big* to Lara, pointing at the him.

"Do you want to see my toys?" Bran asked.

"Oh, yes. Very much."

Bran reached up, took hold of Mathew's hand and led him to the side of the store, where Martin kept a small chest. With some effort he pushed the lid open and took out a gray cloth bag, spilling the contents out onto the floor. It contained about twenty miniature soldiers, their cloaks painted the same deep maroon as the Elgarian Royal Guard. Some of them held crossbows, some had pikes, and some were holding swords. Mathew picked one up and stared at it disbelief.

"Why . . . these were mine," he said.

"I know," Lara replied.

"My father made them for me. I couldn't have been much older than Bran, but I remember painting them."

Lara's smiled. "I know, Mathew—I helped you."

An hour later Martin and Amanda came quietly through the back door and saw Mathew and Bran lying on the floor together playing with the soldiers. Lara had taken a seat and was watching them.

"I'm being ignored," she told her mother.

Amanda walked over and put an arm around her daughter's shoulders. Martin, obviously pleased, folded his arms across his chest and watched the two of them together for several seconds before Mathew grew self-conscious. He got up, ruffled Bran's hair, and went to join the others while Bran continued to play.

"He's a fine-looking boy."

"That's because he takes after his mother," observed Lara.

Amanda slapped her daughter gently on the arm in reproach. "He takes after the both of you. Anyone can see that."

Mathew and Martin nodded to each other in confirmation.

"I've fixed some lunch for everyone," said Amanda. "Why don't we all go to the house and have a bite to eat. We have a lot of catching up to do."

"What about the shop?" asked Lara.

"The shop will survive for an hour or two," Martin replied. "If people want to go to Larsen's, let them."

Mathew frowned. "There's another dye shop in town?"

"There have been a lot of changes since you've been gone, my boy. Let's go eat and we'll talk about it."

Mathew's appetite deserted him halfway through the meal as he listened to what had happened to Devondale since he'd left. The news about the battle at Westrey Bridge and all the deaths that took place there hit him particularly hard. Martin told him that the following year the Vargothans began conscripting young men over the age of sixteen into their military. Mathew's stomach knotted when he learned that Daniel White had been one of the first taken. There had been no word from him since. This, Martin explained, was because of the Vargothans' new policy of not allowing anyone, particularly conscripted soldiers, to return home. Apparently, the number of deserters was becoming a concern, so they put an end to the practice of visitation.

More fortunate than some of their other friends, Collin had received an exemption because he and Lara were living together under the guise of being married. Out of the corner of his eye he saw Lara glance at him when her father mentioned it. He responded by reaching under the table and squeezing her hand to let her know it was all right.

The picture Martin painted of the state of affairs in Elgaria was not completely bleak, however. Mathew had always known his countrymen were a tough and resourceful lot, and it appeared that they were not quite so willing to give up as the Vargothans and Alor Satar had hoped. Bands of resistance and an underground network had formed all across the country shortly after the invasion.

It was only natural for Mathew to ask about Collin, since they had been best friends, but the moment he did he saw another of those looks passed between Martin and his wife.

"Collin won't be back for two days," Lara explained, noting his confusion. "He and five other men from town are out hunting."

"Hunting?"

"For Vargothans," Martin said. "Akin's organized the whole thing. Sometimes a group of us go out, and sometimes the men from Mechlen join us. A week ago we learned that a supply convoy recently left Alor Satar to provision their troops at Ritiba. They're not going to get there."

Lara's father took a bite of his sandwich and said to his wife, "This is delicious, dear."

"I see," Mathew said. "So the men have been going out and hitting the Vargothans. That's good."

This time the look was between Lara and her mother. "The women, too," Lara said.

"You're joking?" Mathew slid his chair back.

"Joking," Bran echoed from the floor. Mathew glanced at him then at Lara.

"Mm-hmm," Lara said, keeping her mouth closed while she was eating. She took a second to swallow then added, "I've been out with them a dozen times. So have mother, Ceta, and a lot of other women."

The food in Mathew's mouth chose that moment to go down the wrong way and he started coughing. "Ceta Woodall's here in town?"

"Poor dear . . . one shock after another," Lara said. She leaned over and kissed him on the cheek. "After Duren's sons traded part of Elgaria to the Orlocks, we were hit by a flood of people fleeing north. Elberton was overrun in a matter of weeks and Ceta lost her inn. She barely got out in time."

Lara got up and went to help her mother in the kitchen,

leaving Mathew sitting there somewhat overwhelmed by the changes that seemed to be falling out of the trees around him. He followed her with his eyes and waited until she was out of earshot. Then lowering his voice, he told Martin what he thought of the idea of women taking part in the fighting, notwithstanding Lara's ability with a sword.

Martin gave him a flat look and pulled a pipe out of his vest pocket. He took his time filling it. "Son, have you ever tried telling an Elgarian woman what to do?" he asked out of the corner of his mouth.

Lara chose that moment to glance over her shoulder at Mathew and flashed him a sweet smile.

"I see your point," Mathew said, smiling back at her. "I'm delighted that Ceta got out all right. So will Father Thomas; he's been worried sick about her."

Martin nodded. "She's doing quite well from what I understand. She owns the Rose and Crown. She bought it from Cyril Tanner's wife after he was killed at Westrey Bridge."

"Ceta owns . . ." Mathew shook his head. "I don't think I can take much more of this. I'd like to stop by and visit with her later." There was a pause as a smile touched the corners of Mathew's mouth. "I'd also like to see the look on Father Thomas's face. Do you think it's possible to keep it a secret for a little while?"

Lara's father thought about that for a second and started chuckling. "Don't see why not, so long as Lara and Amanda cooperate. Ceta's quite a lady."

"Who's quite a lady, dear?" Amanda asked, returning to the table. She handed each of them a piece of apple pie on a plate.

"Ceta Woodall. I was just telling Mat that she owns the Rose and Crown now. He wants to take Father Thomas over there and surprise him."

Both Amanda's and Lara's faces lit up at the same time.

"And speaking of Father Thomas," Martin said, "look who's coming down the alley now."

Everyone turned to see the tall figure of a man walking briskly toward the house. The priest was wearing dark brown breeches, boots, and a loose white shirt. He was also carrying a sword.

Lara let out a squeal, pushed her chair back from the table and ran out to meet him. Amanda and Martin, though not quite as effusive, weren't far behind, leaving Mathew and Bran alone.

"We've been thrown over," Mathew said to his son.

Bran looked out the window at the celebration going on in the alley then got up went out to join the others.

"Hmph," said Mathew.

As Father Thomas had surmised, Mathew was taken aback to learn he had known about his son. The priest, however, was wrong in assuming he would be angry. Until they talked in private, Mathew could only guess at his friend's motives, though it didn't take much to figure them out.

He had always understood that his ring had to be retrieved. It was all the more true now that he had seen his child. Certainly the circumstances had changed, but the world he lived in had not. Vargoth, Alor Satar, and their Orlock friends had to be driven out of Elgaria and the peace restored. That was the beginning and the end of it. There were too many graves in the cemetery to abandon his goal now.

Sitting there and watching the hugging and laughter going on outside, Mathew closed his eyes and swore an oath to another Bran. He swore that he would get his ring back no matter how long it took or the cost involved. Just as he had, his son would grow up in a free country . . . and its name was *Elgaria* not Oridan.

## 22

# Mirdan

IN THE EARLY MORNING THREE MEN WALKED ALONG THE ridge above where Sennia's Southern Army had camped. The eastern sky already showed streaks of crimson and gold, heralding the day's approach. The tall man next to Gawl d'Atherny was dwarfed by the giant figure of the king. The third man walked with a limp.

Atreus Ballinger, on Gawl's left, was commander of Sennia's fabled Phelix Legions and general of the Southern Army. He pulled his cloak a little tighter around him, shutting out the wind. Ballenger was forty-five years old, well-built, with close-cropped black hair. His face was more suited to that of a commoner, which he was, than the general he had become when Gawl promoted him out of the ranks seven years earlier.

Because of his leadership and the bravery he'd displayed in battle over the years, his men remained fiercely loyal to him. They saw Ballenger as one of their own. Down to the last they had defected when their general did, choosing to leave the country rather than serve Lord Guy any longer.

Ballenger himself was a devoutly religious man with a strong sense of right and wrong. Following Gawl's arrest, he had adhered to the rule of law because the Church had endorsed it. That view eroded over time as he watched Edward Guy and the other wine-producing families close Sennia's borders and begin raising prices after they seized power. Higher prices he could tolerate; such things happened. Murder he could not. And Guy's thinly veiled attempt at another trial would be just that.

Torn between loyalty to the country he had sworn to protect and the basic precepts of justice, which were clear and unequivocal to him, Ballenger sought out his priest for advice. They counseled together several times before a decision was reached. The army would defect. Other military commanders had received similar guidance from priests throughout the country.

In the mountain passes between Sennia and Mirdan temperatures were decidedly cooler than those at the lower elevations. Winter came early there. Only two weeks before, the leaves had begun falling, and now they crunched loudly under the men's feet as they walked.

"I'd like to break camp and begin moving as soon as possible," Ballenger said.

Gawl came to a halt and looked at the campfires dotting the valley. "If you would call the men together before we leave, Atreus, I'd like to address them."

Ballenger also stopped walking. "Is everything all right, your highness?"

Gawl, preoccupied, paused before he answered. "We are about to cross the Wasted Lands, a trip some of us won't survive. If we are successful, we'll board ships that will take us to Sennia to fight our own countrymen. No, everything is not all right. I didn't become king for this."

"Then what did you become king for?" James asked.

The question surprised Gawl. "It seemed like a good idea at the time," he replied blandly.

"Really?" James said. "Is that it—it seemed like a good idea at the time? I must remember to mention that to my children. They're quite impressed by you."

Gawl scowled and glanced down at the smaller man. "No, that's not all of it," he said. "When I entered the Olyiad it was because I didn't think anyone could beat me. To be honest, it was a matter of wanting to win the competition—nothing more. The men I defeated were all good men. They wanted to be king—I didn't. Their reasons were all different, of course. A few wanted the power, and some coveted wealth and glory, but one fellow, a man named Richard, said he wanted to make things better. I remember him well. He was not much older than you, James. We talked one night for quite a long time.

"At the end of the fifth day I began to ask myself the same question you just asked me. All things considered, what I was doing at the time was infinitely less complicated than running a country. I thought about abandoning the contest. I bore no rancor for the men around me, and I didn't wish to kill them. It was just a matter of winning, but then I remembered what Richard had said to me. Funny, isn't it, how some people can change your life?"

James reached up and put a hand on Gawl's shoulder. "I was born to this, my friend. There were no decisions where I was concerned. My father is the king, and I will succeed him according to our laws. You had a choice . . . you made the right one."

Gawl, seemingly unconvinced, shook his head.

"Prince James is right, your majesty," said Ballenger. "The men will follow you. Not simply because you head the state—so does Edward Guy. It's because they believe in *you* as a person. Edward Guy is not a man of morals."

Gawl raised one bushy eyebrow. "Do they?" he asked quietly.

"Yes," Ballenger replied, "they do . . . and so do I."

The sun was fully up and breakfast was done when Atreus Ballenger called his troops together. They stood at attention in their respective divisions and waited in the cool autumn air for the king. A variety of colored banners flapped in the breeze, each signifing a different unit of the army. Mixed in with them were five thousand soldiers of the Mirdan army, recognizable by their white cloaks.

*Fifteen thousand men,* Gawl thought, looking out at the troops. He repeated the number to himself. *Some of you will never see home again.*

"Young men," his voice boomed out, "soldiers of Sennia and our friends from Mirdan. You honor me with your presence, and I want you to know that I am grateful—more grateful than you can imagine. I have been a sculptor all my life, a soldier for most of it, and a king for only a part, so let me speak to you today only as one man to another.

"An evil has befallen our world—something insidious and corrupt in nature. An evil that seeks power for its own ends; an evil driven by want and greed.

"Edward Guy has become the puppet of Alor Satar. The men who rule that country hunger for power. They want not to make things better, but they want for the sake of wanting alone. To them power is its own end.

"When I was in Tyraine several years ago, I saw the bodies of a thousand people, many of them women and children, hung from scaffolds by the Vargothans. Their faces have haunted me ever since.

"We have always been a moral people. To be sure there are differences among us, but we live by the words set out in the scripture. To kill children for the sake of teaching a lesson to their parents is a crime so heinous it defies one's ability imagine it. How any person could do so and still sleep at night is beyond me. Edward Guy has aligned himself with these monsters. I tell you now the fight is not about wine. It is not about profits, or jobs, or who the Church might favor on any given day. The fight is about that which is good, and that which is base and vile and hides in the dark.

"So that you know what you are getting into, I tell you that I intend to hang Edward Guy from the first tree I can find. Once that is done we will join with King Delain and Prince James to drive the invaders from Sennia, from Elgaria, and anywhere else they have hidden themselves. We will drive Alor Satar, Vargoth, and the Orlocks beyond our borders and away from our families forever.

"We have been a free people since the Ancient War,

and free we shall remain. We will live our lives as we will and ask no man's permission to do so.

"The task before us is not an easy one. The enemy is more numerous than we are, and the way before us is fraught with danger. Unfortunately, that is our path. After we cross the Wasted Lands, we will board ships to take us to Marigan, where we will confront the traitors. Some of you will not come back. If there are any who do not wish to serve, let them leave now. I will think no less of you for doing so. On this I pledge my word."

Gawl waited for nearly a half minute before he was satisfied. "Very well," he bellowed. "We march."

When no applause or cheering broke out, his first thought was that his speech had failed. As much as it hurt, he was resolved not to show it. He kept his head erect, turned on his heel, and walked back to his horse. Jeram Quinn was there waiting for him.

"Not bad for a sculptor," Quinn remarked, the hint of a smile playing at the corners of his mouth. Suddenly, he gripped Gawl's forearm and looked him in the eye. "You did well," he said, and swung up onto his saddle.

Gawl cleared his throat and looked the other way for several seconds before he followed the constable.

# 23

## Nyngary

THE GUARDS AT THE ENTRANCE TO THE PALACE APART-
ments watched Teanna as she came down the hall. Both
stood at attention and stared straight ahead. The princess's
stride was brisk and the expression on her face serious.
She stopped in front of them.

"Is my cousin Eric in his quarters?"

"Yes, highness, but I believe he has retired for the
night," one of the guards said.

"Please knock on his door and present my apologies.
Tell him I would like to meet with him in the library as
soon as he is able."

"Uh . . . highness, it's possible the prince may not be
alone," the guard told her.

Teanna looked at the man without blinking until he got
the message.

"Yes, highness—at once," he said, with a bow.

Eric Duren arrived in the library in a bad mood. He
wore a heavy wool vest and had a blanket over his shoulders. His white shirt appeared to have been hastily tucked
into his breeches. Teanna, reading a book by the fire, put it
down when he came in.

"What the devil is so important that you had to get me
out of bed at this hour?" he asked, flopping down into a
chair across from her.

"Would you like some tea?"

"Yes, thank you," Eric said. "The fire feels good. This

castle is extremely drafty, you know. Why don't you put in some more of those stoves like we have in Rocoi?"

"I'll speak to father about it."

"Good. Now why are we here?"

"I've just come back from Garivele," Teanna said, handing him a cup.

"I take it your trip had something to do with the meeting between Seth and Shakira you mentioned the other day. After we spoke I asked some of our people to look into it. We should know more in a few days. What prompted you to go there?"

"Because I didn't want to wait a few days. I thought a meeting of that nature was important enough for me to hear about it firsthand."

Eric stuck out his lower lip.

"Oh, don't look like that," Teanna said, making a dismissive gesture with her hand. "You're not the only one who uses spies to gather information."

"This is excellent tea. How do you get it so sweet? It tastes like—"

"Cherries. Yes, I know."

"Really?" he said, looking down at his cup. "And what did you learn in Garivele?"

"That Seth and Shakira not only met with each other, they were accompanied by a priest from Coribar."

Eric looked up at her over the rim of the cup, his pleasant demeanor suddenly evaporating. "Are you certain?"

"Reasonably. The priest was described to me as being around sixty years old with gray hair, possibly faded from red, and pale hazel eyes."

"That would be Terrence Marek," a voice at the doorway said. "I've met him several times and he's not to be trusted."

"Father," Teanna said, getting to her feet.

Eric Duren followed suit. "Uncle . . . what a pleasant surprise."

"Why are you surprised, Eric? I live here."

"It's only an expression, Uncle. I'm always happy to see you."

"Then you should be overwhelmed at the moment," the king observed. "Did I interrupt anything?"

"Eric and I were just discussing that King Seth and Shakira met with each other in Garivele last week. They were apparently accompanied by this fellow Marek."

"Were they?" Eldar d'Elso said. "That's not good. No, not good at all."

"Do you think something's amiss, Uncle?"

"Being condescending doesn't suit you any more than it did your father, Eric. I didn't like him, either."

The mildly amused look Eric Duren generally wore disappeared. "Your majesty," he said, with a small bow. "If you'll excuse me."

Eldar made an annoyed motion with his hand. "Oh, sit down. I may not involve myself in politics very often, but it's perfectly obvious, to me at least, that Teanna's news is of great significance. Whatever you and your brother are, you're still family, as well as our allies. This is something we need to talk about."

Teanna and Eric exchanged surprised glances and took their seats again while the king dragged another chair over to the fire and placed it between them. Her father's reaction was the last thing Teanna expected, and she was curious to see what would develop. Her cousin appeared equally mystified.

"Is that cherry tea you're drinking?" Eldar asked his daughter.

"Yes, Father. Would you like me to make you some?"

"No, no." He smiled. "It's just that your mother used to enjoy a cup on nights like this. At any rate, what do you know of Terrence Marek?"

"Very little," said Teanna. "I've heard the name before, but I can't place it."

"I'll wager Eric can . . . can't you, Eric?"

A pair of hooded eyes regarded the king. In the last several seconds they had become far more intense and very much more aware.

"Marek is the head of the Sandresi Brotherhood on the island of Coribar," Eric explained. "For the last three hundred years they have been the most influential sect within their Church. He is quite well thought of by many of the hierarchy, except, of course, for those who can't stand him."

"Very good," said Eldar.

"The Brotherhood is extreme in their views and rarely come out in the open. They prefer to work behind the scenes whenever possible," Eric added.

"And what else?" Eldar asked.

"They believe theirs is the only true religion and that the various branches found in other countries are all either corrupt or heretical in nature. Their stated goal is to eliminate all opposition to the doctrines they practice . . . *by any means necessary.*"

"Excellent," said Eldar. "I might add they are largely thought to be responsible for the murders of two of the last five Kalifars of Bajan, and if memory serves me right, they also made an attempt on your father's life after he took the throne."

Eric nodded. "I wasn't born then, but Armand told me about it. Father responded by hanging fifty of their priests and leveling the cathedral at Delmont. He thought it would be an effective example."

"All he managed to do was destroy one of the great libraries in the world."

"They tried to murder him, for God's sake," Eric protested. "You think his response was unreasonable?"

"Frankly, I thought it was excessive . . . as well as misplaced. You never attack a country's national symbols, or their church. Your father's actions turned the Sandresi into fanatics. Up until then they were an annoying, but a very distinct minority. That isn't the case any longer."

"What's the point of all this?" Eric asked. "Who cares if Marek met with Seth and Shakira?"

"Obviously they're planning something," Teanna said. "But what?"

"We don't know that they're planning anything," Eric told her. "We only know they've met. I'm not ignoring that it might be important, but I'm not ready to panic over it, either. Heads of state meet all the time, for all sorts of reasons. I think the way to handle this is to tell our people to keep their eyes and ears open and report anything out of the ordinary. I'll see that whatever information comes my way also reaches you."

"Very sensible," said Eldar. "Have you considered the possibility that Seth, Shakira, and Marek are forming an alliance?"

"An alliance? Against whom?"

"Why against you, dear nephew, for a start."

Eric gave a short bark of a laugh. "Not likely. Alor Satar is far stronger than they are. What would they have to gain?"

"That does seems to be the question, doesn't it?"

They discussed the possibilities for another half hour before Eric announced he was tired and going back to bed. He seemed to find Eldar's suggestion of anyone attacking Alor Satar ludicrous. In the end little was resolved, other than that they would remain watchful. There was nothing else they could do. While Teanna believed her cousin was correct, she was not willing to take a passive role and had been on the verge of saying so when she noticed her father shake his head.

The king waited until the library door closed, then said, "Arrogant fool."

Surprised at the vehemence of his words, Teanna looked at him for an explanation. Eldar was normally the most even-tempered of people.

"For an intelligent man," her father said, "your cousin has an amazing blind spot—at least on the surface."

"What do you mean?"

"He either refuses to believe anyone would even consider launching an attack on Alor Satar or he wants *us* to believe that."

"Why would he want to fool us?"

"For the same reasons that the Durens are the Durens. *One country, one rule.* They've been singing that tired tune for the last three centuries. I trust him no more than I did his father, and I like him rather less, if the truth be known."

Teanna blinked. "Such strong words."

"Do you not see the same thing I do?"

There was a pause before Teanna answered. "I think so," she said quietly. "Vargoth now occupies two-thirds of Elgaria, or Oridan, as Eric and Armand want to call it. The mercenaries didn't need to conquer the country, they were invited in. Coribar, which has been quiet for years, suddenly becomes active and seeks to forge an alliance with the Orlocks. Why?"

"Go on," Eldar said approvingly.

"The obvious answer is so they can impose their views on the rest of the world. You've told me they've been willing to kill to achieve this in the past."

"Yes, I did."

"The creatures have also been quiet," she said, "at least up until now. We've had no contact with them since they took over lower Elgaria, and I'll wager Eric hasn't, either, unless he's a better actor than I think he is. The question is, what do *they* want in all of this?"

A slight smile appeared at the corners of the king's mouth, and he rested his chin in his hands, watching his daughter as she worked her way through the problem. "That should be obvious," he prompted.

Teanna's brows came together. "More land?"

"Possibly."

"All right, What am I missing?"

"You've told me that Shakira possesses one of the rose gold rings. Do you really think with that kind of power at her fingertips she'll be content to stay where she is? It seems to me, looking at it from the Orlocks' point of view, having less humans in the world would result in the same thing."

"Less humans?"

"Unless our relations with the Orlocks have suddenly improved, they still hate us as much as they ever did."

"You think they're planning to attack us?"

"I really don't know," Eldar replied. "But we need to increase our vigilance, not only of the creatures, but of Coribar and Vargoth. I also think it would be a good idea to move some more troops to the eastern border. We'll need to keep them at a higher state of alert, at least until we have a better idea of how the wind is blowing."

Teanna took a sip of her tea, made a face, and put it back down again. It was cold. "Thank you for your help, Father. You don't usually show such interest in these things. Has something changed?"

Eldar smiled. "Don't mistake a lack of involvement with a lack of interest. Personally, I prefer reading to politics. There's a good deal more honesty there, at least with some writers. Your mother enjoyed handling matters of this type, just as you do. It works out for all concerned."

"So why your interest now?"

"For three reasons," Eldar said. "First, because I object to being killed by an Orlock. Second, I don't care to climb a tower, bow to the east, and pray three times a day; and last, I don't trust Vargoth any more than I do your cousin Eric."

When the king leaned forward and kissed Teanna on the forehead, the expression on her face must have been obvious. She had always thought of her father as loving, but useless in a crisis. This was a part of him she had never seen before.

"Why don't you trust Vargoth?" she asked.

"Because the opportunity to seize a country and end their dependence on imports is too great to pass up."

"And Eric and Armand?" she asked.

"Quite simply, because they are Karas Duren's sons."

## 24

## Devondale

FATHER THOMAS SAT IN AMANDA PALMER'S KITCHEN, thinking how odd it was that some things changed while some never seemed to. The house was exactly as he remembered it—small, clean, and unpretentious. Akin Gibb, on the other hand, was noticeably different. His friend was still slender and serious in his speech and manner, but he exuded a confidence now that had not been there before.

Just as Martin Palmer had done with Mathew, Akin related what had occurred in Devondale since they'd been away. Some things Father Thomas knew, and some he didn't. Like Mathew, the priest had already concluded that a battle of some kind must have taken place two years earlier; the dates on the tombstones made that apparent. The faces of so many of his friends—his flock, as he thought of them—stared back at him in silent accusation. Perhaps the hollow feeling in his stomach was God's way of reminding him that he had abandoned his duties. He also noticed the many new faces in Devondale.

As they walked from the church, Akin said he had several errands to attend to and left Father Thomas at the town square. The silversmith promised to meet up with him again at the Palmers' home, and Father Thomas had continued on alone.

Now, Father Thomas looked around the little kitchen, closed his eyes, and said a prayer of thanks for the things that didn't change.

"Did you say that Akin Gibb was going to meet us here, Father?" Martin asked him.

"That's what he said. I'm sure he'll be along shortly."

Mathew stood up. "Well, I think we should celebrate this properly at the Rose and Crown," he announced. "It's not every day I return from the dead."

"That may not be the best idea, my son," Father Thomas said. "There are a lot of new people in town, as I'm sure you've noticed, and we should try not to bring attention to ourselves. If someone recognizes you, the word will spread quickly."

"We could use one of the back rooms," Lara suggested.

"And I'd like something stronger to drink than this tea," Mathew added. "No offense, Amanda. It's fine tea."

"Fine tea," echoed Bran.

Father Thomas looked at the boy and chuckled. "What about Akin?" he asked.

"We could leave a note for him on the door," said Amanda. "I wouldn't mind a bit of ale myself."

The priest turned to Lara's mother. "Why, Amanda, I didn't know you drank."

"I don't usually, but this is a special occasion." She put a hand on both Father Thomas's and Mathew's shoulders.

"All right," Father Thomas said, "let's go see how Master Tanner has been faring these past years."

Devondale's only inn was at the opposite end of town, closer to the church than to the dye shop. Before leaving, Amanda wrote a note and placed it on the door. Mathew and Lara walked a little ahead of the others, swinging Bran between them, to his obvious delight.

"It's good to have you back, Siward," Martin said to Father Thomas as they took the back streets toward the pub, to avoid people who might be out at that hour. "How long are you going to stay?"

"Only a day or two at the most."

Amanda and Martin both looked at him at the same time.

"I understand," Martin said. "This is not going to be easy on Lara. She just got him back."

His wife said nothing.

"I'm sorry, Amanda. There's no choice in the matter. Mathew's ring is the only way to neutralize Teanna d'Elso. It has to be recovered."

Amanda began to reply but broke off as a man emerged from a small café across the street. For a moment it appeared he was headed the other way but when he saw them, he changed course and began walking in their direction.

Martin muttered something under his breath that Father Thomas didn't catch and the priest made eye contact with Amanda. He understood her silent message to be careful. Up ahead, Father Thomas saw Lara lean over and whisper in Mathew's ear. Both nodded to the stranger and kept on walking.

The man had a slender face with a large nose, greasy black hair, and a prominent Adam's apple. Father Thomas guessed him to be in his early thirties.

"A word with you please, Martin," the newcomer called out.

Martin came to a halt and waited for him. "What can I do for you, Dermot?"

Father Thomas and Amanda stopped as well.

"It looks like we have some new people in town. Have they registered?"

"They're relatives of ours, Dermot, from Broken Hill. I'll have them come over this afternoon. This is Nicholas Pastor, Amanda's cousin. And that's his son, Thad, up ahead with Lara."

"Nick, this is Dermot Walsh," Martin said, introducing Father Thomas. "Dermot . . . Nick."

"Pleased to meet you," Father Thomas said, holding out his hand.

Dermot hesitated a second and returned a weak handshake. "You need to register."

"Register? I'm sorry, I—"

"Dermot makes a list of people who visit town for the governor once a month," Martin explained.

"That's your job?" Father Thomas asked, incredulous. "We don't have anything like that in Broken Hill."

"I don't like it any better than you do, but it's the law and money's money. You have to register," Dermot insisted.

"Well . . . if it's the law," Father Thomas said. "What do I have to do?"

"Not much. You just sign a piece of paper and give me the address where you'll be staying. You can come to my shop later and take care of it. It's the bakery across from the Rose and Crown. I should be back there in about an hour."

"Does my boy need to come, or can I sign for us both?" Father Thomas asked.

Dermot's Adam's apple bobbed in his throat as he swallowed. "You can do both. I'll waive the three coppers since you didn't know anything about it."

"That's very kind of you."

"Yeah," Dermot agreed. "Will you be staying long?"

"No, just a day or two. We haven't seen the baby in a couple of years, and Amanda's been fussing at me, so Thaddeus and I decided to take a little trip." Father Thomas put his arm around Amanda's shoulders and gave her a squeeze.

Dermot sniffed, took a piece of paper and a pencil out of his pocket and made a few notes on it. "Just a day or two," he repeated.

"Is there an additional charge for that?"

Dermont put his hands on his hips. "No need to be sarcastic. Everyone gets mad at me for doing my job, but times are tough. A man's gotta live, doesn't he?"

"Absolutely," Father Thomas agreed. "I'm sure Martin feels the same way."

Lara's father pursed his lips. "If you say so."

"See what I mean?" Dermot complained.

Father Thomas watched Dermot as he disappeared

around the corner, and shook his head sadly. Some changes were not going to be so easy to deal with. Martin muttered something that earned him a reproachful look from his wife, and they continued walking. Lara, Mathew, and Bran were waiting at the end of the street along with Akin Gibb, who had just joined them.

Before they reached the others, Father Thomas was aware that Amanda was looking at him. "Is everything all right?" he asked.

Several seconds passed before she answered. "I understand about you and Mathew having to leave again."

"Amanda, I—"

"Just see that you do what you have to do, Siward Thomas, and come back to us."

Father Thomas opened his mouth to reply, but before he could, Amanda quickened her pace and went to join the others.

From the expressions on Akin's and Mathew's faces, the priest knew something was amiss even before he reached them.

"Let's go to my house," Akin said as soon as Father Thomas got close enough.

Father Thomas's eyes darted from the silversmith to Mathew, then to Lara and Amanda. "I suppose the Rose and Crown can wait," he replied.

Akin Gibb's house was a good five minute walk from his shop. It had been years since Siward Thomas visited there, and the changes he noticed appeared quite minor. There was a new roof and the door might have been painted, but he wasn't certain about that. Shortly after he and Mathew had ridden into town, he'd noticed that his own house had been touched up and maintained in good repair all these years. He made a mental note to thank Akin. On the lawn, leaves of burnished red and gold blew idly around in circles and stuck in the fence posts.

The first time he'd visited Akin's home had been during his first or second year in Devondale. One of the younger boys in the choir had knocked a silver candlestick off the altar and it had broken. He brought it to their father to be repaired. Unfortunately, the man was away on business that day. Both Akin and his brother, still only apprentices, spent the entire day working on it. When they were finished, the candlestick was as good as new. They refused to accept any payment.

They were *good people*, Father Thomas had thought at the time, and the passage of years had not altered his opinion.

Inside, Akin ushered everyone into his parlor. Bran, Father Thomas noticed, was becoming more at ease with Mathew and settled comfortably onto his lap. When the others had seated themselves, the priest brought out an extra chair from the kitchen and joined them. To his surprise it was Mathew, not Akin, who spoke first.

"Father, we have a problem."

Father Thomas folded his arms across his chest and waited.

"This started out to be a surprise for you, but I'm afraid I have to give you some bad news . . . Ceta Woodall has been living here in Devondale for the past two years. In fact, she owns the Rose and Crown now."

Father Thomas felt his chest constrict. This was not what he expected to hear. A quick glance around the room told him there was more to come. With an effort he mastered his emotions. "Go on, Mat."

"Like I said, we were planning to surprise you. It was my idea, but then we met Akin on the way."

Father Thomas turned to Akin Gibb.

"The Vargothans took her last night, Father. I didn't find out until just a little while ago. Becky Enders has been working at the inn. She found me and told me."

"What?" Father Thomas said, getting to his feet.

"The mercenaries know that you've escaped and about your relationship with her. They arrested her late last night after the tavern closed."

"Arrested? For what?" Martin asked.

"What does it matter?" Akin replied. "They don't need a reason to arrest anybody. They just make something up. The point is they were expecting Father Thomas to show up in Devondale. We need to get him out of town as quickly as possible."

A silence followed. Lara went to Father Thomas and put an arm around his shoulders. The priest's mind was in turmoil. Mathew's revelation about Ceta Woodall being in Devondale had hit him like a blow, but the news of her arrest . . . He should have known that Edward Guy would communicate with Alor Satar, and that was exactly what he had done. Guy also knew about his relationship with Ceta; his daughter Rowena had been at Tenley Palace when their engagement was announced. All the mercenaries had to do was to wait for him to show up, or better yet, use his fiancée as bait to lure him to them. Everyone in the room was talking at the same time. They stopped when he held up his hand.

"Do we know where they took her?"

"The officers' quarters are located on the east side of Gravenhage near the stadium. That's where they usually take most of the women."

Father Thomas frowned. "What are you talking about?"

Akin looked distinctly uncomfortable and rubbed his temples with the tips of his fingers. He looked at Father Thomas as he tried to find the right words.

"I asked you a question, Akin."

"I mentioned it earlier, Father, but I'm not sure you understood."

The silversmith went on to explain that men were not the only ones who had been conscripted since the invasion. When he started to explain how the Vargothans used single women, the priest's face turned to stone. Then, without saying a word, Father Thomas stood up and walked out the front door.

Akin started after him, but Mathew put a hand on his arm.

"Give him a moment. This would be a shock to anyone."

He could see the priest through the window, leaning against one of the old oak trees on the lawn.

Akin sat down next to Martin and conversations in the room resumed, but they were in whispers and without enthusiasm. After several minutes Mathew glanced out the window again at the priest. He hadn't moved.

"I'll be right back," he said. He got up and went out to join him.

# 25

## Devondale

"FATHER, WE NEED TO FIGURE OUT HOW WE'RE GOING TO get her back," Mathew prompted.

Father Thomas did not respond immediately. After several seconds he shook his head. "Impossible," he said.

"What do you mean, 'impossible'?" Mathew asked. "What's impossible?"

"I'm going alone, Mat. Their taking Ceta was no accident. Yes, she's a single woman, but according to Akin, the Vargothans have confined themselves to taking young women under the age of thirty. Ceta is forty-six now."

"That's ridiculous. I'm not going to let you walk in there and hand yourself over. If they don't hang you on the spot, you'll be back in prison before you know what's happened."

"I appreciate that, but this is something I have to do alone."

"There's no way you're going by yourself," Mathew said. "You wouldn't let me, and I'm not letting you."

Father Thomas slowly turned to face Mathew, his eyes intense. "A long time ago I told you there are times when the needs of the many have to outweigh the needs of the one. Occasionally, the reverse is true, but this is not one of them. I have not been there for Ceta in the past . . . perhaps I can rectify that now. You will have to go on to Corrato without me."

Mathew's temper flared. "The ring can melt in hell for all I care."

The priest's face turned cold. "This is not a subject for debate. I'd appreciate it if you would explain to the others for me."

"You're not going, Father. I'm—"

"What goes on here?" Akin asked from the doorway.

Mathew told him.

While he was speaking, Akin glanced at Father Thomas, who did not meet his gaze.

"Let's go back inside where we can discuss this quietly," Akin said. "I don't like standing out here in the open."

Father Thomas considered both men for a moment then headed back into the silversmith's house.

Lara stood up when Mathew reentered the room and went to his side. "What's the matter?" she asked, taking his hand.

Before he could respond, Akin explained what Father Thomas had in mind.

Protests broke out all around the room while the priest stood rigid and tight-lipped. He made no reply. To a person, everyone was in favor of mounting a rescue attempt rather than letting him carry out his plan. Father Thomas however, remained unconvinced and rejected all of their offers to help. Better than his friends, he had already reasoned through the consequences of any direct action against the mercenaries.

"For God's sake, Ceta wouldn't want you to do this," Mathew said, exasperated.

"I know what she would say, Mat," Father Thomas replied.

"I may have a solution," Akin said. "If I understand you correctly," he said, addressing the priest, "you don't want us to go because there are too many mercenaries and more people might get hurt. Is that right?"

Father Thomas took a weary breath. "That's only part of it," he replied. "Though you're correct, the odds *are* too great. According to what you've told me, there are likely to be between twenty and thirty officers in the compound, with the rest of their garrison a few hundred yards away. Mathew cannot risk himself in this venture. His primary task is to get the ring."

Mathew threw up his hands at that. "This is insane."

"What if I could get enough men to even the odds?" Akin asked.

"From where?"

"From Mechlen, from here, and in Gravenhage itself. We could raise eighteen to twenty men with no problem. We've been doing that the last two years on our raids."

"And what happens afterward?" asked Father Thomas. "Are all eighteen of you—or twenty, as you say—going to fight the entire Vargothan army in this region? Their garrison at Gravenhage has at least four hundred soldiers . . . and they'll respond. You've seen what they did in Tyraine."

The corners of Akin's mouth tightened. "Yes, I saw it. I'm sure Delain would want us to wait until we're stronger, but if the Vargothans want to fight, we can match them man for man. It might take a week to get our people together if a real battle starts, but we definitely could do it, Father. We have enough able-bodied men in this province alone. The same thing is true of Lankton and Queen's Provinces."

Father Thomas shook his head. "I appreciate what you're saying, I really do . . . from the bottom of my heart. But the timing has to be right. If we move before Mat has the ring back, everything could be lost."

The protests all started up again, but this time it was Mathew who stopped them, speaking over the rising din of voices.

"I understand what Father Thomas is saying. Since Alor Satar doesn't know that I'm alive, it's got to be Father Thomas they're afraid of. That's why they took Ceta, isn't it, Father? She's the bait."

"Correct."

"The thing is, the Vargothans are expecting you to do

exactly what you're proposing to do. What they won't expect is an all out attack. I agree with Akin on this point. The element of surprise can swing a battle in one direction or another."

Father Thomas folded his hands in front of him. "And what about Teanna?" he asked quietly.

Mathew thought for a moment before he responded. "She was the deciding factor in all the battles before, am I correct?" he asked Akin.

"In *every* battle," Akin replied.

"And without her we were able to hold our own?"

"True."

"Then the best possible thing would be for us to draw her here again," Mathew went on, "because if she's here—"

"Then she's not in Corrato," Akin said, realizing what he was driving at.

"If we act quickly and strike first," Mathew said, "there's an additional benefit to be gained. Without officers to lead them—"

"Their army will be in disarray," Akin said, finishing the sentence for him. He clapped Mathew on the back.

Father Thomas looked from Mathew to Akin and back again. "It might work," the priest said, slowly.

Throughout the conversation Lara had remained quiet. She and her mother exchanged glances while Mathew was speaking, but neither offered an opinion. In the lull that followed, she and Mathew finally made eye contact. Up till then, he had been avoiding doing so. Father Thomas, knowing the young man as well as he did, was certain it was no accident. He was equally confident the next hurdle was about to be reached.

"Why is it necessary for you to go?" Lara asked, speaking for the first time.

The look that passed between Mathew and her bespoke their long familiarity with each other.

"Let's talk outside," he said.

Lara looked down at Bran and said, "I'll be right back. Your *father* and I are going to talk outside."

Bran's eyes got wider and he drew his head back, then went to sit on Father Thomas's lap.

"Wise lad," the priest said under his breath. "Stay out of the line of fire."

While Mathew and Lara were talking, Father Thomas amused the boy by taking a coin out of his ear, putting it in his fist and making it disappear. Bran of course was properly amazed and thought the whole thing great fun. Akin frowned as he watched the magic trick.

"Where did you ever learn to do that?"

"Oh, here and there."

Bran's mouth opened wide in shock when the priest retrieved a copper elgar from his left ear and handed it to him. Confused, he reached up and felt his ear.

Father Thomas glanced into the garden and observed Mathew's gesticulations and the expression on Lara's face. It appeared that his young friend was arguing his case intelligently and calmly, but unsuccessfully.

Martin Palmer also looked out the window, shook his head, then leaned over and spoke softly to Akin, while Amanda contended herself by straightening several of the items on Akin's shelves. Eventually the door opened again, the discussion apparently concluded.

"It's settled," Mathew said. "We're, uh . . . getting married tomorrow and Lara's coming with us."

Both Akin's and Martin's mouths dropped open in shock. They looked at each other, then each took out a silver coin and handed it to Amanda, who accepted them with a pleasant smile and put them away in the pocket of her dress.

## 26

# The Wasted Lands

THE REDDISH-BROWN SAND BLEW IDLY OVER THE TOP OF Gawl's boots, threatening to bury them as it had buried everything else on the plain. Annoyed, he kicked it off and walked a few paces forward, squinting at the horizon. As soon as he stopped, the sand started accumulating again. He wasn't certain when the Wasted Lands had acquired their name, but it was certainly apt. The plain was a sparse, inhospitable place not suited to life . . . any life. Little grew there, except for some dried-out vegetation. The ground itself was pitted and cracked, and as flat as a tabletop. Strangely, though there were few sources of water, the air always seemed unnaturally humid and hung about one's face like a damp cloth. Sweat ran down the back of Gawl's shirt. It was an eerie, disorienting place, with fog banks that moved back and forth over the surface of the land making distances hard to judge.

The last time Gawl had been there was as a young man. Impelled by curiosity, he had wanted to see for himself if the rumors were true. The stories men told of volcanoes and bizarre crystal formations that broke light into a thousand colors had intrigued him. There were also tales about sandstorms of incredible violence, which he would also came to know firsthand. Thirty years later he liked it no better than he had the first time.

It was no longer curiosity that moved him now, but hatred and the desire for revenge. He wanted his throne back from the man who had stolen it. Pitted against that desire was a sense of sadness and guilt. Civil war and death were not things he wished to visit on his people, but he would be damned if he would allow Edward Guy to rule his country one day longer than he had to.

As he watched the sand swirl about his feet he thought about Rowena, Guy's beautiful daughter. He had been a fool to believe that a woman twenty years his junior could have been in love with him. Certainly such things happened, but Rowena had betrayed him just as her father had. Naive or not, pawn or not, she was a traitor. It would have been better for all concerned if she had accepted his offer of clemency four years ago and left the country. The thought of beheading her made his blood run cold. The feelings were still present; he acknowledged that.

When his trial was over, she had come to him and asked that he accept her father as Regent, if only for a little while. She told him that Sennia's borders were being closed again, in order to keep the people free of "outside corruption." Whether Rowena saw this as a pretext or not, Gawl knew the real reason was so that Guy and his cohorts could control the country's wine and copper production without competition. It all came down to money. As intelligent as she was, she had never been able to see her father for what *he* was.

Two nights ago he and James had discussed what was to be done with the Guys and the nobles supporting them. James thought that Gawl's idea of prison was needlessly soft, and he said so.

*How do you cut the head off of someone you loved and not be affected by it?* Gawl thought.

That James could have made the suggestion as blandly as he did still amazed Gawl. Perhaps being born into the aristocracy gave one a thicker skin, he mused. Clearly, he still had a lot to learn about being a king. The problem was, he wasn't sure he wanted to learn it. Killing an enemy in battle was one thing; hiring assassins and murdering people in the dark was something else. Being a simple sculptor had its advantages, he decided.

A footfall behind him pulled him back to the present.

"Did you get any sleep, Jeram?" he asked.

"Some. The building helped block the wind."

Gawl glanced over his shoulder at the foundation of what must have once been a very large structure. Two of the four walls had collapsed eons ago and only portions of those remaining were still intact. The windows were long gone, with only their twisted frames left behind. Over the past three days they had seen several buildings like it, along with portions of a roadway the Ancients once used. With a little imagination, one could picture what they once must have looked like. Now, like the surface of the land, they were pitted and broken.

A few old books had survived the Ancient War, and from the pictures Gawl had seen, he knew how large some of the roads were. The one they were traveling was tiny in comparison, with only two lanes on either side of a natural median.

"You look like hell," Gawl told Quinn.

"So do you."

"I underslept a little."

Quinn smiled and followed Gawl's line of sight. He put a hand above his eyes to shield them from the glare. "Are those hills out there?"

"Mountains," Gawl told him. "The pass we're looking for should be somewhere southwest of that large one on the right. There'll be water at the higher elevations."

"I'd kill for a hot bath," Quinn said, brushing some of the sand from his shoulders. "I've never seen anything like this. Even the sand is the wrong color."

"That's because it's not sand," Gawl explained. "They're rust particles . . . or rust particles mixed with sand. I'm not sure which."

Quinn spit some away from his lips. "Whatever. They're still noxious."

Gawl glanced over his shoulder at the noises coming

from the camp. People were beginning to stir. "How's everyone holding up?" he asked.

"As well as can be expected," Quinn said. "It'll be better once we're out of here. There's something about this place."

"It presses on you."

Quinn nodded and a shiver ran up his spine despite the heat. "How long before we reach the pass?"

"Two days. It will take a half day to get to the other side, and another day to reach the ships at Lipari."

"And then?"

"We will begin our campaign from the northwest. Ballenger wants to hit Camden Keep before moving on the main body of Guy's forces in Barcora."

Quinn thought about it for a few seconds. "Good plan. What do you want me to do?"

"You're not a Sennian, Jeram. You fought with us at Fanshaw Castle, which was more than anyone expected. Lord knows, I'd be proud to have you, but I won't ask it. You've already done more than your part."

"You don't have to ask," Quinn said. "There's not much call for a constable these days, particularly since Elgaria has no government at the moment. Until Delain is back on the throne and our country restored, I seem to be at loose ends. I'll fight with you."

"Good man," Gawl said, putting a hand on Quinn's shoulder. "Let's get some breakfast."

"It'll have to be cold," James said, limping toward them. "All the wood we've found is either rotten or it just doesn't burn. Good morning, by the way."

"Good morning," said Gawl.

"Good morning," said Quinn.

"Well, a cold breakfast is better than no breakfast," said Gawl. "How are the men?"

"They're fine. The sooner we're out of here the better. What in God's name could the Ancients have done to this place?"

Gawl shook his head. "I remember what Ardon Field looked like after Mathew and Duren fought. It was very similar."

James squinted out over the plain. "It's like they killed the land itself. Do you think Mathew will succeed?"

"He'd better, or Teanna will have a field day with us. Either way, it won't make a difference. I don't intend to live under Alor Satar's rule, or the Vargothans, or anyone else's for that matter," said Gawl. "Mathew will succeed, or the man you hired will succeed. Once Sennia is freed, Elgaria is next and we finish this . . . forever."

"Agreed," said James. "You do understand that we will still have one problem left . . . Mathew Lewin."

Gawl and Quinn both turned to look at the prince.

"It wasn't clear to me until we entered this godforsaken spot. It is now. No one person can be allowed to possess the kind of power that can do this," James said, stretching his hand over the land. "No one. Not you, nor me, nor you, constable . . . nor Mathew Lewin. It's far too dangerous."

"If your majesties will excuse me," said Quinn, nodding to both men. He headed down the slope toward camp.

Gawl watched him go for a few seconds and turned back to James. "Explain."

"I believe our military action will be successful. Once it is, things will eventually return to normal. At that point, Mathew must be made to give up his ring or he'll have the entire world at his mercy. I don't intend to be put in that position, Gawl."

"But he's never shown the first inclination—"

"Unlimited power leads to corruption as surely as the sun rises. If we don't act, we will be left with a young man who possesses just that. How long will it be before we have another Karas Duren to deal with?"

"Have you lost your mind?" Gawl snapped.

"I think not," James replied. "The fact is, I'm a realist, and if you plan on holding onto your throne, you'll have to be one, too. Do you think I enjoy having to say these things? I don't."

"What is it you'd like me to do?"

"At the moment, nothing. But when the time comes, we must be prepared. That's all I'm saying."

"Fine," Gawl replied. "We'll talk about it when the time comes." He started walking back toward the camp, but stopped after a few steps. "Understand this: I'm not going to do anything to harm Mathew Lewin, and I'll take it very badly if anyone else tries to do so . . . *very* badly."

A half hour later, after the men had eaten, the officers gave the order to break camp. James and Gawl agreed they would march for about four hours, then rest for the midday meal at an abandoned town Gawl knew. From there they would try for the foothills before darkness.

Though the terrain was level, the heat and humidity made travel difficult. To complicate matters, shortly after they entered the Wasted Lands they found that looks could be deceiving—the lifeless plain was not quite as dead as it seemed. Tremors shook the ground, unexpectedly turning small cracks into crevices and fissures into chasms. The first time one struck, the soldiers froze in their places. Though the episode lasted less than a minute, it put everyone on edge. Nor did it help that formations of crystal columns, some of them eight to ten feet high, would break through the ground without warning. Fortunately, James noticed that a faint high-pitched whine preceded the eruptions and he warned his men to be alert for the sound.

The Mirdanites, Gawl thought, were a stoic lot, and went about their tasks without complaint. Most of them were seasoned veterans who had as little love for Alor Satar as he did. Many had lost family and friends in the last war, when their capital was attacked by Karas Duren. The fact that Edward Guy had chosen to align himself with their old enemy only added to the fire of the long-smoldering hatred.

Since the journey began, Gawl made it a point to walk among the men every day and get to know them. Perhaps it was not the most common practice for a king to follow, but then, he reasoned, he wasn't a common king. Anyone who was willing to fight and die for freedom was a person worth knowing. He was aware of the effect his physical presence had on people. That couldn't be helped. At seven feet tall and nearly 340 pounds, his was an imposing figure. Most people were usually too intimidated to approach him, so he went to them instead. What he found was that the Mirdanites were more sophisticated than he had first assumed. Even the youngest soldier was aware of the shifting political climate in the world and strongly disapproved of what had happened in both Sennia and Elgaria. Like James, they knew it was only a matter of time before Alor Satar turned its attention toward Mirdan.

As far as religion went, they were liberal in their views, particularly compared to his Sennians. Basically, they believed it was better to live and let live. This, Gawl assumed, was because the Church had far less influence in Mirdan. Most surprising to him was that the majority of the soldiers thought that Sennians were provincial and closed-minded. He heard the expression "as narrow-minded as a Sennian" more than once while he was walking. It was an attitude he intended to change. The borders would be open again, and the Church, while it would always play a strong role in his society, would confine itself to moral and not secular matters in the future. The role of religion was to promote understanding and love, not to polarize people. Change for the sake of change was not a concept he embraced, but neither was stagnation.

James and Quinn had gotten used to his sojourns among the men. They generally rode together at the front of the column. Despite the damage to his leg, James never let it hamper him. Overhead, the sky was gray and the clouds were moving rapidly, giving the impression that it might rain any moment . . . but of course it didn't. It rarely rained on the plain, but when it did, you had to take shelter quickly. The drops of water were corrosive and unless you dried off quickly, your skin would begin to burn after a few minutes.

For the last hour Gawl had been talking to a young man named Kevin. He was perhaps eighteen years old and had a pair of mild brown eyes and a head of curly brown hair to match.

"I don't believe in God, your majesty," Kevin told him.

Gawl blinked and looked down at him. "Really?"

"I know it's not a popular thing to say, but a lot of people think the way I do. Bertram, that's my best friend, feels the same way I do."

"Interesting. Do your parents also feel as you do?"

"My parents are dead, Sire. They were killed in the siege at Steormark. But to answer your question they were both God fearing people right up to the time that Duren collapsed the house they were living in on their heads."

"I'm sorry, Kevin," Gawl said. "Is that why you don't believe in God, or have you always felt that way?"

"I've felt this way since I was old enough to think for myself. If there is a God how could he let something like that happen, your majesty . . . or this?" Kevin said looking across the plain. "They were good people who never harmed anyone in their lives. My mother was sewing a dress for my sister's wedding when she died. My father sold paints and never had an ill word to say about anyone, nor they him."

"Terrible," said Gawl, shaking his head. "Truly terrible. And based upon this you've concluded that God doesn't exist."

"I mean no offense, Sire. These are my personal views."

"I understand."

"May I ask you a question?"

Gawl was aware other men around them were listening to the conversation though they were trying not to be obvious about it. "Go on."

"Do you believe in God after what they did to you?"

Gawl smiled. "Yes, I believe there is a God. I confess that I don't always understand his logic or why he does what he does."

"But I'd always heard—"

"That I don't get on well with the church. That's true, but disagreeing with how priests are trying to run things doesn't necessarily equate with rejecting God's existence. I disagree with a lot of people. You may find that hard to believe considering what a pleasant fellow I am."

The smile that Gawl flashed the young man and those around him was distinctly feral.

Kevin blinked and pulled his head back slightly.

"Uh . . . I'll remember that, your majesty."

"I've been obliged to change my view many times throughout the course of my life, young man, and I've found few things are all black or all white. This is just a piece of advice . . . try to keep an open mind on the subject. I have a friend who is very fond of saying that. It's surprising what you might pick up when you do."

"I will, your . . ."

Kevin's sentence broke off as a faint high-pitched hum seemed to come from all around them at the same time. At the front of the column Prince James threw up a hand, halting the men. Like the rest of the soldiers, Gawl stopped in his tracks.

The quake, stronger than any of the previous ones, started gradually and continued to build in intensity for the next three minutes. The ground began to heave so violently, Gawl had to struggle to keep his balance. Then, just as suddenly as it started, it was over.

Gawl looked along the column, spotted James and Quinn and waved to them. Both waved back to signal they were all right. A little more than a half mile ahead he could make out the shattered remains of the old town where they would stop.

"Well," Gawl said, clapping Kevin on the back, "before we were interrupted, you were in the process of telling me—"

The king would have completed his sentence, but the expression on Kevin's face stopped him cold. He twisted around, following the young man's gaze. People were pointing and staring at something on the horizon. To his chagrin, it was what Gawl least wanted to see. An enormous wall of sand had suddenly appeared out of nowhere and was coming toward them. And it was coming fast. He had seen sandstorms before, but this one was at least eight stories high and extended for hundreds of yards in each direction. The sky had taken on a yellowish cast, while the wind around them picked up, causing the flags to crack as they whipped back and forth. At the front of the line the sound of trumpets told Gawl that James had seen it, too.

The soldiers reacted at once, beginning a quick march in the direction of the ruins. After two hundred yards the trumpets blew again, but by then the volume of the wind had increased so much that the trumpets were barely audible at the rear of the line.

One more glance over his shoulder at the storm racing down on them was enough to convince Gawl that any attempt at an orderly advance would result in a lot of people being killed. The sand wall had nearly doubled in size and was pulverizing everything in its path. They no longer had minutes—they had seconds.

Gawl shouted to the men around him, "Make for the ruins!"

The soldiers started trotting. Incredibly, the standard bearers were trying to hold onto their standards and run at the same time. And it was clear then if he didn't get them moving, they were dead.

"*You!*" he bellowed to the nearest soldier, a boy not more than sixteen years old. "Drop that damn thing and run . . . *now!*"

A moment later the king was racing at full speed with

the Mirdanites. Visibility was dropping rapidly as the trailing edge of the storm began to overtake them. Near him, the boy he had yelled at stumbled and fell. Without breaking stride, Gawl reached down and jerked him to his feet. The wind at his back was now so strong the particles of sand striking his neck stung like bees. Gawl gritted his teeth and pounded forward, his long legs covering the ground rapidly. After two hundred yards his breath came in ragged gasps and there was a pain in his side under the rib cage.

*Stop and you're dead.*

With his strength ebbing, he clenched his teeth and re-doubled his efforts, running as he had never run in his life. Ahead in the failing light a low gray shape loomed—the surviving portion of a wall. Gawl made for it and hurled himself over, not knowing what lay on the other side. He struck the ground hard, knocking what little air was left in his lungs out as the full fury of the storm broke over them, the wind rising to a banshee shriek. In desperation, Gawl grabbed for the wall and held on with all of his strength. He had no idea how long he clung there, he only knew that it was getting harder to breath. Sand particles were filling the air. For all he knew, the soldiers around him could have been alive or dead. It was impossible to tell because visibility was almost gone.

The last thing he remembered before a black curtain settled over his eyes was that his knuckles were bleeding.

# ђ enderson

"GUARDIAN," SAID TEANNA.

Her voice seemed louder than normal in the stillness of the cavern. The square that she had materialized in was just as deserted as when she had left it. Several seconds later the air in front of her blurred and began to ripple, then the fireflies appeared.

It was like looking into the water of a pond someone had just disturbed, as the moving air consolidated itself into the shape of a man.

"Greetings, Princess. What is your question?"

"What information can you provide me on Terrence Marek?"

The Guardian tilted his head to one side and assumed the unfocused stare that Teanna associated with talking to a machine. At least that was what she thought he was doing.

"He is the latest Sandresi bishop. Born sixty-eight years ago, he succeeded Artur Mandas. According to the information in my database, he has no living relatives."

"I don't understand what you mean by 'database.' "

"You may think of it as a library. Most of our books were placed into it a long time ago, but new ones are added from time to time, particularly where such information involves ring holders. This is per my programming."

"Programming?"

"The instructions the engineers gave me," the Guardian explained.

Teanna was not sure she understood, but there was no time to waste. "What do you know about the Sandresi?"

The pause was much shorter this time. "The Sandresi are an ancient sect who broke away from the main Church in 3713 to form their own religious order. This was one year after the war was concluded."

"The Ancient War?"

"Correct. They did so because they believed that mankind's lack of morality had resulted in its own destruction. When conventional negotiations to resolve the schism failed, the Sandresi resorted to unconventional means to persuade their brethren that they were correct. At first their assassinations were confined only to officials in the Church's hierarchy; later they were expanded to include anyone who disagreed with the precepts the Sandresi advocated.

"As you may have guessed, such a methodology only polarized things further. The central Church excommunicated their bishop, a woman named Meskhent, and ordered her to leave the country. Unable to find a home in any of the other nations, Meskhent and her followers settled on the island of Coribar, where they established their own Church."

Teanna frowned and thought for a second. "What was it the Sandresi wanted?"

"Basically, they wished for a religious oligarchy headed by their bishop. The Sandresi felt that only by returning to a morally based government could people fulfill the word of God. The morals they espoused were morals of their own construction."

Teanna frowned as she tried to digest what the last phrase meant. Apparently, the Guardian noted her reaction, because he offered an explanation unasked.

"They felt the ritual infliction of pain was necessary to cleanse and purge evil from the soul. Eating meat from animals with cloven hoofs was strictly forbidden, as was the consumption of liquor. One was expected to pray three times a day in order to show proper devotion to God. Failure to do so was punishable as a crime.

"Do you wish me to go on?"

"No. According to what my father told me, the assassinations didn't stop after they settled on Coribar. Is this true?"

"It is."

"So the Sandresi still feel the same way?"

"Any person or group that does not think as they do is considered an enemy. Their clerics teach the populace that killing one's enemies is a holy act. Since, in the past, Coribar lacked the military strength to impose their will on the rest of the world, most of their activities were conducted in secret."

Teanna studied the Guardian for a moment, weighing the meaning behind his words. From previous conversations, she had learned that his meaning was not always obvious on the surface.

"You said Coribar lacked military strength *in the past*. Is this still true?"

"No."

"What changed?"

"They now have a navy and an army of some significance."

Teanna took a breath before asking her next question. "How large an army?"

"Assuming their women take an active role in the combat, a fair estimate would be just under sixty thousand."

"Sixty thousand," Teanna repeated. She had been prepared for a figure five times lower. Coribar now posed a serious threat. And when coupled with the fact that Marek had met with both Vargoth and the Orlocks, the implications were ominous.

"I have another question. Do you know how many Orlocks there are?"

The figure the Guardian gave her nearly caused her to

gasp. Teanna put a hand to her throat and took a step backward. Even if half the creatures were children or female, the size of their army was staggering. More pieces of the puzzle were beginning to fall into place.

"The last time we met, you told me the Orlocks have one of the rings and that I caused it to become active."

"You were not the cause, only the catalyst," the Guardian replied.

A look of irritation crossed Teanna's features but it disappeared quickly. "Why do you play word games with me? Answer the question."

"I did answer the question, Princess. Do you require a further explanation?"

Teanna let out a long breath and composed herself. "Yes."

"Personally, you did nothing. The creatures merely watched in hiding while you altered the brain chemistry of the priest, Kellner. Once they understood what the true function of the Emerald Cavern was, they were able to accomplish the same thing. Four of them died before Shakira made the attempt herself. She alone was successful."

"All right, they have the ring," Teanna said. "Why haven't they tried to destroy us?"

"Speculation is not part of my program, Princess."

"You mean you don't know."

"I mean I don't speculate."

"When I was in the cavern, I came across a number of very odd things. To me, it appeared that Orlocks and men once worked together. Could this be true?"

"It is."

"Then what happened to change all that? Why do they hate us now?"

"That would require a long answer, Princess," said the Guardian.

Teanna walked over and sat down on one of the little benches. "Take your time."

## 28

## Devondale

THERE WERE ONLY ABOUT A DOZEN PEOPLE IN THE church. In another minute Lara would walk down the aisle and they would be married. Mathew wondered whether all bridegrooms were nervous. When her father said something to that effect earlier, he had laughed. People were always saying that sort of thing. The fact that everyone he came into contact with that morning kept asking him if he was nervous probably had a lot to do it, he decided.

*The power of suggestion*, Mathew thought.

Under normal circumstances there would have been more people present, but it was far from a normal situation. Martin Palmer had quietly passed the word around town to a few select people that Mathew and Lara were getting married. The person most obviously missing was Collin Miller, whose absence saddened Mathew. He wished his old friend could have been there.

With a resigned breath, he looked down at his son and smoothed the boy's hair. It was the third time he had done so that morning. Bran made a face and tolerated the unwanted attention well enough, though as soon as Mathew looked away, he ran his hand back through it, returning it to its former disheveled state. A surreptitious glance at his father told him that he was safe.

While they waited for Lara to make her appearance Mathew thought about how their relationship had changed. It was nothing sudden, but the change was fundamental.

When he looked in the mirror, a man's face looked back at him. The boy he felt like was still in there somewhere. He was sure of that. As he wondered how long that feeling would last, a conversation he once had with his grandfather came back to him. He recalled asking the old man when he began feeling like an adult, and the answer surprised him.

"I'm still waiting," his grandfather had said. "For what it's worth, I once asked my father the same thing, and he wasn't certain, either. He thought it was somewhere between eighty and eighty-five."

The memory made Mathew smile.

Father Thomas clearing his throat shook Mathew from his musings and he glanced up. The priest made a small gesture with his chin.

"A fine friend he is," a voice said from the audience. "I'm gone two days and he steals my wife."

*"Collin!"* Mathew exclaimed, spinning around. He was so preoccupied, he hadn't heard him come in.

Collin Miller was seated next to his mother and father, grinning. He got up and met Mathew in the aisle. They both grabbed each other in a fierce embrace, but the celebration was short-lived. The organ music began before either could say anything.

"Go," Collin whispered. "We'll talk later." He gave Mathew a gentle push toward the altar.

Mathew got there in time to see heads turning toward the rear of the church.

Years later, when memories of that moment surfaced again in his mind he recalled his mouth being open at the sight of Lara as she walked down the aisle. She was the most beautiful thing he had ever seen. Murmurs of admiration came from the other women, and the men in the audience nodded in agreement. Her gown clung wonderfully to her figure and she was carrying a small bouquet of flowers. Mathew watched her come toward him, her eyes bright and hopeful. Martin Palmer left his daughter at the altar, kissed her on the cheek, then shook Mathew's hand. He took a seat next to his wife and put an arm around her shoulders. Amanda was crying quietly.

The feeling of love and pride that swelled in Mathew's chest that day would remain with him always.


The dinner in Father Thomas's cottage was one of the nicest Mathew could remember. It was wonderful seeing Collin again. The years and their separation seemed to melt away. When things quieted they moved apart from the crowd to talk.

"When I got word that you were alive, I couldn't believe it," Collin said. "I just couldn't believe it. I rode for two days just to get back, only to find you're marrying my wife."

Mathew squeezed Collin's shoulder. "It's so good to see you. I wanted to contact you and let you—"

"I know, Mat. Akin explained the whole thing to me. So tell me, what have you been doing for the last four years?"

Mathew smiled at the jest. "Not getting any closer to the ring, but there's an opportunity now in Nyngary."

"Fine. When do we leave?"

"I can't ask you to go with me."

"It'll be safer with you than here. Remember, the Vargothans have been taking fellows my age. They took Daniel two years ago."

"I heard."

"Anyway, since Lara and I won't be living together anymore, I don't have a lot of choice in the matter, if you see what I mean. One way or another, I have to leave now."

"Collin, I'm sorry."

Collin looked down at the floor for a moment. "You two were always meant for each other, Mat," he said quietly. "It was the right thing to do. But I will have to leave. I'm not going into the Vargothan army."

"I'd love nothing better than to have you. Are you serious about this?"

"I am. I imagine Lara's also coming?"

Mathew nodded. "Amanda and Martin will be taking care of Bran until we get back. She's going to travel as my wife."

"She *is* your wife, Mat."

Mathew rolled his eyes up and shook his head. "This is still pretty new to me. I called her 'Mistress Lewin' a while ago and she stared at me like I'd fallen out of a tree. I guess she's getting used to it, too."

"Everything will work out fine. She's a wonderful girl and you couldn't ask for a better son than Bran. I wish all of you joy."

Mathew stared at his friend for several seconds and his face turned serious. "Thanks for everything you've done."

Collin gave him a wink. "Let's go back in the dining room."

As soon as they returned to the table, Collin picked up a fork and tapped it against the side of a wineglass for silence.

"I have a toast," he announced, raising his glass. "To my friends Mat and Lara. Their getting married today is something of a relief. Of course, everyone in Devondale has known this day would come for about a decade now, with . . . ah, the possible exception of Mat. Well, it's finally happened and we can all take a deep breath.

"There are certain rumors surrounding this union that I, as their trusted and loyal friend, feel honor bound to dispel. I've spoken to Margaret Grimley and I can assure you that there is no truth to the story that Lara actually picked out her wedding dress ten years ago."

Margaret Grimley, who was standing next to Lara, put her arm around Lara's shoulders and gave her a good-natured squeeze.

"Now everyone in town knows that Mat Lewin has had a sensitive stomach since he was quite young, and I'm here to tell you these unfortunate attacks never once occurred while we were discussing marriage . . . well, almost never. Actually, it only happened a few times. Oh, all right, but fifty percent isn't such a bad average, is it, Father?"

Father Thomas shook his head no and laughed with the rest.

"Perhaps I'm digressing. I've known Mat and Lara since we were young, and they are deeply moral people who have listened carefully to all of Father Thomas's sermons."

Collin paused, looked around the room, made a deliberate show of noticing Bran, who was sitting quietly on the couch. He bent down, picked the child up, and they rubbed noses together.

"All right, all right," he said turning back to the others. "They listened to *most* of the sermons."

The joke brought more laughter.

"In all seriousness, nothing has given me greater pleasure than seeing my two friends where they belong . . . where they have *always* belonged. I join with everyone here in wishing them happiness and the quiet peace of each other's companionship for years to come—to Lara and Mat."

"Hear hear," Akin added.

Collin had barely finished his toast when his glass paused halfway down. He looked out the window and saw a man was staring in at them. The second the man turned and ran, Collin bolted out the door after him, with Father Thomas and Akin close behind. Mathew grabbed his sword and followed. By the time he got to the street he saw Collin holding someone by the back of his neck.

"What's happening?" Mathew asked.

"Dermot here was spying on us through the window," Collin said. "Weren't you, Dermot?"

"I wasn't doing no such thing. I just saw lights on at the priest's house, that's all. You got no right to hold me against my will."

"Your business is several streets away, Master Walsh," said Father Thomas. "What were you doing at my home?"

"Your home?" Dermot repeated. "I knew it was you. Your name's not Nicholas Pastor. You're Siward Thomas."

"You're a very perceptive fellow," the priest said, drawing his dagger. He took a step closer.

The expression on Dermot's face suddenly became fearful. "You're a priest. You can't harm me."

"Really?"

Akin grabbed one of Dermot's arms and Collin grabbed the other. Dermot tried to pull away but they held him fast. His eyes seemed glued to the dagger in Father Thomas's hand.

"You're a priest," he repeated.

"I wonder if your masters told you what I did before I became a priest."

Dermot didn't answer, though his eyes widened as Father Thomas brought the dagger closer.

"No? Let me educate you, then. For eight years I commanded Elgaria's western armies and the Tardof Legions. We had a special way of dealing with traitors. We cut out their tongues to prevent them from speaking, and their ears were removed to prevent them from hearing. Then their eyes were put out to prevent them from seeing."

Dermot's knees sagged. "Oh, God," he gasped.

Mathew was almost ready to intervene. The look on Father Thomas's face was one he had never seen before, and it frightened him.

"Goodbye, Master Walsh," Father Thomas said quietly. He brought the point of the dagger up under Dermot's eye. "I don't think we'll be seeing each other again."

"Mercy, Father," Dermot pleaded.

"Mercy?" Father Thomas repeated, his voice no more than a whisper.

"I'm begging you. I have a wife and two daughters."

"How interesting. What did the Vargothans tell you?"

"Please, Father."

Tears were rolling down Dermot's face now. Akin and Collin looked at each other, not sure what the priest was going to do next.

Father Thomas grabbed Dermot's head and yanked back. He brought his lips close to Dermot's ear. "I'll only ask you one more time."

"They wanted me to keep watch for you and to let them know if you showed up. There's a reward of five hundred elgars on your life." The words came out in a rush.

"And of course you told them I was here?"

"No, I swear to God Almighty."

"What else did they say?"

"Only that you might be traveling with another man."

Father Thomas's eyes darted to Mathew and away again. "Did they say who that man was?"

"No, I swear on my daughters' lives."

The priest's face finally relaxed and he released his grip on Dermot's hair. Akin, Collin, and Mathew all let out a collective sigh of relief when he returned the dagger to his belt.

"Who are you taking your orders from?" Mathew asked.

"The commander of the garrison, a man named Kennard."

"Anyone else?" Akin asked.

"Sometimes the governor."

"Andreas Holt?" Mathew said.

Dermot nodded.

"We'll have to keep him locked up until we get Ceta back," Father Thomas told Akin. "We'll figure something out after that."

"No problem."

Father Thomas turned back to Dermot. "If I were you, Master Walsh, I would change occupations. There's no future in the one you've selected."

## 29

# Outside Gravenhage

AT SUNRISE ON THE FOLLOWING DAY, FATHER THOMAS, Collin, Mathew, and Lara found themselves on horseback on the road outside the town of Gravenhage. A half mile away, Akin Gibb and sixteen other men were concealed in the trees waiting for the priest's signal for them to move. Their objective was a farmhouse the Vargothan officers were using for their compound.

They had appropriated it for themselves when they first occupied the region. Its original owner, Josiah Cassidy, was arrested on the charge of making seditious comments against the present government, and he and his family were all shipped off to Alor Satar. None of them had been heard from again.

Mathew surveyed the scene, assessing the strengths and weaknesses of their position. He imagined Father Thomas was doing same thing. The mercenaries had erected a stone wall at least eight feet high that completely circled a three building complex. The largest, on the far right, was the old Cassidy barn, now converted to a dining hall and sleeping quarters for the junior officers. According to what Akin had told them, the second building, originally the family home, now housed the senior officers and their staffs. The last was a low one-story structure that served as both stable and armory.

Mathew found the wall interesting. It had been constructed wide enough to accommodate a catwalk, with two guards making rounds every thirty minutes. There were two more men at the gate. Through surveillance, they discovered that the mercenaries were keeping Ceta in the main house. Using an updated version of the farsighter their friend Daniel had developed, Collin had watched the home for the better part of an hour before he spotted her in the back bedroom.

The previous night, Father Thomas had laid out his plan. He and Lara would present themselves at the main gate. The men would be split into three separate groups, with Mathew, Akin, and Collin each attacking from different sides when the time came. Their main concern was to get Ceta out and prevent the garrison from discovering what was happening until they were safely away. Everything now stood in readiness.

Father Thomas and Lara climbed aboard a flatbed wagon borrowed from Dermont Walsh, now a guest in Akin Gibb's root cellar, and started off together. The priest would have been hard to recognize. He miraculously had transformed himself into a sixty-year-old, with white hair, thanks to vegetable dye supplied by Amanda, and a crutch. Both Collin and Mathew did double takes when they saw him.

From the shelter of the trees Mathew watched them for several seconds before turning to Collin. "Good luck," he said.

"Take care of yourself, Mat," Collin replied, keeping his voice down. He tugged on the reins of his horse. "See you in a few minutes."

It was a risky strategy, but Mathew had learned to trust Father Thomas's judgment. Given the circumstances, he knew they had little choice in the matter. They either went along with the priest's plan or he would turn himself in to the Vargothans. As soon as the wedding dinner was over, Father Thomas wanted to leave, and he had to be persuaded to wait until Akin got his men together. He was nearly beside himself with worry over Ceta.

Mathew couldn't sleep the night before and insisted on going with Collin to look at the officers' compound for himself. He knew that Siward Thomas was a brilliant tactician, but the priest had taught him that personal involvement could compromise even the most objective mind. As a result, Mathew spent his honeymoon night in the woods above Gravenhage, watching the comings and goings of the mercenaries and studying their weak points. In the end he agreed with Akin that fifteen to twenty men would be enough to take the complex, provided the element of surprise remained on their side. The trick would be keeping Ceta Woodall alive while they were doing it.

Mathew waited until the wagon with Father Thomas and Lara reached the road and then went to join his men. They were waiting on the west side of the complex. Collin should have already been in position on the opposite side. Akin and his men were at the south side. There was enough tree cover to get everyone as close as fifty yards to the wall.

Askel Miller took hold of Mathew's reins as he dismounted.

"Ready?" Mathew asked.

"It's not going to be easy in this wind," Askel replied as he strung his bow. He tested it a few times.

"You're the best shot I've ever seen," Mathew said. "If you can't do it, no one can."

"I'll try. After the first guard is down you'll have to move quickly."

"Where are the others?"

"There." Askel pointed. "They all know not to move until I take the guard out."

"And Lara's off the wagon," Mathew reminded him. "That will be our signal to attack."

"Understood. This is a hell of a way to celebrate your marriage, Mat," Askel whispered. "I'm sorry Adele and I didn't have time to get you a present."

"That guard will do just fine."

Askel glanced at the treetops, gauging the wind for several seconds, then took an arrow out of his quiver and notched it. "Done," he said.

Seconds later he was moving through the trees. Mathew had known Collin's father all of his life, and it was no exaggeration that he was the best shot Mathew had ever seen. Collin was nearly his equal. If the wind cooperated, it would give them the chance they needed. Father Thomas and Lara were now less than a hundred yards from the gate.

Near the end of the treeline, Mathew saw Askel drop down to one knee and take aim. It was hard enough making a shot in dim light, but at fifty yards in a strong breeze . . . he didn't know. Even under the best of conditions it would have been horribly difficult and to complicate matters a light rain had begun falling. The other men in his group signaled they were ready.

Askel used the back of his sleeve to wipe the rain from his face and let his breathing slow. To his right, Garon Lang and Martin Palmer were crouched down on either side of the ladder. On the catwalk above the gate, the guard stopped walking when he saw the wagon approaching and called down to his companions.

Father Thomas and Lara were less then twenty-five yards from the gate when it opened and a soldier came out. He stood in the center of the road waiting and signaled for them to stop.

"What business do you have here?"

"My father is the priest in Devondale," Lara called out. "That's a small village about fifteen miles from here. One of our neighbors told us to come here and present ourselves to you. We didn't know what this is all about, but we came."

"What's your name, Father?" the soldier asked.

"Siward Thomas," Father Thomas replied through a series of coughs.

"My father's very ill," said Lara.

The soldier looked at Father Thomas for a second then called out to one of his companions, "Jack, open the gate, then go get the major. You'd better leave the wagon out here, miss," he added to Lara.

"All right," Lara said. "Let me get your crutch, Father. You'll have to go slowly. I could use some help getting him down."

A frown appeared on the soldier's face and he turned to the other man at the door. "Isn't he supposed to be in his late forties?"

His companion shrugged. "That's what I heard. Must be some sort of mistake."

The first soldier shook his head and came around the wagon to help. "Here, give us your arm and take it slow like your daughter says. Why don't you come around here with his crutch, Miss?"

The moment Lara hopped off the wagon, Mathew's hand came down. *"Now,"* he hissed.

A buzz split the air as Askel Miller let the shaft fly. A second later the nearest guard staggered backward, his hands reaching for his throat. He swayed in place, then silently toppled over the edge of the wall. Acting as a relay from his position in the woods, Akin Gibb signaled for Collin to fire.

Collin leaned against the trunk of a tree, steadied himself, and drew back on his bow. His arrow caught the other guard between the shoulder blades. The man arched backward, his arms going wide. A second arrow hit him just above the first one.

Mathew heard the thuds as the arrows struck and he began running for the wall.

When the second guard's body hit the ground, the soldier who had been helping Father Thomas looked to see what the noise was. Confused, he turned back to the wagon. The moment he did, his head snapped sideways as Father

Thomas's boot connected with his jaw. His companion at the gate never had the opportunity to react. He looked down in confusion to see the hilt of a dagger protruding from his chest. He took two steps in Lara's direction and collapsed to his knees, dying before he hit the ground. Lara calmly removed her dagger, wiped it off, put it back in her belt, she then hurried to get the swords concealed under the wagon's bed and tossed one to Father Thomas.

The priest caught it and looked up at the walls. Both guards were gone. Satisfied, he nodded to her and went in. He reached the courtyard the same time Mathew was dropping over the wall. Akin and the rest of the men followed at the other side of the complex. Using hand signals, Father Thomas motioned one group toward the barn and the other toward the main house. Mathew and his people were to remain where they were to stop any of the Vargothan officers from leaving.

"Askel," said the priest, "take Garon and two men and check that stable. It should be empty except for the horses, but we need to make certain. Arthur, George, Bill, and I, will be at the side of the house. We don't want anyone leaving by the back door and taking us by surprise. Remember, Ceta is our first concern."

There were nods all around as Askel and Garon split off with two of the men from Mechlen.

In the next second a soldier coming out of the main house saw the men in the courtyard, realized what was happening, and raised the alarm.

"We're under attack! All officers to the defense!"

Twangs from three separate Elgarian bows answered him at once and sent him crashing backward through one of the windows.

To Mathew's chagrin, the Vargothans reacted much quicker than he believed possible. There also were a lot more of them than he thought. They began pouring out of the main house and the barn. Most were cut down by the Elgarians in the first rush, but moments later the hand-to-hand fighting began. Across the courtyard Mathew saw Father Thomas parry a soldier running at him with a halberd. The priest sidestepped, ducked under the man's backswing, and slashed upward with both hands. The soldier shrieked as his stomach was laid open. Father Thomas's next blow ended the fight. The priest and two men started forward once again, only to be met by more soldiers coming from the house. Around the courtyard, Vargothans were going down, but so were the Elgarians.

Mathew looked back at the main gate and saw Lara waiting with the wagon. She waved when she saw him.

"All clear," Garon yelled from the back of the stables. Askel Miller and his group emerged from the front door a moment later.

"Help Father Thomas!" Mathew shouted. "The rest of you with me!"

He started toward the main house. Surprisingly, black smoke was already pouring out of the top floor of the barn.

Mathew cursed under his breath. He didn't know who had started a fire, but the last thing they wanted was to send a signal to the garrison. They would have to move fast. Two more Vargothans died with arrows in their chests, killed by Askel Miller, firing as he ran.

Nearby, Collin had engaged one of the mercenary officers, a large man nearly a full head taller than he was. The Vargothan raised a double-bladed axe above his head and Collin's quarterstaff moved in a blur, catching the man in the throat, then across his ankles. He went down heavily and would have risen again, but a roundhouse blow not only fractured his head, it broke the quarterstaff in the process. Collin looked at the piece in his hand, dropped it on the man's body, and drew his sword. He saw Mathew and held up three fingers.

A nearby scream jerked Mathew's attention away from his friend. He spun around and watched in horror as an officer ran his sword through one of the Gravenhage men.

There was something familiar about the soldier, and when he turned, Mathew knew who it was. Their eyes locked.

*"You,"* Kennard said.

The mercenary recovered from his surprise quickly and started walking toward Mathew. *"This* is going to be a pleasure."

There was no point in replying, so Mathew attacked.

Kennard deflected his lunge and riposted at Mathew's chest. Mathew counterparried, redoubled forward, and attacking again. Kennard barely had time to step back. The moment Mathew recovered, however, Kennard came at him. His first feint to Mathew's low inside line was an obvious ploy, so Mathew paid it no attention. Kennard was obviously hoping that he would lower his guard. When Mathew didn't react, the real threat immediately followed. It came just over the top of his forearm, aimed at his rib cage. Using the middle part of his blade, Mathew parried sideways, stepped in, and hit Kennard full in the face with the bell of his weapon. He landed two more blows to the side of the mercenary's head with his other hand. A dagger produced seemingly out of nowhere slashed at Mathew's stomach and made contact with his forearm instead. Searing pain shot up his arm and his shirt went red.

The advantage immediately then shifted to Kennard, who lunged for Mathew's heart. Mathew's blade was pointing at the ground and there was no time for him to execute a chest parry. Off balance, he stumbled back and began to fall. In desperation, he turned his hand down so his thumb pointed at the ground and parried away and to the outside of his body. Using the move his father had taught him many years ago, with a snap of his wrist he executed a flying riposte, and caught Kennard on the side of his neck. It was not a heavy blow and it barely cut the skin. Kennard stopped for a moment and felt the wound, his features twisting with contempt.

"You'll be joining your shipmates in a second, boy. Give them King Seth's regards."

But then an odd thing happened. The moment the mercenary took his hand away, a bright line of blood shot two feet into the air. Mathew scrambled backward on his hands and heels as Kennard advanced on him. The mercenary's next step was more of a stagger, and the third worse than that. Blood squirted freely from Kennard's neck. His eyes widened in shock. Over his shoulder Mathew could see Lara running toward him, her sword drawn.

A look of disbelief appeared on Kennard's face as he took another step and slowly collapsed to his knees. Blood gushed through his fingers and ran down his arm. In the last seconds before he died he may have realized that his carotid artery had been cut. With the last reserves of his strength the Vargothan struggled to his knees and raised his sword above his head. But the blade never came down. Lara, still running at full speed drove her weapon through Kennard's back, knocking him to the ground.

She let go of her weapon and helped Mathew to his feet. "Your arm," she said. "You're hurt."

Mathew kissed her. "I'm fine. Get back to the wagon. I'm going to help Father Thomas."

Lara opened her mouth to protest, but he cut her off. "I'll be all right, I promise, but I can't fight and worry about you at the same time . . . please."

"Worry about yourself," she said. "I'd like my husband back in one piece." Lara looked at the barn, now fully ablaze, and added, "Hurry Mathew—we don't have much time."

She gave him a quick hug, retrieved her weapon, and trotted back to the wagon.

Mathew watched her go, and shook his head. He quickly scanned the rest of the compound. As far as he could tell, they had only lost four men, compared to a score of the enemy. A number of his companions were still fighting, but the odds were definitely shifting in Elgaria's favor.

Across the courtyard Father Thomas finished with the soldier he was fighting and was about to start back toward the house when a movement on the porch caught Mathew's eye. Andreas Holt was there with a dagger in his hand. He threw it at the priest's back.

*"Look out!"*

Everything about Father Thomas moved at the same time. The priest spun and batted the dagger out of the air with the flat of his blade. If the governor was shocked, he recovered quickly enough and ran back into the house, drawing his sword. Father Thomas broke into a full run, and launched himself through the double window.

By the time Mathew reached the house, he found the priest and Andeas Holt engaged in a violent struggle. His friend had placed himself between Ceta Woodall and the governor. On the stairs, behind them, another mercenary was bringing his crossbow to bear. Mathew saw that he would never get to the second man in time in time to stop him, and so in desperation he reached for the power at the precise moment the soldier's finger was squeezing the trigger. The crossbow snapped out of existence. Startled, the man let out a cry, missed his footing, and fell the rest of the way down the steps. He didn't move again.

Holt was obviously an accomplished swordsman. He circled the point of his blade in front of Father Thomas and made a number of feints, testing the priest's defenses. Father Thomas paid no attention to them.

"You made a mistake, Thomas," said the governor. "Our men will be here any moment. Throw down your weapon and we'll let you go."

Father Thomas made no reply nor did he let Holt move any closer to Ceta.

Another feint.

"I've heard a lot about you, priest. It was accommodating of you to come to us. We enjoyed your woman last night, by the way. She's quite the screamer. Unfortunately, she'll probably want to stay here now that she knows what real men are like."

Silence.

"I'm curious," said Holt. "What possesses a general to leave the glory of the battlefield for the obscure life of a priest? Did you lose your nerve?"

Two more feints.

Satisfied that no more mercenaries were coming down the stairs, Mathew started for Holt, but Father Thomas held up his hand. "Stay where you are, Mat," he said, his eyes never leaving his opponent. "There's an old parable I used to teach in church about a warrior who slew his enemies using the jawbone of an ass. That's all our friend is trying to do."

The governor's upper lip pulled back in contempt. "That's right, boy, stay where you are. When I've done with him it'll be your turn."

Without warning, Holt launched a fearsome attack at the priest. Father Thomas pivoted sideways off his front foot. In the split second that followed Mathew heard rather than saw the parry his friend made. It was no more than a flick of his fingers. The priest's arm then shot forward with a riposte, impaling Holt through the chest. The governor's momentum carried him forward, and he grabbed Father Thomas by the front of his robes.

Siward Thomas watched impassively, his face devoid of expression, as Andreas Holt's fingers relaxed slowly. He slid to the floor onto his knees and his head lolled forward. That was the way he stayed.

Father Thomas looked down at him, made the sign of the Church, and turned away as Ceta Woodall ran across the room into his arms.

"Oh, Siward. I knew you would come for me. I prayed for it. I wanted you to come more than anything in the world. What he said, none of it was—"

"Shh," said Father Thomas, stroking her hair. "It's all over, love. It's all over. I'll never leave you again."

Tears rolled down Ceta's cheeks and she kissed him again and again. His hands stoked her hair and he gently touched her face. Father Thomas held her and they stood in the middle of the room, clinging to each other.

Out in the courtyard, the sounds of fighting had finally died down. Most of the Vargothans were dead. Mathew slipped quietly out of the room.

# 30

# henderson

THE MOMENT MATHEW REACHED FOR THE ECHO, TWO heads came up at the same time, though they were a thousand miles apart. Teanna d'Elso knew it was him immediately; so did Shakira. For months the Orlock queen had suspected that he was alive, but this was the confirmation she had been waiting for.

Shakira was old even by Orlock standards. Few of the creatures ever lived past forty—she was nearly fifty. Terrence Marek, Archbishop of Coribar, sat across from her and observed her reaction. One minute they were talking, and the next her eyes went wide and she stared out the tavern window.

Marek waited. He was good at waiting. Like his inhuman companion, he and his people had waited for nearly three thousand years to claim what was theirs. The holy scriptures foretold that victory would be theirs, and Marek believed in the word as it was written. The rest of the world had strayed from the true path. Corruption was rife and morality continued to sink to new depths with each passing day. All that was about to change.

The Orlock finally turned back to him and a cold pair of eyes fixed on his face. Marek neither flinched nor looked away. Politics and necessity made for strange bedfellows. He had learned that a long time ago. There was intelligence behind those eyes he'd learned, and he had gleaned that much from their conversations.

"Is something wrong, your majesty?"

"Lewin is alive." Though understandable, her voice was little more than a hoarse whisper.

"Alive? Are you certain? I thought he was killed years ago."

"I'm certain."

"This presents a problem, don't you think? We had thought to deal only with Teanna d'Elso. Now there are two ring holders."

"Not two. Lewin no longer has his ring. He possesses power of some type . . . different from hers . . . but very weak. It is of no consequence."

"We must leave nothing to chance," said Marek. "I cannot believe his disappearance was an accident. If what you're saying is correct, it's obvious they have been engaging in a hoax of some kind. The question is, why?"

Shakira slowly shook her head.

"No," said Marek. "He cannot be allowed to live. It's too dangerous. What if this is a trap?"

The queen regarded him. "What would you have me do?"

"Kill him. He cannot be allowed to live," Marek repeated. "It would be far too dangerous. Do you know where he is?"

"I know," said Shakira. "The power he possesses is nothing compared to mine."

"Really? Lewin killed thousands of your people, remember?"

The Orlock leaned forward and brought her face closer to Marek's. "Orlocks never forget."

The stench of decay was so strong it nearly caused him to gag, but he did not pull away. "That is well, your highness. May I ask how you know these things?"

"Lewin made contact with the machine. I felt his mind."

"But how could he do that if he no longer has his ring?"

"This I do not know," said Shakira, leaning back again.

"I only know he did it. Sometimes between ring holders it is possible to see through their eyes. Apparently this is still the case with him."

"You can read their thoughts?" Marek asked.

"Only if the person lets down their guard, as he just did. The Nyngary princess is too strong. She blocks out of instinct."

Marek did not understand about blocking, but seeing through another's eyes made sense to him. "What was it you saw?"

"A fight of some kind in a house between the mercenary soldiers and two men; one was a priest, the other was Lewin. A woman was also present, but she was not fighting."

Marek was shocked. "A priest? Can you describe what he looked like?"

"No. It happened too quickly," Shakira said. "I only saw that the priest was very good with his sword—he killed the Vargothan."

Marek stared at her for a moment. "It might be Siward Thomas. I was told that he escaped from prison recently."

The Orlock's brows came together slightly. "Thomas . . . I know this name."

"You should. He was the one who routed Alor Satar at Veshy. Your people were in that battle. He is also the man who lured your brethren into a trap in the town of Tremont several years ago."

A small twitch appeared under Shakira's eye. "Do not push me, Marek."

"That was not my intention. We have both waited a very long time for this opportunity. The scriptures say that at the dawn of the fourth age, the children of the overthrown kingdoms will rise up and cast out their oppressors. When this is done, God's word will reign supreme. This is our time."

"This may be our time, but for different reasons," Shakira replied. "Read your books, priest. See whatever meaning you wish to see in the words. Men wrote those words, and we place no trust in men."

"If I could just show you—"

"The *words*?" Shakira sneered. "We were created by men and it was men who betrayed us. We believe in ourselves, not in any gods that you invented to help you sleep at night."

Marek wasn't sure if the expression on Shakira's face was a smile. It was difficult to tell with Orlocks. But something she said had caught his attention. "Tell me more about how men created you, and about this betrayal. I have never read anything about it."

The Orlock queen didn't reply immediately. Keeping her eyes fixed on his, she took a final bite of the meat she was eating and tossed the bone onto her plate. It was a small, delicate bone that reminded Marek of a child's finger. He shuddered inwardly and forced the thought from his mind. Shakira stood up and pulled her cloak tighter. The material was a deep blue velvet that contrasted with her yellow hair. Marek also stood. They were nearly the same height.

"So . . . you are curious? Have you never thought how Orlocks came to be in this world?"

Teanna was in the process of talking with the Guardian when the image of Mathew Lewin popped into her mind. Like Shakira, she also saw the fight in the house. She recognized Father Thomas immediately. The woman with him she didn't know. Neither was the Vargothan familiar to her. It made little difference. If her cousin wanted to throw his money away employing mercenaries, that was his business. What she was not prepared for were the fleeting visions of Shakira and Terrence Marek sitting together and talking that appeared a moment later.

For the past hour she had been absorbing what the Guardian had shown her. The images made her stomach turn. It was no wonder the creatures hated humans. She understood so much more now . . . so much more. What her ancestors had done to the Orlocks was simply monstrous. Teanna pushed her chair back from the machine and rubbed her face with her hands.

"Do you wish to go on to the next disk?" the Guardian asked.

Teanna took a deep breath and leaned back. She shifted her position to stop the light from passing through him. The Guardian looked better as a solid person, even if he wasn't alive. Having him go translucent in the middle of a conversation was disconcerting. A plate of food she had created a half hour earlier still sat on the table next to the machine, untouched. There was more she needed to see and precious little time to do it. Absently, Teanna picked up the sandwich and took a bite.

"Would you like some?" she asked.

"My operations do not require food, Princess."

"I know," Teanna said, tossing the sandwich back on the plate. "That was a joke."

The Guardian tilted his head to one side and his eyes went blank for a second. "Ah . . . a humorous anecdote or remark. Yes, that could be construed as funny. I shall remember that. My program is designed to learn a great many—"

"Never mind," said Teanna.

She reached forward and passed her hand over the silver disk as the Guardian had taught her to do and a beam of light appeared. Images began to form after several seconds. Like her electronic companion, they were three dimensional, but more translucent. She was looking at a type of newspaper the Ancients had once used. At least that was how the Guardian had explained it. The pictures spoke and moved as if they were alive. It was simply incredible . . . like looking through a window into the past.

Her question about why the Orlocks hated humans

had produced no results, and she turned to the Guardian, puzzled.

"I thought you said this machine could provide answers."

"You must first ask the right question. There are 20,737,605,306 entries in the database."

Teanna took a deep breath. "Those are the number of books in your library, is that what you're saying?"

"In a manner of speaking. Some may be news reports from a particular time period, as well as books, encyclopedias, and other reference material."

Teanna didn't understand the last part, but she wasn't about to say so again. The part about *"news reports,"* however, made sense.

"Are there *news reports* from before the Ancient War?" she asked.

"There are . . . and afterward for a period of ninety-two years."

"But why stop then?"

"All the people who knew how to enter the data had either died or were killed in the first Orlock war."

Teanna thought for a moment. "Then the creatures hatred of us must have started prior to that time. Isn't that right?"

"Relations between Orlocks and their human masters had been deteriorating for many years," the Guardian explained.

*"Human masters?"* said Teanna, shocked. "We owned them?"

"The Orlocks were created as a worker race for humankind."

The news was staggering. Nothing she had ever heard or read gave the slightest hint that her ancestors had created the Orlocks, much less owned them. The very concept was bizarre. She was in the process of working her way through its implications when the hum started. Teanna understood what the sound meant at once.

"Close," she said.

The Guardian inclined his head and promptly disappeared.

She glanced around the room and saw a large gray metal cabinet that was big enough to hide behind.

"Lights off."

A point of white light suddenly appeared in the darkness, and the hum continued to increase. The light expanded into a thin line that gradually thickened and became rectangular. In seconds the air took on a liquid quality. At the center of the rectangle two forms began to take shape. From her hiding place, Teanna watched a human man and a female Orlock materialize. The rose gold ring on the Orlock's finger left no doubt as to who she was. She guessed the man was Terrence Marek.

"What is this place?" Marek asked, looking around. "I've never seen anything so odd."

"You are in a town the Ancients created. This is one of their libraries."

"Astounding."

"It's quite different from the kind humans use today. There are no books or scrolls here, only these machines," Shakira said, pointing to the consoles.

"I don't understand," said Marek. "If there are no books—"

"The machines contain pictures—pictures that move and talk. They can answer almost any question."

Teanna listened as Shakira explained more about the town of Henderson and where it was located. Marek was taken aback at being a thousand miles under the surface of the world, but controled his reaction well. It was equally obvious to Teanna that Shakira was enjoying herself. When she was through with her explanation, she and Marek went to one of the machines and sat down in front of it. The Orlock passed her hand over a silver disk set in the table.

"What information do you require?" a mechanical voice asked.

Marek started when the voice spoke, and he leaned forward and looked on both sides of the machine.

"Orlocks; history," Shakira replied.

For the next five minutes a series of images floated above the silver disk. They showed a group of scientists in an ancient laboratory working on a humanoid body. Teanna looked closer. There were differences in the body's size and shape, but the face was clearly that of an Orlock. Eventually the images shifted to show Orlocks in the role of servants doing all sorts of manual labor.

"Even our name was a joke," Shakira told Marek. "It was taken from a novel one of your ancestors wrote."

Marek shook his head.

"What your people didn't count on was our ability to develop emotions and think for ourselves. At first the humans refused to accept this. Hundreds of my people were taken to laboratories and their brains were removed so your scientists could study them."

A montage of images appeared over the disk, showing the most gruesome operations being conducted on the creatures. Watching from the shadows, Teanna grimaced, but did not look away. Marek had much the same type reaction.

"In the end, the proof was irrefutable," Shakira went on. "Even the most adamant of humans could no longer deny it, but still the Orlocks were kept as slaves. After two hundred years, groups of your people began to petition their governments to free our people from their servitude and afford them rights as living creatures. I would tell you the date this occurred, but it would be meaningless to you. Do you understand what you have seen so far?"

Marek nodded and passed his hand through the images floating over the disk, then looked at his palm. "I understand. Is there more?"

Shakira laughed to herself. "Do you know what the words *sepratus t'equi* mean, human?"

"Separate but equal. It is the old language."

"Separate but equal," Shakira repeated. "An interesting concept, wouldn't you agree?"

Marek turned in his chair to face her.

"The protests over freeing the Orlocks continued for eighty years, becoming more and more violent."

More images appeared over the disk.

"Toward the close of the second age a resolution was finally passed which all governments agreed to. Orlocks were to be given status as sentient beings—equal to humans. The only stipulation was that we were banished to live under the earth . . . where your people would not have to look at us."

"In places like this?" Marek asked.

"No . . . not like this. This town is quite different from any of the others. Perhaps I'll show you why one day. No, we lived in caves and in underground caverns. That's where we built our cities.

"Continue," Shakira told the machine.

Once again a series of images appeared, showing dozens of Orlock towns and buildings under construction.

"I don't understand," Marek said. "What happened?"

"Deprived of their servants, your ancestors began to look for something to replace them. Not far from here there is another machine. It took your people a hundred years to develop it, and another thirty years to create this cavern. That machine reaches into the depths of the planet."

Shakira held up her hand to show Marek her rose gold ring. "It is the reason why these rings function. It has the ability to turn thought into matter."

"I know all of this, your majesty."

"Do you?"

"Yes, I do. I've studied the ancient books. The Church of Coribar has known about the machine since it was built."

"Do your books tell you what happened after it was built?"

"If you mean the war, everyone knows about that."

"Once the machine was awake, if your ancestors wanted something, all they had to do was to think about it. They needed nothing—least of all Orlocks."

Teanna knew what Shakira was about to show Marek, and this time she averted her eyes. There was no need to view the atrocities she had witnessed again.

"On the pretense of giving my people more rights, conferences were set up in all the great caverns and in stadiums on the surface. There, the Orlocks assembled, and there they were slaughtered . . . male, female, and children alike. The killing went on until the humans were satisfied their *mistake* had been corrected. An experiment that should have never been done, they called it."

Marek shook his head sadly as he watched the images flash above the disk. Teanna put her hands over her ears to shut out the screams.

"I am so terribly sorry, your highness," he said. "I had no idea. None of this appears in any of our books. A great wrong has been done to your people. The holy scriptures say that all of God's creatures shall live together in peace and harmony."

"Words," said Shakira. "Humans find it easy to use words."

"It is not too late," Marek repeated. "The revolt has already begun in Elgaria and in Sennia. Alor Satar will respond by sending its armies to crush the rebellion, but it's they who will be crushed. Once the sinners are gone, we shall all live together as God intended."

"In peace and harmony," Shakira said.

From the shadows Teanna could see the cold smile that appeared on the Orlock's face. It never touched her eyes.

* * *

Teanna waited until they were gone. She was still in shock from the things she had learned. It was now clear to her that Marek, Shakira, and Seth were planning a trap. She knew that Marek was right when he said that her cousin Eric would respond to a rebellion in Elgaria with force. The mercenaries, she assumed, would be the ones to draw Alor Satar in. That, however, was not the least of her problems. Marek was so blinded by the opportunity for his Church to prevail in the coming conflict he was willing to sacrifice humans beings to the Orlocks.

Any fool could see that Shakira had no intention of living peacefully with anyone other than her own people.

It was no longer a matter of going along with Eric. If Alor Satar were destroyed, they would target her country next. Each of the three had their own reasons for doing so. The Orlocks wanted no more humans to betray them. If men killed men, so much the better—there would be that much less work for the creatures to do. Coribar wanted its doctrine to reign supreme, and anyone who stood in their way were enemies. Her father's theory about Vargoth's motives was also correct. The mercenaries saw a chance to end their dependence on imports from other countries, and Elgaria was rich in natural resources.

*How nicely everything fits.*

"Guardian," Teanna said.

As before, it took the Guardian a moment to materialize.

"Princess," he said.

"How can I reach Mathew Lewin?"

"I cannot provide that information to you."

"It's extremely important that I find him. I know he's alive, so you don't need to pretend."

"That would be a human emotion. I am not programmed to pretend nor can I give you the information you are requesting."

"But it's imperative that I speak with him. Why won't you tell me where he is?"

"My programming prevents me from giving you that information."

"That's ridiculous. You told me that 'programming' means instructions. Whoever built you did it three thousand years ago. They couldn't know anything about me, because I didn't exist at the time, nor did Mathew."

"The reason this information is restricted is because you attempted to harm another ring holder. It's a safeguard the planners built into the machine."

"A what?"

The Guardian folded his hands in front of him. "When your ancestors first created the rose gold rings, they were not blind to human failings. They knew there were some among them that would try to harm others, so they took precautions against it. When evil thoughts were detected, thoughts of doing harm, the machine shut that person down—*forever.*"

A wave of panic swept over Teanna and she reached for the power. On the other side of Henderson was the laboratory she'd discovered on her first visit. The needle on the first gauge moved slightly when she did.

She could feel the power was still there. The machine hadn't cut her off after all.

"Nothing's happened to me," Teanna said.

"That is because your ring lacks the restrictions built into all the others. So it is with Mathew Lewin's ring. It is also true of Shakira's and the ones remaining in Alor Satar. They are all part of the original eight," the Guardian explained.

"Then if there are no restrictions—"

"Only one. You may think of it as a system of checks and balances. When you tried to kill Mathew Lewin, the machine knew this. It will not aid you in doing so again."

"But I don't want to kill him," said Teanna. "I was very angry at the time. I don't feel that way now. I just want to talk with him. Can't you understand that? What happened between us was four years ago. I overreact sometimes; I admit it. It's imperative that I speak with Mathew. We're in great danger."

The Guardian didn't respond. After several more seconds it became apparent that he wasn't going to.

Exasperated, she fixed the image of her bedroom in her mind and disappeared.

## 31

# The Wasted Lands

GAWL D'ATHERNY OPENED ONE EYE AND LOOKED around. Then he opened the other. He deemed the fact that he wasn't dead a good sign. Inside what remained of the building's foundation, the soldiers were just beginning to stir. A groan from someone on his left attracted his attention. Prince James sat up and spit out some sand. Quinn was about fifty feet away.

"Well, that was fun," said James, getting to his feet. He put a hand under Gawl's arm to help him up. "What the hell was that?"

"A sandstorm," said Gawl, brushing his arms off.

"It wasn't like any sandstorm I've ever seen," James replied. "How often do they happen here?"

Gawl didn't answer right away. Instead he looked out toward the horizon. "We'd better check on the men and see if anyone was hurt. It would be best if we get everyone to shelter as quickly as possible."

"Why rush now that it's over? If that didn't kill us, nothing will."

Gawl looked at the prince and lifted his eyebrows.

"You can't be serious," said James.

"They usually come in groups."

"Oh, this is marvelous. This is just wonderful," James said, throwing up his hands. "Why didn't you tell me about this before?"

"You never asked," Gawl replied. "Anyway, we were lucky. Some of them are really violent."

Gawl clapped him on the shoulder, and James limped off to see about his men, muttering under his breath.

As it turned out Gawl was right, they had been lucky. On his first visit to the plain years earlier, the storm that had hit his company killed six men. The memory still sent a shiver up his spine. The winds were like nothing he'd ever encountered. It was so bad, the men were unable to breathe and choked to death on the sand. Given James's present mood, he decided to keep that information to himself.

Throughout the day the heat continued to climb and the sky resumed the same gray metal appearance. Dark clouds moved slowly overhead as Jeram Quinn sat down next to Gawl. By the time they stopped to eat the constable was sweating profusely. He accepted a bottle of water from Gawl and took a drink.

"This is an incredible place," said Quinn. "How is Prince James?"

"Not in a very good mood. I think he wants to reach Sennia and get things over with as quickly as possible."

"Don't you?"

"Certainly. Hanging Edward Guy is one thing, but it won't be confined to just him, or even Ferdinand Willis and his crew. Sennians set great store by their priests, and a lot of my people will believe Guy is in the right just because Willis tells them he is. I've been giving the whole business some thought."

"And . . . ?"

"And I'm thinking now there might be another way to handle things. If Guy is a traitor, then we should put him on trial and let the law deal with him. James thinks I'm crazy. He says that the king *is* the law and to hang him and have done with it. Things aren't as clear-cut as they were a few days ago, Jeram. I suspect your influence may be rubbing off on me."

"I'll take that as a compliment."

"I'd like to ask you a question," Gawl said. "Would you be willing to preside over a trial?"

Quinn was shocked. "Me? I'm not even from your country. I'm an Elgarian."

"But you fought with our men at Fanshaw Castle. A lot of people will remember that, plus you're a constable. Who better to conduct a trial than a judge with no personal stake in the outcome?"

Quinn looked at Gawl for several seconds. "Are you serious about this?"

"Completely."

"You understand that any trial would have to be managed according to the law, whatever the result."

"Whatever the result," Gawl agreed.

Quinn took a deep breath. "I'll have to give it some thought. You're a remarkable fellow, your majesty."

"As I keep telling people."

After an hour the men were rested. A brief debate took place between Gawl and James as to whether they should try to make it to the mountains or camp for the night since the ruins were in relatively good condition. It was settled as soon as Gawl told the prince about the possibility of corrosive rain. James kept muttering the entire way.

They managed to avoid any more sandstorms, but were unfortunate in that just before leaving the plain another quake struck. It opened a mile-wide fissure in the earth. Two men were standing directly over it when it happened. Both fell in and were killed. Their deaths left a pall over the expedition.

As they moved into the higher elevations, the temperatures dropped to more tolerable levels. Gawl located the path he was looking for without difficulty. It was just a narrow tract that ran along the edge of the mountain. He glanced at the rubble littering the ground with some unease and then up at the rocks above them.

James looked as well. "Is this way safe?" he asked.

"I think so," said Gawl, squinting upward. "It appears solid enough. We should pass the word for the men to be cautious just in case."

"How long before we reach the summit?"

"A little over an hour. There will be a number of streams coming out of the rocks and two tiny waterfalls about a half mile ahead. Under no circumstances should any of the men drink from them. Once we're over the top, the path descends into a valley. The water down there is fine, but for some reason these streams—"

"Look, if this is something that's going to depress me again, I don't want to hear about it," James said. "I'll tell the men to be careful."

"We'd better get going," said Gawl. "I don't want to be caught up here at night."

"Oh, for God's sake," James said, stomping off.

Gawl looked at Quinn. "Touchy sort, isn't he?"

The rest of the journey went without incident. It appeared the Mirdanites were as anxious to get off the mountain as their prince was. Compared to the plain, the valley looked like a perfectly pleasant place. The farther in they moved, the more grass and vegetation they saw. There was even a rapidly flowing spring that ran alongside the path.

James, as Gawl knew, was an experienced outdoorsman, and despite his grumblings about earthquakes and poisoned water, he understood at once what was wrong there. No sounds of life could be heard anywhere; not from the birds or from any insect. Twice the prince walked to the edge of the stream and looked down at it. Though the water was perfectly clear, he could see no fish nestled along the banks. Unfortunately, not everyone was convinced and heeded Gawl's warning.

A young corporal ignored his captain's instructions and refilled his canteen in one of the streams that flowed out of the rocks when no one was looking. He died in convulsions an hour after taking a drink. Another soldier, who was walking at the rear of the column, popped a handful of blackberries into his mouth. His face broke out in boils, and in a short while, it was so swollen he couldn't see and had to be helped along by his friends. The following morning a fever took him and he was buried within ten miles of their goal.

It was the greatest relief to both Gawl and James when they finally left the Wasted Lands and came at last to the sea. It stretched before them to the horizon. The expedition had climbed for most of the day and was now atop a cliff that looked out over the Gardic Ocean. The sky changed from gray to sharp cloudless blue, and they saw the sun for the first time in six days. White gulls glided gracefully through the air, their cries reaching the men below.

Gawl took a deep breath, pulling the welcome salt air into his lungs.

*If I never set foot in that miserable place again, it will be too soon,* he thought.

Out of an abundance of caution, James sent two scouts on to Oglive Bay, where they were to rendezvous with the Mirdanite fleet. He wanted to make sure all of the ships were there and it was safe to bring the men forward. It took the scouts nearly four hours to make the trip and the return. They reported that forty ships had dropped anchor approximately fifteen miles from their present position. Ten more ships were expected in the morning.

James then gave the order to make camp.

Once Arteus Ballenger was satisfied his men were properly settled, he posted sentries and went to join Gawl. They walked together in silence along the sandy shore for nearly twenty minutes before Gawl said anything.

"I think you ought to know about my conversation with Jeram Quinn."

"The Elgarian constable?" Ballenger asked.

"Yes. I've asked him if he would preside over a trial for Edward Guy and Ferdinand Willis."

"I see."

"I know how you feel," Gawl said, "but I think I've come to the right decision."

He went on to tell the general about his plan for dealing with the traitors. Ballenger occasionally nodded but didn't interrupt. Gawl couldn't tell if that signified agreement or not, so he continued with his explanation.

"I think it's a good plan, sire. A soldier's job isn't to make war, though I would have no objection to doing so where the Archbishop and Lord Guy are concerned. I think they're the worst thing that has ever happened to Sennia. My job is to see you back on the throne, and that's what I intend to do."

" . . . but something bothers you."

"I don't know this Quinn very well. He seems like a good man, but he's not a Sennian. Do you think the people will accept that?"

"I believe so," Gawl replied. "I've promised to give him a free hand. The trial will be conducted with a jury of commoners and barons according to the law. I intend for it to be held in public, not in a closet as Siward Thomas's or mine were. His job will be to preside over it and make sure that things are run correctly. If the outcome is good, it's good. If it's bad, it's bad, but it will be a fair trial."

"The army will support you, sire. You have *my* word on that."

"Good man."

The following morning an army composed of fifteen thousand Sennians and Mirdanites made their way to Oglive Bay and began boarding the ships. The horses presented a problem and special slings had to be installed in the ships' holds to accommodate them. It was a slow and tedious process.

Gawl stood in the prow of James's flagship listening to the wind moving through the rigging. He watched the activity down on the beach for a few minutes before his mind drifted to Rowena and the thought of putting her on trial. Under Sennian law, the penalty for treason was death. It was not something he wanted to dwell on.

*Why couldn't they have accepted my offer of clemency? This must be what happens when you get old. You go soft. Gawl of Sennia going soft on his enemies.*

The thought made him laugh.

## 32

# The Road to Nyngary

NEARLY A WEEK HAD PASSED SINCE THEY'D FREED CETA
Woodall from her captors, and as Father Thomas had predicted, the Vargothans struck back violently. Despite the
fact that none of their officers had survived the attack at
Gravenhage, the mercenaries proved to be amazingly
well-trained. When the main garrison realized what was
happening, they organized quickly and launched a coun-
teroffensive, burning half of Gravenhage to the ground. It
was not so much a show of strength as an attempt to teach
the Elgarians a lesson. Unable to find anyone who would
give them information about the assault, the Vargothans
then moved on Mechlen.

But without experienced officers to guide them, the
mercenaries were a less effective fighting force than they
had been. Three hundred fifty Elgarian militia under Akin
Gibb's command met them at a place called Mirasal Valley. No Vargothan survived the encounter. Whether King
Delain liked it or not, the rebellion *had* begun.

Mathew learned about the battle secondhand. In the
confusion following Ceta's rescue, it was decided that he
and Father Thomas would take advantage of the enemy's
disarray and immediately head for Nyngary. It was no
longer possible, of course, for either Ceta or Collin to remain in Devondale. Even the dullest Vargothan would be
able to piece together what had occurred.

At Father Thomas's suggestion, two more of Dermot
Walsh's wagons were appropriated, and were now being

used to support their disguise as traveling wine merchants. For a brief period Mathew considered trying to talk the women out of coming, but following a heated conversation with his new wife, he gave up on the idea. Lara and Ceta had made up their minds, and arguing further would be pointless. Mathew and Lara did agree to leave Bran in Devondale where he would be safe. It was not an easy decision, but a necessary one. He would be safer there. Goodbyes were said and they rode out the following day. The little boy's face was somber as he watched them go.

The town of Bell's Ferry, where they stopped, was colorless. It bordered the Roeselar River and, like most towns, had an inn.

They'd traveled most of the day over roads badly in need of repair and their progress had been slow. Exhausted, and with evening coming on, they decided to take rooms for the night. Father Thomas and Ceta were at the end of the hallway, and Collin was next door. If everything went as planned, they would be in Nyngary in less than a week. That was the easy part.

Sleep came quickly, but it didn't last. For the third time in as many nights Mathew awoke in a cold sweat. The dream was back again. He'd been having the same dream off and on for the last four years, but for some reason, he was having it more often of late and the details were richer than in the past. He was now as familiar with their content as he was with his own face. In all of them he had found himself inside a cave.

Lara was sleeping quietly by his side when he awoke and sat up. He had no idea what time it was because it was too dark to see the clock. Some time after midnight he guessed. A quiet rain was falling against the windowpane. Mathew put his head back down on the pillow and tried to recall as much about the dream as he could before the memory faded.

The cave was dark and he had been carrying a lantern.

Without it there would have been no light at all. That much he remembered clearly.

For the next hour he stared up at the ceiling waiting for sleep to return. It didn't. Too many thoughts were keeping him awake. As he lay there he pictured his son playing on the floor of Martin and Amanda's house. A few days ago he was single—now he was married and with a child.

*Things were changing. His life was changing.*

It wasn't that he objected to them. Bran was a good boy. He could tell that right away. He desperately wanted to get to know him better and be the right kind of father. Mathew smiled in the dark.

The minutes wore on slowly and his eyes grew heavier until sleep finally overtook him. Then the dream started and he found himself back in the cave again.

He could feel the rough stone on the walls when he touched them, but something was different. For the first time he realized that he wasn't alone. Collin was with him and they were traveling the narrow path together. The way was not marked, but he could see an opening in the rocks where the path disappeared. They decided to keep going. No spectacular colors were revealed when the lantern's light shone on walls. They were dull and tan. Somewhere in the distance he could hear the sound of water dripping.

"Do you know where we are?" Mathew asked, uncertain if people could talk dreams.

"No idea," Collin replied.

They had to squeeze their bodies through several irregular rock formations as they continued along the path. After some time, it widened into a circular area about two hundred feet across. High above them a subterranean waterfall cascaded down into a pool. The dream shifted and he found that he was climbing once again. As a boy he had never cared for heights, and it was no different now, dream or not. The only reason he climbed at all was because his friends had and he was afraid of being laughed at. They continued to climb for another fifteen minutes until they were far above the cave floor. Mathew reminded himself that it was better not to look down, did, and was immediately hit by a wave of vertigo, which caused his stomach to tighten. He clung to the side for a moment until his breath came back.

After Mathew recovered, he suddenly found himself standing on the ledge of a cliff with Collin.

He also knew why they were there. The echo's pulsations had been increasing throughout his body for some time. His ring was near.

Compared to what he had once been able to do, the echo's power was feeble. This was both a blessing and a curse—on one hand, it had enabled him to save Father Thomas's life; on the other, it was a constant reminder of what he had lost.

They both saw it at the same time. On the other side of a fifteen-foot chasm, a door was set into a sheer rock wall. It was rounded at the top and made of heavy oaken planks that had been reinforced with iron bands and nails. The cavern floor lay more than two hundred feet below them, and there was no way to get across it without building a bridge.

Mathew held the lantern higher to get a better look and let out a yell of surprise, stepping backward out of reflex. In the shadows were three Orlocks. Two of them were males, the third was a female. The woman was as tall as the men. She had the same white skin and yellow hair, but her eyes were gray. He knew it was Shakira.

Collin drew his sword, but the Orlocks didn't react. Mathew put his hand on his friend's arm. They could run from the creatures, he thought, but where would they go? The Orlocks could have easily killed them while they were climbing, and yet they hadn't.

"An interesting place Teanna has chosen to hide the ring, wouldn't you say, human?" Shakira asked.

Mathew glanced at the door across the chasm and took a step forward. "Is my ring in there?"

"It is."

"You're Shakira, aren't you?"

The Orlock queen inclined her head.

"I'm Mathew Lewin. This is my friend, Collin Miller."

"I know who you are."

"How could you know me? We've never met."

"There is enough power coming from you even now to see as much."

"What is it you want?"

"The same thing you do," Shakira replied.

"But the ring can only work for one person," Mathew said. "Each one is unique. It would be useless to you."

Shakira laughed to herself. "You have a great deal to learn."

"So people keep telling me. It's the truth though. The rings *can* only work with one person. It has something to do with the chemicals in the brain. I'm not even sure they would work with an Orlock."

"Mat," Collin interrupted, touching him on the arm.

Mathew pulled his arm away. "Look, I know how you feel about us, but Orlocks and humans didn't always hate each other. I was in the Emerald Cavern and I've seen what's down there. If you would just let—"

"Mat," Collin said again.

*"What?"* Mathew asked, turning to him.

Collin motioned with his head toward the Orlocks. The two males stood silently, their chests rising and falling. Shakira folded her arms across her chest and said nothing. It was a second before Mathew noticed the rose gold ring on her right hand.

The look of shock on his face must have been obvious, because Shakira smiled.

"How?" he asked.

"There is a good deal more to the cavern than you saw during your visit," Shakira told him. "You are right in one respect, our races did work together . . . once, but that time passed into the shadows three thousand years ago."

"You came here for my ring?"

"Your ring by chance, not by right."

Mathew thought rapidly. Something about the conversation wasn't adding up.

*If Shakira already has one of the rose gold rings, she could easily have killed us and taken the other one. So why are we standing here passing the time of day?*

"You know, you're probably right," said Collin. "If you'll just excuse us, my friend and I will just be running along now. It's been nice to meet you."

"If the ring is in there," Mathew asked, "why don't you get it yourself?"

Shakira's silence spoke volumes to him, and he looked at the door again. The fact that it was across a drop shouldn't have mattered to her, but for some reason it did.

Collin picked up on the same thing. "Maybe they don't like heights," he said under his breath. "Let's get out of here."

Convinced that something was wrong, Mathew studied the door closer.

He hadn't seen anything before, but now he could just make out something in front of it. The air was not quite transparent . . . at least around the edges. Some sort of blur ran completely around the frame.

Mathew bent down and picked up a pebble. He glanced at Shakira and the other Orlocks then tossed it across the chasm at the door. It never made contact. A bright orange flash and a loud crack made everyone jump.

"You can't get to it," Mathew said.

"But *you* can. Retrieve the ring for me and we will let your people live. The time of the Orlocks has come and there is nothing you or anyone can do to stop us."

"What's around the edge of the door?" he asked.

"A ward Teanna d'Elso has placed there."

Mathew thought about that. It made sense that Teanna wouldn't leave the ring unprotected. But what Shakira was saying made no sense. Did she expect him to simply get the ring and give it to her? The moment he put it on, they would be equal. *No*, he decided, *there was something else going on.*

"Why don't you get it?" he asked.

"You know very little about how the rings work," said Shakira. "Whatever she has placed there cannot harm you. This is not true for us."

"You've already pointed out my ignorance," Mathew said. "I'll need some time to think about this."

Shakira's eyes fixed on his. "For you there is no more time. Kill them."

Both of the male Orlocks drew their weapons and rushed forward. Caught unprepared, Collin and Mathew managed to avoid the initial attack but couldn't stop the creatures from running into them. Bodies met and Mathew found himself hurtling through the air. He was so close to the Orlock that its smell nearly overpowered him. Even as they fell, it tried to bite him. Sharp teeth sunk into his shoulder and he screamed in pain.

He came awake with a start, his sudden movement waking Lara.

"What is it?" she asked, putting a hand on his back.

"It's nothing. I was just having a dream."

"A nightmare?"

Mathew swallowed and lay back down again. He reached out and smoothed her hair. "Yes, I'm fine now. Go back to sleep."

"You first."

He slipped an arm around her shoulders and she snuggled closer, resting her head on his chest.

The following morning they met Father Thomas and Ceta in the common room for breakfast. Collin was there with them.

"Both wagons will be ready as soon as we are," Collin announced.

"My, you've been busy," Lara remarked, giving him a kiss on the cheek before she sat down.

"I decided to get up early and see that everything was in order. Say . . . this egg toast is pretty good," he said, taking a bite of his food. "Bran loves egg toast. I generally make it for him in the mornings, particularly when it's cold out."

It seemed to Mathew that he was about to say something else and then thought better of it and changed the subject.

"It's not as good as yours, Ceta," he went on, "but it's definitely not bad."

"Thank you, Collin," Ceta replied. "We didn't hear you come in last night. That floor in the hallway squeaks so."

"Well . . . I was trying not to disturb you."

The kitchen door opened then and a pretty, auburn-haired serving girl came out carrying a large glass of orange juice and a plate of eggs. She set it down in front of Collin with a smile, introduced herself to the others as Hilde, then took their orders. She made a point of trailing her fingers across Collin's neck on the way to the kitchen. Ceta and Lara exchanged glances. Seated between his wife and his friend, Mathew noticed it as well, but prudently said nothing. Lara however, made a point of leaning around him and looking at Collin, who seemed to be concentrating on his eggs with more attention than was strictly necessary. After a few minutes he excused himself and said he would meet everyone at the stables later.

Father Thomas watched Collin go out the front door. "As soon as we're all done eating," he said, "I'd like to get started. If the weather holds and we keep up a reasonable pace, we should reach the Cut just after midday and be in Alor Satar before nightfall. There's a town called Ardosta where we can stop."

"Will it be safe?" Ceta asked.

"I'm not sure anyplace is safe. The Vargothans are certainly going to try and find us once they get organized again. And it's safe to assume that Alor Satar will send troops to support them. Our job will be to avoid both groups, which may be easier said than done."

Ceta nodded.

"Then I suppose we'd better purchase some more wine," said Ceta.

"We have wine," Father Thomas replied.

"We have two barrels, dear. Since we're supposed to be traveling wine merchants, it might look better if we actually had a reasonable stock to sell in case we're stopped. From what I've seen, the prices are pretty reasonable here—we might even turn a profit."

"Maybe we should let Collin do the negotiating," said Lara. "He seems to have developed a rapport with the locals."

Father Thomas, Ceta, and Mathew all turned to see what she was looking at. Outside the window, Collin and Hilde were talking to each other, their heads close together. She looked up at him and smiled.

"How fickle," Ceta said to Lara. "The first time you turn your back he takes up with another woman."

"If you'll excuse me," said Father Thomas, pushing his chair back from the table. "I'll see if I can find out where we can buy the wine. Mat, would you care to join me?"

"Lara and I can do it," Ceta said quickly. "You men get the things loaded up. It shouldn't take us long."

"What's wrong with my doing it?" Father Thomas asked.

"My dear, you're a wonderful priest and who knows what else, but as a wine merchant, well . . . "

Father Thomas's expression turned wounded and he looked to Mathew for support. Unfortunately, he didn't find any there. "I think I've done very well so far," he said, somewhat offended.

"If you pay what you did in Sarroy," Ceta explained, "we'll be bankrupt before we reach Nyngary. We don't have that much money left."

It seemed that Father Thomas was going to argue the point but decided against it. Instead, he folded his arms across his chest and said, "Fine. Mathew and I will load the wagon."

Ceta and Lara both got up. "It's settled, then," said Ceta. "We'll meet you in two hours at the stables."

Both exited the room, leaving a perplexed Father Thomas behind. "Was I that bad? I thought eighteen elgars a barrel was a fairly good price."

"Let's go rescue Collin before you have another wedding to perform," Mathew replied, changing the subject.

Ceta and Lara returned to the stables. They were followed by a fellow on a flatbed wagon being pulled by an old horse.

Ceta introduced him. "This is Cedric. He sold us our wine and was nice enough to bring it here."

Father Thomas, Mathew, and Collin all shook hands and then helped him load eight barrels onto their wagons. It wasn't until later that Father Thomas found out that Ceta had negotiated a price of eleven elgars a barrel.

# 33

## New Raburn

THE CUT, ALSO KNOWN AS COLE'S PASS, WAS A SEVENTY-yard-wide opening, nearly five miles long, that ran through the mountain range separating Elgaria from Alor Satar. Mathew had heard stories about it from his father and then later from Gawl, both of whom had been ambushed there during the closing days of the Sibuyan War. Bran Lewin had taken two arrows that day and was pulled to safety by Father Thomas. But this was the first time Mathew had actually been there. The towering white cliffs were every bit as big and imposing as he'd pictured them. He scanned the terrain, trying to visualize what a fight in that narrow enclosure must have been like.

*Awful*, he decided, and wondered if Father Thomas was thinking the same thing.

Collin rode alongside the wagon on his horse. Their eyes met and a silent communication passed between them. Askel Miller had also been caught in the same trap. From conversations around the Millers' dinner table when he was young, he knew that Collin's father had exhausted an entire quiver of arrows within the first few minutes of the battle in order to give his companions cover as they crossed the river. Like most young boys, he'd been fasci-nated by stories about the war, but after seeing more than his share of battles over the last seven years, the Cut took on a new perspective to him. Men had fought and died on this ground, and there was nothing terribly romantic about it.

Overhead, a few clouds were beginning to appear in the sky. Massive rock walls on either side of them added to the ponderous, claustrophobic feeling. Eventually they would emerge in Alor Satar, cross that country into Cincar before reaching Nyngary.

Collin's voice pulled Mathew back to the present.

"I'm going to ride up ahead and see if the way is clear. I'll be back in a few minutes."

"Good idea."

"Be careful," Lara called out.

"I wish I had brought a spare horse along," Mathew said as he watched his friend disappear around a corner. "It hasn't been much of a honeymoon for you, Mistress Lewin."

Lara leaned closer and nibbled on his earlobe. "I'm glad we're together," she whispered. "You can make it up to me later." To emphasize her point she trailed her fingers up his thigh.

"Uh . . . I wonder how Bran is doing," Mathew said.

"He's fine. He adores Mother and Father. They spoil him, though. He'll probably weigh a hundred pounds by the time we get back."

Mathew smiled. "It's a funny thing having a child, isn't it?"

"You should try it sometime, if you think it's so funny."

"I didn't mean it that way. I meant one minute I wasn't a father . . . and the next I was. It takes some getting used to."

Lara looked up at him.

"Don't get me wrong. I love him. I really do. But between you and me, the whole thing's a little scary . . . I hope I . . . be a good father."

"You will," Lara said.

"I've been thinking about it. Once you're a parent, you start looking at the world differently. Does that make any sense? I mean, I'm still the same person, but I find myself thinking that when we get back there are so many things I'll have to teach him. I'd like to show him how to sail and navigate a ship, and about weather signs, and tracking, and numbers, and fencing, too, of course . . . I'm babbling aren't I?"

Lara smiled and put both arms around him. "I love you," she said. "But you do owe me a honeymoon." Mathew smiled again and put his arm around Lara's shoulder and they rode awhile in silence until the sound of Collin's horse returning reached them.

"Trouble," he said, pulling up on the reins. "There's a column of Alor Satar soldiers coming up the pass. They're less than three minutes behind me."

"Tell Father Thomas," Mathew said.

"Right."

"What should we do?" Lara asked.

"Continue being wine merchants." Mathew glanced over his shoulder at his sword, lying on the floor of the wagon.

Collin returned a moment later, and Mathew felt the back of the wagon dip as his friend climbed in.

"Father Thomas says when we see them, we're to pull the wagons off to one side and give them the road."

Shortly, Mathew came around the bend and caught sight of the soldiers. His first estimate was that the column was closer in size to a full battalion, of at least five hundred men and horses. Father Thomas's prediction about Alor Satar's reaction had been accurate. As instructed, he pulled his wagon off to the side, with the second wagon following.

Two scouts were riding well ahead of the main body of troops. Both saw the wagons at the same time and came to a halt. One of them rode forward while the other turned back to report.

The scout came to a halt in front of the wagons. He was joined moments later by two men on horseback. Both were well-dressed and wore insignias on their cloaks, marking them as officers. Mathew picked the leader out right away, a man in his late fifties with gray hair and sharp features.

"Good morning," he called out.

The soldier didn't respond immediately. Instead, he looked at the other wagon and gave a curt nod to the scout, who spurred his horse forward and proceeded down the pass.

"May I see your passes, please?" the officer asked without preliminary.

"I'll get them," Lara replied. "They're in here."

She started to get up but stopped when he snapped, "Wait." To the man next to him, he said, "Check the back of the wagon."

The soldier nudged his horse around to the rear of the wagon and looked in. "Just barrels," he said, "and another young man."

"Very well. You can get your passes now," the leader told Lara. "My name is Julian Thierry and this is Hilton Brown, my second in command."

While they were talking, Father Thomas pulled his wagon alongside them. "Morning, Colonel," he called out.

"Good morning. My thanks for the promotion, but I'm a major. And you would be?"

"Joshua Lane, a seller of fine wines. This is my wife Elise, and I see you've already met my son Thaddeus and his wife Linda. That's my brother's boy, Mark, in the back. Why all the activity?"

The major nodded a greeting in their general direction. "My men and I are on our way to a town called Gravenhage. There's been some trouble there."

"Must have been a lot of trouble," Father Thomas replied, glancing down the pass at the soldiers. "Looks like you brought the whole army with you."

Thierry smiled. "Not really. This is only a battalion."

"Here are the passes," said Lara, emerging from the wagon. She handed them to Thierry.

"It says here you're from Melfort and are heading for Corrato in Nyngary."

"True enough," replied Father Thomas. "Would you or

your men be interested in some good quality Elgarian Red? I could let you have it at a good price."

"The correct name is *Oridan*," Thierry told him.

"Oh, for pity's sake," Father Thomas answered. "You can't go changing the name of the wine, too. Everyone calls it Elgarian. Folks won't know what I'm talking about if I say 'Would you like to buy some Oridan Red?' "

"You have a point," Thierry agreed, "but unfortunately it's the law."

Father Thomas shrugged. "Whatever you say, Col— Sorry, Major. We're just simple people trying to make a living. Can I offer you a sample? It really is top quality."

"No, thank you very much. It wouldn't do for my men to see me drinking while they're waiting in the sun. Tell me, Master Lane, did you happen to see or hear of any problems on your way in from Melfort?"

"Can't say as I did," said Father Thomas. "But to be honest, we didn't get near Gravenhage on this trip. Between you and me, it's not much of a town. The people there try to squeeze the blood out of you. How are the roads into Alor Satar?"

"They're fine for traveling, if that's what you're asking."

"That means they're still not safe at night," Father Thomas said to Ceta. He then turned back to Thierry. "I thought you people were going to do something about the brigands. We've heard all kinds of stories about them, I can tell you. It's getting so a person can't go out anymore. A little help from the army would go a long way toward keeping prices down. If I get robbed, we just wind up passing the costs along as part of doing business, and no one likes that. Prices go up and—"

"I'm sure something will be done as soon as we've settled the trouble in Gravenhage," Thierry interrupted, handing the passes back to Lara.

"Say," said Father Thomas, "is there any chance you could let one or two of your men ride along with us until we get to Ardosta? I'll throw in a barrel at half price."

The offer produced a small gasp from Ceta, who touched Father Thomas on the arm and tried to get his attention.

Thierry laughed. "I don't think so. Besides, I don't think your wife would approve."

Father Thomas started to say something, but the expression on Ceta's face obviously changed his mind. She leaned forward and said something in his ear. In a second they were both whispering angrily back and forth to each other.

Mathew observed the entire interchange in silence. He thought the act his friends were putting on was a little dramatic, though it definitely looked genuine. Apparently, Major Thierry thought so as well, because he was now searching for a way to end the conversation and get it back to the original topic.

"At any rate," Thierry said, trying to interrupt them, "my men and I will be going now. Good luck to you all."

If Father Thomas or Ceta heard it they gave no indication. They were still arguing when the last man in the column passed. As soon as he rounded the bend, however, they burst out laughing and hugged each other.

"Our first argument," Father Thomas said, wiping a tear from his eye.

Ceta tucked a strand of hair behind one ear and took a deep breath. "Oh dear," she said, raising a hand to her chest.

"You had me convinced," Collin told them. "That major nearly left skid marks trying to get out of here."

"I'm afraid we didn't set a good example for the children," Father Thomas said, which started them both laughing again.

The priest gave the reins a flick while Lara, Collin, and Mathew exchanged bemused glances.

When they emerged from the Cut, Father Thomas pulled his wagon to a halt and waited for Mathew to draw up alongside. Collin was back on his horse. The priest pointed at the black storm clouds behind them that were rolling in from the west.

"I don't think we have much time before we get wet," he said.

"How far is it to Ardosta?" asked Collin.

"Another four hours at least. There are some ruins we can take shelter in just over that ridge. I haven't been there in years, but many of the buildings were reasonably intact."

"I don't want anything to do with ruins," said Collin. "The last time I visited one, someone tried to blow me into the next province."

"We don't have much choice," said Mathew. "That storm's coming in fast."

Collin twisted in his saddle and studied the horizon for several seconds. The clouds *were* moving in their direction rapidly. A rumble of thunder apparently changed his mind. He muttered something under his breath and turned back to Father Thomas.

"I'll ride up ahead and check them out. Over that ridge, you say?"

"Correct. You'll see them as soon as you get to the rise. We'll meet you there."

Collin kicked his horse to a full canter while the wagons followed at a slower pace.

The ruins were more extensive than those Mathew had seen in Argenton, closer in size to a small city than a town. At least eight tall buildings were still standing, along with a host of smaller ones. The biggest was over forty stories. Near the outskirts were the remnants of two of the Ancients' elevated roadways. One ran completely around the city's perimeter. At some point in the past a portion of it had caved in, leaving a pile of rubble at the base. The other, which they were on, was supported by a series of huge cement columns and approached the city across an open plain, that spanned a dried-up riverbed. Much of the concrete was pitted and cracked, forcing the wagons to proceed slowly, but given its age, the surface was more than serviceable. Lightning flashes now lit up the sky behind them, accompanied by thunder that was much closer than before.

At the opposite end of the bridge Mathew caught sight of Collin and waved to him. Collin responded by pointing at the horizon and signaled for everyone to hurry. Mathew didn't like what he saw over his shoulder. The sky had taken on an ominous yellow tinge, and parts were nearly black, making it look more like night than day. A haze over a section they had just passed through indicated that the rain was coming. Mathew flicked the horse's reins and quickened their pace. He estimated they had perhaps five minutes before the storm broke on top of them. Father Thomas's wagon also picked up speed and bounced over the road's surface.

Thunder crashed again, and this time Mathew felt its vibration through the wagon seat. In the last few minutes the temperature had dropped at least ten degrees, and he could smell the storm in the air. They were nearly at the end of the bridge, where Collin was struggling to keep his horse under control. The whites of the animal's eyes were showing.

"Make for that big granite building on the next block," Collin yelled.

The wagons sped down the roadway, with Collin leading the way. Mathew's mind registered details on the buildings as they went by. Drops of rain were already falling and stronger gusts of wind were pushing the wagon sideways. Lara gasped once when two of the wheels lifted off the ground. Ahead, Mathew could see the building looming like a giant stone sentinel. Collin galloped past the main entrance and around to the side, motioning for the wagons to follow. At the end of the building, a cement ramp led down to an open area beneath it. Mathew brought the wagon to a halt, then slowly followed Father Thomas's wagon down the slope, keeping one hand firmly on the brake to prevent them from gathering too much speed.

Halfway down the ramp the rhythm of the raindrops splattering against the wagon's roof suddenly changed. Mathew looked up and winced as something struck the side of his face. Hail. It was falling in pellets the size of tiny pebbles.

*Well, this is great.*

Lara pulled the hood of her cloak over her head and moved closer to him. By the time they reached the bottom of the ramp, the ground had turned completely white. He had seen hail in Devondale when he was growing up and again in the Great Southern Sea, but never any of this force. He climbed down off the wagon, brushed some pieces out of his hair, and went around to help Lara. The horse snorted at him as he passed.

"Sorry," Mathew mumbled.

Lara had been the better climber of the two since they were children and got down on her own. "What is this place?" she asked, looking around.

"Some kind of basement," said Father Thomas, coming to join them.

"It's so large."

"Why are all those lines painted on the floor?" asked Ceta.

Mathew looked and saw a series of faded yellow lines running perpendicular to the walls. At the far end of the basement was another ramp, similar to the one they had just come down, that descended to a lower level.

"I think this is where they stored their vehicles," said Father Thomas.

Ceta blinked. "There must have been hundreds of them. How many people lived here?"

Father Thomas looked up at the ceiling and shook his head slowly. "I don't think this was a residence, dear. The old books show pictures of buildings like these . . . People worked in them."

Ceta opened her mouth to say something and closed it again.

While the others waited near the opening watching the hail fall Collin located a stairway in the corner. He disappeared into it and returned two minutes later.

"Hey, c'mon," he said. "You've got to see this."

The rest followed up a flight of stairs, and found themselves in the middle of an enormous, six-story glass atrium. Outside, the hail had finally let up, but the rain was back, moving up the street at an angle. With nothing else to do they began exploring. In the center of the room was a bronze sculpture of a heavily muscled man who stared down at them with a stern expression on his face. He was holding a trident.

"I wonder how Gawl is getting on?" said Collin, looking up at it.

Mathew assumed the remark was because Gawl was a sculptor, and said so.

"No, it's not that," Collin replied. "The arms remind me of his."

They spent the next several minutes looking around the lobby and found nothing remarkable there. It was just a large empty room that could have held at least a thousand people. Against the far wall Collin found a series of metal doors with four tiny rooms behind them. Each contained several rows of numbered buttons on a wall panel. The highest read *42*.

"I saw something like this in Argenton," Collin told Mathew. "The Ancients used them to go up and down the building."

"You boys can keep exploring if you like," Lara said. "It doesn't look like the storm is going to let up. I'll get the food and our sleeping rolls."

"I'll go with you," Ceta said.

To everyone's surprise, the women returned a short while later not only with food, but with a small gray cat.

"Look what I found," Lara said. The cat was cradled comfortably in her arms, its paws resting on her shoulder.

"Where'd you find him?" Collin asked.

"He was in that basement place. He meowed when we came down. I'll bet he's starving."

Collin looked at the cat and frowned. "He doesn't look like he's starving. He looks kind of chubby."

Lara made an exasperated sound. "Don't listen to him," she told the cat.

The cat glanced at Collin for a second and dismissed him, putting his head back on Lara's shoulder.

"Hmph," said Collin.

Ceta took the basket Lara was carrying, set it on the floor and, with Father Thomas's help, spread the blankets out. When she was through, they all sat down to eat, including the cat, who waited patiently for leftovers, which Lara was more than happy to give him.

"Do you think he lives here by himself?" asked Collin.

The question hung in the air for several seconds. It was answered when Father Thomas slowly got to his feet and drew his sword. Ceta's gasp startled the cat, which skittered across the floor and disappeared into the shadows. No one moved.

Standing outside the glass windows were at least fifteen men.

## 34

## Çorrato, Nyngary

TEANNA D'ELSO WAS SURPRISED TO FIND BRYAN OAKES coming out of the palace apartments.

"Good morning, your highness."

"Good morning, Bryan. Is my cousin in?"

"No, the prince and his escort left earlier this morning. My captain asked me to check the rooms."

"They've gone?"

"I believe so. Is there something I can do for you?"

"No," she said, annoyed. "Do you know if they were returning to Alor Satar?"

"Prince Duren didn't choose to confide in me, majesty, but I did overhear him say that they were going to crush the rebellion out of existence, if that helps."

"It does," said Teanna, "a great deal."

"Are you certain there is nothing I can do to be of help?"

Teanna shook her head. "No, but I may call on you later."

"I am at your service," Bryan said, with a small bow.

Fifteen minutes later Teanna found herself in her father's private library. The king was there reading a book, and he closed it when she entered the room. "Is something wrong?" he asked, noting her expression.

"Father, I need your advice. We have a problem."

"Is this regarding our discussion yesterday?"

"Yes. I needed to speak with the Guardian, so I visited the town."

"May I ask why?"

"There were things I was curious about. I wanted to know more about the Orlocks; about where they came from, and why they hate us as much as they do. He showed me, Father. It was horrible."

Teanna proceeded to tell her father about the Orlocks' origins and about how men had tried to exterminate them. The king listened in silence.

"Interesting," he said. "And the problem you spoke of?"

Teanna looked at him. It was always difficult to tell what her father was thinking, but oddly, he seemed to be taking the news far more calmly than she expected he would.

"I'm not insensitive to what you are saying, daughter. What happened to the Orlocks sounds terrible. Unfortunately, these events occurred three thousand years ago. And to be perfectly blunt, I feel no responsibility for something my ancestors might have done . . . assuming we are related at all. The present, I *can* do something about. So, I'd like to hear the rest of what you have to say."

Teanna took a deep breath and continued. "There is a machine the Guardian has that shows pictures. It's like reading a book, but you actually see things that happened. I was watching it when Shakira and Terrence Marek appeared in the cavern. I hid myself and heard what they were saying. They're planning to lure Eric into a trap.

"The Vargothans have sent him a message that a rebellion is in progress in Elgaria, and they need more troops to put it down. They think Eric will respond by sending his soldiers. Once that happens, they're going to turn on him."

"I see," Eldar said.

"That's not the worst of it, Father—"

"Yes, yes, yes—the Orlocks and Coribar are going to join them," Eldar said, finishing the sentence for her. "You're right. We do have a problem. The question now is, how we should deal with it?"

"How could you know that?"

"A guess based on our conversation the other day." Eldar pushed himself out of the chair and went to the window. "In all likelihood Eric is already in Elgaria, or whatever your cousins are calling it these days, so it may be too late to do anything to help him. My concern is whether we should get involved at all."

Teanna's mouth fell open. "You mean, we should do nothing?"

"Alor Satar is perfectly capable of defending itself. They're the most powerful country in the world. Seeing them get their comeuppance wouldn't be entirely a bad thing."

"Father—"

"In fact, it might go a long way to equalizing the military balance of—"

"*Father,*" Teanna said. "I didn't finish what I was telling you. Shakira also has one of the rose gold rings, as well as a million Orlocks at her command. Marek doesn't care what means she uses, if they can eliminate whoever opposes him. He's so blind to get what he wants that he can't see that she's lying."

"Interesting," Eldar said.

"Interesting or not, we need to warn Eric. The Orlocks aren't going to stop in Elgaria. If anything, they should be better disposed to Alor Satar than the rest of us. It was Eric who kept his father's bargain with the creatures."

Eldar thought over the possibilities for several seconds. "I suppose we had better prepare the country for war. I'll see to it the border garrisons are placed on alert."

"And what about Eric and Armand?"

"My dear, one less Duren in the world won't make much of a difference, but if it makes you happy, I'll send riders out to intercept them . . . unless you have a faster way of doing it with your ring."

Teanna shook her head. "I'd have to know where they are to transport myself. Send the riders."

"Good. Then we're agreed." The king kissed Teanna on the forehead, picked up his book and started for the door.

"Father . . ."

Eldar stopped in mid-stride, turned around and folded his hands in front of him. He listened as Teanna told him that Mathew Lewin was alive.

"You're quite sure?" he said.

"Yes."

"And I assume Shakira is capable of using her ring, just as you can?"

"I don't know how strong she is or the extent of her powers, but she was obviously able to get to the cavern. My guess is that we are dealing with a very dangerous opponent."

"In Lewin or her?" Eldar asked.

The question caught Teanna off guard. "Mathew doesn't have his ring anymore, Father."

"I understand that. Have you considered the consequences if he did? Two against one?"

Teanna didn't answer immediately. She walked over and stood near the fireplace, letting the heat warm her back. "Mathew would never side with the Orlocks against humans."

"Are you willing to bet our lives on that?"

Teanna was preoccupied as she walked through the garden toward the sculpture. She needed time to think. It was already late in the afternoon, and the temperature was dropping. What had started out as a mild autumn day was going to melt into a cold night. Winter was coming. A movement near one of the benches stopped her. It was Bryan Oakes.

"Forgive me, your majesty, I didn't mean to startle you."

"You didn't. I was just thinking."

"I will leave you alone, then," he said.

"It's all right, Bryan. You're welcome to stay. What are you doing here?"

"The palace commander wanted me to check the apartments again."

"Aren't they empty?"

"Quite," Bryan said. "You were the only person to show up there today. I'm afraid I'll have to report that. One can never be too diligent."

Teanna giggled. "I'll be sure to tell Captain Jervis about your work." It felt good to laugh.

She saw her father up on the balcony watching them and gave him a small wave.

"Should I wave, too?"

"Oh . . . do you know Father?"

"No, but I thought he might like it if I waved to him."

The comment caused Teanna to laugh again. She looked at Oakes more closely. He was definitely a handsome man. He had wide shoulders, a slender waist, and warm brown eyes. She liked his eyes.

"I'm glad I could get you to smile. You looked so serious a moment ago . . . besides, I felt I owed it to you."

"Owed it to me? Why?"

"I've always been curious about what beautiful young princesses do in their spare time, and now I know. They walk in their garden and think."

Teanna stopped. "I do more than that."

"Such as?"

She started walking again. "Running a country, for one. You may think it's all fun and games, but I can tell you . . ."

Her voice trailed away as a buzz cut the air. It was followed by a dull thud and a sound from Bryan. She turned and to her surprise saw him stagger. A heartbeat later there was another buzz, then Bryan hit the ground face first, two arrows sticking out of his back.

Teanna was in shock. Three soldiers from the palace guard were racing toward her with the king close behind them. One of them was Captain Jervis, the officer in charge of the royal bodyguard.

"Father, what?" she gasped.

Eldar went to her and put his hands on her shoulders. "Are you all right?" he asked, searching her face.

"Yes," she said.

Teanna's shock widened further when the captain rolled Bryan's body over and she saw that he was clutching a long needle in his right hand. Jervis used the toe of his boot to kick it away, then took out a handkerchief, bent down and picked it up. He held it to his nose and sniffed.

"Poison," he said, looking at the king.

## 35

## Sennia

IT TOOK THE ARMY NEARLY A FULL DAY TO DISEMBARK the ships. Gawl had only visited the port city of Mardell in western Sennia once before and he knew little about it. To his surprise, they met absolutely no opposition from Lord Guy's forces on their arrival. In fact, the soldiers were notable by their complete absence. Ballenger insisted on landing one ship farther up the coast and another about fifty miles below the town to ensure that they weren't sailing into a trap. Neither encountered the slightest bit of resistance. Stranger still were the reports they brought back. It appeared that Lord Guy had withdrawn his troops two weeks earlier.

A delegation of people, led by the town's mayor, came down to the docks to meet them. Gawl took James's advice and waited in his cabin with Ballenger until Colonel Haynes could report on what they wanted. James stayed with him. The colonel returned fifteen minutes later.

"It appears the people are quite happy you're back, Sire," Haynes said. "They'd like to talk with you."

Gawl and James looked at each other. "Just like that?" said Gawl. " 'We're happy you're back. Sorry about you being in prison the last four years.' "

"Well . . . uh, yes," said Haynes. "That's pretty much what they said. Both the mayor and the head of their council confirmed that the garrison stationed here left for Barcora ten days ago. The mayor also told me a small number of the Archbishop's guards fled to the monastery when they saw our ships pull in."

"Do you trust what he said?" asked James.

"I do," Haynes replied. "I grew up quite close to here. The mayor and my father were friends."

Gawl pushed himself up and promptly thumped his head on one of the beams. "Goddamn these little ships."

For a second it appeared that James was going to laugh, but the smile forming on his face vanished when Gawl looked in his direction.

"If he knew Shelby's father," Gawl said, rubbing his forehead, "he's got to be at least a hundred years old."

"Thank you," Haynes said, giving him a flat look. He held the cabin door open for the monarchs, as they went out, adding, "Mind your head," as Gawl passed by.

Gawl chose to ignore it, though a smile twitched the corners of his mouth.

Dan Kirk, might not have been a hundred, but he wasn't far from it, at least in Gawl's opinion. Despite his age, the man's eyes were sharp and bright. His face was nut brown from the sun, heavily lined, and his hair snow white. He and the other members of the council bowed when they saw the king approaching. Gawl introduced James and Arteus Ballenger.

"If we knew you were coming, your majesty, we would have arranged for a better reception," Kirk said, shaking Gawl's hand.

"Quite all right," Gawl replied. "What news have you from the rest of the country?"

The mayor rubbed a jaw that was badly in need of a shave. "There's still some fighting going on between your supporters and Lord Guy's people, but for the most part it looks like it's over."

"*Over?* We've only just gotten here."

"Are you saying Lord Guy's troops gave up and ran?" James asked.

"I don't know whether they ran or not, but they didn't

waste any time leaving. They lost three battles in succession to that general of yours and took off for Barcora."

Ballenger frowned. "What general is that?"

"Some girl who took over after word got out that you escaped. That's when all the riots started."

"*Melinda,*" Gawl exclaimed.

"That's the one. A big blond girl . . . curses like a drunken sailor. I met her when she came through here."

"How many people did she have with her?" asked Gawl.

"Couldn't say for sure, sire. My guess would be upward of five thousand men, and a good number of women, too."

Gawl started to chuckle.

"I know this woman," said Ballenger. "She commanded a regiment during the Sibuyan War."

"And fought with us at Fanshaw Castle," Gawl added. "She's something."

"Yes, indeed," Kirk agreed. He reached into the pocket of his vest and pulled out a letter. "She asked me to give this to you if you showed up."

Gawl carefully unfolded it and started reading. A second later he burst out laughing and clapped the mayor on his shoulder. "Thank you very much, my friend. I'm going to send some men up to the monastery to have a word with the Archbishop's guards, unless you and your council object to it."

"No," said the mayor.

"Good. From this moment on the Archbishop's Guard are illegal in Sennia. There are no exceptions. I will see that their weapons are turned over to you."

"Does this mean you're back to being king again?" asked Kirk.

"I suppose it does," said Gawl. "That is my first law."

"Are you in the mood to make another law, sire?"

"Such as?"

"Well . . . the prices of wine, copper, and coal have all doubled since Guy closed the borders. My guess is that a little competition wouldn't be such a bad thing. The Ashot priests keep telling us we'll all go to hell if we let foreigners settle in Sennia and trade with us. Personally, I have my doubts on this point."

"Do you?"

"I do. Seems like young James here doesn't have any horns growing out of his head. No offense intended, sire," he said to James. "I've always thought that an ally who shows up to help when you're in need is a person to be cultivated."

"Thank you," said James, with a small bow.

Gawl stared at the old man for a space then slowly drew his broadsword from the scabbard. Grasping it just under the hilt, he held it at arm's length and pitched his voice so it would carry to all around.

"I, Gawl Alon d'Atherny, King of the Ten Provinces, Ruler of the Eastern Islands and all territories lying therein, do hereby declare the borders of Sennia now to be open. Our neighbors and friends may pass in and from our country without fear of molestation or excessive tariff."

After a quick glance at Dan Kirk and the rest of the town's council out of the corner of his eye, Gawl added, "And so on and so forth. This sixth day of Ocandell, in the year of our Lord, 6265."

The members of the council appeared to be all suitably impressed and nodded to each other. Then they bowed to Gawl and James, and headed back to work. Kirk shook Gawl's hand and invited him to stop by his home for dinner along with Prince James when they had the time.

James watched them go and moved closer to Gawl. "And so on and so forth . . . that was my favorite part," he said, under his breath.

In the week that followed, Gawl, James, and the Southern Army engaged in only one battle. It lasted less than an hour before the Earl of Chambertin's men threw down their weapons and surrendered. Of Edward Guy, no sign could be found. The army scoured the country for him

without success. It was Ballenger's opinion that he had retreated to Barcora to consolidate his position and get his
men ready for the coming fight.

Each town the army went through gave them much the
same reception they had received in Mardell. Most people
were glad Gawl had returned, and more than pleased that
the borders were once again open. The news that drew the
greatest reaction, however, was the announcement that
Archbishop Willis's guards were officially disbanded. No
one they met voiced the slightest objection. Nor did they
object when Gawl let it be known that a system of courts
were to be established throughout the country, with each
town, city, and province having a court of their own to
deal with local matters.

Sennians gathered in town squares and inns to read the
king's proclamation. They discussed it and argued its mer-
its. The new law provided that the people were free to
elect from their own ranks any person, male or female,
they felt qualified to act as a judge.

Along with this, another announcement was posted de-
claring Edward Guy and his daughter traitors and informing the people that they would be tried before an impartial
magistrate when found. Resistance quickly began to
erode, even among Edward Guy's supporters, and by the
time Gawl and James reached the town of Bexley, people
were lining the streets and cheering for him.

At the Abbey of Barcora, ten miles from Bexley proper,
Archbishop Ferdinand Willis looked up when there was a
knock on his door. He had taken over Paul Teller's study
for his private offices four years earlier, and it was not a
shock to see the former abbot enter the room with three
members of the Ecumenical Council. Willis was the one
who had expelled Teller from the abbey, and there was no
love lost between them. In his view, Paul Teller was a
commoner and unfit to hold the office of abbot. He eyed
Teller with distaste and listened calmly as Teller read the

council's proclamation removing him from office, signed by all eleven members.

"I do not recognize your authority," Willis said when he was through. "My office is held by divine right. Lest you have forgotten, I remind you that I am a prince of the Church. You will all leave here at once, or I shall call the guards and have you removed."

The men in the room exchanged glances, but no one moved.

"There are no guards, holiness," said Teller.

"Ridiculous," Willis snapped. "Jacomo, Bertrand, come in here at once."

When no one responded to his call, the silence in the room grew heavier.

"They've all gone," Teller said. "The king is waiting downstairs."

"Liar," Willis replied, pushing past him. He opened the door to his study and yelled more loudly, "Jacomo! Bertrand!"

After several seconds Ferdinand Willis turned around and stared at the solemn faces of the priests. Then he straightened his cassock and walked to the window. In the courtyard below, the figure of Gawl was unmistakable. There were at least a hundred armed men with him. It was impossible to say whether he and Gawl saw each other then, because neither reacted. Willis laughed once to himself and turned around.

"I need a few minutes alone, Fathers, if you don't mind," he said. "I will be down presently."

The other members of the council looked to Paul Teller, who nodded in reply.

Gawl was waiting by the side of his horse along with Prince James, Colonel Haynes, and Arteus Ballenger when they came out of the main building. He turned his palms up to Paul Teller in a silent question.

"He'll be down in a few minutes," Teller said.

Gawl started to reply and then stopped. Seeing a movement at the third floor window out of the corner of his eye. There was no scream or sound of any kind as Ferdinand Willis's body tumbled out, save for a rather horrible thud when he hit the cobblestones. He landed ten feet from the nearest soldier, nearly causing the man's horse to rear. The soldier immediately got down out of his saddle, and ran to the Archbishop. He stood up a moment later and shook his head.

"He's down," said Gawl.

Tenley Palace was located twenty miles ride from the Abbey of Barcora and both Gawl and James insisted on riding with the advance scouts to see what defenses Edward Guy had prepared. To their surprise, they found none—no soldiers, no battlements, nothing. It was a complete mystery. The troops followed, shortly thereafter. The anticipation of the pending fight was becoming harder and harder to deal with. Prevailing thought was that Guy intended to make his stand at the palace, a well-fortified structure that would have afforded him the advantage of an elevated position.

Three miles from the palace, Ballenger sent out reconnaissance patrols to assess the situation. They returned a half hour later and reported seeing no evidence of Guy's troops. They also said the palace gates were open.

"They've fled, sire," the head of one patrol told Gawl.

"Fled?" Gawl repeated, incredulous.

"Yes. They're gone."

"Are you certain of this?" asked James.

"I went as far as the palace gates myself," said the soldier. "An elderly fellow named Alexander came out to meet me. He told me to tell his majesty that dinner would be at seven o'clock and that Lord Guy would not be attending."

"Is this some kind of joke?" asked Gawl.

"I think not, your sire. It seems that Lord Guy and most of his cabinet boarded a ship for Alor Satar four days ago.

The commander of the palace garrison came by while we were talking and confirmed it. He said to tell you 'welcome,' by the way."

"Welcome," Gawl sputtered, looking at James.

"I should have stayed home and gone fishing," said James.

"What about Guy's army?" asked Gawl. "Did they just go home, too?"

"No," said the soldier, "but they have returned to their posts in the north and along the border. At least that's what the commander told me."

Gawl put his hands over his face and shook his head. "I spend four years in jail and the cowards run away . . . amazing, simply amazing."

There was a great deal of discussion about what to do next, but in the end it was decided that Tenley Palace would be a more appropriate place to conduct it. Gawl passed the news on to his general, and Ballenger in turn told the men about Lord Guy's defection. A cheer went up that continued for nearly five minutes.

When they rode into the courtyard, Gawl and James found that Alexander had assembled everyone to greet them, one hundred and thirty people in all. No one spoke until Gawl dismounted and embraced the little chief of staff. Then they, like the soldiers, also began to cheer.

Alexander waited until they were well inside before he handed Gawl a letter from Delain.

## 36

## New Raburn

"BRIGANDS," COLLIN SAID UNDER HIS BREATH.

Mathew nodded and moved a little apart. Behind him Lara cursed under her breath. "I left my sword in the wagon. All I have is a dagger."

"Easy," Father Thomas said, putting his sword back in its scabbard. "They may or may not be."

Outside the window none of the men had yet moved. They were standing under the portico of the building watching them, silhouettes against the light. When Mathew saw the priest put up his weapon, he looked at the men more closely. He could see no evidence of weapons.

"What are they doing?" Collin asked.

"The same thing we are, it seems," said Father Thomas.

"Well, it doesn't make any sense to stand here and stare at each other," said Lara. "Come inside if you want to," she called out.

Mathew wasn't sure if her voice would carry beyond the glass, but apparently it did, because a second later the men started moving toward the doors at the center of the room.

"Do nothing until I do," Father Thomas cautioned.

As it turned out, the men were neither brigands nor soldiers, as Mathew thought they might be. They were ordinary people who lived in the ruins. Many of them were close to his age; a few were nearer to Father Thomas's. They had fled their homes rather than face conscription by the Vargothans.

The leader was a man named Garvin, a tall, hulking fellow with a red beard and an accent that marked him as coming from the southern part of Elgaria. He introduced only himself to the others and did not offer to shake hands.

"We've been living here nearly three years now," Garvin said, in response to Father Thomas's question. "What made you pick this place to stop, if I might ask?"

"The storm drove us in," Father Thomas explained. "We were on our way to Ardosta."

"And you're a wine seller?"

"That's what I said."

Garvin held Father Thomas's gaze for a second then looked over his shoulder at the man behind him, who glanced at the priest and nodded slightly.

"I don't like calling a man a liar," Garvin said, "but you're no wine merchant, you're Siward Thomas. Stokes here served with you at Jeremy Crossing."

Only Father Thomas's eyes moved, fixing on the man behind Garvin. Stokes stepped forward and took off his hat.

"Kendall Stokes, General. I was a sergeant in the third infantry under Colonel Myers. I recognized you right off . . . meaning no offense, sir."

Father Thomas looked down at the floor and smiled. He looked up several seconds later. "It's good to see you again, Stokes. I apologize for the deception, but for the next few days, at least, we really are wine merchants."

"I heard a rumor that you left the army and became a priest, but that was years ago," Stokes said.

"You heard correctly. I have a small church in the town of Devondale. This is Ceta Woodall. And that's Collin Miller, a friend of ours."

"A pleasure, ma'am," Stokes told her, with a small bow. "Your servant."

"And who would these others be?" Garvin asked, gesturing to Mathew and Lara with his head.

"This is Thaddeus and Lara, also from my hometown."

"Do they have last names?" Garvin asked.

"Let's leave it at that," said the priest. "I give you my word that there are good reasons for it."

Garvin, however, was having none of it. "Here, Harry," he said to one of the men with him, "bring that light over. I'd like to know who I'm talking to."

The man he referred to as Harry was carrying a storm lantern and started forward. A slight shake of Father Thomas's head stopped Collin from reacting. Harry held the lantern higher while Garvin and another man looked at Collin, Lara, Ceta, and Mathew in turn. Taking the priest's example, Mathew stood there quietly until their examination was over. For a moment a flicker of recognition seemed to appear in Harry's eyes, but it was gone again just as quickly.

When it happened, Mathew was sure the game was up. He stared impassively back at the men until they dropped their eye contact and looked away. It had been four years since he was Mathew Lewin, and he was twenty pounds heavier, two inches taller, and now had dark hair.

In response to Garvin's silent question, Harry shrugged.

"I suppose being a priest, you have your reasons," Garvin said. "You can stay for the night, but in the morning you'll have to leave. Are any more of your friends likely to show up?"

There was a silence.

"You're Elgarians," Father Thomas began, "so I hope you'll understand what I'm about to say. People are looking for us. I'm fairly certain we haven't been followed, though I can't swear to it. All I can tell you is that we left Elgaria out of necessity because my companion was taken by the Vargothans. We got her out."

The comment immediately produced a buzz among the men, and Garvin motioned for silence. They moved off to the side of the room and began talking in low tones. From the gesticulations, it was obvious that an argument was going on. Unfortunately, there was nothing to do but wait and see how it turned out. Once the conversations died down, several hands were raised.

*Eleven out of fifteen*, Mathew said to himself.

Garvin turned back to Father Thomas. "You can stay until the storm lets up, but after that, you'll have to go. I know that sounds harsh, but we've got women and children to protect and we can't risk bringing the Alor Satar army down on our necks. That was our vote."

"I don't see anyone but you," Collin told him.

"There's over three hundred people living in these ruins, son," Garvin explained. "Most are from Elgaria, but we've got 'em from Alor Satar, Cincar, and Nyngary. We've even got a few from northern Vargoth . . . them with families who don't like the conscript any more than we do."

"That's very kind of you," said Father Thomas. "We'll be on our way when the storm is over."

"If you're willing to donate a little of that wine you're carrying in the wagons, you can stay to supper," Garvin told them. "Everyone contributes what they're able here."

"All three hundred of you eat together?" Mathew asked.

"'Course not," Garvin said, "but this is the second night of Saint Trista's Feast and the ladies put together a celebration. You're all welcome to attend." Turning to Father Thomas, he added, "We haven't had a regular priest here in quite some time, so if you want to say something, I'm sure a lot of folks would appreciate it."

Father Thomas smiled back at him. "I'd be happy to, friend."

"It's settled, then," said Garvin. "Harry will stay here and show you the way. The underground passages can be tricky if you don't know them."

In conversations with Harry over the next hour, Mathew learned that the ruins actually had a name. At various points in the past they had been called R'hailbin, Raibon, and finally Raburn City. They were now called New Raburn, though it was only by the people who lived there. Essentially, the city had been refounded three years earlier by a group of eight families fleeing not only the Orlock invasion, but also the mercenaries. Shortly thereafter other people began to arrive and the population swelled.

Because New Raburn was well off the main thoroughfare and almost entirely self-sufficient, they had managed to keep it secret. It was a situation, Harry said, their council knew wouldn't last forever. If Alor Satar became aware of their existence, they would almost certainly send soldiers to remove them. So far they had been lucky.

The wind continued blowing with as much force as it had when the storm began. Water ran down the gutters and disappeared into a sewer system. The sky no longer had a yellow cast to it, but evening was coming on quickly. Mathew stood at the window of the building and watched raindrops splattering on the glass. There were no signs of other people outside—not that he expected them to be in this weather. If Garvin was telling the truth about three hundred people living in New Raburn, they had to be living farther back in the ruins, he thought. He glanced up at the sky and could not see how anyone could hold a party, given the weather.

In the distance he saw an outline of the mountains they'd passed through earlier, jagged fingers along the horizon. The largest of them reminded him of a mountain in his dream. He was so deep in thought that he jumped when Collin put a hand on his shoulder.

"Sorry," Collin apologized. "I didn't mean to startle you."

"It's all right. I was just thinking."

"About what?"

"Nothing special. Just about a dream I had."

"About the ring, right?"

Mathew turned away from the window and stared at him. "How did you know?"

"It doesn't take a genius to figure it out, Mat. You've been so damned preoccupied the last few days, it's pretty obvious it's been on your mind . . . besides, I talked to Lara."

Mathew nodded. "Did she send you over?"

"No. I decided to check on you myself. It's good to have you back again. I missed you."

"I missed you, too," Mathew said. "I wanted to write and let you know I was alive, but it was too dangerous. I hope you're not angry."

"I understand. You did what you had to."

"And you took care of Lara all these years and a son who wasn't yours. I know it's not nearly enough, but thanks, Collin."

Characteristically, Collin brushed it aside. "Bran's a good boy and Lara's a fine woman. See that you take care of them, okay?"

There was something in his tone that Mathew wasn't quite sure he understood, and he looked at his friend closely. "I've never asked you . . . are *you* okay?" he asked. "Things have changed pretty quickly."

"Me?" Collin scoffed. "I'm fine. As soon as this sorry business is over, I'm going to take a long trip and see what the rest of the world has been up to. There are plenty of opportunities for an enterprising fellow like me. In fact there was a man who came through town a few weeks ago. We spoke for quite a while and, um . . ."

Collin's words trailed away, and Mathew watched him. What was wrong was just beginning to dawn on him.

When Collin spoke again his tone was uncharacteristically somber. "She chose you a long time ago, Mat. That's the end of it."

Mathew started to say something but didn't get the chance.

"I said that's the end of it," Collin repeated. He started walking back toward the lobby.

"Collin," Mathew said quietly. "Thanks for always being my friend."

Collin paused for a moment then kept on walking.

## 37

# New Raburn

THEY WERE FOLLOWING HARRY ALONG A MUSTY SMELLING corridor somewhere under the city of New Raburn. Every fifty feet or so an ancient light globe spilled yellow light onto the floor. Small halos formed around the globes. Some of them were working and some were not. From Mathew's standpoint, it was amazing that anything worked at all, considering the age of the place. A number of large pipes suspended from the ceiling ran the length of the corridor, and the walls were painted a flat gray. Their voices echoed when they spoke. It was not a comfortable place, he decided.

Now and then they passed a sign written in the old tongue. Some of the words he knew and some he guessed the meaning of. Some made no sense at all.

*"Pressure Relief Valve,"* Mathew said aloud. He looked up and saw a valve atop one of the pipes.

"Those bring hot water and heat into the buildings," Harry explained, pointing to the pipes. "And in the summer those bring cold air."

"How can that be?" Collin asked.

Harry shrugged. "We don't know exactly how they work, or even *why*, after all this time," he said. "Garvin and two others tried following them for a full day and gave up. They go down ten levels and come out in a crawl space that runs toward the mountains."

"But how do they know when it should be hot and when it should be cold?" asked Ceta, looking up at the pipes.

"Can't say, mistress. We're just glad they work. It can get plenty cold here in the winter."

"Are there many of these tunnels?" Ceta asked.

"At least twenty," Harry explained. "You can get anywhere in the city using them. We don't have far to go. The meeting place is just around that corner and up two levels."

"What does this one say, Mat?" Collin asked, pointing to another sign.

When Lara kicked him in the shin, Collin shot her a puzzled look. It was a second before he realized his mistake. He mouthed a curse and then the word *Sorry* to her. All three of them glanced at Harry, who was up ahead talking to Ceta and Father Thomas. Fortunately, he didn't seem to have heard.

The meeting place turned out to be a massive hall in a low two-story building at the far end of New Raburn. It was the biggest single room Mathew had ever seen—palaces and cathedrals included. Only Barcora's stadium could have rivaled it in size, he thought. He was positive that if everyone in Devondale, Gravenhage, and Mechlen had stood shoulder-to-shoulder along the walls, they wouldn't have gone around the room's perimeter. The ceiling was at least forty feet high, and it contained a series of lamps in the ceiling that put out a brilliant white-blue light making it look like daytime. You could only stare at them for a few seconds.

Fifty yards away a celebration was going on, though it only took up a small part of the hall. Families with children were milling about talking or strolling up and down rows where merchants sold different food from little stands. A platform had been erected near the middle of the gathering, and on it three men and a woman were playing music. Mathew remembered celebrating the Festival of Saint Trista the week they had left Devondale, and he found it comforting that people were still celebrating it in this odd place.

"This was once used to hold great conventions," Harry told them.

"It's enormous," said Collin, staring up at the ceiling, open-mouthed. "The whole city must have met here."

"I doubt it, young fella," Harry said. "Bekham Marsh, one of the men who lives over on South Street, figures there were over fifty thousand people living here once."

Mathew kept his face straight when Lara glanced at him. He knew what his wife was thinking. She'd made it plain enough in the past that cities were not her favorite places, and from Ceta's expression, he guessed she was probably in agreement.

"Well, it looks like just about everyone's here," Harry said. "I can take you around and introduce you, or you can wander and get to meet some folks for yourselves."

"We'll wander," said Father Thomas. "Thanks for the hospitality."

"No problem, Gen— Sorry, do you want me to call you 'Father' now?"

"I think that would be best," Father Thomas told him.

Harry nodded. "Garvin said to tell you he would have your horses fed and the wagons brought over. There's a tan building two blocks from here where you can stay for the night. It's no inn, but it's a far sight better than the Red Tower, where you were. There's no heat or running water there."

"The Red Tower?" Father Thomas repeated.

"We don't know what the proper name is, so that's just what we call it," Harry explained. "Anyway, you'll find most people here are pretty decent sorts. They'll be happy to have a priest to talk to, if you don't mind, that is."

Father Thomas shook his head. "I don't mind at all. Why don't I use that platform in the center to deliver my sermon? You can let me know when. Afterward, anyone who needs to see me can come by to speak privately if they're comfortable."

During the next hour Lara and Mathew strolled along the aisles, talking to people and looking at the merchandise for sale. In various conversations, they learned that everyone in New Raburn lived within the city itself. In fact it was the law. One man explained that was because the governing council wanted to prevent anyone from knowing about the city for as long as possible.

From what Mathew could see, their plan was working. Once a month a different group of men would leave New Raburn to trade with towns along the Elgarian–Alor Satar border. They brought back whatever supplies were needed. The people, he thought, seemed realistic, knowing the situation would change one day, but they were determined to nurture it as long as they could. The reason they all lived in the buildings suddenly began to make sense. To a casual passerby, New Raburn looked exactly as it had for hundreds of years—an abandoned ruin.

Perhaps the most amusing thing he and Lara heard about was New Raburn's plan for discouraging visitors. The men who went to trade in the border towns spread rumors that the buildings were haunted and inhabited by the dead. Personally, Mathew had never believed in ghosts, but he had met a fair number of people who did. Whether that was an effective deterent or not was still up in the air.

Twice during their walk through the aisles they passed Harry and another man. The two seemed to be deep in conversation, so they didn't greet them. The third time they came upon them, however, the man with Harry looked directly at him.

"Uh-oh," Mathew said under his breath. "I think they may have recognized me."

To Lara's credit she didn't turn. "They're probably jealous because you're so handsome," she said.

"I'm not joking."

"I know," she said calmly. "I saw them look at you when we passed them earlier. We should let Father Thomas know when we find him."

"We found him," Mathew said, looking toward the platform.

Lara followed his gaze and saw Garvin and Father

Thomas walking up the steps to the platform. The musicians stopped playing and on the floor heads turned in their direction. Garvin held up his hands for quiet.

"I'm sure most of you know that we have guests with us tonight. This being the second night of Saint Trista's Feast, and us being without a priest for the last three years, I've asked Father Siward Thomas if he would mind delivering the holiday sermon, and he agreed. He and his friends hail from Devondale in middle Elgaria, so let's make them as welcome as possible."

When Garvin finished introducing him, Father Thomas got up. At some point during the evening he had changed to his black robes. The last time Mathew had seen the priest speak to a congregation was at his father's funeral.

"First," Father Thomas began, "I would like to thank you for the hospitality you have shown us. These are difficult times and it is nice to know that common courtesy still survives. We sincerely appreciate the many well wishes and your generosity in providing food and shelter to us.

"This evening I have met Vargothans, Alor Satarans, Elgarians, people from Cincar, and families from Nyngary. Yet when I look out on you now, I see none of these. I see no different countries, no uniforms, no biases of culture or ancient hatreds—I see only people. People who wish to live their lives quietly. People who wish to raise their families without the threat of war and death hanging over their heads, and people who have come here to avoid being conscripted into an army and forced to fight.

"Perhaps you are right. Perhaps establishing New Raburn was the wisest thing to do. You are free and happy here—for *now*. Those whom I have talked to seemed to be intelligent people. In each instance I posed a question. I asked whether you think your situation here will last, and I was told, no. Many of you said, 'It's fine for the time being.'

"There is a parable in the scriptures that instructs us that it is better to teach a man to fish than to feed him. The slogan is simple, and one your parents probably taught you, but have you ever considered the meaning behind it? Obviously, if a man or woman can fish, their future is secured because they will never go hungry.

"The true message in those words however, is that a temporary solution is fine *for the time being*, but it won't ensure the future."

Mathew saw that people were listening carefully to the priest's words.

"Most of you have families," Father Thomas went on. "The children standing by your side and playing at your feet are not just your future, they are the future of our world. You have given them a fish by coming here and founding New Raburn, but you have sacrificed their future.

"Freedom, my friends, does not come cheaply. It is always dearly bought and difficult to hold on to. There are those who wait in the shadows to take it away. It has been this way throughout history. A storm is coming, and it will sweep our lands. When one country trods people underfoot, the small community of nations in our world can either say how fortunate they were that such things didn't involve them . . . or they can act to correct the problem.

"Strike at freedom and you strike at the foundations of what we are as a people, regardless of borders or religious beliefs. To look the other way is but a temporary solution, because the next day they will come for you.

"As parents our job is to protect our children. As God-fearing men and women, can we do less when our neighbor is hurt? I submit to you that the answer is *no*.

"That, my friends, is the true meaning of the parable. Look not just to today, but for what the future may bring. Your children will bless you for it."

A long silence followed Father Thomas's sermon. Many people had broken up into small groups and were talking among themselves. Garvin didn't look happy, nor did several other men. A number of people were waiting at the bottom of the platform to speak to the priest.

Mathew didn't have long to consider the situation because Harry and two other men, he recalled from the Red Tower were approaching him.

"Your friend's a good speaker," Harry said. "He's got a lot of people talking."

"Yes, he is," Mathew agreed.

"Can we talk over on the side for a minute?" Harry asked.

Lara started to object, but Mathew spoke first, saying, "I don't have any secrets from my wife. She can come with us or you can say what you want to say right here."

The men looked at one another and nodded their agreement.

"All right," Harry said. "We'll all go."

Mathew and Lara followed them into a shadowed area away from the noise.

"I suppose I should introduce everybody," said Harry. "This is Gordon Baker and Alfy Denholm. They're both members of our council."

The moment Mathew introduced himself as Thaddeus Lane, it was obvious they knew he was lying.

"I'm not meaning to offend you," said Harry, "but I recognized you a while back. You're Mathew Lewin, aren't you?"

He knew there was no point in trying to hide it any longer, so he answered, "Yes."

"Gordon here was at Ardon Field, and Alfy hails from Tremont. I wasn't in either of those battles, but there were enough pictures of you posted all over the country a couple of years back. We heard you were dead."

"Well, he's not," Lara said. "Now what do you men want?"

"We don't want anything, ma'am, except maybe the truth," said Gordon. "We certainly don't mean you or your people any harm, if that's what you're asking. The thing is, we have families to protect, and if there's going to be trouble, we think we have a right to know about it. Is that unreasonable?"

The explanation seemed to mollify Lara. "No, that isn't unreasonable," she replied.

The three of them turned back to Mathew.

"All right," he said. "First, I have no reason to believe our being here will put you in danger. We told you that at the Red Tower. Second, if you know who I am, then you know why my identity has to remain a secret, as do my plans."

"This has something to do with the rings, doesn't it Mat?" Alfy asked. "I was on the wall at Tremont when you and your friend came tearing in there with about a thousand Orlocks chasing after you. I recognized Siward Thomas earlier, just like Harry did, but I wasn't going to say anything. He did a hell of a job for us that day."

"And I saw you fight Karas Duren at Ardon Field," Gordon told him. "That explosion at the end knocked me down, and I was two hundred yards away. Duren would have roasted us alive if it wasn't for you."

Mathew returned a tight-lipped smile. "Look, I'd tell you men what we're about if I could, but the fact is I can't. I will say this . . . there's a reason for those rumors about my being dead. I can also tell you is that if it suddenly gets out I'm alive, what I have to do will be a whole lot more dangerous—not only for me but for everyone around me. Have you mentioned this to anyone else?"

"Only Alfy, Gordon, and I know," said Harry. "I wanted to make sure before saying anything."

Mathew looked at the other two and they both nodded.

"Good, and I give you my word that no one will hear about New Raburn from my lips once we leave here. Personally, I think Father Thomas has a point, but if that's the way you want it, then that's the way it'll be."

"Excuse us for a second, Mat," Gordon said, and the

three men moved a few feet away and conferred privately for nearly a full minute. While they were talking, Alfy looked back at his hands. Mathew made no effort to hide the fact that his ring was missing, but neither was he going to bring their attention to it, even if he thought they had already figured it out.

Alfy approached him once the conversation was over. "There's no denying everyone in this room owes you a debt," he said, "at least those from Elgaria. I don't know exactly what happened in Sennia between you and Teanna d'Elso, but your secret's safe with us. If we don't see you again before you leave, good luck."

He held out his hand and Mathew took it. Gordon and Harry waited for Alfy to join them, and the three of them walked back to the celebration together. Mathew put an arm around Lara's shoulders as he watched them go.

"They're good men," he said.

Father Thomas and Ceta were talking to a group of people, and Collin was off to one side watching the dancing. While Mathew waited for the priest to get free, Lara spoke with Collin. Mathew saw her whisper something in his friend's ear. They both turned to look at a little boy who was walking with his parents. The child reminded Mathew of Bran. Collin said something back to Lara and they both laughed.

It might have been their demeanor, or because their heads were close together. Whatever it was, Mathew felt a twinge of jealousy. Nor did it help when he saw Lara kiss Collin on the cheek.

Mathew watched them out of the corner of his eye for several seconds more, trying not to be obvious. After a moment or two he became angry at himself for his reaction. Lara was his wife now and Collin was his best friend. They had been together for four years and probably still had feelings for one another, he decided. It was petty and stupid of him to be annoyed. But he could not entirely convince himself.

It took an effort to keep his expression neutral as Collin approached.

"You heard?" Mathew asked his friend.

"It was bound to happen sooner or later, Mat. Your face was everywhere for at least two years. We'll probably run into a lot of people who remember you. Maybe you should grow a beard or something."

"I had one and just shaved it off a few days ago. I think the best thing for us to do is get out of here as soon as possible and continue on to Nyngary."

They both glanced out the window. It was still raining and the wind seemed to have picked up again.

"The storm ought to blow itself out by tomorrow," said Collin. "We can be on our way at first light. I'm guessing, our friends here won't be sorry to see us go."

"You're probably right. What were you and Lara talking about?"

"There was a little boy who reminded her of Bran. They both walk the same way. Garvin told me a couple of the ladies fixed up rooms for us across the way. There's a tunnel that will take us directly to it."

Mathew nodded.

Whether it was to make sure they didn't get lost or to prevent them from wandering around New Raburn, Garvin had two men escort them to their building. It was nowhere near as large as either the Red Tower or the convention hall, but was certainly big enough. Both the food they had brought in their wagon and their bedrolls were waiting for them on the second floor. The men explained that the building had once been used as a residence and that there were five more like it in the city. Some of the people they'd met earlier lived on the top three floors. The second floor, the one they were on, was empty, the men said, so they were free to sleep wherever they chose. The only requirement was that the room had to be on the inside of the building rather than facing the plain, to prevent any lights from being seen by passing travelers.

After saying good night, Mathew and Lara spent a few minutes exploring their new lodgings. It was an apartment consisting of six rooms and equipped with the same type of yellow light globes they'd seen in the tunnels, except these were sensitive to movement. As soon as you walked into a room they came on. The first time it happened, both of them froze and looked around before they figured it out. The lights did the same thing in the other rooms. It was disconcerting until they got used to it. Lara solved the problem when she found a switch on the wall that controlled them and flipped it down.

Whatever furniture that might have been in the apartment was carried off years earlier. Even the cabinets that once hung on the kitchen walls were gone, their outlines visible on the faded paint. A set of windows looked out into a street that faced the interior of the city and another building directly across from them. The wind was still blowing hard and the rain showed no sign of letting up. It was an interesting place, Mathew thought, but he couldn't imagine living there for any length of time. Obviously, that was not the case for the people of New Raburn.

He and Lara discussed this for several minutes after they lay down.

She felt the same way he did: Under the best of circumstances, living in rooms like these was a compromise of life. Nevertheless, she conceded that protecting one's family came first and she said she admired the sacrifices that the people there had made. Mathew didn't agree but said nothing. They went on talking for a while before sleep overtook them.

# 38

## Rocoi, Alor Satar

ERIC DUREN SAT IN HIS LIBRARY, WEIGHING THE RECENT turn of events. The implications of Eldar's letter were staggering. There was now little question that Vargoth and Cincar had formed some type of pact with the Orlocks. That much he had already deduced from his conversations with Teanna and the information his own spies had been able to procure. What he was not prepared for was the size of the Orlocks' army or the navy Coribar was now said to possess. He had almost laughed out loud when he read the figure in Eldar's letter saying that Shakira intended to pit a million Orlocks against them. But while Eldar might be a book-reading fool, Teanna was certainly not. His niece possessed her mother's intelligence and cunning, and according to Eldar, she had heard the information from Shakira's own lips. To complicate matters, Eldar went on to say that the Orlock queen now possessed one of the rose gold rings. By itself that would have been enough to worry him, but Eric was also privy to the fact that Vargoth had recently acquired cannons from Felize.

Momentous things were afoot and the political landscape was changing rapidly. He was no stranger to power plays of this type. They were inevitable, and something to be dealt with if one wanted to maintain an empire as vast as Alor Satar's. His father had been an excellent teacher in that regard. For years Eric had planned how his country would react when the attack came. It was like the game of kesherit. If one did not anticipate his opponent's moves, the game would end quickly. Like his father, Eric was an excellent kesherit player. His strength lay in his ability to think five or ten jumps ahead.

Betrayal by one's allies was a possibility all monarchs anticipated. He had always known that Vargoth would acquire the cannons and black powder, just as other nations would in time. As a result of several well-placed bribes to Felizian sea captains, Alor Satar had had those weapons for the past two years.

Eric, of course, kept this a secret.

The sea captains, unfortunately, had all met untimely ends. He looked on their deaths not as a waste of good money, but as a means to level the playing field. Anyone who turned on Alor Satar would find them more than ready. But Eric had not counted on the Orlocks acquiring one of the rings, or the size of their armies. His brother Armand was already gone by the time he had returned home. Once news of rebellion in Elgaria reached him, the king had assembled his men and rode off to support the Vargothans. Armand's temper was as famous as his vaunted military acumen.

That was five days ago, and they had heard nothing since. The riders he sent out to warn him had not returned yet, so Eric sat and fretted. He glanced down at the book he was reading and flipped the page back again. He'd read the same paragraph three times now and he had no idea what it said. He was considering whether to send more riders out when the door to the library banged open.

Armand was standing there, his brother's face streaked with dirt and his cloak torn. There was blood on his arms and chest and he looked ready to collapse.

"Good lord," Eric said. Jumping to his feet, he went to Armand, put an arm around his waist and helped him to a chair. "Are you all right?" he asked, pouring a glass of brandy.

Armand downed it in a single gulp. "I'm fine."

"What happened?"

"The Vargothans betrayed us. We arrived in Anderon to

reinforce them and they led us into a trap. Most of my command was wiped out. We lost nearly a thousand men."

Eric's eyebrows went up. "Are you injured?" he asked, looking his brother up and down.

"It's nothing. We need to gather our commanders immediately."

"First tell me what happened," Eric said. "I need to know everything."

Armand leaned back in his seat, closed his eyes and began to speak slowly. "The commander is a man named Jonas Carmody. He sent a messenger saying that Delain and a force of just over five hundred men launched an assault on their northern garrison two days ago. He confirmed the reports we'd been getting about a general uprising throughout the country. When I got Carmody's letter, I left as rapidly as I could. He wrote there was no way the occupation force could keep things under control.

"When we arrived, Carmody told us that his men had followed Delain to a place called Kelsey Church and blocked his escape route back into the mountains."

Eric thought for second. "I don't know this Kelsey Church."

"It's a small town near the border. You get to it by going through a valley surrounded by mountains on both sides.

"The Vargothans had nearly two hundred men, fully equipped and ready to go, so we combined forces and marched, thinking to meet Delain. When we got to the valley, we found another five hundred of the mercenaries waiting for us, along with several hundred Orlocks. They fell on us from all sides. My rear guard sacrificed itself so I could get out."

Eric poured himself a glass of brandy and sipped it slowly. "I'm glad you're in one piece, brother. We're going to need your military abilities now more than ever. You understand that what happened was just the beginning. They're not going to stop there."

"Let them come," Armand said. "I intend to teach those lying bastards what we do with traitors. If the Orlocks and the Vargothans want a war, we'll give it to them."

"It won't be that easy," said Eric. "Coribar is also involved now. Let me tell you what I've learned in your absence."

For the next fifteen minutes Eric filled his brother in on the news in Eldar's letter. To his credit, Armand calmed down, sipped his drink and listened.

"You think they mean to come for us?" Armand asked when his brother was through.

"I do," Eric said. "If you study history, this is inevitable. Fortunately, we're well-prepared."

"The cannons?"

"That, and our dear cousin Teanna," Eric answered. "Whether Eldar sends troops is up in the air, but Teanna will almost certainly support her family, particularly now that an attempt has been made on her life."

Armand was shocked by the news. "Someone tried to kill her? Is she all right?"

"She's fine. We haven't spoken yet and they don't know who sent the assassin. He was killed before Eldar could interrogate him, but it's a safe bet either Coribar or one of the Western nations were behind it . . . James, most likely. It doesn't fit Delain's style."

"Why would James act now?"

"Because he's an opportunist. It's obvious that he and Delain think the time is right. With Teanna out of the way, their path would be clear. James knows the landscape as well as anyone."

Armand made a dismissive gesture. "It won't make any difference if Mirdan enters the fight. We could have beaten the lot of them at Ardon Field. I was a fool to listen to Teanna. We should have finished them when we had the chance."

"If we do," Eric said, "it will have to be by ourselves.

By the way, we've acquired some new house guests . . .
Edward Guy, his daughter, and five barons from Sennia."

"Oh, this just gets better and better," Armand growled.
"What the hell are they doing here? We need them in the
south. They share a common border with Mirdan. Guy
should be getting his army ready."

"If wishes were horses," Eric replied. "The fool was so
anxious to rid himself of Gawl d'Atherny he announced
another trial—for treason. Most of his army commanders
rose up and threw Sennia into a state of civil war. Guy had
to flee and Gawl is now back in power."

Armand ran his hands through his hair. "This is rich. If
Sennia's lost to us and Nyngary can't be counted on, it
looks like we'll have to go it on our own. Vargoth may
have the Orlocks with them, but they'll have to contend
with Delain on one side and us on the other. We'll deal
with whichever of them survive."

"What we need now is intelligence," Eric said. "We
need to know how many troops Seth has committed and
how many of the Orlocks are supporting him. We'll also
have to get Teanna here to deal with Shakira."

Armand thought about it for a few seconds and nodded.
"A good plan. Send for Edward Guy. He can start earning
his keep."

## 39

## Bacora, Sennía

THE ORIGINAL PLAN HAD BEEN FOR JAMES TO RETURN TO Mirdan once Gawl was back in power. Though the king was less than pleased by Edward Guy's defection, it came as a welcome surprise to everyone else. Satisfied that all was in order, James was in the midst of his preparations to leave when another letter arrived from Delain. He and Gawl read it together in the palace's small dining room.

If the news about Vargoth turning on Alor Satar came as a shock, it was nothing compared to Delain's revelation that Orlocks had joined in the fight. Even more shocking was the news that Shakira held one of the rose gold rings. According to the reports Delain passed on, the Orlock queen had set Anderon Palace ablaze while hundreds of her creatures stood by and cheered.

He went on to report that nearly a hundred citizens had been carried off by the Orlocks.

The thought sent a shiver up James's spine. He and Gawl discussed the developments over dinner. Both were in agreement that honor and friendship dictated they help Delain. Gawl was for setting out immediately, but James opted for learning more about how many of the creatures they would be facing before they went. As much as Gawl hated it, he was forced to agree. Vargoth alone could be dealt with, they decided, but Orlocks added another factor to the equation. Consequently, the commanders of both the Sennian and Mirdanite units were instructed to remain

on alert. James also sent a message back to his own country telling his soldiers and citizens to prepare for war.

"Is there any way to stop your assassin?" asked Gawl.

James shook his head. "We've been through all this,"
he said, taking a bite of food. "We'll have to deal with
Teanna eventually. We might as well do it now."

"We *have* discussed it," Gawl agreed, "but things have
changed radically, in case you haven't noticed. I would
rather deal with a human wearing one of the rings than
with the creatures. Their eating habits leave a great deal to
be desired."

James's fork paused halfway to his mouth. "Point taken.
Unfortunately, there's no way to get in touch with him."

"What if we send word to the Nyngary court and let
them know?"

"Let Eldar d'Elso know that we sent someone to murder his daughter? 'By the way, Eldar, our decision with
that assassin was a bit hasty. Apologize to Teanna for us,
would you?' I can just imagine how he'll react to that."

"Well, we've got to do something. We can't just sit
around on our asses."

"I'm open to suggestions. You know, it's possible we
could . . ."

The Prince's words trailed away when a high-pitched
whine started in the room. He and Gawl both came to their
feet as a point of white light appeared out of nowhere and
hung suspended in front of the fireplace. A moment later it
expanded into a single line. Then the line thickened, forming into an opaque rectangle, with something dark at its
center, when the shape resolved into the form of Teanna
d'Elso. James started to reach for his sword.

"I've seen this before," Gawl said, stopping him. "She's
not really here. We're looking into a window of some kind."

*"What?"*

"Trust me. I saw Mathew Lewin do the same thing in a
forest outside of Tremont several years ago."

James made a face, but relaxed.

Teanna glanced around the room and saw them standing there. "Your majesty," she said, bowing her head to Gawl.

"What is it you want?"

"Only to talk. I do not believe I know the gentleman next to you."

"This is Prince James of Mirdan. James, I present Teanna d'Elso, Crown Princess of Nyngary."

James looked at Gawl as if he had just lost his mind. After a moment he shook his head and bowed to the image floating in front of him.

"Forgive me," said Teanna. "I know communicating this way can be unsettling, but it was imperative that I speak with you. It's doubly lucky that you're both here."

Still uncertain about what he was seeing, James peered at the window of light more closely. Behind Teanna he could see a bed, a dresser, and a mirror.

"I have no idea what I'm looking at," he said. "But if you *are* Teanna d'Elso, why should we listen to anything you have to say?"

"Because it's important to all of us," Teanna replied.

"There is nothing you have to say that would interest me," Gawl added. "Go back to wherever you came from. I don't speak with liars."

Teanna's eyebrows arched in response, but she did not move, nor did the window disappear.

"Perhaps I deserved that," she said. "If saying I'm sorry for what happened would make any difference, I would do so now. I know that you've suffered, but what I did was four years ago and I took no part in your overthrow. I didn't learn of Eric's plan until after it was set in motion."

"Your words ring false, Princess," Gawl said wearily. "We trusted you . . . *I* trusted you. You came as a friend and an ally and betrayed us. You would have killed Mathew Lewin in the Emerald Cavern if it wasn't for Jeram Quinn."

"I reacted out of anger," she said. "You're right about Mathew. I came to Sennia with a plan to avenge the deaths of my mother and uncle, but then things became confused."

"And afterward you sided with Edward Guy and your cousin by taking Fanshaw Castle apart stone by stone with your fireballs," said Gawl. "Your deeds give lie to your words."

"You have every right to be furious with me, sire, but I hope you can understand that I was nineteen and found myself in a position of having to support my family or abandon them. What would you have done?"

"You weren't nineteen when you took part in the battle at Tyraine, or at Anderon, or a half-dozen others," said James. "It seems to me that had it not been for your intervention, the West would still be intact."

"We can go over what I did and why I did it for the next year and it won't change a thing. I'm not asking for your forgiveness. I was raised to believe that one's family comes before all else, and I lived up to my obligations. Fortunately, I'm also not nineteen anymore."

"And now you've changed your mind," said Gawl. "Pardon my being blunt, but I would as soon bed a rattlesnake as trust you, Teanna. Get out of my house."

"You don't need to trust me. I'm only asking you to *listen* to what I have to say."

Gawl looked at James, and the prince responded with a small shrug.

"Speak," said Gawl.

Teanna began, and was in the process of recounting essentially what Delain had reported in his letter when Gawl cut her off. "We already know all of this. Why are you here?"

"I'll answer that question in a moment," she replied. "Let me finish. I'm sure by now you know what happened in Anderon between the Vargothans, the Orlocks, and Alor

Satar, but that is only part of the story. Vargoth's alliance also includes Coribar."

"Go on," said James.

"You face a greater peril than you can possibly imagine."

"We already know about Shakira and her ring," said Gawl. "We'll figure out a way to deal with her when the time comes, just as we'll figure out a way to deal with you."

"Brave words. But will you also figure out a way to deal with a million Orlocks? Because that's exactly what she has at her command. I swear on the honor of my house that I'm speaking the truth," Teanna said.

Neither Gawl or James said anything for a while.

"Fine," Gawl finally replied. "You're speaking the truth. That doesn't answer why you're here."

"There are two reasons. Just as you, I love my country and I don't want to see it destroyed. I can do a great deal with this ring," she said, holding up her hand, "but I can't be everywhere at once and I'm not invulnerable."

"And the second reason?" prompted James.

"I know that Mathew Lewin is alive. I want to talk with him."

Gawl's face went cold. "I have no idea what you're talking about. Mathew's been dead for four years now."

"It's no use pretending, Gawl. I know he's alive. I've felt his mind."

"And you'd like to apologize for trying to kill him," said Gawl. "Pardon me, but my patience with this charade wears thin."

Teanna looked at James who stared back at her but made no response.

"I repeat, I was younger then. People grow up. Yes, I'd like to apologize for what I did. It's not just my country or your country or Alor Satar that are in danger right now—it's everyone. Have you ever asked yourself why the Orlocks hate us as much as they do? This may be difficult for you to accept, but there is a machine under our planet that makes the rings work. I know that sounds incredible. Our ancestors built it, but before that was done they *created* the Orlocks. Do you understand what I'm saying?"

"No," said James.

"It's true, I swear it. The creatures were meant to be a slave race. Once the machine became active, our people didn't need them anymore and began to destroy them in the most horrible ways. I've seen the proof with my own eyes. I can take you to the Ancients' town and prove it to you if you like."

"What town would that be?" asked James.

Teanna took a breath before continuing. "It lies thousands of miles under the earth in a cavern. I've been there myself, many times. If you'll let me, I'll—"

"Come back tomorrow," Gawl said. "We'll be here at the same time."

Teanna looked like she was going to say something else but thought better of it. The rectangle of light moved inward until it became a line, then compressed itself into a single white dot and promptly winked out of existence. The sound of a far off chime slowly died out in the room.

As soon as she was gone James turned to Gawl. "Why did you stop her?"

"Because something she said jogged my memory. Several years ago I had a talk with Mat Lewin and Siward Thomas. It took place here in the palace after two of my statues came to life and tried to kill him. At the time, we didn't know that a priest named Aldrich Kellner was controlling them. He also had one of the rings. At any rate, Siward, Mat, and I spoke for quite a while, and Mat mentioned the underground town. Teanna may be telling the truth."

"Or part of it," James pointed out.

"That's possible as well," Gawl agreed. "But if she's right about Shakira having a million Orlocks . . ." He sighed heavily. "Well, this is serious and I want time to think things through."

"An excellent idea," said James. "So do I."

## 40

## New Raburn

THE DREAM BEGAN DIFFERENTLY FROM THE OTHERS. Mathew saw the mountain in front of him and the entrance to the cave as he climbed the hill, but now there was a bay in the distance. He couldn't tell what bay it was. As he climbed higher, the masts of different ships anchored there came into view. On the opposite side of the bay a town stretched up into the hills. It was not a large town and it resembled none of the ports he had visited while on the *Daedalus*. One prominent structure—a castle, by the look of it—sat on a hill above the town. It was too far away to make out anything in detail other than two prominent watchtowers.

Collin was already at the cave entrance fifty feet above him. The opening was little more than a rift in the rock, and one had to stoop to enter it. The same sick vertigo took hold of him during their climb as it had done before. Eventually he found himself on the ledge facing the Orlocks once again. Shakira was there.

"So, human," she rasped. "Have you considered my offer?"

*So much for the preliminaries,* Mathew thought. "What do I gain by getting the ring for you?" he asked.

"Your life and the lives of your friends, to begin with."

"And what's to stop me from killing you once I have the ring back?"

"Nothing. Except you would also be killing your friend."

Mathew was about to reply when he realized that

Shakira was looking at something over his shoulder. He turned around to see two more Orlocks standing in the shadows, dressed in black leather armor and pointing crossbows directly at Collin.

"If you try reaching for the power," Shakira said, "your friend will die. You have my word on that."

"Don't listen to them, Mat."

Mathew felt his heart begin to race. No other dream had been as clear as this one or possessed its detail. He could see the pores on Shakira's face and the veins on the back of her hands.

"We've done nothing to you," he said.

"Nothing?" Shakira repeated. "You were responsible for the deaths of three of my people in Elberton, and twelve in the forests of lower Elgaria. It was *you* who closed the mountain tunnels outside of Tremont, killing hundreds more, and you say you've done nothing? Shall I go on?"

"Those things are true," Mathew said, "but it was your people who attacked us. We were only defending ourselves."

"Is that what you call it, human? Defense? You are the greatest mass murderer in three thousand years. Karas Duren was a child compared to you. You have one minute to make up your mind."

"No, Mat," Collin told him. "Once she gets the ring, she'll kill every human she can."

One of the Orlocks stepped out of the shadows and clubbed Collin across the back of his head with its fist, knocking him to the ground. Mathew went to him. Collin was unconscious but appeared unhurt. With his hand on the hilt of his sword, he rose to his feet.

"Think, human," Shakira said. "It's four against one. You'll just get both you and your friend killed."

"Perhaps," Mathew said. "But you still won't have the ring. Why do you need it, anyway, if you already have one?"

"To ensure my people's safety. It is too great a risk to

allow these rings to float free in the world. Each one is a danger to us."

"You can't believe Teanna d'Elso will simply hand hers over, can you?"

"We will deal with the Nyngary princess when the time comes. Give me your answer."

Mathew glanced at the two Orlocks standing with their weapons trained on Collin's back. One word from Shakira and his friend would be killed.

"I'll get it," Mathew said.

He walked to the edge of the chasm, looked down and shuddered. Then he studied the door and the area surrounding it more carefully. There was no way to get across the gap and only the smallest of ledges running below the door to stand on. The air around it had the same blurred quality he remembered from the other dream.

Out of curiosity, Mathew picked up a rock about the size of a pear and threw it across at the opening. Even though he was prepared for it, the flash of light and the noise still caused him to jump.

Mathew awoke on the floor of the apartment, propped himself up on his elbows and looked around. He was in his bedroll, Lara beside him. Outside, the rain beat against the windowpane and a spectacular lightning display lit up the sky. He chided himself about his imagination and settled back down again, staring up at the ceiling, wide awake now. Except for the lightning, it was pitch-black outside. He tried to think about the disturbing dreams. They had been occurring with increasing intensity over the last weeks and he wondered if it was because he was getting closer to his ring. According to Delain's man, the ring was in Teanna's palace, which made far more sense than in a cave. She would want it close where she could protect it. The idea of what an Orlock might do if they could actually make a ring work kept him awake until the sky grew light.

\* \* \*

They were all eating breakfast in Father Thomas's rooms when Garvin came to visit. After passing a few polite comments about how they had slept, he got right down to business.

"The council and I discussed your situation last night and again this morning," he said. "As you can see, it's still raining, so we'll not be asking you to leave in this kind of weather. You got a lot of people talking last night, Father. I'll say that."

"That's a priest's job, my son. I've always thought it's better to get people to think than to tell them what to think."

"I'll be honest," Garvin went on. "I don't agree with everything you said, but there was certainly some truth in it. At any rate, the council asked me to tell you that if you want to stay, you'll be welcome . . . all of you."

Father Thomas smiled at him. "That's very kind and I'm deeply touched. If the circumstances were different, we might be inclined to accept your offer, but our business is urgent and we've lost enough time already."

"Understood," Garvin said. "I'll let the others know. You're free to wander around the town and explore. Stick to the tunnels with lights, if you do. They'll take you just about anywhere you want. You'll find a blue square painted on the wall every sixty feet or so that'll keep you from getting lost. Just follow the one you came in on last night and you'll be fine."

"I know the hall's on one end; what's on the other?" asked Collin.

"The residence buildings mostly. Each one has its own color. There are eighteen in all," Garvin explained. He then went through the list and told them he could be found in Green 560.

"I don't get what the numbers mean," said Collin.

"We think that's what the Ancients called the buildings . . . in place of a name. The colors were our idea. It didn't seem right calling a building by a number. Almost all of them have numbers. You can see 'em above the main doors or in the lobbies. We've never been able to find any proper names for any of the streets, so we just use the numbers and colors."

"Strange," Collin replied.

Garvin chuckled. "It takes some getting used to. I lived in Tyraine before I came here, and all of our streets had names, even the little ones."

"I heard it was pretty bad there," said Ceta.

"It was. After Elita's forces surrendered, soldiers from Alor Satar came through every day for two weeks, telling us to leave. They said Orlocks would be occupying the city and all the country as far up as Lake Larson. Of course, we didn't believe them at first. No one wanted to leave their homes or their businesses. By the fifth day they started clearing people out of the South Quarter and the Orlocks began moving in. That was enough to convince me. I got the wife and my boys and we left. Some folks were never convinced."

"I owned the Nobody's Inn in Elberton," Ceta told him. "I lost it when the creatures took over the town."

A smile lit up Garvin's face. "Why, I've been there a number of times. It was a fine inn. I'm sorry for your loss, mistress," he added.

"Thank you."

"At any rate, you're all invited to the midday meal today. It'll be back at the convention hall. We'll have a lot more vendors than we did last night. Some good artists, too. If you need help, I can send one of the men to guide you. No one'll ask you to make any speeches today, Father, unless you're wanting to."

"No, no," said Father Thomas. "I think we'll give everyone a rest. I imagine we can find the hall again on our own."

"Any chance the weather will clear?" Mathew asked.

Garvin shook his head. "It's hard to say, son. I was up in the Red Tower's observatory earlier and couldn't even make out the mountains. Normally, if it's a clear day you can just about see Ardosta from up there."

"Then we'll probably just wander around and take in the sights, if that's all right with you," Father Thomas said.

"That's fine, Father, but if you go exploring, stay away from the lifts. They're a bit dicey. Sometimes they work and sometimes they don't. The stairs are a safer bet."

"I'm sorry," Mathew said. "What are lifts?"

"It's those little rooms with the buttons. When they're working they'll take you up to any floor you press. The problem is, they're hit or miss. Two of our boys got stuck in Yellow 350, and it took us most of an afternoon to get them out."

"Thanks for the warning," said Father Thomas. "We'll walk if we feel adventurous."

They said goodbye to Garvin and promised to meet him at the celebration. A half hour later they were making their way through the tunnels and speaking in hushed tones. There wasn't any reason for lowering their voices, it just seemed like a natural thing to do in a tunnel. As luck would have it, Collin missed the last blue marker and they found themselves back at the Red Tower again.

"Sorry," he said. "I suppose we'll have to backtrack."

"As long as we're here, I'd like to see that observatory Garvin mentioned," Mathew said.

Father Thomas looked up at the ceiling for a moment. "How many buttons did you say were in those lifts yesterday?"

"Forty-two, Father," Collin replied.

"That's what I thought. I think I'll let you two young men go. You can tell me all about it when you come down."

Neither Lara or Ceta were overwhelmed by the prospect of climbing forty-two flights of steps and also declined, so he and Collin set off by themselves. Halfway up, Mathew's legs began to tire and he began to reconsider the wisdom of his decision.

"I don't see how Garvin made this climb," he gasped.

"I'll bet he took one of those lifts he told us not to take," Collin said.

"There's no power in this building, remember? What floor are we on?"

"Twenty-eight," said Collin, wiping the sweat off his face. He came to a halt on the next landing, rested his head on his forearm and took a moment to regain his breath. Mathew slapped his friend on the back and trudged upward.

Collin muttered something under his breath that Mathew didn't catch and started after him. They reached the roof ten minutes later and waited for their heart rates to return to normal.

The observatory was a glass enclosure completely covering the top of the building. At the moment, there wasn't much of a view—in the last hour, fog had closed in on New Raburn, turning the world gray. Even the lower portion of the building was shrouded. It was the highest up Mathew had ever been, and what little they could see made the climb worth it. It felt like he was looking down from the sky. He gazed out at the swirling clouds for a minute and stepped away from the edge. It was the same thing in every direction, though for a moment he thought he could see a break in the clouds to the west. The opening, if it was one, disappeared quickly.

Near the center of the roof was a plain looking rectangular structure containing four doors which appeared to be made of the same material as those in the lobby—a strange type of metal, Mathew thought, not silver, though their color reminded him of it.

"Can you read this sign, Mat?"

Mathew looked at where Collin was pointing and saw a small brass plaque written in the ancient tongue. " 'Observation Deck,' " he said.

"Great. It's not like a person couldn't figure that out for themselves."

He and Mathew spent a few minutes exploring and

didn't find anything remarkable except for two more of the rectangular structures at either end of the roof, each containing the same silverlike doors they had seen in the lobby.

"We'd better get back down," Collin said. "It doesn't look like there's much up here."

"I suppose you're right. Thanks for coming with me."

They began heading back to the stairway when Mathew abruptly stopped. "Now that's curious."

"What is?"

"That one has six doors."

"Huh?"

"You see that structure in the middle?" Mathew pointed. "It has six doors. The others have four."

Collin shrugged. "So?"

"And those two on the right are different from the others. I didn't notice it until just now."

"Maybe they needed more lifts for the people in the middle of the building," Collin suggested.

Mathew started walking toward them.

"What's the big deal if they're different? C'mon."

"I don't know," Mathew answered. "It's strange."

"What? That those two are made of glass? Maybe they got bored, or maybe they ran out of the silver metal. Who cares?"

"Hang on a minute," Mathew said. He ran his fingers over the surface of the door. "This isn't like any glass I've ever seen."

Collin looked closer. "Hmph . . . I guess you're right. But I still don't see— Whoa!"

Startled, both of them jumped back as the the door suddenly slid open to reveal a tiny cubicle inside. It was approximately the same size as the lifts they had looked into, but there was something different about it.

"I thought Garvin said there wasn't any power in this building," said Collin. "That just about scared me to death."

"Me, too."

They moved closer and craned their necks in. It took only a glance for Mathew to decide they were not looking at a lift. A familiar shiver coursed through his body—the same feeling he got when he accessed the ring's echo.

On the wall facing them was a small sign written in the old tongue:

SPEAK DESTINATION CLEARLY OR
USE KEYPAD TO TYPE IN CODE

Mathew translated the words for Collin. Just below the sign there was a black glass window approximately twelve inches square. Seemingly suspended on the inside of it they could see what looked like several rows of letters with a single row of numbers. It was the oddest thing either of them had ever encountered. *"Key-pad,"* Mathew said.

"What's a key-pad?" Collin asked.

Mathew shook his head. "I think that's it," he said, pointing at the window.

Collin frowned, then walked to the back of the structure to examine the window more closely. "It doesn't come out on this side," he said. "Someone must have painted those letters inside the glass."

"I don't think so," Mathew said. "I think this is a machine of some type. It has something to do with the ring."

His mention of the ring stopped Collin in his tracks. "How do you know?" he asked, coming back around.

Mathew explained about the sensation he had just gotten. "I felt it as soon as the doors opened."

"Are you positive?"

"Definitely."

Mathew stared at the walls of the cubicle. There was something odd about their appearance. "Do you know, I don't think the insides of this are glass at all," he said. "I think they're some type of crystal."

"What's it supposed to do?" Collin asked. "There are no buttons, so it can't be one of the lifts."

Mathew vaguely recalled a reference in one of the Ancients' books that had something to do with his ancestors being able to cross the world in minutes using specialized machines. His initial impression had been that the book was referring to the old airships, but now, looking at the silver disks in the floor, he wasn't so sure. He glanced up at the ceiling and saw six more just like them.

"Mat," Collin said, touching Mathew on the arm, "there's a glow coming from the window."

Both of them immediately stepped away from the opening. There was a faint red glow and it was also coming from the walls. Collin and Mathew looked at each other and waited. Nothing happened. The glow remained for nearly a minute, then faded away, and the doors closed with a hiss. Out of curiosity, Mathew took a step toward them again. They opened and the glow reappeared.

"I can't be certain, but I think this may be one of the Ancients' transporting devices."

"Transporting what?" asked Collin.

"Uh . . . themselves, I think," Mathew said. "That's what the sign is talking about."

"I thought '*destination*' meant going to the ground floor or something like that."

"It could, but I suspect that's what the lifts do. If I'm right, this thing could take you to another city or even another country."

Collin's look was skeptical. "You mean you just ask it to take you to Anderon or Barcora and you go?"

"Theoretically . . . assuming it still works. I don't know when it was used last, and the names of places change over time," Mathew told him. "The machine would have to know what you were talking about if we try it."

The last was too much for Collin. "That's ridiculous," he said, making a dismissive gesture. "How can a machine know anything?"

When Mathew took a step closer to the doors, Collin grabbed him by the elbow.

"You're not going in there until we know more about it. I can hear you thinking, Mat Lewin, so get it out of your head right now. I'm not going back and explain to Lara that her new husband stepped into a magic room and disappeared."

"But—"

"*No,*" said Collin. "I mean it. Let's get some more information. Maybe Garvin can scare up some books for you to read."

"I guess," said Mathew, "but I don't want to approach Garvin with this. We can ask Harry. He and two other men recognized me last night. I think they would be willing to help."

They argued about it all the way down the stairs.

## 41

## Tenley Palace, Sennia

MATHEW AND COLLIN WERE NOT THE ONLY ONES ARGU-
ing. Fifteen hundred miles away Prince James of Mirdan
was trying his best to persuade Gawl to hear Teanna out.
And 650 miles to the southwest in the city of Tyraine, Terrence Marek sat across from King Seth of Vargoth, and
was doing his best to convince him the time was right to
launch a full offensive against Alor Satar.

Seth however, was reluctant. In his view it was better to
weaken the enemy by attacking their border garrisons.
Shakira listened but did not participate in the conversation.

"We can have all of our ships assembled in less than a
week, highness," Marek insisted. "My people are prepared
to die for our cause."

Seth looked at him and slowly explained his position
again. "And that's exactly what they will do if we march
on Rocoi before the time is right. Armand Duren in no
fool, Marek. According to the reports, they've been
shoring up their borders for the past two weeks. We can't
simply march and hope no one will notice. These things
take time. All we've won is a single battle, and I guarantee
you Armand Duren and his brother are going to strike
back. The only questions are where and when."

Their argument went on for another fifteen minutes before Marek turned to Shakira and asked what she thought.

"How nice of you to include me in your plans," she said.

"We meant no offense," Seth said. "It's just that—"

"Orlocks are best at being told what to do."

"Shakira—"

"Or perhaps it's that we are incapable of understanding the complexities of the situation?"

"No, no," Seth replied quickly. "You have my apologies. It won't happen again."

Marek dropped his eyes when Shakira turned to him. "Forgive me, your majesty, I meant no offense. The fervor of my faith sometimes carries me away."

Shakira looked at Marek for several seconds and laughed quietly to herself. "Our numbers are far greater than theirs. The Orlocks are ready to move. Let us destroy their border defenses then move on Rocoi."

Seth thought about it for a few seconds before making up his mind. "Fine . . . we'll move," he said. "But there is another matter that needs to be settled. The situation here in Oridan is far from stable. It would be insanity to attack Alor Satar with Delain at our back . . . *all* of our backs. This is simply good military sense. Our people are having a hard enough time with them as it is."

"I have never cared for the name Oridan," Shakira said. "It was the name of Karas Duren's father."

After discussing their options for fifteen more minutes, they settled on a plan. The king called for a bottle of wine and poured each of them a glass. He wasn't certain if it was the right thing to do as far as an Orlock was concerned, but Shakira accepted it, keeping her eyes fixed on his. It was a disconcerting habit, which he ignored. He held the wine up to the light, examining its color.

"After the country is ours and our friend's Church is established," he said, with a nod toward Marek, "I suppose we can find a more appropriate name. Alor Satar will be divided, as we have agreed, but I'm curious about something, Shakira. We have been referring to your land as the 'Orlock Territories.' Do you plan to leave it that way?"

Shakira's smile was cold. "For the time being."

\* \* \*

James sat on the veranda above the Tenley Palace gardens waiting for Gawl to arrive and resume their latest discussion. Below, workmen were busy putting back the statues Edward Guy had taken out. James had seen examples of Gawl's work before and he found them impressive. The subtlety and attention to detail were astonishing.

Earlier, he, Quinn, and Ballenger had been given an impromptu tour of the grounds by Gawl. It was pleasant to be with the other men, and for a while he managed to forget the mounting tensions that seemed to hang in the air, until they came to a pond and saw a sculpture of two nude women holding a pair of horses on tether. It was a beautiful piece that immediately caught his eye. He had started to ask about them, but stopped when Jeram Quinn shook his head. Gawl gradually slowed and stared at the statues without speaking, then excused himself and went back into the palace. As soon as they were alone, he and Ballenger turned to Quinn for an explanation. The constable told them that the woman on the left was the Lady Rowena.

The king's sudden departure left James with the job of informing the others about Teanna's visit. He also told them how Gawl felt about it. As he surmised, both men were in favor of hearing what she had to say. Privately, he suspected that Gawl would come to the same point of view in time, but mistrust ran deep.

James was still marshaling his arguments when Gawl entered the room. His friend was dressed in a pair of worn black breeches and a brown vest that was covered in marble dust. His shirt was green with long sleeves. After they shook hands Gawl plopped down in a chair across from him and tossed a letter on the table.

"What's this?"

"Read it."

James picked the letter up, looked at the writing for a moment, then reached into the pocket of his shirt, pulled out a pair of glasses and put them on. When he finished reading, he laid the letter facedown on the table.

"It came about an hour ago," said Gawl.

"This is serious. I hoped we would have more time. It appears Teanna may have been telling the truth."

Gawl gave him a look. "If Delain is set to move against the Vargothans, he'll need all the help he can get. They'll throw everything they have at him."

"Yes," James said. "But there's something else going on here."

"How so?"

"It's all well and good that the Orlocks and Vargothans have turned on Alor Satar. Delain sees this as an opportunity for himself in spite of Shakira having one of the rings. He told us that much in his last letter. But the fact is, even if he could prevail against both the creatures and the Vargothans, he'll lose against her."

James picked the letter up again and read it through one more time. "He says here that only a few hundred of the creatures were involved in the battle and that they fell back when his people attacked using the new cannons."

"That doesn't make sense," said Gawl.

James thought for a moment. "Don't you see? The Orlock's retreat was a ruse to draw him in. From Delain's perspective, it appears that he's the beneficiary of a rift in the enemy camp. Vargoth has turned on Alor Satar—good. Better would be having them go at each other, with Vargoth fighting a war on two fronts. Seth is too experienced to let himself be caught in this kind of position."

"So they need to take care of Delain first," said Gawl.

"Exactly. Shakira's burning Anderon Palace was meaningless. A palace has no military value, only emotional."

"Particularly to Delain," said Gawl, as he began to understand what James was driving at.

"Right. Delain responds by attacking, which is exactly what they wanted him to do. The Orlocks retreat, even though they could win. It's all for the purpose of getting him to follow with the bulk of his forces, and then . . ." James slowly closed his fist.

Gawl's face went pale and he leaned back in the chair. "He doesn't know how many creatures he's up against."

"No," said James. "Cannons or no cannons, he won't stop a million Orlocks."

"If we march, we can get there—"

"Too late. It would take us at least a week. He says he's going to move in five days."

"Goddammit," said Gawl, "there's got to be something we can do."

"There is."

The king's eyes fixed on him. "You want to form an alliance with Teanna."

"She's the only person who can get word to him in time. If he goes charging after Vargoth, the Orlocks will destroy him."

"Do we tell her about Mathew?"

James rubbed his temples with his fingertips and thought. "Let her prove herself first. If she succeeds in stopping Delain, we can deal with that question later."

# 42

## New Raburn

ON THEIR WAY TO THE CONVENTION HALL MATHEW TOLD
Father Thomas and the others what he and Collin had
found. The priest listened carefully and thought it was best
to leave the machine alone until they knew more about it.
Privately, Mathew was inclined to agree, but he was frustrated at being cooped up and wanted to do something.
The whole thing put him in a sour mood.

Using the colored tunnel markers, they found the hall
with no difficulty. A number of long tables had been set
out and people were just sitting down to eat. Garvin motioned them over and introduced them to his wife,
Leanne, and their children, two twin girls and a boy. The
girls curtsied to Father Thomas, while Garvin's son, who
was six and had the same red hair as his father, made a
stiff little bow and promptly returned to his meal.
Mathew snuck a glance at Lara and wondered if she was
thinking of Bran.

The dinner conversation centered mostly on the weather
and other innocuous subjects. While they were eating, one
of the twins, Mathew noticed, kept stealing surreptitious
glances at him. The third time she did so, he responded by
winking at her. Her color heightened by two shades and
she stared down at her plate. Her sister leaned over and
whispered something in her ear, which prompted a stern
look from their mother.

"It's not polite to stare at our guests," said Leanne.

"I'm sorry," the girl mumbled.

"It's all right," Mathew said. "New faces are always interesting."

"Are you going to live here?" the girl asked.

"No, we're on our way to a place called Nyngary. Do you know where that is?"

"Mm-hmm. My friend Gabriele comes from there."

"I see. And you are . . ."

"Suzzette," she reminded him. "We're from Tyraine. Where do you live?"

"Well, my friends and I come from Devondale. It's about five hundred miles to the north of Tyraine."

"Christa says she's seen you before," said Suzzette. "Were you ever in Tyraine?"

"I was," Mathew answered, "but that was a long time ago."

Garvin's wife put an end to the questioning by telling the girls to finish their meals and run along. "I'm sorry," she apologized. "We don't get a lot of new people here and children are always curious."

The topic of conversation, at least between the women, shifted to the subject of children and child caring. When it appeared that it would stay there awhile, Mathew, Collin, and Father Thomas excused themselves to go for a stroll. Garvin managed to slip away unnoticed and joined them. Their presence didn't seem to be missed.

A number of people were leaving the tables and drifting toward the front of the room where various merchants had their stands set up. As he walked, Mathew, however, continued to think about the odd machine in the Red Tower. It was strange that Harry had said there was no power in the building, and stranger still that no one in the city had discovered it was still functioning. More interesting to him was that the doors had opened when he approached them. None of the others reacted that way.

Collin fell back to join him while Father Thomas and Garvin drifted ahead. After a minute of getting only perfunctory responses to his questions, his friend seemed to read his thoughts.

"Get it out of your head, Mat," he said in a lowered voice. "If you try using that thing, I'll knock you down."

The comment finally brought a smile to Mathew's face. "Sorry. I'm just preoccupied. It's frustrating being cooped up like this. As soon as the rain lets up I want to leave."

"We will," Collin said. "Say, those pastries over there look pretty good. Want to split one?"

Mathew followed Collin's gaze to a small cart where a man was selling cone-shaped cakes sprinkled with powdered white sugar.

"You go ahead. I couldn't eat a thing."

Collin shrugged. "I'm not hungry. I was just trying to get your mind off the topic."

Mathew thumped Collin with his shoulder. After all the years his friend probably *could* read his mind. They continued along the aisles looking at the merchandise and the various wares. The merchants of New Raburn were a resourceful lot, and offered everything from pots and pans to boots and jewelry.

A quick glance back at the tables confirmed that Lara and Ceta were still engaged in their conversations; moreover, it appeared that three other women had now joined their group. Mathew made a mental note to check back on her later. It suddenly occurred to him that in their rush to leave Devondale, he hadn't had the time to get Lara a wedding gift; so he decided to remedy the situation by stopping at a small stand that was selling handcrafted jewelry. The owner, a heavyset fellow, introduced himself and invited him to take his time.

"What are you doing?" asked Collin.

"I thought I'd surprise Lara with something," Mathew said, picking up a silver and turquoise bracelet.

"Better go with one of the necklaces. She's not partial to turquoise."

Mathew started to reply when he remembered that Collin probably knew her tastes better than he did. Nevertheless, the comment annoyed him. He put the bracelet down.

The next stall had a number of finely crafted wooden boxes with flowers inlaid onto the lids. Mathew thought they were attractive and exactly the sort of thing a woman would like. The first one he opened was lined with red velvet and had several small compartments.

The stall owner was with another customer at that moment. So Mathew patiently waited for her to finish.

"Lara's already got one like that," Collin told him. "Her mother gave it to her for her birthday two years ago."

"What?"

Collin shrugged and turned his palms up.

Exasperated, Mathew handed him the box and walked to the next stall where they were selling perfumes. Up ahead, Father Thomas and Garvin had been joined by a third man. Mathew purchased a bottle that smelled like fresh flowers and stuck it in his vest pocket before Collin had a chance to comment. He glanced over his shoulder and saw that his friend had also acquired additional company—a tall blond girl. They seemed to be getting on well together so he kept going.

The next aisle contained stands selling paintings, pottery, and a variety of decorative glassware. Mathew walked past them and stopped at one where several other people were watching an artist doing a charcoal sketch of a woman. She was seated in front of him on a chair. The image on the pad didn't look very much like her, in his opinion, but he kept the observation to himself.

Hung on canvas at the back of the stall were different examples of the artist's work. These were mostly landscapes and coastline views of homes with colorful flowers on balconies. He recognized two of the coastlines. One was of lower Elgaria, and the second was a view of Barcora's harbor from Tenley Palace. On the whole, he thought they were quite good, and felt the artist would be better served if he concentrated on landscapes rather than portraits.

After a while he decided it might be time to check on Lara again. He had only gone a few steps, however, when he stopped and turned around. At the top left corner of the booth he saw another coastline scene. On the hill above was a castle with two watchtowers overlooking a small bay. He stared in disbelief. It was the same castle in his dreams, right down to the color of the walls and the tile roof. Even the watchtowers were identical. He was suddenly conscious that his heart was pounding, and he looked around for Father Thomas. The priest was two aisles away talking with a group of men. Collin and the girl he'd been speaking to were just coming around the corner.

The number of onlookers around the artist had increased, by several people who were interested in seeing the portrait he was working on. It was all Mathew could do to keep himself from interrupting the man. He had to know where that castle was located. He stared at the painting again. He'd never seen the coastline before, but it was definitely the same castle.

Moving closer, he looked over the artist's shoulder. At best the man was only halfway finished with the sketch. He cursed under his breath and looked around. Several booths away he spotted Harry and a woman, chatting with a vendor who was trying to sell them some pottery. Mathew forced himself to walk slowly toward them. He wanted to run.

"May I have a word with you?" he asked, touching Harry on the shoulder.

Harry turned around and smiled when he saw him. "Hello, Thad. Are you enjoying the festival?"

"Yes, it's very nice. I need to ask you a question. Do you know the artist over there?"

"That's Ben Walsh. He and his family moved here about two years ago."

"From where?"

Harry scratched his head and thought for a moment. "I believe they're from Alor Satar . . . one of the eastern provinces up near the Nyngary border, if I recall right. Is something the matter?"

"No," Mathew said. "Would you mind introducing me to him? I'm interested in one of his paintings."

Harry turned to the woman he was with and excused himself, then he and Mathew walked to the artist's booth. They waited until the artist finally put down his charcoal and held the pad up for his subject to see. The woman and her companion exchanged pleased smiles, paid the man, and went happily on their way, as did the rest of the crowd.

"Ben, I want to introduce you to Thaddeus Lane," Harry said. "He was walking by your booth and saw one of your paintings."

"Which one?" Ben asked, shaking Mathew's hand.

"That one in the left corner." Mathew pointed.

"That's Leola Bay," Ben said. "I did it quite a while back."

Mathew searched his memory for a second and couldn't place the name. "Leola Bay," he repeated. "Where's it located?"

"About ten miles from where I grew up. My father was the d'Elso's head groundskeeper. That's Rivalin up on the hill . . . their summer palace. If you like the painting, I can give you a good price on it."

"How much?"

"How about ten elgars?"

"How about six?" Mathew countered.

Ben frowned and looked down at his feet for a moment. "Tell you what . . . let's make it eight and I'll throw in a charcoal sketch of you and your lady. You're the newcomers, right?"

"Right," said Mathew. "Make it seven and I'll save you the trouble of doing a sketch."

Ben took a deep breath and held out his hand. "Done."

While the painting was being wrapped Mathew asked for more information on Leola Bay.

"It's up in the North Country," Ben told him. "About a day's ride from Knightsbridge. There's not really much up there except Rivalin and some small towns. I've got a map here, if you want to see."

"I'd like that very much," said Mathew.

He was aware that Harry was listening to the conversation, but he didn't care. Their eyes met as he bent over the map and Harry winked at him. "I'll let you two talk. I'd better be running back to the wife before I get in trouble." He gave Mathew a friendly slap on the shoulder and departed.

"Good man," Mathew said, watching him go.

"That he is," Ben agreed. "Will you and your friends be staying with us?"

"No, I'm afraid not. We'll be leaving very soon."

## 43

## Tenley Palace, Sennia

WHEN THE HUM STARTED AGAIN, NEITHER JAMES NOR Gawl were surprised, but something was different this time. A brilliant white point of light appeared and rapidly expanded itself into the form of a woman. When the hum stopped, Teanna d'Elso was standing there.

"My," she said, touching her face with her fingers.

Gawl and James looked at each other. This was no image. She was actually there in front of them.

"Good morning, sires," she said, with a small curtsey.

"Teanna," Gawl replied stiffly.

"Your highness," said James.

"I apologize for coming this way, but I thought it would be better for us to meet each other face-to-face."

"Isn't that what we did the other day?" asked Gawl.

"In a manner of speaking, but it's not quite the same thing. At any rate, I've brought a letter from my father."

Teanna reached into the pocket of her dress and pulled out a yellow parchment envelope bearing the royal seal of Nyngary and handed it to James.

"Would you like me to step outside while you read it?" she asked.

"What? No," said Gawl.

Teanna folded her hands in front of her and waited while they read the letter. Twice Gawl looked up at her, but her face was unreadable.

"Your father proposes that we form an alliance with

Nyngary and Alor Satar . . . incredible," Gawl said, shaking his head.

"I've already spoken with Eric and Armand. They'll go along with it and acknowledge the sovereign right of your countries to exist."

"How generous," said Gawl.

"I understand how you feel. They will also abandon their family's goal of 'one nation, one rule.'"

"Forgive me, Princess," said James, "but in the past your family has proven to be somewhat forgetful when it comes to the promises made in their treaties."

"They will honor this one. I will swear it by my family's name. Moreover, I will be the one to enforce it should the terms be breached."

Gawl made a derisive noise and looked out the window.

James went silent as he considered the proposal. Clasping his hands behind his back, he limped to the fireplace and sat down in one of the chairs, motioning for Teanna to do the same. She glanced at Gawl, whose back was still to her, then went over to join the prince.

"The fire feels good," she said.

James nodded absently. "Why?" he asked after nearly a minute.

"Four days ago forces from Alor Satar fought a battle with Vargoth, two hundred miles northwest of Rocoi at a town called Epps Crossing. The Orlocks were there as well. I found out about it last night.

"Armand placed twenty thousand men in the field along with two hundred of the new cannons. Less than six thousand returned home. Vargoth also has cannons, though far less of them than my cousin. He thought they would be the key to their victory. He was wrong. The Orlocks attacked in waves for two days straight. They charged straight into the guns, running over the bodies of their own dead. It was a slaughter. Those who were killed were lucky."

Gawl finally turned around, walked over, and stood

behind James's chair. "How do we know we can trust you?" he asked.

"That is a reasonable question," Teanna answered. "Sires, you are intelligent men. I know there has been mistrust between us. Some of that I am responsible for, some my family has engendered, but it is time to put our history aside. I want my people to survive and to prosper. Moreover, I want my country to survive. I am capable of protecting them, but I cannot protect everyone. Ruling a world of corpses is not a future I relish. We are fighting for our lives. Not just Alor Satar or Ningary, but Cincar, Sennia, Elgaria, Bajan, Felize . . . anywhere there are human beings. The Orlocks will not stop with the crumbs Vargoth throws them, and Coribar is too blind to see the truth. Our race will be extinguished unless we act."

"I ask again," said Gawl, "how do we know we can trust you?"

There was a pause.

"I am prepared to give Mathew Lewin back his ring."

Her announcement took both monarchs by surprise, yet neither was willing to acknowledge that Mathew was still alive.

In the end it was decided to put her to the test. Against his better judgment, Gawl revealed what Delain was planning and asked if she would use her powers to communicate with him about the trap that had been set. Teanna readily agreed.

"I can only communicate with him if I know where he is," she said. "I need to form a picture of the place in my mind's eye."

"He's in Anderon," Gawl told her, "but precisely where in the city, I don't know."

Teanna made a clicking noise with her tongue as she thought. "I was a little girl when we visited there. I seem to remember a wide boulevard with iron lamp posts and a fountain in the middle. At one end was a brown building with lots of steps and columns at the top. I believe the royal palace was at the opposite end."

"That's right," said Gawl. "Can you do that thing with the window again?"

"I could, but he would have to be there when I appear. If he's not, we'd just wind up talking to an empty street or scaring some poor citizens half to death."

Gawl smiled at the image. "Fine. What do you suggest?"

When he recalled that moment later, he resolved to never again ask such a question. Before he and James knew what was happening, the hum began. From somewhere far off he heard Teanna say, "You might want to close your eyes. This sometimes makes the stomach feel a bit queasy."

"Queasy" was an understatement. One moment he and James were talking to Teanna d'Elso, and the next they were being sucked into a tunnel of white light. Wind pushed Gawl's hair back and a tremendous rushing sound filled his ears. Fleeting images of trees, mountains, sky, and stars shot by so fast it made him dizzy. Then, just as suddenly, the vortex disappeared and they found themselves standing in water up to their calves. They were in the middle of a huge fountain.

In front of them was a street lined with a series of ornate iron lamp posts. They were in a circular intersection. Four other streets, coming from different directions, ran directly to the intersection where they were standing. The brown building with the steps Teanna had mentioned was facing them three blocks away. At the other end was all that remained of Anderon Palace. Even from where Gawl was standing he could see the blackened stones. Only three of the walls were intact.

Gawl stepped out of the fountain and reached back to help Teanna out.

"I'm sorry," she said, bending down to wring the water out of her dress. "I got an image of the fountain fixed in my mind."

James muttered something under his breath and sat down on the edge of the retaining pond. He pulled off one of his boots, and poured a stream of water out. "The next time you decide to do that, I would appreciate some advance warning," he said.

"If I told you, you wouldn't have agreed, would you?"

"Actually . . . no," he replied, taking off his other boot.

"Are you both all right?" Teanna asked.

Gawl put his hand over his stomach and said, "I probably won't eat for a week."

The comment brought a smile to Teanna's face. "My father said the same thing the first time he and I tried it."

"And you're still on speaking terms?" James asked, pouring water out of the other boot.

"Oh, yes. We're very close. Now, how shall we find King Delain?"

Finding the king turned out to be a lot easier than they thought. Four soldiers on the other side of the intersection were standing there, watching them, their mouths open. Teanna was the first to notice.

"Oh, dear," she said.

Gawl and James turned to see what she was looking at. For some reason, the scene struck James as funny and he began to chuckle. Now all they had to do was convince the soldiers that they were the monarchs of three different countries, he thought.

Teanna, apparently realizing what they looked like, started laughing herself. At first Gawl was annoyed, but even his face eventually creased into a smile.

"They probably think we're ghosts who have lost their minds," he said, trying to contain himself.

It brought a fresh round of laughter from James, who nearly fell back into the fountain. Meanwhile, the soldiers drew their swords and gathered enough courage to cross the street. Still trying to regain his composure, all James could do was motion for them to come closer.

"Gentlemen, I'm Teanna d'Elso," Teanna called out. "Please don't be afraid. We are here to see King Delain."

Their reaction was exactly what James expected. They all looked at her as if she were insane. James started laughing so hard, he slipped off the lip of the fountain and landed unceremoniously on his rump. Gawl sighed, then reached down and helped him to his feet.

"You shouldn't be in that fountain," said one of the soldiers. "It's public property."

"My apologies," Gawl replied, drawing himself to his full height, "but the lady was telling the truth. She *is* Teanna d'Elso and I'm King Gawl of Sennia. The soggy fellow next to me is James Genet, Crown Prince of Mirdan. I know what we must look like, but we really are here to see Delain. I'd appreciate it if you would take us to him."

One of the soldiers, a tough-looking sergeant, put his hands on his hips. "And I'm King Seth of Vargoth. Why don't you run along now and and sleep it off? We can have the peace conference later."

Gawl closed his eyes and opened them. He looked at James, who was still trying to control his laughter and was completely worthless at that moment, then at Teanna, and shrugged.

"You can't blame them, can you?" he asked.

Teanna took a deep breath. "I suppose not," she said. "Are you men sure there's nothing we can do to convince you?"

"You just go home and change into dry clothes, missy. I'll be sure and tell the king all about it."

"I really hate to do this," she said under her breath.

A moment later the expression on the sergeant's face turned to one of shock as he lifted off the ground and found himself suspended ten feet in the air. All three of his companions followed.

"Gentlemen, as King Gawl said, I *am* Teanna d'Elso. This is neither magic nor witchcraft and I assure you that we mean you no harm. What you are seeing is the Ancients' science . . . how they traveled, if you will. Unfortunately, I miscalculated a bit on where we were to appear, but I give you my word that we are here on a matter of the greatest urgency. We need to see King Delain immediately."

With that, Teanna gradually set the soldiers back on the ground and folded her hands in front of her.

"This one's big enough to be Gawl," one of the men said to his sergeant.

"And that one looks like James," another said. "I seen him at the battle of Ardon Field several years ago."

The sergeant placed his sword back in his sheath, not taking his eyes off the newcomers. "Dan, go get Colonel Morrisey," he said, over his shoulder.

Twenty minutes later Gawl, Teanna, and James found themselves walking up the steps of the brown building, flanked by a squad of twenty men.

## 44

# New Raburn

FATHER THOMAS WAS TALKING TO A GROUP OF MEN WHEN he saw Mathew round the corner. His instincts immediately told him something was amiss. Instead of the more measured pace he was accustomed to, his young friend was walking rapidly. He excused himself and started after him. His first thought was that Mathew had heard the news about the Vargothans turning on Alor Satar and Delain's attack in Anderon. There was no question now that the country was at war. Events were unfolding quickly. Several aisles away Collin Miller noticed the same thing. They both caught up with Mathew at the same time. He was so deep in thought he barely noticed.

Pulled from his reverie, Mathew looked up to see the priest and Collin. "Delain's man is wrong," he said. "The ring isn't in Corrato."

The priest took his elbow and stopped him. "How do you know?"

Mathew quickly told them about the artist and the painting, as he pulled the paper wrap off the painting and held it up for them to see. Father Thomas gently lowered his arm, and they started walking again. "Let's go someplace where we can talk," he said.

They moved to a corner of the hall, where Mathew recounted the dream he'd been having.

"So you think Delain is wrong about Teanna keeping the ring at her palace?" Father Thomas asked.

"I do. According to Delain, his man only had a general

idea about where she was hiding it. He saw her place her own ring in a book, but that was it. He never actually saw my ring. We've all been assuming all along that they're both there. Do you know where this Rivalin is, Father? The mountain's got to be close by."

"I do," Father Thomas replied, slowly nodding. "As soon as this storm lets up—"

The priest didn't have a chance to finish what he was saying. A tremendous bang nearly deafened all of them. It was followed by a concussion and a blast of hot air that knocked them to the ground. The entire forward wall of the meeting hall had just exploded. Outside, horns started blaring. Dazed, Mathew got to his knees and looked around. People were running and screaming and there were dead everywhere. He alone knew what was happening, having felt the tremendous surge of power when Shakira struck.

At the front of the building, Orlocks were pouring through the shattered opening. Pandemonium broke out as the men of New Raburn tried to rally.

Mathew helped Father Thomas and Collin to their feet and drew his sword.

"It's Shakira," he said. "She knows I'm here."

"We've got to get the women to safety," Father Thomas told them.

Mathew's eyes went wide. In the confusion, he'd completely forgotten about Lara and Ceta. All three of them started running.

Out of nowhere a snarling Orlock wielding a double-bladed axe rushed toward them from the shadows, and two more of the creatures followed him. Without breaking stride, Collin launched himself into the Orlock. Both went down in a tangle of arms and legs. Collin came up on top and plunged his dagger into the creature's heart. Without warning, a powerful shove from Father Thomas threw Mathew sideways, as two arrows whizzed past his head, missing him by inches.

The Orlock who had fired was no more than five feet away. Father Thomas knocked the crossbow aside, with his sword spun sideways, and beheaded the creature with a single stroke. Mathew recovered his balance in time to see a third Orlock level a pike and charge straight for him. With little time to react, he pulled his sword from the scabbard and parried upward, deflecting the point away from his body as he sidestepped. The Orlock's momentum carried him forward, only to find his victim was no longer in the same spot. Mathew's circular riposte caught the creature across its shoulder. Steel bit into muscle and bone. The Orlock screamed and whirled around, swinging the pike back at him in a wide arc. Mathew moved inside the blow and lunged for its heart. The creature's eyes opened in shock and a second later they glazed over. It fell, still reaching for Mathew as it died.

Through the commotion of battle he saw Lara, Ceta, and several other women about fifty yards away. Four men from New Raburn were in front of them, fighting a group of Orlocks. Lara had a sword in her hand. Once again Mathew started for them. He saw a young mother go down with an Orlock blade in her stomach as she tried to defend two young children behind her. One was a blond-haired young boy, not more than five or six, and the other a girl of about eight. Without stopping to think, Mathew changed direction and sprinted for the children.

What happened next would be burned in his mind forever. Holding a toy sword, the little boy stood his ground before the Orlock. Dead black eyes filled with hate for all that was human turned on him and the creature ran his sword through his chest.

Mathew screamed, "No!" still too far away to help. From out of nowhere a man beside himself with frenzy, armed only with a dagger, launched himself at the creature. He stabbed the Orlock in the chest over and over before both of them fell to the ground. Mathew couldn't count how many times the man stabbed the creature, but in

the end the Orlock was dead. When he got there he helped
the man to his feet then picked up the frightened girl and
handed her to him.

"Take her to safety," he said.

It took a second before the man's eyes focused. Then
he nodded and hurried off toward the rear of the hall,
clutching the girl in his arms.

Over the rubble of the shattered front entrance more
Orlocks were rushing into the room. Desperately, Mathew
searched the hall for Lara and Ceta, spotted them again,
and started making his way through the press of the fight
Collin, Father Thomas, and a group of men from New
Raburn had engaged twelve of the creatures and were trying to defend a small cluster of children, huddled behind
them. They were fighting their hearts out, but were gradually being driven backward.

Everywhere he looked people were dying.

His heart nearly stopped when one of the Orlocks broke
through. Lara stepped directly into the creature's path,
smoothly parried its blade, then pierced it through the chest
and moved out of its reach. The Orlock died on the spot.

Everything seemed to be happening in a rush as Mathew
fought his way across the floor. He felt someone grab his elbow and turned to see Harry, a large gash across his forehead and his arm was bleeding freely from a wound. Before
he could say anything, a series of explosions snapped
everyone's head around. Dust and smoke soared into the air
and flooded the hall as a thirty-story building collapsed in
on itself. Out in the street, for one brief moment, Mathew
caught a glimpse of a tall female Orlock. She was standing
quite still despite the destruction going on around her. Then
she was gone, obscured by the gray smoke.

"You've got to get out of here!" Harry was shouting.

"What?"

"Take your people and get out! We'll hold the creatures
as long as we can. Follow the tunnels and stay to your left.
They'll take you out into the mountains."

"I'm not leaving," Mathew said. "These people will die without help."

"They're dead already. Can't you see that? New Raburn's lost. You've got to get out, now."

"No," Mathew said, yanking his arm away. "No . . . we'll stay. We'll fight with you."

Suddenly Lara, Father Thomas, Collin, and Ceta were by his side. Lara grabbed him by the front of his shirt with both hands. "Mathew, he's right—we have to leave."

*"No."*

Alfy and two other men joined them. They were breathing heavily and their faces streaked with dirt. He put his hand on Mathew's shoulder. "Get going, boy," Alfy said. "You don't have much time."

It was the second time in Mathew's life that he had run away from a fight, and the thought consumed him with shame and self-loathing. In his mind he was nothing more than a coward, saving himself at the expense of others. He wanted to put his hands over his ears to shut out the screams coming from the great hall. They followed him down into the tunnels as they ran. They followed him for the rest of his life.

Harry had cautioned them to keep to the left. Above the ancient light globes spread their odd yellow light onto the walls and floors. For ten minutes the five of them followed the corridor, until it split off in three different directions.

"We need to take that one," said Collin, who was bleeding from a cut on his thigh.

"Shh," Father Thomas said, making a sharp hand gesture.

Cautiously the priest poked his head around the corner and looked down the tunnel. It ran in a straight line for better than three hundred yards until it disappeared in the shadows.

"Orlocks," he whispered.

Ceta gasped and put her hand over her mouth, and Collin gently slid his sword out of its scabbard.

"How many?" Collin whispered.

In answer, Father Thomas shook his head and drew his sword.

Mathew's mind was working furiously. Along the way they had passed a number of other tunnels. He touched the priest on the shoulder and pointed back down the corridor they had just come from. "Everyone take off your boots and follow me," he whispered.

With the others following, Mathew led them past two intersections and eventually came to a third one that angled off to the right. Collin grabbed him by the arm.

"That way leads back to the Red Tower, Mat."

"I know."

They came out in the basement where they had originally taken shelter from the storm. The rain was still coming down, though nowhere near as heavy as it had been during the first two days. Thanks to the ramp, a large puddle now covered most of the floor. There everyone stopped to put their boots back on while Collin checked the opening. He returned a moment later.

"The street's crawling with Orlocks," he said.

Mathew felt his heart sink. "Is there any chance we can—"

Collin was shaking his head before he had finished his sentence. "There are too many."

Mathew looked at his friend, then at Father Thomas, Lara, and Ceta in turn.

*Without you, our son won't have a chance to grow up.* Lara's words echoed in his mind. *Up . . .* He looked at the stairway in the corner of the room. *Up . . .*

"Collin, take point," he said. "We'll have to cross the entrance one at a time."

Once Collin was in position, he held up a hand for them to wait. A moment later he waved Ceta across. Lara followed her, then Father Thomas.

*So far so good,* Mathew thought. He crouched at the side of the entrance and waited for a group of Orlocks to pass by. A hand signal to Collin set him in motion. Once he was there they headed for the stairs.

Everyone was out of breath and their faces covered with grime by the time they reached the roof. Collin was the last one up the steps.

"Trouble," he gasped, pointing down the staircase.

Father Thomas and Mathew glanced at each other then threw themselves at the door and bolted it. Less than a minute passed before the Orlocks started pounding on it.

"What are we going to do?" Ceta asked. She went to the edge of the roof and looked down.

Mathew already knew the answer. The lifts were out of the question. They would only take them back to the Orlocks. He had no idea if what he had in mind was going to work, but it was the only chance they had. The hinges on the door were already weakening; it wasn't going to hold much longer. Thud after thud reverberated in the silence as the creatures hammered against it.

"Follow me," he said.

He stopped when they reached the structure's six doors and quickly explained what he remembered about the Ancients' machine.

Father Thomas grasped the concept at once. "Are you sure it will work, my son?" he asked, keeping his eyes on the rooftop door.

"I don't know if it will work at all. We'll find out in the next few seconds."

"You find out," Collin said. "I'm not getting in there. I'll buy you as much time as I can."

"We all go or we all stay," Mathew told him.

The two locked eyes before Collin cursed under his breath and sheathed his sword. As before, the crystal door slid open when Mathew drew close. The rooftop door finally gave way, falling with a loud crash.

"Each of you stand on one of these disks," Mathew said, pointing at the floor.

*"There!"* the first Orlock shouted. It started running toward them with an awkward loping stride. Five more of the creatures followed.

After a second's delay, the red glow behind the sign appeared and the doors closed with a soft hiss. The creatures began pounding on it. Through the crystal their faces seemed even more distorted and misshapen than ever.

Lara reached out and took hold of Mathew's hand.

"Devondale," Mathew said out loud.

Nothing happened.

Collin and Father Thomas turned to look at him.

"Corrato," Mathew said next, as a crack appeared in the door.

A second later one of the creatures thrust his sword through the opening. It stopped just short of Collin's stomach. Collin looked down at the blade and sucked in a breath.

"I really wish you'd hurry with whatever you're doing," he said over his shoulder.

The answer occurred to Mathew a moment later. He had said as much himself the day before. In all likelihood the machine had been created long before Devondale and most cities and towns of the modern world ever existed. There was only one place he was certain of.

"Henderson."

For the second time in less than a minute Collin Miller's eyes went wide and he began to yell. It was difficult later for Mathew to describe exactly what sound his friend had made, but it was similar to how someone might sound if they had just jumped off a very tall cliff. A smoky white light enveloped them and a hum came from what seemed everywhere at the same time. The light abruptly went black and he felt himself being drawn into a long twisting tunnel. Shapes and colors rushed past him at incredible speed and he felt a dropping feeling in the pit of his stomach. He had the feeling of tremendous speed, and of wind on his face.

All at once the darkness was gone, as was the room. They were in the middle of a small park. Collin, still yelling, jumped nearly a foot when Mathew touched his shoulder.

"Where are we?" Lara whispered.

"This is the town of Henderson," Mathew replied.

## 45

## Anderon

DELAIN WAS SITTING AT HIS DESK SPEAKING WITH TWO OF
his generals when Teanna, Gawl, and James entered the
room. On the wall behind them was a map of Elgaria. A
number of pins were stuck in various places along the borders and around the major cities. One glance was enough
to tell Gawl they represented enemy troops.

It was obvious from Delain's reaction that he had been
advised of their presence.

"Your Grace," Delain said, getting up to embrace Gawl.

"My liege," Gawl responded, returning the hug.

Delain greeted James in a similar fashion before he
turned to Teanna.

"My lady," he said, bowing. "To what do we owe the
unexpected pleasure of your visit?"

"It would be better if all four of us could speak in private," Teanna said.

Delain nodded to the men with him, and they both left
the room. As soon as the door closed he turned back to
Gawl.

"What the hell is going on? They told me three drunken
magicians were swimming in the Memorial Fountain pretending to be Gawl, James of Mirdan, and Teanna d'Elso.
If I didn't recognize you with my own eyes—"

"Teanna's the only magician," Gawl said, helping himself to a glass of wine from a bottle on the table. "Though
I can't say much for her aim."

"Excuse me?"

"The fountain was an accident," Teanna explained. "It's been years since I've been here, and I just got the image fixed in my mind. I'm sorry if I caused a fuss."

"You're sorry if you caused a fuss. Fine. Now would one of you please explain what this is about? The last time I checked," he said to Teanna, "we were supposed to be enemies."

"We're here to stop you from launching an attack against the Vargothans," James told him.

"And the Orlocks," Gawl added.

"And the Orlocks," James echoed.

"Am I supposed to be friends with them, too? Perhaps we could all sit down and have dinner together."

Teanna spoke up, quickly explaining about Coribar's involvement and the alliance it had formed with Vargoth and the creatures. Delain's face grew somber and he sat on the edge of his desk and listened to her. When she got to the part about how many Orlocks were arrayed against them, he glanced at Gawl, then at James. Both nodded in affirmation.

"All right, I understand," Delain said, when she was through, "but that doesn't explain why you are here, Highness."

"Teanna will."

Gawl listened to the princess's explanation for a second time and had to give her credit for courage. He knew that apologizing was no easy thing for someone of her disposition. Part of him wanted to trust her, and part of him would never be fully convinced. Still, she had responded to their test without hesitation, even though her method left a lot to be desired. The trick now would be to convince Delain.

"I can't fault you for wanting to save your people," Delain said. "But you'll understand that trusting what you say is somewhat difficult for me. Your family were the ones who sold my country to the Orlocks, and now you would like us to help you rescind that bargain. Why should I believe you?"

Teanna's answer about giving the ring to Mathew Lewin surprised him,

"What makes you think he's alive?" Delain asked.

"It's not a matter of my thinking it. This is a fact—like the sun coming up in the east. An affinity exists between ring holders," she explained. "Under certain circumstances it's possible to feel the other's mind."

"But how, if he no longer has his ring?"

"That part I don't understand. Perhaps there is a residual effect from wearing them. Perhaps Mathew is different. I only know that he still lives and that between the two of us we might be able to stop Shakira, Coribar, and the Vargothans. Alor Satar cannot win by itself. My father thinks that wouldn't be such a bad thing, but I believe if the link in the chain breaks . . ."

Delain held her gaze for a time. "You tried to kill Mathew Lewin once before, how do I know you won't finish the job the first chance you get?"

What Teanna did next surprised everyone in the room. She pulled the ring off her finger and tossed it to Delain. "You can give it back to me once you're satisfied I'm not lying."

Delain stared at the rose gold in his palm and hefted it a few times. "Heavy," he said, half to himself. "This is the second time I've held one of these. It might have been better if they had never been created at all."

"We can debate that later," said Teanna. "At the moment, there are a million Orlocks moving on Alor Satar. Next, they'll turn toward Elgaria, or perhaps Cincar, or Nyngary, or Bajan, it doesn't make a difference. Coribar is moving its fleet from the south. Mathew and I could stop them."

"We're far from defenseless," Delain pointed out.

She responded by taking a deep breath. "I assume you're talking about the cannons. Eric and Armand also have them and so does Vargoth, so the field is even. My cousins used the weapons at a place called Epps Crossing and recently lost. What they didn't have—and what you don't have—are a million men to repel Shakira's attack. Vargoth and Coribar soldiers raise that number even higher."

Delain looked at James, who lifted his eyebrows in reply.

"Let me ask you a question," Gawl said. "Couldn't you simply destroy their forces?"

"Possibly," she answered, "but it's not as simple as that. Using the power drains you; the body needs time to recover. Shakira is not going to sit by while I attack her army. I'll have no choice but to deal with her first. If I'm successful, there's a reasonable chance I'll be powerless to do anything about her followers for several days, and by then it would be too late. That's why we need Mathew."

Their discussion went on for the better part of two hours, and in the end Delain asked her if she would excuse them so that he, Gawl, and James could speak in private. She inclined her head and they stepped into the next room.

Each scenario the three men considered was as dismal as the next, as far as Gawl could see. If they were able to convince Bajan to join them, their number would still come to less than seven hundred thousand.

"We're in trouble," he said.

"Mankind is in trouble," James corrected.

When they reentered the room, Teanna was seated in a chair by the fire, reading. She looked up, closed the book, and put it on her lap. Without saying a word, Delain tossed the ring back to her. She caught it in midair.

"What makes you think your cousins will go along with an alliance?"

"They have no other choice," Teanna said, slipping the ring back on. She closed her eyes for a second and waited until the shiver passed. "It's a matter of survival now. Eric and Armand are no fools."

Delain shook his head. "This is very difficult. We've been at odds with them so long. Trust doesn't come easily."

"The most important thing is getting Mathew's ring back to him. Where is he?"

"Unfortunately, I don't know," said Delain. "He and Siward Thomas left for Nyngary over a week ago. We've had no word since."

One of Teanna's eyebrows arched at the mention of Siward Thomas's name. "I assume they went there to get the ring."

"Correct. They should already be in Corrato."

"That's a shame."

"What?"

"I'd tell you to ask Bryan Oakes for your money back, but he's dead."

Delain and James exchanged glances.

"That was my doing," said James.

"Both our doings," Delain corrected.

Teanna looked from one to the other, and they met her gaze without flinching. She understood why they had conspired to have her killed. She also knew that it was time to put old hatreds aside. This was easier to say than do, but there had to be a starting point.

She nodded. "I assume we'll have no more Bryan Oakeses," she said. "I've given my word and I'll keep it. I expect you to do the same."

# henderson

Nothing appeared to have changed since the last time he had been here. Nothing moved and there were no sounds. Mathew looked up and could see clouds moving against what seemed to be a blue sky, except he knew it wasn't a sky at all. If you stared at it long enough, you would eventually realize it was a giant dome.

A sharp intake of breath from Ceta told him she had just discovered the sky wasn't real.

"I've told all of you what happened to me after the battle of Ardon Field," he said. "This is where Teanna took me. We sat at that café over there."

Lara made a sound under her breath that he ignored.

"What made you pick this place, my son?" asked Father Thomas.

"It was the only place I thought the machine would recognize. That's why the other names didn't work when I said them. They were built after the machine."

"Fine. How do we get out of here?" asked Collin.

"Uh . . . actually, I'm not sure," said Mathew. "We need to pick someplace the machine knows. Do you know any, Father? Any places or buildings that survived from the ancient time and still have the same names?"

Father Thomas frowned. "Hmm, nothing comes to mind. Give me a while to think about it. I'm sure there must be a good many of them."

"Well, find one soon," said Collin. "This place gives me the creeps."

"Will you look at that?" Lara said.

They turned to see what she was staring at. In a dress shop directly across the way, two female manikins were in the window. They both wore dresses so short, they had nearly made Mathew blush the first time he'd seen them.

Collin's eyes opened wider and he let out a low whistle.

"I have got to see this closer," said Lara.

"Me, too," said Ceta.

Both women crossed the street, followed by Collin and Father Thomas. Mathew sighed and went to join them, but paused partway there to stare at the single white line painted down the middle of the street. A series of dashes ran parallel to it, creating four separate lanes. The surface felt odd under his feet, and he bent down to examine it more closely. The material was smooth and black and it was unlike any of the ancient roads he had come into contact with. Out of curiosity, he tested it with the point of his dagger and found that he was able to pry a bit up.

"What in the world is this stuff?" he asked no one in particular.

He was about to mention it to the others when he noticed a shadow on the ground. A man was calmly standing there, watching him, a pleasant smile on his face. He was oddly dressed.

"Asphalt," the man said.

"Excuse me?"

"The surface of this road is constructed of asphalt."

"Oh, well thank you. You startled me."

"My apologies," replied the Guardian. "It's taken you a long time to get here."

"I beg your pardon?"

"I said, it's taken you a long time to get here. Shall I increase the volume of my voice?"

"No, I heard you. How could you possibly know about me?"

"Because I've been sending you messages for nearly four years now, Mathew."

Mathew blinked. "I haven't gotten any messages from you. I don't even know who you are. How do you know my name?"

"It's my job to know things and to facilitate the transfer of information."

The conversation finally caught the others' attention, and they came back to join them.

"Who's this?" asked Father Thomas.

"Well, I don't know exactly. I just looked up and he was standing here."

"Indeed?" said the priest. "Perhaps we should all introduce ourselves. I am—"

"Father Siward Thomas of Devondale, Elgaria. Behind you are Collin Miller, Lara Palmer, and Ceta Woodall."

"Lewin," Lara corrected. "May I ask how you know who we are, sir?"

The Guardian didn't answer immediately. Instead he tilted his head to one side, and his face appeared to go blank for a moment. "Ah, I understand . . . the ceremony of marriage. A legal state. You were referring to your last names. In marital relationships, it is customary for females to assume the male's last name."

Lara, Ceta, Father Thomas, and Collin all exchanged puzzled glances.

"Something like that," Lara answered, "but you haven't told us how you know who we are."

"Or your name," Ceta added. "Do you live in this place?"

"This is my place. I am the Guardian. It is my job to know things and to facilitate the transfer of information."

"Yes, you said that before," Mathew told him.

"And the answer is equally true at this moment."

"All right, it's your business to know things," Mathew said. "Apparently you know a great deal more than I do. But what about these messages you've been sending me. I haven't—"

"He hasn't received any message from you," Collin said, finishing the sentence.

"Yes, I have," Mathew said, as it finally dawned on him. "It's the dreams, isn't it?"

The Guardian inclined his head and smiled.

"*You've* been sending me the dreams?"

"In a manner of speaking. I could provide further details, but I fear the capacity to understand them would be beyond you at this time."

The condescending tone rankled him. "Really?" Mathew said. "Try me."

The Guardian took a breath and launched into a brief explanation of how he had been communicating.

"You're right, I don't understand," Mathew said, dejected.

He received a pleasant smile in return. What he *did* understand was the Guardian's explanation about the echo—the dreams, he remembered, had started four years earlier. The machine had been trying to speak to him.

The concept itself was overwhelming, but then, everything about the rings and Henderson was incredible.

"Look, I know the Ancients were a bit odd," said Collin, "but why stick a town way down here in the middle of the earth?"

"Come with me," said the Guardian. "It will make more sense if I show you."

He led them across the square, away from the shops and toward a one-story gray building. The giant crystal Mathew had seen on his first visit rose up and disappeared into the roof. It was in the shape of an octagon and was as smooth as glass. The closer Mathew got to it, the more he felt the echo's power growing in his body. A faint red light glowed at its base. All of them slowed as they passed it. They were heading down a street Mathew had not been on before and it ran directly away from the town center. Collin, walking with Father Thomas, slowed up to allow Mathew and Lara to catch up with him.

"Mat, I can see right through this fellow," he said, lowering his voice.

"I don't think he's lying," Mathew answered. "Some of the things he said make sense. In fact—"

"No. I mean I can actually *see* right though him. Look for yourself."

Mathew did look, and his mouth dropped, as did Lara's. All of them were unsure of what to do or say until Lara solved the problem.

"Sir," she called out. "May I ask you a question?"

The Guardian stopped and turned around.

"You're not really alive, are you?"

Father Thomas and Ceta stopped dead in their tracks.

"No, I am not alive at all," the Guardian replied. "I am an image, if you will . . . an interface between machine and people such as yourselves."

"An image," Father Thomas repeated, trying to digest the concept. "Do you mean you are an image of one of the Ancients?"

"One of the designers of the machine, to be precise . . ."

Curious, Lara took a step closer. She reached out and touched the Guardian's face with her fingertips. There was a faint sizzling sound as her hand passed through his head and she pulled it back quickly.

"I'm sorry. Did I hurt you?"

"Not at all," he replied. "Follow me, please. We only have a short way to go."

The street led them into the darkened recesses of the cavern. They walked for five minutes then turned onto another street which ended at a metal catwalk with handrails on either side. A faint thrumming sound grew progressively louder the farther they went. The Guardian came to a halt and pointed. Stretching before them was the machine of the Ancients.

Like the giant crystal they had passed it was shaped like an octagon, and was so immense that Mathew couldn't see where it began. A series of orange lights pulsated up and down the shaft of the machine at regular intervals. There were other catwalks below them, so many that he lost count after several seconds. The sight took him aback and all he could do was stare. The others had the same reaction.

"My God," Collin whispered.

"We are at Maintenance Level One," said the Guardian. "There are fourteen thousand others like it. The last level is 226 miles below us."

Collin shook his head and looked over the edge of the railing. "What makes it go?"

"The machine's energy source derives from the planet's magma. The answer to the question you asked earlier is that this town was created to house the workers and engineers who lived here. At one time over thirty thousand people were in residence."

"Amazing," said Father Thomas. "Is there a reason you're showing us this?"

The Guardian seemed offended by the question. "Most people find this fascinating."

"Indeed," said the priest, "but that doesn't answer why you've brought us here."

"There are a number of fascinating things in Henderson that I can show you if you wish. Is there other information you require of me?"

Mathew was aware the Guardian didn't answer the question, but his instincts told him not to press the matter just then. Their discussions with him lasted for nearly four more hours before they took a break. The Guardian walked back to the square with them and said they would find food waiting at the café. Before anyone could ask another question, he announced that he would return in one hour and promptly disappeared.

In retrospect, Mathew found the information he had provided invaluable. It was difficult to say which was more enlightening: who the Orlocks were and how they came to exist, or why all the rings did not work in the same way. He had long suspected the latter to be true. Each ring had its own peculiarities, which explained why the dragon's tail had passed through Teanna when they were in the Emerald Cavern. It wasn't something he was capable of.

After their dinner the Guardian reappeared and took them to the gray building where he showed them images of people long dead and a litany of events that had taken place in the shadows of history. In some form or fashion, almost all of it was related to the rings.

At Mathew's request, he displayed pictures of the eight members of the Ancients' Western Ruling Council. Their bodies long gone to dust, they stared back at him across the centuries. One in particular, a dark-haired woman with intense eyes, caught his attention, and he asked who she was.

"Elaine Lasker," the Guardian responded.

Mathew nodded slowly as another mystery was solved. Most of the writing engraved on the inside of his ring had been worn smooth over time, but he had always been able to make out the letters E and L.

Collin asked which other people had visited the town. Teanna d'Elso was one, as Mathew already knew, but the revelation about the Orlock queen and Terrence Marek came as a shock. Father Thomas supplemented the answer by explaining who Marek was, and provided everyone with a quick history of the Sandresi.

While he spoke, the dome gradually changed from daylight to evening and ultimately to night. Stars came out and there was even a hint of moonlight on the horizon.

Collin looked up and shook his head. "They could have done a better job on the stars," he said through a yawn.

"That sentiment was shared by many of the people who once lived here," said the Guardian. "I assume you will all want lodgings."

No one objected, and he led them to a residential street and told them to pick any houses they wished.

*  *  *

It felt strange to be in someone else's home, Mathew thought as he and Lara walked through the rooms. They were far from empty. The occupants were long dead of course, but there were plates in the sink and even articles of clothing still hanging in the closets. It made it seem that whoever had lived there might return at any moment.

When they sat down on the couch together and she rested her head on his shoulder.

"This is such an odd place," Lara said. "I don't like it."

"Neither do I. We got a bit sidetracked today, but first thing in the morning I'll ask him how I can get my ring back and we'll leave."

"What do you suppose they were like?"

"The Ancients you mean?"

"Mm-hmm."

"I suppose they were people just like us."

"Mmm," Lara said, snuggling closer and putting an arm around his waist.

The moments in his dreams when he held her in his arms, came back to him now, and he was afraid he would wake up and find her gone. Of course, he didn't. This was real.

They kissed, and it was exquisite, filling his senses, as the years of separation melted away once again. So many emotions were surging through his mind, it was hard to separate one from another. He only knew that Lara was there, fresh and clean, and smelling faintly of flowers.

When they finally separated, she lay in his arms until their breathing slowed.

"Don't ever leave me again, Mathew," she whispered, looking up into his eyes.

"I won't."

"Ever," she murmured, drifting away.

She might have heard him say, "Never." Or she might have already passed into sleep. It didn't matter.

An hour passed, and then another, and Mathew lay

there staring up into the darkness. He thought about a lot of things, of Collin in particular, and how his return must have affected him. He had caused his friend pain by coming back and turning his world upside down.

Collin would say nothing about it—of that he was sure. Their brief talk in New Raburn was all the conversation they would ever have on the topic. That was just his friend's way. In the morning Mathew decided that he would ask him to be Bran's godfather. Collin clearly loved the boy and he owed him that much.

Nor had he and Lara spoken about their living together for the last four years. They might one day, but for the moment, some things were better left unsaid.

There was enough light coming through the bottom of the door, Mathew studied Lara's profile. He loved the way she looked and the way she smelled. Cautiously, he pushed a strand of hair away from her eyes. And then Lara's words, *people just like us*, came back to him. He disengaged her arm and got up as quietly as he could. There was a blanket in the next room that he got, covered her, and slipped quietly out the front door.

The silence and lack of movement on the street were the first things that struck him as he headed back toward the square. *Thirty thousand people once lived here*, the Guardian had said. He knew the Ancients had destroyed themselves and that their end came faster than any of them had ever imagined. It was frightening. Even with fifty thousand years of accumulated knowledge, they were still powerless to avoid what occurred. Their science, capable of creating miracles, had failed, and in the end it was their own dark thoughts that sealed the bargain.

"They were people just like us." He said the words aloud and kept walking.

The Guardian was waiting for him at the town square by the theater.

"You didn't answer Father Thomas's question earlier," Mathew said. "Why did you show us the machine?"

"Can you think of no reason?"

Mathew stared at him for several seconds. "No."

"Really? Perhaps the answer will come to you later."

"Who are you?" Mathew asked.

"I've already told you that."

Mathew thought for a moment. "You're not simply an image, are you?"

The Guardian smiled. "No . . . I'm quite a bit more than that."

"Who are you?"

"Think of me as an echo, Mathew. The real Malcolm Henderson died three thousand years ago. I'm all that's left of him. He designed this complex." The Guardian paused and looked around. "I was the last resident of this place."

"You didn't leave with the others?"

"No."

"You died here?"

"I was murdered here . . . by Elaine Lasker, or her subconscious thoughts, to be precise."

*"Murdered?"*

"Elaine was the chief administrator of the Meria Project. That was what this complex was called," he said, looking up at the dome. "We wanted to bring light to mankind; to free people from manual labor so that man could reach his true potential. It almost worked.

"When the deaths started, we knew that something was wrong. My team and I worked around the clock to identify the problem. Unfortunately, we weren't immune to what was happening. At first we thought the deaths were accidents, but it soon became obvious that they were really attacks, attacks that grew more and more violent . . . and open.

"I came to realize that all of the safeguards we had built

into the rings were directed toward *conscious* thoughts. We neglected to account for what the mind did while we were asleep.

"I prepared a report on the subject to the Ruling Council recommending that we shut Meria down until the problem could be corrected, but by then it was too late. The East launched their attack on us without warning, killing millions, and our council responded. They thought their only option was to remove all restrictions from the rings and fight back.

"Elaine and I quarreled on this point. She was in favor of removing the safeguards and I was vehemently opposed to it. You can guess the rest."

Mathew had heard bits and pieces of the story while he was at the Abbey of Barcora, but this filled in a great many blanks. "So you changed the rings," he said.

"Eight of them, but not quite in the way the council wanted. In my time we had a system known as 'checks and balances.' It was designed to prevent any one branch of government from becoming too powerful. The echo is one of those—so is the ability to receive images about where your ring is located."

"You mean the cave."

"Correct."

Mathew nodded. "Can you help us get there?"

"I can."

"What about the door? In my dream there was something around it."

"Yes. Teanna set up an energy field to keep others away. Unfortunately, I cannot tell you how to remove it."

"Teanna," Mathew said, shaking his head. "It appears that you and I have something in common. She tried to kill me."

"I know," said the Guardian. "You may find that she has changed in some regards."

"I doubt it."

"Change, Mathew, is a fundamental. If people are not

capable of change, then we wasted a great deal of time in building this. If there is no change, there is no hope."

"Do you think people have changed enough so the rings can be used?" Mathew asked quietly. "That's why you showed me the machine, isn't it?"

A faint smile appeared on the Guardian's face. "Come with me."

He led Mathew into a laboratory past the huge metal doors that once guarded the entrance. They were badly damaged. Mathew glanced at them as they passed trying to imagine what kind of power could have twisted them that way. He wondered if this was where the Guardian had died.

"Those things on the wall are called 'gauges,'" the Guardian told him. "They measure the machine's output—its power, if you will. Each one represents ten times the power of the one before it, and so on, and so on."

Mathew counted them. There were twenty in all, but only the one at the extreme left side of the room showed any movement.

"Please say your name out loud," the Guardian said.

"What?"

"Say your name out loud please."

"Mathew Lewin."

There was a second's pause before a mechanical voice in the console next to him repeated: "Recognize, Lewin, Mathew D."

"This room is the control center of the complex," the Guardian went on. "From here you can speak directly to the machine, as you have just done. The expression is not entirely accurate, but it will suffice for the time being. The commands are voice activated. To shut down Meria, you must say the following words in sequence: 'Override . . . Henderson . . . 68272 . . . Terminate operation.'

"Can you repeat that?"

"Yes, I think so," Mathew said repeating it.

"You will be asked to say those words in the exact or-

der I have just told you. After that, you will have thirty
seconds to get to the transport pads before the power is
cut. Do you understand?"

Mathew felt his pulse quicken. "I'm sorry, maybe I
don't understand after all. If the machine shuts down,
won't that destroy everything—all the knowledge?"

"Part of it would continue to function, and the knowledge might still be recovered at some point in the future.
The rings, however, would cease their operation."

"I see. Why don't you do it, then?"

"Because that is not part of my instructions. When you
recover your ring, you will need to decide if your people
have changed enough to accept the responsibility that goes
with them. My generation improved our science, but we
forgot about improving ourselves. Perhaps this is no longer
the case; perhaps it still is. Only you will be able to deter-
mine that."

The implications of what the Guardian was suggesting
were staggering. Who was he to decide mankind's fate?
He'd spent four years searching for the ring, and now he
was being handed a choice to destroy the very thing that
made it work. It was too much.

"I don't want this," Mathew said, taking a step backward.

The Guardian watched him.

"No," Mathew insisted. "It's not my place."

"Yours and yours alone."

"You're crazy. Don't you know what the rings can do?"

The words sounded dumb as soon as he said them. Of
course the Guardian, or Henderson, or whoever he was,
knew what they could do. He knew better than anyone
else.

They talked for an hour, and during that time the
Guardian did nothing to persuade him one way or the other.
In the end it felt as if he were arguing more with himself
than with an image of the long dead Malcolm Henderson.
He wanted very much to get Father Thomas's advice.

"I can't decide any of this right now," Mathew said. "I need time to think."

"That is your prerogative. My program—my instructions in this regard—are now fulfilled."

"Great," said Mathew. He turned to go, but only took two steps before the Guardian stopped him.

"There is more I have to tell you."

*Oh, for God's sake,* Mathew said to himself. "See here, why don't I go and get Father Thomas, and you can tell him whatever you have to say. He's very good at this sort of thing."

One of the Guardian's eyebrows went up.

Mathew took a deep breath. "All right, fine."

"I showed you how the Orlocks came to exist for a reason. Like the machine, they were a failed experiment. Man's betrayal and their attempted extermination of the species are things that have stayed with the creatures over the centuries. Even as we speak, thousands of them are marching on the borders of Alor Satar along with soldiers from Vargoth and Coribar. Shakira's forces are legion—the greatest military force ever assembled . . . more than a million in all."

Mathew couldn't believe his ears. "Are you serious?"

The Guardian's gaze became unfocused for a moment and then was clear again. "Gawl of Sennia moves from the south to intercept the creatures, and James Genet of Mirdan strikes from the west. Nyngary and Cincar are marching from the east."

"War."

"War," the Guardian repeated. "But this is no longer just a war to free your country. The trap the Orlocks have laid has been a thousand years in the making. Understand this, Mathew Lewin—the battle that is coming is not for land or wealth or political ideology. It is for the survival of man. The nations of both the East and West now seek to form an alliance to meet this threat. In this Teanna d'Elso has been instrumental.

"If men survive, all of the accumulated knowledge that you asked about will still be here. You can return the world to what it was or let things resume their natural course. The ultimate decision will be yours. I give you this warning, however: Should you emerge as the victor, people will seek you out. It will make no difference whether they are capable of controlling the ring or not. The lure of power will draw them. Conceivably, they will be content to let one person possess such power, and then again . . .

Mathew sat on the edge of a console.

"Maybe they won't," Mathew said, finishing the sentence. "But how can I stop a million Orlocks? Even if I retrieve the ring, there are limits to what I can do."

The Guardian stared at him for a long time. "No, there aren't," he said softly.

Gradually, an image of the last time he fought Karas Duren began to surface in Mathew's mind. The terrifying power that built up inside him had been almost too great to contain and he pulled himself back from the precipice at the last possible moment. He had seen in his mind a kaleidoscope of devastation and destruction on a scale that was barely imaginable. There were times at night when the thoughts still frightened him.

Mathew shook his head. "My ancestors nearly destroyed the world. Do you know what you're asking? I've read about what happened in the books . . . about their weapons."

Without warning a picture formed above the disk on the console to Mathew's right. After several seconds it was replaced by another picture. Then more followed, one after another, and the horror of what he was seeing closed around his heart like fingers of ice.

"There has to be another way," Mathew whispered when the pictures finally stopped. "Why did you show me this?"

"I suspect you already know the answer," said the Guardian. "You have known for a very long time."

"But I have a wife and a son, now."

"I know," the Guardian said quietly.

"No, it's not possible."

The Guardian watched him.

Seconds passed before Mathew finally reached his decision. "Can you tell me how to reach Rivalin?"

## 47

# Alor Satar

ERIC AND ARMAND DUREN SAT IN THE COMMAND TENT
of Alor Satar's elite Northern Battalions, on the heights
above the Roeselar River. Teanna d'Elso was with them.
She had just delivered an ultimatum to her cousins, and
neither was happy. Either they swore an oath and joined
the new alliance, she told them, or they could meet the Orlocks and Vargoth on their own.

It was late morning on a clear autumn day, and the
camp was alive with activity. Fortifications were being
constructed all along the ridge and sentries had been
posted. Horses pulling cannons moved past the tent opening in a constant stream. This was where Armand Duren
intended to make his stand.

Three miles away, on the east side of the river, the Vargothan and Orlock armies were engaged in their own
preparations. Teanna had been in military camps before,
but she had never seen anything on this scale. The Northern Battalions had been reinforced with units of Alor Satar's border command, and they now numbered eighty
thousand men. Supply wagons came and went with regu-
larity as more soldiers arrived on the scene.

"You should have consulted with us about this first,"
said Eric. "We've spent too much money and time acquiring Elgaria, and you give it away just like that." He
snapped his fingers.

"We're still able to defend ourselves," Armand added.

"We have better than five hundred cannon along the heights and the advantage of higher ground."

Teanna looked from one to the other. "I can't believe you two are this thick. Don't you see what's happening? Bajan has sided with Delain, and Lirquan and Felize are providing him ships to meet Coribar. You're all alone. If you weren't family, I'd wash my hands of the both of you."

"But it's insanity giving Mathew Lewin back his ring," said Armand. "As soon as the war is over he'll turn on us."

"Mathew Lewin will not break his word. My problem is finding him in time."

"And you have no idea where he is," Eric said, "other than someplace in Corrato."

"That's what Delain told me. He's with Siward Thomas."

Eric leaned back in his chair and stretched out his legs. "You took that statement at face value and call us stupid? Delain could be playing you for a fool—pretending to form an alliance so he can let us take the brunt of the attack."

"I don't think so," said Teanna. "I've met with him as well as James and Gawl. I think they're sincere. This is a threat to all of us."

"Do you know what I think, cousin?" Eric said, picking up an apple and cutting it in half. "I think your infatuation with Lewin has clouded your judgment. He killed your mother and our father, in case you've forgotten."

Teanna locked eyes with him. "No, I haven't forgotten, but there comes a time to put the past aside. The important thing now is to preserve our countries and our people."

The brothers looked at each other.

"What's the next step in this grand plan of yours?" asked Armand.

"Delain wants to meet in Bajan at Arkasha in three days time so we can plan our strategy. The treaty will be signed there."

Armand's smile was sardonic. "Why doesn't he come here?"

"Because he trusts you no more than you trust him," Teanna replied. "Bajan has agreed to host the summit."

Armand laced his fingers together and considered the proposal. He was a methodical man whose skills as a military commander were known far and wide. Unlike his brother, he tended to be plainspoken and usually said what was on his mind. The key was not to rush him.

Teanna's face assumed the masklike aspect that she had seen her mother employ when negotiating. Eric continued to cut the apple into slices, not taking his eyes off her.

"All right," said Armand. "Tell Delain we'll meet. Our scouts say it will be at least five days before Shakira can bring her troops up from the south. She'll have to pass this way or be caught in a vise."

Two days after his return to Tenley Palace, Gawl walked among the smoking ruin that was once the Abbey of Barcora. Jeram Quinn and Arteus Ballenger were with him. Two of the abbey's buildings had been reduced to rubble, and sunlight now flooded through enormous rents in the walls. The main gates, torn from their hinges, lay shattered on the ground. Everywhere Gawl looked there were the dead; not just soldiers, but teachers and scholars, young boys and old men. The priests had tried to defend the abbey, but their efforts had made little difference. Most of them died horribly. Gawl could see that. A force of five thousand Vargothans and Orlocks had landed in a cove twenty miles to the south of Barcora in the dead of night and launched their attack.

After twenty-eight years of being a soldier, Gawl thought the sight of death was something he would grow used to. He was wrong. The smell alone nearly turned his stomach.

"They had no warning, sire," Ballenger said. "One of the young novices escaped and found a patrol of ours. He told the lieutenant what was happening, but by the time my people returned it was over."

Gawl nodded slowly. "Where are they now?"

"We followed them as far as Nicola Cove. Apparently, Coribar's fleet was waiting there to take them off. Two women from Bexley described their flag accurately enough so there's no doubt."

"But why attack an abbey?" asked Quinn.

"This is Terrence Marek's doing," Gawl replied. "Eliminate the competition."

Quinn spat on the ground.

"How long before the cannons are ready?" Gawl asked.

"Two more days," Ballenger answered. "We'll need at least another five days to train the men."

"And how many ships do we have?"

"With the ten that Prince James left us, forty in all."

A short distance away three women were struggling to unload a barrel from a flatbed wagon. Gawl stepped away, picked up the barrel, and set it on the ground. When the women saw it was the king, they started to bow, but he shook his head to stop them and returned to Ballenger and Quinn.

"Do we know where their fleet is heading?" he asked.

"The best information we have is from a merchant vessel that docked in the harbor last night," Quinn told him. "Their captain sighted a huge flotilla heading north a hundred and thirty miles southeast of Tyraine. It's got to be them.

"We also know that a large contingent of Vargothans left Palandol two days ago and was seen heading along the coast road toward Cincar. In all likelihood they'll cross the border tonight."

Gawl looked at his general. "How did we get this news so quickly? It doesn't seem possible."

"Teanna d'Elso appeared at our headquarters last night and furnished us the details," Ballenger told him. "It's a bit disturbing to have her pop out of a ball of light and disappear again."

"You should try traveling with her sometime," Gawl replied. "Did she say anything else?"

"She said the Orlocks are moving everything they have toward a place called Balengrath. It's located on the other side of—"

"I know where it is," said Gawl. "This is what we'll do . . ."

Gawl called for a map and spread it on the ground. Then he described his plan to Ballenger and Quinn. The Sennian army would to be divided in half. One half, under Ballenger's command, would take the mountain passes and intercept the Vargothan and Orlock attack force that had destroyed the abbey. The remaining half would board the ships and head for Tyraine.

"Understand this," said Gawl. "We may be too late to stop the mercenaries and creatures from getting off those ships, but I intend that Coribar's ships will not leave the Tyraine harbor. Do I make myself clear? The passes will let us out well to the north of Tyraine and ahead of their army, so the lead is not as great as they think. Once we have destroyed them, we will join forces at Ritiba and converge on Balengrath."

Ballenger snapped a salute and headed back to see to the preparations.

Gawl and Quinn resumed their walk amidst the wreckage, helping where they could. Some two hundred men and women from Bexley and the surrounding towns had already arrived with wagons and were loading the dead onto them. It was a somber and depressing sight.

Without a word, both men stopped to right a sundial in the main quadrangle that had been knocked over during the fight and their eyes met.

Jeram Quinn spoke first. "You haven't said where you want me."

Gawl was silent for a moment. "It seems your career has been sidetracked, Jeram. Guy, Rowena, and the barons have fled the country, so the trials will have to wait.

Mathew and Siward Thomas are who knows where?"
Gawl shrugged. "We can only pray they'll be successful."

"Under the circumstances, I think it best to release you
from your pledge. You're an Elgarian and you belong with
your own people."

"That's very considerate," said Quinn. "Several years
ago I led a cavalry charge at Fanshaw Castle. Do you remember?"

Gawl nodded. "Of course. I didn't hear your speech to
the men, but they told me about it afterward."

"I meant what I said. Coribar wants to destroy anyone
who opposes their way of thinking, and I'm opposed to
anyone who tries to force their views on me. Vargoth
wants Elgaria; I'm equally opposed to that. The Orlocks
want mankind exterminated. Unfortunately, I have moral
objections to being murdered and eaten, so it seems I'm at
loose ends at the moment. Whether I fight here or there
will make no difference in the great scheme of things."

Gawl looked down at the constable and started to
chuckle. Then he put his arm around Quinn's shoulders and
they walked through the front gate of the abbey together.

## 48

# Ten Miles Outside Rivalin

THEY FOUND THEMSELVES STANDING ON A HILL IN THE middle of an old castle. All that was left were two walls and a portion of a third. A gate that once guarded the entrance now hung sideways on its hinge. Grass grew between the cracks of what must have once been a courtyard and the wind whistled through the broken foundation.

Lara brought her hands up to her face as if to make sure it was still there. "I can't say I care for this way of travel."

"Nor I," Ceta agreed. "It makes the stomach feel funny."

"Where are we?" Collin asked.

"Somewhere above the town of Rivalin, I should say," Father Thomas said, looking out over the nearest wall.

Mathew joined him. In the distance were the watchtowers of his dream and the bay. He turned a slow circle studying the landscape. Most of it consisted of jagged peaks and heavy forest, but he could see no sign of a cave. It was still early in the morning, the sun barely over the horizon, bathing the mountains in warm reds and golds. If the situation was different, he might have stood there admiring the view, but at the moment all he cared about was locating the cave entrance.

"Any idea where it is?" asked Collin.

Mathew shook his head and tried to recall the angle of the watchtowers from his dream. Lara put an arm around his waist and looked with him. Father Thomas and Ceta took one side and Collin the other.

"Maybe we should go down to the village and ask somebody," Collin suggested.

"It's got to be around here somewhere," Mathew said, half to himself.

"There," Ceta said, pointing.

"Where?" asked Father Thomas.

"Just between that clump of trees and a little to the right. I can make out an opening."

Mathew shielded his eyes from the glare and followed the line of her arm.

"What do you think, Mat?" asked Father Thomas.

"That's it. I'm sure of it."

Father Thomas gave Ceta a kiss.

"Well it won't be easy getting there, and I don't see any roads," said Collin.

Mathew turned to face the others. "There's something I want to say to all of you. I haven't told you everything about my dream. This is something I need to do alone."

The others listened as he explained the part about Shakira and the Orlocks. Even Collin was uncharacteristically quiet. When he was through, Father Thomas was the first to speak.

"Did you mention this to the Guardian?"

"Yes, but he only knew about the ring being in the cave."

Father Thomas thought for a moment. "Dreams are strange things, Mathew. Your brain could be playing tricks on you."

"I'm aware of that. But the point is, I can't take a chance with your lives. I'm going by myself."

The statement produced a storm of argument that lasted ten minutes. Lara was adamant about going; so was Ceta. Surprisingly, it was Father Thomas who decided the issue.

"I think Mathew is right," he said. "Lara, you are not only Mat's wife, but a mother as well. It would be bad enough if something happened to one of you. This makes it all the more imperative that the other survives for your son's sake. We've talked about this before, and it's just as true now. Ceta, my darling, you are many things, but unless you have concealed your skill with a sword from me, going would place you in grave danger, and that I will not allow."

Father Thomas then turned to Collin. "And as for you—"

"And as for me, I'm in the dream, right?" Collin said. He turned to Mathew. "Right?"

"Well, yes, but—"

"You said that in your dream both of us climbed up to the door in the cave, didn't you?"

"Sure, but—"

"Then it's settled. Father Thomas can take the women into the town and get horses for us. We'll meet them there once we have the ring."

There were more protests from Lara and Ceta, but they were less forceful than before. Father Thomas stayed out of it and eventually motioned for Collin and Ceta to come with him. They walked to the opposite side of the courtyard, leaving Mathew and Lara alone together.

Mathew took her by the shoulders and looked into her eyes. "You know I'm right," he said, keeping his voice down, "so for once in your life, please don't argue with me. We don't have much time. I love you and Bran with all my heart and I'd have you with me if I could. But I can't. You must understand that. I'm not going there to die—I'm going there to get the ring back. I want you to wait for me in the village. I'll come to you, I swear."

The tears that welled up in Lara's eyes nearly broke his heart. He thought of Bran and of Devondale and how she looked standing at the altar in the church that day.

Lara settled the matter by pulling him to her and kissing him. Then, without another word, she turned and walked to Father Thomas.

She and Collin said something to each other that Mathew couldn't catch before his friend rejoined him. The two of them stood atop the broken foundation and watched the others walk down the hill until the trees finally blocked their view.

"Let's go," said Collin.

The terrain was uneven and difficult to negotiate. It took them two hours just to reach the base of the hill where Ceta had seen the cave. There, they took a short rest. The opening was about a hundred feet up and barely visible from where they stood. There was a narrow ledge below it. Above the entrance was nothing but sheer rock that ended in a plateau.

Mathew checked the area for any sign of Orlocks.

"Anything?" Collin asked.

Mathew shook his head, tight-lipped.

"So far so good."

Another half hour of scrambling up a steep incline brought them to the ledge and breathing hard from the exertion. Mathew looked out and caught a brief glimpse of Lara, Ceta, and Father Thomas well below them, making their way along a narrow path toward the village. He waved even though their backs were to him, then turned to consider the cave entrance.

"This is it," he said, taking a drink from his water bottle.

"Great. What happens next?"

Mathew stared at him over the lip of the bottle.

Collin's shoulders slumped. "More climbing?"

"If I'm right, once we're inside we'll find a narrow path that leads to a circular opening in about three hundred yards. There'll be a waterfall and the door will be directly above that."

"How directly?"

Mathew responded by poking his forefinger up a few times.

Collin sighed. "I need a vacation."

The climb for Mathew was exhausting physically and mentally. At any moment he expected to see the creatures staring back at him from the darkness. Added to that was the anticipation of finally recovering his ring and the fear of losing it forever to the Orlocks. He peered into the shadows and saw nothing. Thoughts of Lara and Bran filled his head. What would become of them if he failed? What would become of everybody?

The weight of that responsibility grew heavier with each passing yard. He still couldn't see the door, yet he knew it was there. He thought about what his ancestors had done to the creatures: the lies, the deceptions, and the final betrayal. Men had tried to exterminate them, and they were now returning the favor.

Did he bear responsibility for something that had happened three thousand years ago? The Orlocks seemed to think so. He didn't. The bones of the people who had led the Orlocks into a trap had long since turned to dust. The creatures' hatred lived on.

Hatred. Until a few years ago it was only a word, loosely applied to such things as food he didn't like or the music lessons his mother and old Father Halloran had tried to force on him. The word had little meaning then. It didn't any longer. It was a vile thing to hate, he decided, unavoidable perhaps, because people like Karas Duren, Berke Ramsey, and Teanna d'Elso populated the world. He didn't want to hate, but if that's what he needed to steel him, so be it.

The Guardian had implied that Teanna had changed.

*We'll see,* he thought, shaking his head. *One thing at a time.*

That was his father's philosophy. At the moment the physical effort was stopping him from thinking clearly, so he concentrated only on the climb. He remembered about not looking down and did anyway. Collin was moving steadily and, annoyingly, with less effort than himself.

The Orlocks, if they were there, would not catch them by surprise. All they had to do now was to find a way to get past Teanna's door and the wards she'd put in place.

Collin reached the ledge first, put his light stick on the ground and reached down to help Mathew up the last few feet. The sticks had been a gift from the Guardian. They weighed only a few ounces and provided a cold light that threw back the darkness.

"Anything?" Mathew asked, propping himself up on one elbow.

"We're the only ones up here, if that's what you're asking. The door's on the other side of that chasm," Collin said, motioning with his head. "It's at least eighteen feet across."

Mathew looked around the ledge and saw nothing. "Strange," he said. "Everything else in the dream is accurate. I wonder why the Orlocks aren't here."

"Be thankful for small favors," Collins said. "How do we get to that door?"

"I don't know. Teanna's put something around it to keep people out."

Collin picked up the light stick, held it aloft, and peered across the chasm. "I don't see anything."

"Watch," said Mathew.

He grabbed a few pebbles and tossed them at the door. A series of bright orange flashes and loud pops lit up the cave as the pebbles made contact with the ward.

"Damn," said Collin, stepping backward.

"There must be a way to get in."

For the next few minutes they threw pebbles at the door from every possible angle. Each one produced the same result. Finally, Collin lobbed the last one underhanded, which arched up over the top of the door, hit the wall, and dropped straight down untouched.

They both looked at each other.

Collin tried it again with the same result. A little more experimentation revealed a small opening over the door's center that extended approximately three feet out from the wall. They began to search for some way to bridge the gap.

"Look there," Collin said, pointing upward. "Do you see how the chimney narrows the farther up it goes?"

"I see it."

"There's an overhang. If we can secure a rope, one of us could climb down and drop behind whatever Teanna's put there."

"It might work," said Mathew.

"Let's try," Collin said, slinging the rope.

Collin got it across his shoulder. "We can leave the water bottles and our cloaks here to cut down on the weight. I think the light sticks will throw off enough light to see by if we prop them up on the edge. In fact . . . What's the matter?" he asked, noticing that Mathew hadn't moved.

"Something's wrong," Mathew said.

"What is?"

"Everything's been happening just the way I dreamt about it, with the exception of the Orlocks. That's the only difference."

"So? The last time I checked, that was a good thing."

"The Guardian said that after Teanna tried to kill me, the machine made some kind of adjustment. That's part of what the echo is—a 'safeguard,' he called it."

Collin folded his arms across his chest and waited for Mathew to finish. But it was a while before the voice trailed off. After several seconds, Mathew shook his head in annoyance.

"It's right there and I can't get a hold of it," he said.

"Just relax," said Collin, squeezing his shoulder. "It'll come to you when you least expect it. Right now we need to get moving before your friends really do show up. You or me?"

"Me," said Mathew. "I'm thinking that maybe the echo will have some effect on the ward."

"All right. I'll stay down here and anchor the rope. Are you sure about this?"

Mathew nodded and took the coil of rope from Collin and put it over his shoulder. He unbuckled his sword, placed it on the ground, and started to climb. The knob of rock jutting out above him looked a long, long way off.

"You're doing fine," Collin called up. "Just keep concentrating."

After five minutes Mathew's shoulders were aching badly and sweat was running down his back. The chimney narrowed quickly, which made it difficult to maneuver freely. The overhang was still fifty feet away.

*Don't let go of a foothold until you have a solid handhold,* he told himself.

As time passed he began to measure his progress in inches. He looked up. *Thirty feet to go.* The walls were barely four feet apart now, so close he could almost put his foot on one side and brace himself against the other.

*What do I do once I get there?* he asked himself.

If he couldn't get over the knob and find a place to anchor the rope, there was no way he could lower himself down to the door. His hands were raw from the surface of the rock. It was cool to the touch. He put his cheek against it and took a second to rest.

"C'mon, Mat, you can do it," Collin called up.

Mathew wanted to answer him but didn't have the strength. Faces of friends and family came and went in his mind: his father, Giles Naismith, Captain Donal, Rodney Blake, Daniel, and so many others. They urged him forward. He was now directly under the knob. In years to come he could never quite remember how he had gotten there. The rock stuck out above his head and effectively blocked him from going any farther.

"Is there anyplace you can tie the rope?" Collin yelled up to him.

Mathew was so exhausted he could only shake his head.

"All right, find a handhold and pull yourself up to the

top. There's bound to be something up there, but take a moment and get your strength before you try it."

Mathew braced his back against the wall, wedged both feet against the opposite wall waiting for his heart rate to come down. He glanced up at the rock and found encouragement for the first time. There were enough cracks in the surface for him get his hands in, though once he did, there was no going back. He would be hanging in midair with only the strength of his fingers to support him. He waved to Collin, letting him know that he was ready.

*Here we go.*

Mathew pushed himself off the wall and twisted around so he was looking directly up at the overhang. He tried to swallow, but his mouth was dry. One deep breath . . . two deep breaths, and . . . with a sudden heave of his legs he thrust himself outward. A brief moment of panic seized him before his fingers found a tiny opening. Biceps, arm, and back muscles tensed, and with all the strength he had left he began to pull himself upward. Some part of his mind was aware that he probably looked ridiculous hanging there with his long legs. One more thrust upward and he found the next handhold. Inch by inch his upper body moved higher until at last he lay on the lip of the overhang.

"I'm up," he croaked.

Seventy-five feet below, Collin sagged to the ground in relief and took a deep breath. "Are you all right?"

Mathew gave an exhausted wave, though Collin couldn't see it.

"Mat?"

"I'm fine. Give me a moment. I'm going to tie the rope off and start lowering myself down as soon as I can breathe again."

Above his head the chimney continued on, growing progressively more narrow until it ended at the ceiling. Surprisingly, the base of the knob was covered in coarse sand. Mathew secured the rope around a small boulder, tested it a few times, then picked up a handful of sand and stuck it in his pocket.

"I'm coming down now," he called out.

He shuffled to the side of the knob and tossed the rope over, then flexed his fingers a few times. They felt stiff and his shoulders hurt. Mathew took a deep breath, placed the rope behind his back, and began to lower himself.

When he was five feet above of the door, he took half the sand out of his pocket and sprinkled it down. The moment it made contact with the ward it produced a series of sparkles that lit up the surrounding rock. The part closest to the door, however, fell straight through.

"The gap looks wide enough," he said to Collin.

"Did you remember to bring a key or a good pry bar?"

Mathew lowered himself a little farther.

He had no idea if the echo would open the door. If it didn't, he wasn't sure what he would do now. The closer he got, the more the sensation grew, building throughout his body. He could feel the ring now.

Hanging suspended from the rope, he scanned the door from top to bottom for a lock. There were only heavy oak planks with iron bands reinforcing them. There wasn't even a handle.

"There's no lock," he said.

"There has to be. Look closer."

"I'm telling there's nothing here."

"Well, wave your arms at it," Collin said. "Do something magic."

"Do something magic," Mathew muttered. He turned back to the door and concentrated, drawing on the echo.

"Open."

Nothing.

Mathew expelled a breath. "Please, open."

Still nothing.

For the next few minutes he tried saying the word in the old tongue, in Cincar, and even backward. Nothing worked.

"All right, Teanna," he said, to himself, "what did you do to the door?"

To his surprise, the moment he spoke her name there was a faint click and the door moved several inches. Mathew blinked, looked at Collin, and got a thumbs-up sign in response.

Slowly, carefully, Mathew slid down the rope until he could reach the top of the door. Despite its weight, it swung open with only the slightest pressure on his part. Careful to avoid contact with Teanna's ward, he eased himself down, dropped onto the threshold, and looked in.

# 49

## Tyraine

JUST BEFORE DAWN, FORTY SENNIAN SHIPS OF WAR MADE landfall under the rocky cliffs ringing the Tyraine harbor. Gawl d'Atherny stood on the quarterdeck of the flagship *Reliant* and pulled his cloak tighter to keep the chill out. Fog covered the water like a shroud and light rain was falling. It promised to be a dismal, overcast day.

Edmund Bain, the ship's captain, stood next to the king. He was a slender man whose sharp blue eyes missed nothing, at least where his ship was concerned. Now fifty-two, he had been in the Sennian navy for forty years. After receiving his orders, he had drilled his crew day and night to master their use of the cannons. Though far from satisfied with their progress, Bain was ready to concede that the men were proficient enough for what his king intended.

The night before, the entire fleet had dropped anchor in a northern cove. And there Gawl met with the ships' captains while Bain dispatched a sloop to gather what information it could on the whereabouts of Coribar's fleet. An hour earlier the sloop had returned. It appeared the enemy had spent the day disembarking its Vargothan and Orlock allies, the same group that had attacked the abbey and murdered the priests. They were gone, the sloop's captain reported, but the ships were still there, reprovisioning.

"Does everyone have their orders?" Gawl asked.

"They do, your highness," said Bain.

Gawl nodded and looked down at the black cannon next to them. "Filthy thing," he remarked.

"The world is changing, your highness," Bain replied. "I don't like these things any better than you do, but it will be a lopsided battle without them."

Gawl nodded. "I'm no sailor, Edmund. You'll need to get me close. I'd like to have a few words with Terrence Marek."

"I'll try. The latest report said he's in their temple near the heart of the city. It won't be easy."

Gawl looked across the water and squinted. "What happened at the abbey was not an act of religious or political difference," he said quietly. "It was murder and perversion, nothing more. I respect the beliefs of all men. They can worship rocks and trees if they want to, but no one has the right to kill.

"Have your ship land me farther up the coast. Once the fighting starts, my guess is that Marek won't risk returning to his ship. He'll make a run for it inland, toward Vargoth. If he does, there's only one road he can take."

"Your majesty—"

"Those are my orders, Edmund. I'll take fifty men with me. You can select them. We'll meet at Victoria Point tomorrow. None of those ships are to reach the open sea. Do you understand me?"

"Yes, your majesty," the captain replied.

Two hundred fifty miles away, the other half of the Sennian army, under the command of Arteus Ballenger, was emerging from the mountain passes northwest of Tyraine. Advance scouts reported that the enemy had camped for the night at a place called Catera Valley. There was nothing but heavy forest between them.

As much as he wanted to press on, Ballenger knew that his men needed rest. He had pushed them hard and they were exhausted. Reluctantly, he gave the order to make camp. Four hours would have to suffice. In a war, he knew, that battles tended to have a cumulative effect. Some were more critical than others, which was only to be expected.

If the Vargothans and Orlocks were expecting reinforcements at Stewart Vale, they were going to be sorely disappointed. He would see to that.

An hour later Ballenger walked with his junior officers, and spoke with the men, giving a word of encouragement here and there. Judging from their faces, they seemed relaxed. Most knew what was at stake and were grimly determined.

Earlier, the scouts had reported seeing a number of cannons in the Vargothan camp. That was something else they would have to deal with. In the interest of speed, he had been forced to abandon their own cannons. The breeches had been spiked and barrels mortared so that if the enemy ever found them they would be useless.

Despite the fact that they were at the base of the foothills, it was an unusually mild night. Tomorrow would be an interesting day, he thought.


Farther north, Darius Val, Kalifar of the Five Tribes of Bajan, waited for Delain and his delegation to arrive. The Durens and Teanna d'Elso were there already. She looked as beautiful as her mother always had, and they looked sullen and unhappy.

Val was a man just above middle height, whoses head was shaven. As a matter of personal choice, he had never embraced the traditional head-covering the rest of his countrymen wore. Eric and Armand Duren were directly across the table from him. He knew them by reputation, but he had never met either one until earlier that morning. Delain was yet to arrive.

For the first time in six hundred years Bajan and Elgaria were about to become allies. Since the war had ended four years ago, his primary goal had been to maintain his country's neutrality and avoid being pulled into the problems of the West or the plots of the East. That also was about to come to an end.

He sighed inwardly.

For Vargoth and Coribar to have sided with the creatures against their own kind was madness. Could the fools not see that once you had a lion by the tail you could never let go? Avarice and greed were the most deadly of combinations.

The Nyngary princess was at the end of the table, and their eyes met briefly before she turned away. Having known her mother and uncle, Val wanted as little to do with their family as possible. Still, it was the girl who had proposed the meeting. Such foresight was unusual in the young. After studying the matter from all angles, he agreed that if Alor Satar were to fall, it would only be a first step. The Orlocks would not stop there, nor would the fanatics of Coribar's church. The danger they presented was insidious. It was not land or riches that their church wanted. Their goal was simplicity itself—abandon your beliefs and think as we do.

Like Ra'id al Mouli before him, Darius Val was a religious man. Though a soldier by training, he was also a scholar and not inclined to give up his right of free thought. They would deal with Coribar soon enough, providing any of them survived the coming battle.

An announcement by the majordomo turned everyone's head toward the door. Val got up and went to greet the newest arrival.

Delain was dressed as a plain soldier. Perhaps this was appropriate, Val thought, because the ultimate ownership of his country was still up in the air. The Durens might well be willing to renounce their claim, but it was unlikely that Vargoth and the Orlocks were as charitably disposed.

"Forgive my keeping you waiting, Kalifar," Delain said, placing a hand over his heart and bowing in the traditional manner of Bajan.

Val bowed in return and then embraced Delain, kissing him on both cheeks. "Welcome to my home. I am pleased that you arrived safely, my lord."

"Thank you."

"I trust that you already know Teanna d'Elso, Crown Princess of Nyngary, who is here as her father's representative."

Delain started to bow, but Teanna surprised him and everyone else in the room by putting out her hand. They shook, and like Val, she kissed him on both cheeks. Eric and Armand were the last to get up. Each offered their hand, and to Delain's credit he took them, after the smallest of pauses.

Val gestured for everyone to be seated and called for more wine and fruit to be brought in.

"I am glad that we could all assemble today," he said. "The reports we've been getting are ominous." He turned to Armand. "Perhaps you could enlighten us further?"

Armand took a drink and set the goblet down on the table. "Our forces have suffered two major defeats in the last week. For safety, our people have been pulled back to Kolb Ferry, where we are dug in. From the information Teanna has been able to provide and from what our scouts have brought back, we believe the next attack will come very soon. Cincar and Sibuyan are sending reinforcements, but even with the addition of their people it is unlikely we will prevail."

There was silence in the room.

"Nyngary's border garrisons should arrive in three days," Teanna said.

Armand smiled. "Even another thirty thousand men will make little difference. The Orlocks are simply too numerous. We had better than two hundred cannons at Epps Crossing and the advantage of an elevated position. It made no difference."

Val folded his arms across his chest and sat back. "Bajan will enter the war with each of the five tribes contributing twenty thousand men."

"And I will be there," Teanna added. "I was too late to meet Shakira at the last encounter; she went into hiding immediately after the battle."

"Gawl is moving north from Sennia and James is swinging around the top of Elgaria to join us," Delain said, speaking for the first time. "As soon as they arrive we can begin our offensive, assuming we are all in agreement."

Eric leaned forward, resting his elbows on the table. "I appreciate that, Delain. What's your price?"

If the question surprised Delain, he recovered quickly. "I hadn't thought to put a price on the survival of the human race. To be blunt, I have more reason to hate your family than anyone here, but I'm willing to put that aside. As your cousin said, we must all pull together, or be pulled apart."

An amused smile played at the corners of Eric's mouth. "But surely you want a little something out of this for the help you're so generously offering."

Delain's face turned to stone and he started to rise.

"Stop," Teanna snapped, looking hard at Eric. "My cousin likes to play games. Unfortunately, this is not the time or place for that. Alor Satar agrees to relinquish any and all claims on Elgaria forever. They will do whatever is necessary to help you secure your borders against Vargoth *and* the Orlocks. Nyngary will lend whatever support may be required, as will Cincar and the Sibuyan. In return, Elgaria's forces and those of Sennia and Mirdan will ally with us to repulse the pending threat.

"Have I stated it correctly, cousin?"

Eric gave her a sour look. "I suppose so."

"Prior to your arrival," she said to Delain, "I asked the Kalifar to have his scribes prepare the necessary papers to seal the treaty."

Delain glanced at Val, who nodded in reply. He then turned to Armand. "And you're prepared to support this?"

Several seconds passed before Armand pushed his chair back from the table and stood up, extending his hand to Delain. "We have an accord."

There was almost and audible sigh of relief around the room. Even Eric managed a smile and shook Delain's hand. While the documents were being signed, Val asked Teanna if there had been any news of Mathew.

She shook her head. "I have my people scouring Corrato for him, but there's been no word yet."

"An interesting young man," Val said. "I should very much like to meet him again."

"As would I," Teanna replied.

## 50

## The Cave at Rivalin

IT TOOK A MOMENT FOR HIS EYES TO BECOME ACCUS-
tomed to the dark. There was just enough illumination
from Collin's light stick. The room was small and square
and had seemingly been carved out of the rock itself.
Mathew's brows came together. In the center was a large
oblong object at least six feet in length. It looked very
much like a crypt, except it was made of glass rather than
limestone. Curious, he moved closer and saw a dark shape
inside.

*What in God's name is that?*

A second later the answer became apparent. The shape
was that of a woman. Mathew stared at her for several seconds and could detect no sign of her breathing. It was impossible to tell her age.

*Young*, he thought. *Perhaps in her late forties.*

Nevertheless, something about her profile was familiar.

"Mat, are you all right?" Collin called out, startling him.

"I'm okay, but there's someone else in here."

*"What?"*

"It's the body of a woman. I don't think she's dead,
though."

Collin threw his hands up. "Just find the damn ring and
let's get out of here."

Mathew nodded and looked around the room. Except
for the crypt, it was quite empty. Since there didn't seem to
be any other place for the ring to be hidden, he grimaced

and pushed the lid aside. He had definitely seen the woman before, but *where*? Her face was beautiful, framed by a mass of dark hair.

*She's definitely not dead,* he thought.

Mathew swallowed and cautiously touched her shoulder. There was no response. He placed his fingertips against her cheek, thinking she might wake up, but again nothing happened. The skin was cold.

*So odd,* he said to himself. *What's she doing in this godforsaken place?* He took a step back and looked at the rest of her. The moment his eyes came to rest on her hand, his question was answered. A rose gold ring on the third finger of her right hand glinted dully in the light. He suddenly knew where he had seen her. It had only been one time and quite by accident, as a result of his first experiments with his ring. He was looking at Teanna's mother, Marsa d'Elso.

Mathew's heart was thumping so hard in his chest he was certain Collin could hear it out in the cave.

*Get out,* his brain shouted.

"Mat, are you all right?" Collin called again.

It took a moment for Mathew to find his voice. "Yes," he said, but it only came out as a hoarse whisper. "Yes," he said back a second time.

"Is it there?"

"I don't know yet. I'm looking now."

The thought of touching Marsa paralyzed him. If she woke up, she would kill him in an instant. Seconds ticked by, how long he couldn't say, but somehow he managed to make his hand move.

Her arms were folded across her chest in a state of repose. He carefully lifted her right wrist. There was a second ring resting beneath her palm. His eyes flicked to Marsa's face then back to the ring. He stared at it, not believing what he was seeing. Holding his breath, he reached out and took it.

The familiar shiver coursed through his arm the moment his fingers came into contact with the rose gold. Gently, he placed Marsa's hand back in its original position. Mathew squeezed his eyes shut and clutched the ring to his chest. Seconds passed. They turned into a minute and then another as he stood there, immobile. He was so giddy he wanted to laugh. Collin's voice eventually pulled him back to reality.

"Have you found it yet?"

"Give me a moment."

He pushed the lid back into place and put the ring on. Teanna was bad enough, he thought, but the prospect of having to fight both mother and daughter sent a shiver up his spine. He was thinking about that when separate images of Shakira and Teanna flashed into his mind.

*You fool,* he nearly screamed.

He'd completely forgotten about blocking them. Furious, at his his own stupidity, he shut his mind to further contact.

*Well, congratulations, Mathew. There's no question they know you're alive now. Why didn't you just send them a letter?*

Halfway to the door the answer came to him. However brief, his image of Teanna had been, it was clear and bright. She was sitting in a room somewhere with four other men. Shakira's vision, however, was dark and shadowed, and there was rock behind her, as if she was standing in a . . . *cave.*

"Collin, they're here!" he yelled.

Collin spun around, drawing his sword in time to see Shakira and two of the creatures literally step out of a rock wall twenty feet from him. Mathew came to a skidding halt at the threshold—Teanna's ward was still there. He had no idea how she had created it or how it worked and there was nothing he could do to remove it.

"Get out of here," he yelled to Collin.

It was now obvious why Shakira had hidden herself. It

was unlikely that she could harm him, but she could certainly hurt his friends and family. The creatures advanced on Collin, their weapons drawn.

"We didn't come here to hurt you," Mathew shouted. "Leave him alone!"

The Orlock queen said something to the creatures he couldn't hear and they stopped. Both stood there glowering at Collin, who wisely backed away and put some distance between them. Shakira glanced at him and then looked at Mathew.

"You cannot pass through the ward, Lewin," she said. "You will have to return the way you came."

"Will you give me your word not to hurt him?"

There was a brief delay before Shakira answered. "Come," she said, gesturing with her fingers. "You have my word."

Mathew reached for the rope, but then stopped. "Or me?" he added.

"Or you."

Mathew stood there, uncertain what to do.

"Orlocks do not lie, human."

He wasn't so sure about that, but there didn't seem to be much choice in the matter. They could continue to stare at each other, or he could try and find a way out of their predicament.

"You need only climb to the top of the ward. I will create a bridge for you," Shakira told him.

Out of nowhere a stone bridge appeared, spanning the chasm. Mathew pulled himself up and tested it with his foot. It seemed solid enough, so he put his other foot down and crossed over. The bridge promptly disappeared.

He half expected to be attacked as soon as he reached the opposite side, but nothing happened. The Orlocks were still where they were and Collin still had his sword out.

"Thank you," Mathew said. "My name is—"

"Mathew Lewin. Yes . . . I know who you are."

"And you're Shakira. I'm pleased to meet you." He

knew it sounded stupid, but he didn't know what else to say under the circumstances, particularly to an Orlock.

"Are you indeed?" Shakira asked.

"Actually, I am. I've had so many dreams about you and this cave," Mathew told her, looking around him. "I feel like we know each other."

A frown appeared on Shakira's face at the mention of the word *dream*, but it disappeared just as quickly. "It's always good to meet an old friend," she replied with a smile that had no warmth in it.

Mathew chose to ignore the sarcasm. "I know you hate us—humans, I mean—but it wasn't always like that. A long time ago we worked together. I've seen the Emerald Cavern—Taritna, your people call it. I've also seen the floating pictures of what my ancestors did to yours. It was monstrous, and I'd change it if I could, but the fact is, I can't. We don't want to hurt you. I give you my word."

Shakira seemed to find that amusing. "Your word of honor?"

"I can't speak for everyone," Mathew said, "but Collin I don't hate you and most people I know don't, either. They're just afraid of you."

"They have good reason to be afraid."

"Fine. They have good reason. What is it you want?"

"I want you to turn your ring over to me. Do it and I will let you live."

Mathew's eyebrows went up in surprise. "Just like that?" he said. "Turn over the ring and have a pleasant day. I'm able to protect myself, Shakira, and my friend, too, if necessary. I'm not going to simply hand my ring to you."

"Your ring by accident."

"Accident or not, it makes no difference," Mathew replied. "It's in my possession now and I'm not giving it up. Isn't it possible for people to live in peace? What happened three thousand years ago was something we had nothing to do with."

"Peace is an interesting word coming from you, human," said Shakira. "You are responsible for the deaths of hundreds of my children at the town of Tremont, in Elberton, and in the Elgarian Woods."

Mathew's temper rose. "That wasn't something I wanted," he said. "They were coming to kill us. I was only trying to protect myself and my friends. Look, we can argue about this until the sun stops moving, but it won't change a thing. I'm not giving the ring up and I doubt that you have the power to take it, so I ask again, what is it you want?"

"An arrangement," Shakira replied. "You said you want to live in peace—so be it. Your friend can go free, as can your wife and the companions traveling with her. *You*, however, will remain with us."

The expression on Mathew's face at the reference to Lara made Shakira smile.

"Yes, Orlocks are not nearly as stupid as you think. We have been watching this area for some time and we knew the moment you arrived. The priest and the two women are now our . . . *guests*. If you would like to see them again, I suggest you cooperate. At a word from me, they will be killed, along with your son and all the other humans in your village."

"Don't listen to her, Mat," said Collin. "She's trying to trick you."

Shakira's gray eyes shifted to Collin for a second before settling on Mathew again. In reply, she reached into the pocket of her dress, pulled something out, and tossed it to him. Mathew recognized the object at once—the necklace he'd given Lara on her birthday years ago. It was something she wore constantly.

"The choice is yours," Shakira said. "The time of the humans on this world is at an end. You may delay the future, but you will not stop it. You will accompany me back to Taritna. There, I will link your ring with mine. Once the war is done, the remainder of your race will be removed to the Wasted Lands. They can stay there forever as far as we're concerned. The less we have to do with you, the better. I will have your answer now."

"Well, here's *my* answer," said Collin. And without warning he pulled his dagger from his belt and threw it at the Orlock.

Shakira did no more than glance at it and the dagger disappeared into thin air.

"Stop," Mathew said quietly, hold up his hand.

Collin stared at him in disbelief. "You're not thinking of doing what she says, are you? You can't trust an Orlock. She's bluffing."

"Maybe," Mathew said quietly, before he turned back to Shakira. "I need more time to think about this. Showing me a necklace doesn't prove anything. You could have made a duplicate, for all I know. I'll need to see my wife and her companions for myself. Where are they?"

"They were seized by my people and are unharmed. You may look if you wish."

Her plan was clear now. By linking their rings together she could control both and double her power. Not even Teanna would be able to stand against her. He desperately needed more time. Mathew fixed the image of Lara in his mind and concentrated.

"It's no good," he said after a several seconds. "That's something I've never been able to do. All of the rings are slightly different, and mine doesn't work that way. I want to see them in person. You can block me if you want. I won't do anything to stop you."

That surprised the Orlock, nevertheless, she nodded to the creatures and they withdrew into the shadows.

"I will meet you at the bottom of the hill, Lewin."

The moment they were alone, Collin spun on Mathew. "Are you out of your mind?" he snapped. "If you let her block you the way Duren did, you'll be defenseless."

"It's already done," said Mathew. "She can maintain it only as long as she keeps her concentration intact."

"And then what? She might have a hundred Orlocks

down there waiting for us. What are we supposed to do, challenge them to a name-calling contest?"

"I need to see that Lara, Ceta, and Father Thomas are all right," Mathew whispered fiercely. "Just follow my lead and stop arguing."

## 51

## Tyraine

THE PATH UP THE HILL HAD RARELY BEEN USED. IT WAS narrow and barely wide enough to accommodate two men at a time. Gawl and Colonel Haynes were in the lead with forty-eight fully armed soldiers behind them.

Gawl pulled the watch from the pocket of his vest and looked at it. "Sunrise in half an hour," he whispered to Haynes.

The old colonel nodded and pointed ahead of them. Less than a mile away the gold dome of Coribar's church rose up, unmistakable against the city's skyline. So far they had been lucky. Gawl knew little about the sleeping habits of Orlocks nor did he have any idea where in the city they now lived. He and his men were on the outskirts of Tyraine, close to where the coast road began.

It was eerie to look down at the buildings and see no lights. Only the church showed any signs of life. Still, the scouts had reported seeing Orlocks there earlier that day.

The king raised his hand. If everything went according to plan, Edmund Bain would be bringing the ships into position in approximately thirty minutes and the attack would begin. It had been several years since he'd visited Tyraine, but he remembered the city's layout well enough. Nearby were a number of houses. He didn't know whether they were inhabited, because the scouts had been unable to get close enough to find out. That information was now imperative. As much as he wanted Terrence Marek dead, he was not willing to throw his men away in a foolhardy attempt to reach him.

"Haynes," he whispered, "I want you to take five men and set fire to those houses down below us. We'll wait ten minutes and see if any rats come out of their nests."

Haynes nodded and disappeared into the dark with his men. The rain had turned into a cold blowing spray that penetrated the bones. Gawl wiped his face and motioned to the rest of his men. Silently, they moved off toward the nearest home and waited. Their wait was short-lived.

Less than five minutes later the first tongues of flame could be seen coming from the houses four streets below them. Then the shouting started as Orlocks ran from their dwellings carrying buckets of water. Gawl waited a while longer, observing. There were no signs of movement along the street they were on.

*So far so good,* he thought. *The creatures haven't come up this far yet.*

Two minutes later Colonel Haynes and his men reappeared.

"Good work," Gawl said. "It looks like we'll have a clear shot from here. Take half the men and move to the other side of the street. In five blocks you'll come to a large plaza with a fountain in the middle. Three streets run into it. The one on the extreme right leads you up to the temple. If I should fall, do whatever you have to, but make sure Marek doesn't leave there alive. You'll need to find your way back to the coast road and from there to Victoria Point. If everything goes well, Bain will be waiting to take you off."

"*Us* off," Haynes corrected. The colonel turned to go, but Gawl put a hand on his shoulder.

"Thank you for always being there, Shelby."

In the dim light the old man smiled. Seconds later he was gone.

The trip to the temple lasted less than ten minutes, but

they were the longest of Gawl's life. Shortly after they had started up the street a series of explosions could be heard coming from the harbor. From their vantage point he saw the Sennian ships moving in two lines toward Coribar's fleet, which still lay at anchor. At the head of each line was a fire ship.

The forts at either end of the harbor responded quickly. Cannonballs streaked across the sky, joined moments later by the catapults. Thus far all the shots had fallen short, but that wouldn't last long. Trumpets were blowing near the city center and there was a great deal of activity going on down at the docks as the Coribar ships tried to get under way. Gawl had no more time to spare. His business was at the temple. Priests were coming outside to see what the commotion was about.

Gawl had never laid hands on a priest in his life, and part of him recoiled at the idea now. Possibly these were innocent men and possibly they were not. He didn't know the answer, and circumstances weren't going to permit him time to dwell on it. The fury of battle rose in his chest. Quite probably he would go to hell for what he was about to do, but so be it. At his signal, the archers on both sides of the street opened up.

Gawl rose to a low crouch and sprinted for the church door, fifteen yards ahead of the nearest man. Two white-robed priests who weren't cut down in the initial flight of arrows ran back inside and were attempting to bar the door when he hit it with his shoulder. Though made of heavy bronze, the door flew backward, knocking one of the men unconscious. The other produced a pike from somewhere and charged.

Gawl easily parried his attack and could have killed the priest, whose back was now exposed. Instead, a blow from his fist knocked the man senseless.

Colonel Haynes and two other men joined him, stepping over the priests' bodies. The other soldiers flooded into the temple from the side doors.

"Is everyone all right?" Gawl asked.

"Sire," one of the soldiers answered, pointing toward the altar.

Gawl turned and looked.

There, at the front of the temple, were three more priests. The one in the center was elderly and completely bald.

"You have come to do murder in God's house," Terrence Marek called out. "Put up your weapons and leave this place at once."

The soldier nearest Gawl notched an arrow, raised his bow, and would have fired, had Gawl not stopped him. "Marek, you will come with us."

The Archbishop stayed where he was. "I know you, Gawl d'Atherny. You will never leave this place alive. The Lord protects his followers and his retribution shall be swift and terrible."

"No doubt," Gawl replied. "We can debate the matter when we meet Him, but right now you're coming with us."

Both of the priests immediately stepped in front of Marek, drew their daggers and started down the steps toward Gawl. Neither reached the bottom. At a gesture from Colonel Haynes, the soldiers fired, killing them both. Marek hardly glanced at them. Instead, he reached into the pocket of his robe and produced a glass cylinder approximately six inches long. It was filled with a black liquid. Before he could throw it, four arrows in succession buried themselves in Marek's chest. A puzzled look appeared on Marek's face and he took a step forward, then slowly collapsed to his knees and fell over onto his side. The vile shattered on the floor and the liquid changed into a yellow-tinged mist that began to spread and creep down the steps.

"*Poison!*" Haynes shouted. *"Don't breathe in the fumes, sire!"*

Foam and spittle filled Marek's mouth. A second later convulsions racked his body. One of his hands, claw-shaped, reached out toward Gawl.

*"Out!"* Haynes ordered. *"Everyone out, now!"*

Whether Terrence Marek died from the arrows or from the thing he had just released inside the church, Gawl never knew. He felt no joy at his passing, only a grim determination to rid the land of the other pestilence that was inhabiting it.

"Get the men together, Shelby," he said, speaking to the colonel. "We go to Victoria Point and on to Stewart Vale."

"And then?" Haynes asked.

Gawl looked down the hill toward the bay. The Cincar ships were burning and it looked like the lower portion of the city nearest to the docks was also on fire.

"And then we end this," he said.

# 52

## Outside Rivalin

THE MOMENT MATHEW REALIZED THAT SHAKIRA WAS IN the cave, he understood the nature of the trap she had set, and his thoughts immediately turned to Lara, Father Thomas, and Ceta. They were the real targets, not Collin or him. In the fleeting seconds before he closed his mind, he saw the Orlocks take his wife and friends as soon as they crossed the stone bridge.

His choices then were simple: go to their aid and lose Collin, or stay and try to find a way out of their predicament. It was unlikely the Orlocks would harm them, because they were more useful as hostages.

By letting Shakira block his access to the ring he had done two things: The Orlock queen would believe she had won, or was about to, and he had gained additional time so he could explain his plan to Collin. He only hoped the creatures didn't look under the bridge.

Shakira and her two Orlocks were waiting for them at the bottom of the hill. In daylight she looked even taller than she had in the cave and a great deal older. He had heard that Orlocks didn't live very long, but she was obviously the exception. Her skin had a translucent quality and it seemed to be stretched across her skull.

She watched them approach, unblinking. The expression on her face was enough to tell Mathew how hard she was concentrating to maintain the block. Neither said anything to the other as he passed, In fact, Shakira barely seemed to notice him at all.

"This path will take you to the bridge, humans," the nearest Orlock rasped. "We will follow behind you."

The path was not in the best condition. For the first half hour they descended down the hillside into a forested valley. Through the trees Mathew occasionally caught glimpses of the stone bridge, at least a mile off.

It soon became clear that Shakira was having difficulty negotiating the trail. Several times Mathew and Collin found themselves having to wait for the Orlocks to catch up.

From what he could tell, the path would emerge into an open area, with the bridge about a hundred yards beyond that, and spanning a deep river gorge. He didn't know the river's name.

"There's the bridge," Collin said. "And there's Lara, Father Thomas, and Ceta."

"With three Orlocks," Mathew added. "Do you still have your pipe?"

"Sure, but—"

"Let me borrow it, would you?"

Collin looked at Mathew like he'd taken leave of his senses. Nevertheless, he pulled the pipe out of the pocket of his vest and handed it to him. "When did you start smoking?"

"I didn't," Mathew said. "As soon as we get to the bridge I'm going to slow down to light this. I want you to keep going, and whatever you do, *don't stop.* Do you know anything about black powder?"

"Only what I've heard."

"It makes a hell of a bang, and when it does, you don't want to be anywhere around. There's a keg of it under the base of the bridge right now."

"That's impossible."

"No, it's not," Mathew said. "I created it and placed it there once I knew what Shakira had in mind. They were after Lara, Ceta, and Father Thomas all this time. That's why I let her block me."

Collin held Mathew's eye for a moment. "So what happens now?"

"I'm going to set it off. I don't know how long the fuse will burn; that's why you need to be off that bridge."

"You're a rather sneaky fellow, Mat Lewin. Has anyone ever told you that?"

"Several people, actually," Mathew replied, giving his friend a push to get him started.

Collin took two steps and stopped. "What about you?"

"I'll be fine. I've worked with black powder a hundred times. Just make sure you're on the other side thirty seconds from now."

As soon as Mathew reached the bridge, he stooped down and pretended to tie his bootlace. Collin continued on without him. Shakira and her Orlocks were at least fifty yards behind them. On the opposite end of the bridge the three creatures waited with Father Thomas, Lara, and Ceta.

Mathew stood up, walked to the side, and casually glanced down. Just beneath the foundation of the bridge was a trail of black powder. He couldn't see the keg, but he knew it was there. When he told Collin that he'd worked with black powder before, he omitted mentioning that his past experiences were with cannons and cannonballs; still, he judged the principles were about the same.

Shakira was forty yards away when Mathew took the tin of matches out of his pocket. He made a show of lighting Collin's pipe, though there was no tobacco in it, then casually dropped the match over the edge, praying it would stay lit. It did.

Twenty yards, Mathew broke into a trot and then a full sprint.

The explosion was deafening. Stone and dirt flew skyward and a hot blast of air all but lifted him off the ground. Arms and legs wheeling, he launched himself for the opposite bank as the bridge was blown to pieces. One minute it was there and the next it was gone. He hit the bank chest first, clawing for anything he could get a hold of. Lara dove to the ground and grabbed him by the back of his shirt.

Collin, who was ready for the explosion, charged directly at the stunned Orlocks, driving his sword through the nearest creature's stomach. It let out a terrible scream. Father Thomas grabbed its companion by the wrist and twisted outward sharply. The bone broke with a snap. He wrenched the sword from the creature's fingers and slashed backward. For one horrible moment a headless body swayed on its feet in a macabre dance before it collapsed to the ground.

The third Orlock finally realized what was happening and rounded on Ceta, its axe raised. The killing blow never arrived. Not knowing what else to do, she kicked it between the legs. The creature let out a grunt, its eyes going wide, and slowly sank to its knees. Collin clubbed it across the back of its skull and pushed it over the side of the hill.

He looked down for a moment and nodded his approval to Ceta.

In the meanwhile Father Thomas went to help Lara. They got Mathew up without difficulty. On the opposite bank Shakira and her two Orlocks were lying on the ground. Mathew couldn't tell if they were dead or simply unconscious as the the power flooded back into his body.

Collin explained what had just happened to the others while Mathew continued to stare at the opposite bank.

Lara went to join him. "Are they dead?" she asked.

Her presence jarred him back to the present and he kissed her cheek. "I don't know . . . maybe."

"Is everyone all right?" asked Father Thomas.

Lara and Ceta both nodded.

"I'm fine," Mathew answered over his shoulder.

"Why don't we talk while we're walking?" Collin suggested. He cupped his hands around his eyes and searched the surrounding countryside and hills. "I think we should get out of here before any more of her friends show up."

"Agreed," said Father Thomas. "This path appears to

head in the right direction. If we can get to the docks we should be able to book passage on a ship."

Lara had to tug on Mathew's elbow to get his attention again. He was still staring at the Orlock bodies on the opposite bank.

On the way into town Father Thomas filled Mathew and Collin in on what had happened to them. Six Orlocks took them by surprise.

"But there were only three when we got there," said Mathew.

"Father Thomas killed two," Lara told him. "And Ceta and I killed the other."

That nearly caused him to miss a step, and he looked from Lara to Ceta, only to be met by a pair of enigmatic smiles. It occurred to him that he might ask exactly how they had killed the Orlock, but he decided that his life would be just as rich if he didn't know.

The terrain flattened out quickly once they reached the valley floor, which enabled them to make better time. No one talked much during the trip, especially Mathew. He responded to Lara's questions with nods or one word answers.

The village of Rivalin was small enough so they had no trouble finding the tavern. As a precaution, Father Thomas sent Collin on ahead to make sure the way was clear before he let the others follow. Once there, they took a table in the corner of the common room.

While they were waiting for their food, Father Thomas leaned over and whispered to Mathew, "A word with you please, my son."

Mathew, preoccupied, seemed to notice Father Thomas for the first time. He pushed his chair back from the table and followed the priest.

Once they were outside, Father Thomas folded his hands across his chest and leaned back against the side of the building, tucking one leg up under him. "Are you all right, Mat? You seem distracted."

"I'm sorry, Father," Mathew replied. "I was just thinking—"

"About what happened back there. Yes, I know. It would have been wrong to kill a helpless enemy, even an Orlock."

Mathew looked at the priest sharply. "I don't have the luxury of always knowing I'm right. A lot of people are going to die because I didn't act."

Father Thomas looked down at his feet and smiled. "You'd be surprised how many times priests are wrong, my son. Am I correct that you believe Shakira survived the explosion?"

"She's alive. She regained consciousness a little while ago, and she's not in the best of moods."

"Pity. You're certain of this?"

Mathew nodded and stared at the street. It was small and unpaved and reminded him of the way Devondale used to be when he was growing up.

Father Thomas watched him for several seconds before he spoke again. "Mathew, you can no more change your nature than a river can change its course, or that horse over there can sprout wings and fly. You are the child of a good man and a good woman. Both were friends of mine and they raised you to be a certain way. Your life experiences have tempered this, but the mold was set a long time ago. Something that is morally wrong does not become right because circumstances seem to call for it."

"But—"

"*But* people will die, as you have said. That is unfortunate and tragic. A war is coming. That is also tragic. It would be more tragic still if the first casualty proved to be your soul. I'm proud that you stayed your hand when you could have struck. The end does not justify the means. It never will, my boy."

Mathew let out a long breath. "I'm going to have to fight her, and probably Teanna, too. I'm not sure I'm strong enough to manage it."

A strange look passed over Father Thomas's face at the mention of Teanna d'Elso, but it disappeared quickly.

"You will do what you must. That is all anyone can ask. As for fighting Teanna, let us deal with one situation at a time. You told me the Guardian said she has been instrumental in rallying the East and West to meet the Orlock threat. Perhaps we should keep an open mind where she is concerned."

"The last time I trusted her, she nearly killed me. I won't give her a second chance."

Father Thomas nodded. "Nor should you. Protect yourself first, of course. I only suggest that it is possible for people to change. If what we have heard about Teanna is true, this threat is one that faces all humans. I ask only that you look at things objectively."

"And how am I supposed to do that?"

"There's no easy answer to that question," said the priest. "I wish there were. You will have to judge for yourself. She is a very unusual young lady, so this is the best advice I can give: Her mother was a great influence on her in the past. As we both know, this is no longer the case. Perhaps she has learned something over the last four years."

They talked for several more minutes, but Mathew was still confused.

"Was this all that was bothering you?" asked Father Thomas.

"Not really."

"Would you like to talk about it?"

"No . . . yes. Father, even if Teanna doesn't try to kill me again, there's still the problem of the Orlocks. The Guardian said this war is for our survival. I think he was telling the truth. You said as much yourself a moment ago. I don't have the strength to fight them all. There are too many."

"Mat—"

*"Listen to me,"* Mathew said, taking a step toward the

priest. "He showed me things the Ancients did—that their weapons did—things that scared me. I admit that. Those weapons are still around. Did you know that? I don't . . . I don't want to use them."

It was several seconds before Father Thomas spoke. "Your father was my best friend, and he once told me that heroes and cowards are both afraid. The difference lies in how they deal with it."

"He told me the same thing and I'm no hero."

"Nor are you a coward, my son," Father Thomas said quietly, taking Mathew by the shoulders. "I have no question of this. You doubt yourself more than others do. When the time comes, and the decision is before you, you'll know it. Trust in yourself."

Mathew looked away. "Father, will you promise me something? If anything happens to me, will you take care of Lara and Bran if I'm not there to do it?"

The words struck at Father Thomas's heart. And he looked at the young man, but Mathew continued to stare down the street at nothing.

"I promise," said the priest, "but it will not come to that. In this you must believe."

There was still no answer.

"Let's go back inside now, Mat. The others will think we're lost."

"I'll be in in a little while."

Father Thomas's words usually helped to put things in perspective, but this time they didn't. Mathew thought about what the Guardian had shown him, and the contempt for his own weakness grew larger in his mind. He thought about Teanna d'Elso. Both the Guardian and Father Thomas had their own views on her, though where they were getting them from was a complete mystery to him. The simple fact was that she *had* tried to kill him. Moreover, she had manipulated Father Kellner in Sennia four years ago and was indirectly responsible for the deaths of at least three other people.

The whole business was confusing. People who were the enemies were now allies. *Sure, trust them*, he thought. *Maybe when the war was over they could all take in a play together.*

Mathew leaned against the post. So many balls were up in the air, it was difficult to tell which one to watch. He supposed the answers would come sooner or later. For him, it was just a matter of getting to the later part. After five minutes of considering the possibilities, nothing presented itself and he went back inside.

Almost as soon as he walked into the common room a man approached him. He was in his late forties, well-dressed, and appeared unarmed.

"Excuse me," he said. "Am I correct in that I'm addressing Mathew Lewin?"

Father Thomas and Collin got up and came over to join them.

"My name is Julian Tesh and I'm a member of his majesty, King Eldar's staff. Let me assure you that I mean you no harm. I apologize for not knowing who you are, young man," he said to Collin, "but I assume you are Father Siward Thomas."

"What is it you want?" asked Mathew.

"I have been instructed to invite you to the summer palace. His majesty is in residence and requests an interview with you."

"*Requests?*" Mathew said. It had been his experience that kings and princes generally did more telling than requesting.

"His majesty was very specific. If you decline to meet with him, no one will stop you from leaving. I pledge my word of honor on this."

Mathew looked at Father Thomas and then at Collin, who shrugged.

"How did you know we were here?" Father Thomas asked.

"We have been watching this area for the last month in

the hope that you would arrive. Unfortunately, we had no idea when that would be. The Princess Teanna would have been here herself, but she is detained in Bajan at the moment."

One of Mathew's eyebrows went up. "Really?"

"Yes," said Tesh. "The recent explosion was something of a giveaway. May I assume you are Mathew Lewin?"

There didn't seem much point in trying to carry out a charade, so Mathew simply answered, "I am."

He introduced Lara, Ceta, and Collin to Tesh, who appeared to be the very soul of courtesy. He bowed to the ladies and shook hands with the men.

"What is it King Eldar wants?" asked Father Thomas.

"Only to talk," Tesh assured him. "I don't know how well-informed you are, Father, but we are at war. One week ago waves of Orlocks and Vargothans attacked all along our western border. They killed nearly three thousand people before they were driven back. Similar battles are being fought in other countries. His majesty will fill you in on the details if you agree to come."

"And if we don't?" Collin asked.

"Then I will bid you good day."

Mathew searched the man's face and could see no sign of deceit there. A slight nod of Father Thomas's head was enough to seal the decision.

"We'll come," he said.

## 53

## Rivalin

TWELVE OAKS, THE SUMMER PALACE OF THE D'ELSOS, WAS a large compound built on a promontory which overlooked the town. A stone wall surrounded four separate buildings and the watchtowers in Mathew's dream. Other than being big, it reminded him more of a sprawling hunting lodge than a castle.

As he walked toward the main entrance he tried to recall what he had heard about Eldar d'Elso. The king was said to be an intellectual man in his late sixties who rarely involved himself in either politics or the day-to-day running of his country. According to what Teanna had told him, her father was content to leave those things to her mother, and then later to her. Though both women were intelligent and had strong personalities, it was an odd thing for a king to do, he thought. The d'Elsos had been in power for more than five hundred years, a difficult feat to accomplish under any circumstances, without strong leadership. He mentioned that to Father Thomas.

"Don't be deceived by Eldar's manner," the priest told him. "He may appear laconic, but he is an extremely intelligent man. What power Marsa had was only because he chose to permit it. I assume the same thing also applies to Teanna. He is content to let others lead because it suits him to do so."

It was a curious observation, and Mathew wondered how his friend had come to it. He knew of Father

Thomas's background, but once again it amazed him at how far reaching the priest's experiences were.

They found the king waiting for them in the great hall, and he did not fit the mental picture Mathew had formed of him. Eldar d'Elso was several inches shorter than Collin and easily thirty pounds overweight. He tried forming an image of this man and the statuesque Marsa d'Elso as being married to each other and couldn't. Nor could he imagine him as Teanna's father. Still, he had seen more unusual families in his time.

"Thank you for coming, Siward," Eldar said, addressing Father Thomas. "I bid you and your companions welcome to my home. I am Eldar d'Elso."

*Siward?* thought Mathew. He and Lara exchanged glances. Ceta must have reacted the same way, because the king turned to her and surprised everyone by bowing.

"I am informed that you are Siward's lady. Please accept my good wishes."

"Why, thank you," Ceta said, with a curtsey.

"And you are Mathew Lewin," he said, turning to Mathew. "I have heard a great deal about you from my daughter."

"Uh . . . yes, your majesty," Mathew replied. "May I present my wife, Lara Palmer . . . I'm sorry, I mean, Lara Lewin, and this is my friend, Collin Miller."

Eldar chuckled. "I made a similar mistake for a number of weeks after I was married. Marsa finally had a mug engraved with her name on it as a reminder. I am pleased to meet you both. Thank you all for coming. I understand that Julian interrupted your midday meal. Perhaps you'll join me in the dining room?"

It was not so much a question as a statement, because Eldar didn't wait for a reply. He nodded to Tesh, who promptly excused himself and disappeared through a doorway at the end of the hall. The king led, with the others trailing in his wake.

Their meal was a pleasant affair and Eldar a courteous

host. He asked a number of questions regarding the explosion and listened carefully when Mathew described what had happened in the cave.

"So, Shakira wanted to combine your ring with her own to use against my daughter and the human nations. Interesting."

"Yes, sir."

"You are an exceedingly resourceful fellow, Mathew, but I already knew that. I assume you noticed that your ring was not the only thing inside the cave."

"If you mean the crypt, yes I noticed it."

"And what was your reaction?"

"I was shocked," Mathew replied simply. "I had thought Marsa . . . your wife, was dead. I'm glad she isn't."

Eldar d'Elso leaned back and considered Mathew for a moment. "That's a strange thing for you to say. She tried to kill you, as did my daughter, and you say you're glad that she's not dead."

The topic made Mathew uncomfortable, but now that it was broached, he had no choice but to deal with it.

"I didn't want to kill your wife, sir. I didn't want to kill anybody, for that matter. Under the circumstances, the only choice I had was to protect myself. I'm very sorry if I caused you pain."

The king put the tips of his fingers together and leaned back in his seat. What he said next surprised not only Mathew, but everyone in the room.

"Marsa was insane, as was her brother. Oh, I don't mean that she howled at the moon, but insanity can take many forms. Ruling the world was something their grandfather drummed into their heads from the time they were little. It was an ill-conceived concept then, just as it is now."

Looks were exchanged around the table at the directness of the king's comments. Only Father Thomas sat quietly observing. Mathew stared down at the wine in his goblet.

"I meant what I said before, your majesty. I know Marsa's not dead, but she's not alive, either . . . at least not as far as I could tell. Is this the reason you brought us here?"

"I said that you are a resourceful young man, but you are also clever," said Eldar. "The answer is 'partly.' My wife would certainly be dead had it not been for Teanna's intervention at the last moment. Regardless, she suffered an injury to her brain that the doctors do not understand. These past years, Teanna has sought to find a cure for this ailment, though without avail. I would like you to help restore her if possible."

Mathew blinked. Of all the things he was prepared to hear, that was quite possibly the last one. The memory of a wall of fire a half mile wide and hundreds of feet high roaring at him flashed through his mind. Next were the thunderbolts and a ball of fire Marsa had created, which came hurtling down on Collin, Akin, and himself as they stood on the cliffs above Tremont. He realized that his mouth was open and he closed it, but before he could speak, Eldar continued.

"I am aware of what happened in Elgaria four years ago, and I am also aware of what transpired between you and my daughter in Sennia. Know that I would have prevented them if I could. The unfortunate fact is that they did happen.

"You would be completely justified in refusing me, and if you do, that will be the end of our discussion. Before you give me your answer, however, there is something else I must tell you.

*Wonderful*, thought Mathew. *He's going to tell me Karas Duren's stopping by for dinner.*

"Over the past few years my daughter has matured a great deal. She is still impetuous and has to work to control her temper. But the fact is, she *has* changed. Her focus has turned outward and she now looks for ways to improve the lot of our people. She has labored to improve conditions in this country, and I feel these are admirable things. Whether this mind-set was there all the time or is something she has learned with the passage of time, I do not know. Perhaps a combination of both."

Eldar darted a quick look at Father Thomas, but the priest showed no reaction, and he turned back to Mathew again.

"The world is now at war and Vargoth and Coribar have aligned themselves with the Orlocks. As we speak they are attacking Alor Satar, Cincar, Sibuyan, and our own country."

"We've heard this," Mathew said.

"Did you also know that Teanna has rallied the forces of the West and those of the East to repulse the threat? Since the war began she fought in a dozen battles. She will be here soon and I'm sure she'll have much more to tell you."

"You say she's coming here?" Mathew asked, surprised.

"I did," Eldar replied. "I would like you to give me your word that you will take no action against her. I am not asking this as a king, but as a father."

A storm of emotions assailed Mathew. He looked around the table and met Lara's eyes. She smiled at him.

"Your majesty, I had a similar talk with Father Thomas a short while ago," he finally replied. "I certainly don't want to fight a woman, but I'm not going to give her another chance to finish what she started. I want you to be clear on that."

"Understood. I just want you to hear her out."

"I'll listen."

Eldar d'Elso pushed his chair back from the table. "You have my gratitude. Now if you will all excuse me, I would like to speak with Father Thomas alone, with your permission, of course, ma'am," he added to Ceta.

If having a king ask her permission was a surprise to the

lady innkeeper, she managed to conceal it well enough. "Certainly," she said.

"You are all free to roam where you wish," Eldar told them. "Should you need anything, my staff will be happy to provide it."

# 54

## Stewart Vale, Alor Satar

A LONE RIDER CHARGED ACROSS THE VALLEY FLOOR ON
the border between Alor Satar and Elgaria, keeping his
horse close to the treeline. Nearly a full regiment of soldiers from Vargoth and two Orlock squads followed in hot
pursuit. The rider's face was caked with grime, and blood
ran down his left arm from the arrow shaft lodged in his
shoulder. His horse's flanks were flecked white with foam.
The rider was one of the few soldiers who wore glasses.

Since he had been taken by the mercenaries two years
earlier, Daniel Warren, late of Devondale township, had
served with the Vargothan intelligence unit. Like many of
his countrymen conscripted into the army, Daniel knew
about the war breaking out and was appalled to find that
Orlocks were Vargothan's new allies.

The mercenary commanders had made the fundamental mistake of assuming that higher pay for their men
would translate into higher loyalty. They were wrong.

The battle that had just been fought along the banks of
the Roeselar River resulted in another victory for the Vargothans. Hopelessly outnumbered, Delain's forces fought
bravely, but the end was never in question. All afternoon a
steady stream of riders came and went from the command
tent, bringing reports of what the enemy was doing and
where their main force were camped. Daniel was alone in
the tent when the last piece of intelligence was delivered.

The rider told him that Delain had assigned units of
the Elgarian militia to hold the northern flank under the

command of a man named Akin Gibb. The militia, he knew, were not regular soldiers, but farmers, merchants and shopkeepers from all across the country. The soldier also reported their scouts had discovered a path through the mountains that could bring them up behind Gibb and his men.

"Excellent," Daniel said, clapping him on the back. "Get something to drink and return to your regiment. I'll inform General Caspar at once."

The messenger only got two steps before his eyes bulged. Daniel clamped a hand over his mouth and held the dagger in place until he felt his knees collapse. He dragged the body to the back of the tent, upended one of the cots, and covered it. The soldier's horse was just outside the opening.

"Rider coming in!" one of the sentries called out.

Akin Gibb looked up from the map he was studying, picked up his farsighter and trained it toward the valley.

"There's a whole lot of folks after that fellow out in front," the sentry said.

Several other soldiers and officers stopped what they were doing to watch.

"What the hell's happening?" one of the officers asked.

Akin narrowed his eye and peered through the lens. They were moving so fast it was difficult to tell who the lead rider was, but there was something familiar about him.

"You men at the front lines get ready!" Thom Calthorpe yelled. "Cannoneers, you will fire on my command."

"Good Lord," Akin whispered, putting the farsighter down. "Hold your fire men!" he shouted. He started running toward the cannons. "Let that rider through. Thom, have the archers provide covering fire for him. That's Daniel Warren from our village."

Chunks of earth flew from the horses' hooves as they tore across the valley. Daniel's horse never broke stride approaching the Elgarian line. For one frozen moment it appeared to Akin that animal and rider were suspended in midair as it leapt the nearest cannon, causing the soldiers there to duck. He and another officer caught Daniel as he slipped from the saddle, and gently lowered him to the ground.

Daniel glanced at the farsighter hanging from Akin's neck and then up at his friend.

"Interesting invention," he said.

He managed to deliver the rest of his report before he lost consciousness.

Twenty miles to the south of where Akin and his men were camped, another report was being delivered to Armand Duren.

"My lord, the creatures have broken through our first line of defense. James of Mirdan is attacking their rear line and Delain is shifting his Fifth Battalion to meet them."

"Teanna?" Armand asked.

"Nearly spent, my Lord. The princess was magnificent. She managed to repulse the mercenaries' first three onslaughts, but there are simply too many. They came in waves along with the creatures. She is resting in her tent now."

"Darius Val?"

"The last word is that he is still a day's ride from here. Gawl and his men are two days behind him. The bulk of the Sennian army arrived several hours ago, but they are badly in need of rest."

Armand studied the map on his table. "Send word to General Krelco that the Second Army is to abandon their position on the heights and move all cannons to either side of Skeffington Pass. Tell him that they must be in place by nightfall. Sentries along the lines are to be doubled. We will have to hold until the reinforcements can arrive. If the Orlocks want us, this is where they'll have to come," he said, jabbing the map with his finger.

"Yes, my lord," the man said, saluting.

Armand turned to his brother as soon as they were alone. "Do you think our southern garrisons will be able to hold?"

"They'd better," Eric answered. "If the Orlocks get through, our position here is lost. They'll have a clear march to Rocoi."

Armand took a deep breath. "I'm going to see how Teanna is feeling."

"You understand what Seth and Shakira are trying to do?" Eric said, stopping him in the doorway.

"By initiating different actions along a hundred mile front, they force her to expend her energies. Each time, it takes longer and longer for her to recover. We *must* buy her time."

Armand raised his eyebrows, took a deep breath, then walked rapidly to Teanna's tent. The soldier stationed outside came to attention.

"Teanna?" Armand called out.

There was no answer.

"Teanna," he called again.

He moved the flap aside and stuck his head in. To his surprise, it was empty.

# 55

## Rivalin

MATHEW STOOD IN THE KING'S GARDEN LOOKING AT
Teanna's fountain, his hands clasped behind him. A breeze
passing threw the water pouring from the horses' mouths
created a spray that hung in the air. A short distance away,
Lara sat on a small stone bench watching her husband.
Eventually, she got up and came to his side.

"Do you want to talk?" she asked quietly.

"I'm sorry," he said. "I don't mean to be so distracted."

"I know."

"This whole business is very confusing."

"It's not really."

Mathew frowned and looked at her for an explanation.

"I only know what you've told me about Teanna and
what I've heard," Lara said, "but if the Guardian and her
father were telling the truth, it's possible that she's
changed. People grow up."

"I suppose so," Mathew said. "I'm a bit frightened of
her, that's all."

This time it was Lara's turn to be surprised. Taking his
hand, she led him back to the bench. His eyes had their faraway look again. Nearly a minute passed before he spoke.

"The rings don't make you invincible," he said. "If
Teanna hadn't gotten Armand to call off the attack at Ardon
Field, we'd have lost. It's as simple as that. Even Delain
says so. To this day I don't know why she did it. Do you
know what the Guardian told me?"

Lara shook her head.

"He said Shakira's army stands at one million . . . *one million*. And that doesn't count Vargoth and Coribar. I can't fight that many."

Lara finally understood. "Mathew, I married you because I love you. I also believe in you. When Father Kellner locked me up in the Emerald Cavern, I prayed that you would come for me, and you did. You were magnificent then, just as you were when you fought Karas Duren at Ardon Field. You're not alone.

"Our people aren't ready to hand the world over to the Orlocks and their friends. Bran deserves a chance to grow up. You can only do the best that you're able."

Mathew opened his mouth to reply, but never got the chance. The hum, which began softly and gradually grew got louder and a point of pure white light appeared out of nowhere hanging suspended in the air.

Mathew knew what it was at once and he got to his feet and stepped in front of Lara as the light expanded into a line and then grew into the shape of a rectangle.

Teanna d'Elso swayed on her feet and took a halting step toward him. "Mathew . . ."

He caught her before she fell.

Dinner passed largely in silence that night. Collin glanced at his friend several times and started to speak, but a look from Lara forestalled him. Father Thomas was equally distracted and spoke hardly at all. Eldar d'Elso sent his regrets at not being able to join them. The message was delivered by Julian Tesh, who told them that Teanna had still not regained consciousness. Her father and his physicians were with her. He also said that rooms had been prepared if they wished to stay the night.

Later, unable to sleep, Mathew lay awake in bed again. After two hours he gave up, dressed, and slipped out of the room. Lara opened her eyes as the door closed and considered going after him. It took an effort to stop herself from doing so.

Mathew knew he needed to walk. The corridors of the palace were narrow and he wasn't sure which way to go. After one turn he came to the balcony and double staircase that separated the guest quarters from those belonging to the royal family. The staircase led to the main hall and the dining room. An ornate gold clock on a table at the top of the stairs said it was two in the morning. He stood there for several minutes looking down at the hall before he decided to try the opposite direction.

At the end of the hall he turned and found himself in a different corridor with rooms on either side. A few pictures hung on the walls. One more turn brought him to still another corridor, where he stopped. Voices were coming from the room at the end.

Tone deaf he might be, but there was no mistaking Father Thomas's voice. The royal crest above the door told him the room belonged to Eldar d'Elso. Curious, Mathew moved closer and listened.

"I don't blame you, Siward," the king was saying. "I never have. Marsa's tastes always ran to younger men, and she knew children were important to me. I couldn't give them to her . . . and you weren't a priest then."

"Do you think she knows?"

"She knows. Marsa was very forthcoming with her daughter . . . in all things."

There was a pause.

"I thought as much," Father Thomas replied after a moment. "Teanna and I had a conversation in Gawl's palace several years ago. I said nothing, of course, but her anger spoke volumes. If you think it's best, I'll leave before she wakes."

"No, no," Eldar said. "I meant what I said earlier. You'll find that she has matured a great deal over the past few years. She might even be happy to see you."

A rueful laugh was Father Thomas's answer.

"I'm quite serious," said the king.

"That would be a nice thing. I certainly have feelings for the girl. I always have, but the fact is that *you* are her father, Eldar. You were the one who raised her, and it's you whom she loves. This is as it should be. I was never here, nor could I have been under the circumstances."

"Yes," the king said. "Ceta seems like a fine woman. I hope you and she will be happy together. I wish you both joy. It's a shame that you abandoned your former occupation. We may need your services before long."

"We shall see," said Father Thomas. "How bad is it?"

"Bad. We've managed to repulse their first attacks, but they were only the initial forays. Their strategy was to catch us unprepared. Since they didn't, they've had to regroup and rethink things, which means sending for reinforcements."

"Can your people hold out?"

"I think so," the king said. "If they weren't already committed to Stewart Vale, Vargoth would come at us from the south. That's where the war will be won or lost. Should Alor Satar fall, we'll be fighting on two fronts, and that won't be good. Mathew and Teanna must work together."

"Agreed," Father Thomas said. "If her ring works the way his does, she'll recover her strength quickly. I've seen this before with Mathew. She should be all right in a day or two."

"Assuming we have that much time."

Mathew was in shock. *Teanna was Father Thomas's daughter?*

But he'd heard it with his own ears. Suddenly, bits and pieces of different events and conversations began to make sense: Gawl's remark about Father Thomas knowing Marsa in his studio after the statues had come to life, and the odd expression that had crossed the priest's face; and the look that had passed between Teanna and Father Thomas the night the assassins tried to steal his ring.

There had to be at least a half dozen other details that now fell into place.

Mathew stood there, uncertain what to say or do. The whole business was insane, and becoming more so by the minute. Without question Father Thomas had to be the most complex man he had ever met. He suddenly felt very embarrassed being there. Some things were private and meant to remain that way. If Father Thomas chose to talk about it, that would be his decision. Mathew quietly walked back down the hallway.

He knew that sleep was not going to come that night, and he didn't want to disturb Lara. One look at his face and she would start asking questions, he went downstairs to have a drink—a good stiff drink.

To his surprise, he found Collin seated by the fire in the library. His friend hooked a leg around one of the chairs and pulled it closer. Mathew walked to the sideboard first, picked up a decanter of something, and sniffed.

"Try the one on the right," Collin suggested.

"What are you doing up so late?"

"I might ask you the same thing."

"Couldn't sleep," Mathew said, flopping down into the chair with the decanter. He offered the bottle to Collin.

"I've had enough," Collin said, stretching.

Mathew looked at him.

"I ran into one of Teanna's ladies-in-waiting after dinner and she offered to show me around. Nice girl. Very interesting place they have here."

Mathew nodded and decided to leave the topic where it was. The liquid felt warm as it went down and left a slight aftertaste that reminded him of almonds.

"What are you doing up at this ungodly hour?" Collin asked.

"I've been seriously considering becoming a monk and moving to an island."

Collin chuckled. "Have you talked to Teanna yet?"

"No, she's still too weak," Mathew said.

"I ran into Julian Tesh. He told me that she forced Eric and Armand into making a treaty with the West."

Mathew gave him a flat look.

"You don't believe it?" Collin asked.

"I don't know what to believe," Mathew told him. "I know we'll have to talk, but it's hard being cordial to someone who tried to kill you twice."

"Twice?"

"That dragon in the cavern was her invention."

"Mmm," Collin replied. "What are you going to do?"

"I don't know," Mathew answered, stretching out his legs. "I've heard that things are getting pretty bad."

"Between you and her, you could take Shakira, couldn't you?" Collin asked.

Mathew shook his head. "Maybe. It's not as simple as that. If Shakira really has an army of a million creatures, it's going to be hard. The rings don't make you invincible. There's only so much power you can draw on, and doing it drains you. Once that happens—"

"Right, right," Collin said. "Well, you'll think of something. If you let the creatures have a look at that homely face of yours, it might send them screaming back to their caves."

Mathew poured himself another drink, and the two friends sat talking about politics, philosophy, books, women, and a dozen other things that young men talk about as the sky grew light. The years apart from each other seemed to melt away, and for a while they both forgot the storm that was gathering in the west.

Lara was brushing her hair when she heard a knock at the door. She did up the last two buttons on her dress and went to answer it. Expecting Mathew, she was surprised to find a dark-haired woman standing there. The woman was tall and quite beautiful. She was dressed in a pair of brown leather pants with a matching vest. Her boots added an additional three inches to her height, and her shirt looked like a man's garment.

"Good morning. I'm Teanna d'Elso," she said. "May I speak with you?"

"Of course. Come in. I'm Lara Lewin."

Lara's uncertainty about whether to curtsey was quickly settled when Teanna held out her hand. "Thank you for seeing me," said Teanna. "Have you had breakfast yet? I can call for something."

"That would be fine," Lara replied. Teanna both was and wasn't what she expected. "Perhaps we should sit."

Teanna nodded and they walked to a pair of love seats on either side of the doors leading to the balcony.

"This is difficult for me," Teanna began. "Princesses don't generally apologize for making asses of themselves, but that's what I'm here for. I was hoping to find you alone. We've met before, you know."

Lara's brows came together. "Really?"

"You weren't conscious at the time, but I lifted some blocks of masonry off you in an underground cavern."

"Oh," Lara said. "Thank you for that."

"I know you and Mathew were recently married and that you have a child now, so let me first wish you both happiness. I don't know what he's told you about me, but I really do want to apologize. At one time I thought I was in love with your husband."

Lara blinked. She knew a great deal about Teanna and about the things she had done, but the candor of this statement caught her off guard. And yet, one look at the expression on the princess's face was enough to convince her that she still held feelings for Mathew. Coming here, she knew, had to be painful for Teanna. She didn't know what prompted her to do so, but she reached out and took her hand.

The two women spoke for the next half hour. Breakfast came and went and they still continued to talk. It was difficult for both of them.

* * *

It's safe to say that the last thing Mathew expected when he came back to his room was the sight of Teanna and Lara sitting on the couch together giggling like old friends.

Lara got up and came over to kiss him. "Teanna and I have just been chatting," she said.

"So I see."

"I'm going to leave you both alone together," said Lara. "I know you have a great deal to talk about. Teanna's been telling me about what's happening at Stewart Vale. It's terrible, dear. You have to help."

Mathew opened his mouth and closed it again. "Of course," was all he managed.

Later, when he and Teanna entered the dining hall, everyone was there. Collin and Father Thomas got up and bowed, while Ceta and Lara curtsied.

"We'll be leaving shortly," Mathew announced.

His statement came as no surprise, because Lara had already prepared the others for it. Though not fully recovered, Teanna said she felt strong enough to take Father Thomas and Mathew with her to Stewart Vale. Ceta, Lara, and Collin would travel to the battle site with the king's escort.

The rest of the news was grim. Teanna told them that every man, woman, and child of fighting age had been flocking to Stewart Vale for the last two weeks, at a place called Balengrath. They were coming from countries and towns everywhere. Whatever the outcome of the battle, it would decide the fate of mankind for generations to come.

"Your majesty," Mathew said, addressing Eldar. "When this is all over I will return here with Teanna and we'll see what we can do for your wife. I give you my word on that. We would try now, but I think it's important that we both conserve our strength."

"That's understood," Eldar said. "My gratitude and prayers will go with you. We will join you at Balengrath in one week's time."

The goodbyes were more difficult than Mathew

thought they would be. He felt a pang in his heart when Lara whispered, "You are my life . . . come back to me."

Father Thomas and Ceta's parting was equally difficult. They stepped away from the others and spoke privately. When they returned, the priest and Teanna made eye contact, but Mathew only saw polite nods pass between them. Then he and Father Thomas took their places on either side of her.

Transporting always made him slightly nauseous. And he was glad the whole process lasted less than a minute. Once he got his breath back he decided that if he needed to go someplace in the future, it would be by conventional means.

## 56

## Stewart Vale

THEY MATERIALIZED ON A HILLTOP A SHORT DISTANCE away from an enormous gray citadel. The flags of Bajan, Alor Satar, Nyngary, Cincar, and his own beloved Elgaria were flying from the battlements. To his left was a broad valley, easily two miles wide, where a battle was in progress. Cannons were firing all along the hills and on both sides of the valley. A smoky haze hung in the air.

"Princess," a soldier called out, running up to them. "You are needed. The Orlocks are attacking the eastern flank."

"I'll come," Teanna said.

"I'll come with you," Mathew said.

"Where can I find Delain?" Father Thomas asked the man.

"He is in the main hall with Darias Val and Armand Duren. "I believe Kalifar is with them."

Father Thomas thanked him and turned to Mathew and Teanna. "I must familiarize myself with the situation here. Do what you need to do, but make sure not to expose yourselves unnecessarily. I would like to see each of you when you are through."

Teanna's expression turned cold and she opened her mouth to say something, but the priest cut her off.

"There is much you and I need to talk about, but this is neither the time nor the place to do it. Right now our people need you. We'll speak later."

Father Thomas spun on his heel, walked toward the entrance, and disappeared into it.

"He gets that way sometimes," said Mathew.

"I wouldn't know," Teanna replied coolly.

Fifteen minutes later it seemed to Mathew that he had been dropped into a maelstrom. Across the valley floor thousands and thousands of Orlocks, supported by an army of Vargothans, were advancing on the Alliance's men. Along the ridge, Alor Satar's cannons continued to tear into the enemy. The Vargothans answered with their own cannons and field catapults. Fountains of earth flew skyward as the balls struck home. On the right side of the field, near where the trees began, two groups of soldiers on horseback were engaged in violent combat. From the color of the cloaks, Mathew could tell one group was from Alor Satar and the other from Vargoth. The Alor Satarans were clearly outnumbered.

He grasped the situation at once. "We need to buy those men down there some additional time," he told Teanna.

"How?"

"Like this."

He formed a picture in his mind and concentrated. Startled gasps came from the soldiers manning the cannons as well and those on the field as a fifteen-foot-high wall appeared out of nowhere. It stretched from one side of the valley to the other, effectively cutting the two armies off from each other. Elgarian reinforcements charged forward to help the embattled Alor Satarns against the enemy now trapped behind the wall.

Teanna's mouth dropped open and she grabbed his arm excitedly. "I never thought of that."

"It won't last long," he told her. "Either the Vargothans or Shakira will knock it to pieces before long, but at least it gives us time to think."

Teanna smiled at him. "You seem to think very well, Master Lewin."

Mathew steadied himself and blinked a few times to clear his vision. The headache was starting again. "I'm fine, but it does take a little out of you."

Teanna nodded and started to ask another question, but broke it off as a group of riders came galloping up the hill toward them.

"You are about to meet my cousins, Armand and Eric," she said.

Armand skidded his horse to a halt and jumped off. "Brilliant, Teanna. Just brilliant," he said, hugging her.

Before Teanna could answer, he turned to the soldier next to him, "Have the cannons concentrate their fire on the enemy's center." Then he turned back to Teanna and added, "That was the first bright spot I've seen in—"

"Armand, this is Mathew Lewin," she said. "The wall was his idea."

The smile faded from Armand's face, but after a brief hesitation, he put out his hand and said, "Thank you for your help."

Mathew returned the greeting and bowed. "You're welcome, sire. I'm glad that we're fighting on the same side."

Armand looked at him for several seconds. "Yes. This is my brother, Eric. I assume you know Val and Delain."

"Pleasure," Eric said, from horseback with a small wave. "Well done, young man."

Darias Val's greeting was far more enthusiastic. He dismounted, threw his arms around Mathew then kissed him on both cheeks. He was dressed in a belted black tunic and pants that came just below the knees, to the top of his boots. The curved sword he carried was common to his country.

"It is good to see you again, my friend," said Val. "You fought bravely against the creatures that night in Tremont."

"It's been a long time," Mathew replied.

"One of these days you might consider making a less dramatic entrance," Delain said as he got down off his horse. He was also smiling. "Well met, the both of you."

Delain shook Mathew's hand and touched cheeks with Teanna.

"Simply amazing," Val said, as he scanned the scene. Many of the enemy who were caught on the wrong side of the wall had surrendered and were being taken prisoner. "This will give Seth something to think about."

"It won't last," said Armand. "The enemy's already knocking holes in it."

Everyone looked toward the field. The Vargothans had retrained their cannons and were now concentrating on the wall. Large rents were beginning to appear.

"Simple enough," said Teanna.

She extended her arm toward the wall and closed her eyes. A second later it was as good as new and she gave Mathew a wink.

"Uh . . . did Father Thomas find you?" he asked Delain.

"Yes. He's studying the maps and talking with our commanders. It might be a good idea for us to get off this ridge. One lucky cannonball and Bajan, Alor Satar, and Elgaria will be looking for new rulers."

"Agreed," said Armand. "We can meet at the fortress and let them know what's been going on."

"Do you need horses," Delain asked, "or will you, ah . . ."

"We'll ride," Mathew told him.

"Good. Ten minutes," said Armand. "I'll have a patrol escort you back."

Father Thomas was waiting outside the main gates for them, his face somber. Mathew barely had time to dismount before the priest pulled him aside.

"We are in trouble," Father Thomas said without preliminary. "Delain's commanders are competent men, but they were not the ones who chose this site. This position is indefensible."

"Why?" Mathew asked. "We have the higher ground

and the enemy has to cross the valley floor to get to us. I don't know how many cannons we have along the ridges, but there's certainly a lot of them."

"Akin Gibb just sent word that he received a report from Daniel Warren about a path through the mountains the enemy has learned about."

"Daniel!" Mathew exclaimed. "Where is he?"

Father Thomas hesitated a second. "With the doctors right now, Mat. He was badly injured trying to get to us."

Mathew felt his stomach sink and he gripped the priest's arm. "Is he all right?"

"They tell me he'll live, but he took two arrows in the back."

"Where is he?" Mathew asked, looking around. "I want to see him."

"He's at the militia infirmary two miles from here. They're camped at the base of that mountain." Father Thomas pointed. "Go and see him, but come back as soon as you're able."

While they were talking, Teanna had discreetly stepped aside and was waiting patiently for them to finish.

"A friend whom I haven't seen in a long time has been hurt," Mathew explained to her. "I need to go to him."

Teanna glanced at Father Thomas then back to him. "Do you want me to come with you?"

"No. You don't know him," Mathew said, swinging up into his saddle. "But thank you for asking. I'll be back as soon as I can."

She watched him ride down the road, then turned back to Father Thomas, her face once again masklike.

"You said you wanted to speak with me."

"I did," Father Thomas replied. "Perhaps we should walk."

"Can't you say what you want right here?"

"I could, but I would rather not."

Teanna's eyebrows went up and she let out an exasperated breath and started walking. Father Thomas clasped his hands behind his back and joined her.

"Your father and I spoke the other night, Teanna. He told me that you are aware of our relationship."

"Thank you for calling him my father. I've known about you since I was eight."

"I see."

"I asked my mother about it one day because I could see so little of Eldar in me and she told me the truth."

"And do you still see little of him in you?"

The question seemed to surprise Teanna and her pace slowed for a moment. "It would be unusual if I did, since we're not related."

"You don't need to be. My question was, 'Do you still see little of him in you?' "

Teanna looked at Father Thomas, puzzled.

"Eldar d'Elso is the one who raised you, Teanna, not I, and it was to him you ran when you were hurt or frightened as a little girl, not me. I didn't know about you until you were nearly four."

"And it obviously made no difference once you found out."

"On the contrary, I wanted to come and see you, but your mother was against it. Her reasons were good ones. She explained that your father wanted an heir but unfortunately was not able to conceive. By then you had already been declared Nyngary's crown princess and Eldar's daughter. Had I acknowledged you publically, it would have placed you in danger of being ousted, and perhaps thrown the country into a civil war. You know better than anyone else there are no shortage of nobles who would like to lay claim to the royal throne. So I gave her my word, and I have kept that word through the years. Do you understand what I'm saying?"

"I understand that you never made an effort to see me."

"That's what keeping one's word is about," said Father

Thomas. "By the time I learned of you, I had already taken my vows as a priest. Your mother wrote to me and told me that you were happy and growing into a beautiful young lady. I still have those letters."

Teanna nodded. "And now you feel the need to tell me this."

"I tell you this only by way of explanation. I was unaware that you knew of me until your father and I spoke the other night. Only the three of us know the truth, and I will never speak of it to anyone else."

Teanna wasn't quite sure what to think. Over the years, she'd formed an image of what her real father would look like and what she would say to him if they ever met. Father Thomas did not fit that image at all. Her belief had always been that she was abandoned. She needed time to think.

"Thank you for your discretion," she said. "I really must be getting back to the camp now."

She turned and headed back up the path.

"Teanna," Father Thomas said, to her back. "I want you to know that I am proud of what you are doing. Caring about one's fellow man is no small thing. I would like to think the blood in your veins has played some small part in this.

"There are differences in the way your cousins and you look at the world. This is as it should be. Your father is a good man, but you should know that I will also be here for you if you desire it."

Teanna didn't move. She stood where she was after Father Thomas finished speaking. After several seconds she walked back in the direction of camp.

The large tent where they were keeping Daniel had been converted into a makeshift field hospital. All of the cots were taken up by the wounded. Daniel was unconscious when Mathew arrived. His friend's spectacles sat on a little table next to the bed. Akin Gibb stood close by, watching as the doctor applied bandages to Daniel's wounds. When they saw each other, Akin put a finger over his lips and motioned for Mathew to join him outside.

"How is he?" Mathew asked when they were out of the tent.

"He's lost a lot of blood, but the doctor says he'll live."

Mathew closed his eyes and said a silent prayer of thanks. "What happened?"

"I don't have all the details. He'd been serving with the Vargothans, and it seems that earlier today he intercepted a message from one of their scouts about a path through the mountains. If the mercenaries took it they would come out behind us. Daniel stole a horse and made a dash across the valley for our lines with about a dozen of them on his heels. He took two arrows in the back."

Akin opened his hand and showed Mathew two arrowheads. Both had dried blood on them.

Mathew grimaced. "Do we know where the path is?"

"Our men found it a little while ago; they're watching it now. Unfortunately, that's only part of the problem. A fellow who lived in this area claims that all the hills around here are honeycombed with caves."

It took Mathew a second to understand Akin's point. "Tunnels," he said.

"Right."

"That isn't good. The Orlocks could come out anywhere."

"We know. I passed the information on to Delain, but he says it's critical for us to hold this position."

"And run the risk of being caught in a vise? That doesn't make sense. We have to do something."

Akin folded his arms across his chest. "I'm open to suggestions. Until Gawl and James arrive there's not much we can do. The last report we had said they're still days out. We're badly outnumbered, Mat. All we've been doing is hanging on."

"But if the creatures get behind us—"

"Those are the orders," Akin told him.

Everything was happening too fast, Mathew thought. His head was pounding, and try as he might he could not tell if Shakira was in the vicinity. It was possible that she had been hurt worse than he initially thought, but something told him she wasn't.

For a moment he considered asking Akin to show him the path across the mountains, then rejected the idea. The enemy obviously knew that it was now being defended, and probably wouldn't try it. The caves concerned him far more.

"Is the man who told you about the caves around?" he asked.

"I think we could find him," Akin replied. "Why?"

"I'd like to see one or two of them. I'm thinking that if I can seal the entrances, it might prevent the Orlocks from getting behind us."

"Good idea. Wait here. I'll be right back."

Fifteen minutes later Akin returned with a stocky fellow who had a lump of tobacco in his cheek. "This is Spencer," Akin said, introducing him.

"You know about some caves in this area?" Mathew asked, shaking his hand.

"Yep," Spencer said between chews. "I grew up in Telfair Province. My hometown's about five miles from here."

"Do you think you could show me them?"

"Sure. But there's at least twenty or thirty, maybe more. They're all connected like an ant colony. How many do you want to see?"

"Just a couple," said Mathew.

Spencer looked up at the surrounding hills for several seconds then spit a brown stream of tobacco juice onto the ground, then reached for his tobacco pouch. He took a large pinch out, stuck it back in his cheek, then offered the pouch to Akin, who shook his head.

"Uh, no thanks," Mathew said when the pouch came around to him.

Spencer frowned. "You Elgarians are strange folks. This'll put some hair on your chest."

"Maybe later," Mathew told him.

Spencer shrugged and put the pouch away. "Suit yourself," Spencer said, putting the pouch away. "There's a cave close by. See that waterfall up on the hill? The opening is right behind it."

"And you're sure they're connected?"

Another stream of tobacco juice hit the ground. "Can't say every one of them is, but the ones I know are. We used to camp out up here when we were boys. Mind if I ask you a question?"

"Sure," Mathew said.

"If you're gonna do some of your magic, is it okay if I stay and watch?"

Mathew considered telling Spencer about how the rings worked, but his head was throbbing and he didn't have the patience for it just then. "No problem," he replied.

They sent word back for Teanna and waited until she arrived. Mathew introduced her to the other men, who bowed. Interestingly, Akin tended to stammer in her presence and had trouble meeting her eye, which was curious to Mathew because he had never seen his friend like that before. Akin was not an aggressive man around women, but neither was he particularly shy. Teanna, for some reason, seemed to find his behavior amusing, and they struck up a conversation together as they walked along the path.

Spencer had been correct—they couldn't see the cave until you got behind the waterfall, so they had to inch along a narrow ledge and hug the wall, which meant getting wet. Once behind it, cascading water formed a white curtain, cutting them off from the rest of the world, the noise drowning out everything else.

It took a little over twenty minutes for them to reach the cave entrance. When they were inside, Teanna produced a floating ball of blue light and lit the interior. Like the others, she had gotten soaked, and took a moment to wipe the water from her face with her hands. In the middle of doing so however, she noticed Akin staring, and readjusted the material on her shirt so it no longer clung to her breasts. In the dim light, Mathew couldn't be sure, but he thought his friend's color might have gone up a shade when Teanna caught him looking. Oddly, she didn't seem upset.

"This goes quite a way back," Spencer told them. "I haven't been here in thirty years, but if I remember right, this passage comes to a wall about a hundred feet in, then turns off to the right and connects with another cave."

"Exactly what are we doing here?" asked Teanna.

Mathew was looking up at the ceiling. "I wanted to see how wide the opening was," he said. "I thought there might be some way to divert the flow of the waterfall and flood the caves, but now that we're here, I don't see how we can do it."

"What if all that rock wasn't there anymore," Teanna asked.

"There's got to be at least a hundred feet of it, ma'am," said Spencer.

Teanna raised her eyebrows and looked at Mathew, a silent communication passing between them.

"Do you think we could?" he asked.

Teanna stared up at the rock for several seconds then nodded. "I think so."

The two of them moved aside to discuss it further. In the meanwhile, Spencer wandered back along the tunnel. He returned less than a minute later interrupting their discussion.

"Orlocks," he whispered.

Teanna's ball of light promptly faded out and the four of them scrambled back out the opening and along the ledge. In their haste, Teanna missed her footing and would have slipped had Akin not grabbed her.

They were all breathing heavily by the time they reached the bottom of the hill.

Mathew looked up at the waterfall again. Spencer's estimate of how much rock was there was about a hundred feet short. In addition to the rock there were tons of earth above the opening. Mathew turned to Akin and said, "You and Spencer drop back a bit. We'll join you in a minute."

"What are they gonna do?" Spencer asked.

"That magic you were asking about earlier," Akin said, taking him by the elbow.

The smaller man's eyes widened and he didn't ask any more questions. He and Akin moved along the path until they were a safe distance away.

"Do you still remember how to link, Mathew?"

"I do."

"Fine. Clear your mind and let me control it."

Mathew took a deep breath and looked into Teanna's eyes, letting his mind go blank. He heard her talking, but the words now seemed to come from far away. Other sounds also receded into the distance . . . the wind moving through the trees, the birds chirping. Eventually, only Teanna's voice remained, growing more distinct inside his head.

He felt the power surge within him the moment she said, *"Now."*

Seventy-five yards away Akin saw a beam of white light shoot from the princess's hand and strike the point where the waterfall crested the hill. A tremendous bang followed, and he felt the shock running through the ground. As water and incalculable tons of solid rock were blasted into the air the beam of light bore into the hill. So intense was the explosion that Akin and Spencer were forced to retreat from the flying debris.

When it ended a minute later Akin could scarcely believe his eyes. A section of the hill thirty feet wide had been ripped away. The water was no longer pouring past the cave's opening, but was now pouring directly into it.

He and Spencer raced back up the path. Mathew was holding Teanna up, but he looked groggy and disoriented.

She was barely conscious. Akin took the princess in his arms while Spencer helped Mathew.

Akin carried her the entire way back to the militia camp. It came as something of a shock when he glanced down and saw that Teanna's eyes were open. And she was watching him.

## 57

# Citadel of Balengrath

FOR THE NEXT FIVE DAYS, MATHEW AND TEANNA ALTER-
nated their defense of the citadel at Stewart Vale. They
were both exhausted and badly in need of rest. In the in-
terim, though more and more Orlocks continued to arrive.
There was still was no sign of Shakira.

Akin and Teanna seemed to be getting on well together.
He stayed with her while she recovered from the
headaches, and she visited his camp a number of times.
They were frequently seen walking together.

Not surprisingly, Armand Duren had as little to do with
Mathew as possible. Whenever Mathew entered a room, Armand left it. His brother Eric was less aloof and engaged
Mathew in conversations from time to time. He seemed
genuinely concerned about how he and Teanna were doing
under the trying circumstances. He was also worried about
their troops' ability to hold out until Gawl and James arrived
with reinforcements. According to Eric, the odds were on
the enemy's side and their prospects were bleak.

All of that changed on the sixth day. A scout rode in
through the citadel's rear gate and reported that Gawl and
his Sennians were only an hour away. A short while later
another scout brought news that James was expected later
that evening.

A conference was hastily convened in the great hall to
discuss their strategy. The consensus among the commanders was that it was time for them to take the initia-
tive. The army of Mirdan would begin attacking the

enemy's rearguard at first light. Delain was to swing west and hit the Vargothan flank, while Alor Satar would begin its spearhead toward their center, supported by Teanna. The Sennian army, with Mathew, would shore up Akin's militia, who were the Alliance's weakest link.

Afterward, Mathew went up to the parapet to get some fresh air. The Citadel of Balengrath was laid out in the shape of a square, with watchtowers at each of the corners and in the middle of its massive walls. All of them had conical spires. A dried-up moat that hadn't been used in over eighty years surrounded the castle, that had been Alor Satar's capital before Gabrel Duren moved it to Rocoi.

A number of guards on duty along the citadel's outer curtain nodded when he passed by. Some patted him on the back or uttered words of encouragement, despite the somber mood.

Mathew looked out across the valley at the enemy campfires and a shiver went up his spine; tomorrow was not going to be an easy day. To his surprise, he found Teanna and Akin were also there, talking. Not wishing to intrude, he was about to go back the other way when they saw him and waved him over.

"I didn't mean to interrupt," he explained as he approached.

"You didn't," Akin said. "I was just heading back to see that everything is in order with my men. I'll see you tomorrow, Mat."

He gave Mathew's shoulder a squeeze and said good night but only got a few feet before Teanna hurried after him and kissed him on the cheek.

"He's a sweet man," she said when she returned. "You and he have many of the same qualities."

"He's a good man. I've known him forever."

Teanna smiled and looked out at the valley. "So many," she said softly.

Mathew rested his forearms on the wall. "There are."

"I got word earlier that my father and our army will be here tomorrow," she said.

"That should help," Mathew said.

In truth, he was hoping that Eldar and his people would be late. He missed Lara terribly, but the last place he wanted her was in Balengrath.

"But you don't think it will, do you?" Teanna asked.

"I honestly don't know. The two of us can slow the enemy down, at least. But I'm puzzled as to why Shakira hasn't shown her face yet."

Teanna shook her head. "We'll have to conserve our power," she told him. "I've been so tired all week."

They started walking and eventually found themselves back at the keep. Despite the late hour, people were still coming and going.

"Oh, look," Teanna said, "Eric's talking to someone down there."

Mathew couldn't make out who it was in the pale moonlight. It gave the courtyard a silver cast.

"I spoke with Siward Thomas the other day," she said, changing the subject.

"Did you?"

"He's not what I expected."

*That's the understatement of the year*, Mathew thought, though he kept the observation to himself. "No, he's not. If anyone can help win this battle, it's him."

"Mmm."

"It's getting late," Mathew said. "I should probably turn in for the night."

"I'll walk down with you."

Eric was still in the courtyard, talking, when they reached the bottom of the steps. He saw them and nodded.

Mathew was in no mood to start another conversation, so he waved back and said good night to Teanna.

"I'd better go and say something to him or his feelings will be hurt," Teanna said. Good night, Mathew.

He was about halfway across the keep when Teanna screamed his name.

Mathew spun around and saw Teanna and Eric standing about fifty yards away. She had her arm extended toward him. A moment later something whizzed by his ear. To his horror, Eric drew his sword and brought it down across Teanna's arm, severing her hand from her body.

Teanna shrieked and went reeling backward, blood spurting from the wound as Eric reached down, picked up the severed hand, and pulled the ring off its finger.

The whole thing happened in seconds. Recovering from his shock, Mathew ran toward her, intending to help.

*"Behind you!"* gasped Teanna.

He barely had time to react as a man rushed at him from the shadows, brandishing a sword above his head. Anger surging in Mathew's chest, as he realized what was happening. The man with the sword stopped and grabbed his head. A moment later he fell to the ground, dead, blood draining from his ears.

When Mathew looked toward Teanna again he saw Eric smash her rose gold ring under the heel of his boot. The princess was down on her knees, rocking back and forth in agony. Blood was everywhere.

Eric's voice carried to him. "This is how our family deals with traitors," he heard him say. "You should never have sided with them."

Somewhere in the keep people were shouting. Mathew was aware of it as he began walking again toward Eric, his pace neither slow nor fast. It did not quicken as he watched Eric's sword go up and heard him say, "Goodbye, cousin."

The sword never came down. It merely disappeared from Eric's hand. Startled, he turned then to see Mathew standing a feet away.

"Still alive, Lewin?" he sneered. "I must really learn to pay my people—"

Those were Eric Duren's last words. A white light appeared out of nowhere, enveloping him. In the last seconds that he lived, he screamed, but the sound ended abruptly as the light disappeared. Somewhere in the distance a chime faded away.

Armand, Delain, and Father Thomas came running.

"What did you do with my brother?" Armand demanded.

Mathew stared at him for several seconds, slowly then glanced up at the moon before turning his back on him and stooping down to help Teanna.

## 58

## Stewart Vale

SHE LAY THERE UNCONSCIOUS, HER LIFE EBBING AWAY AS the blood pumped out of her arm.

"Someone send for a doctor!" Mathew shouted.

"We've got to find a way to stop that blood or she'll die in minutes," said Father Thomas.

"How?" Mathew asked.

"The arteries must be closed and the wound cauterized. Here and here." Father Thomas pointed to show him.

Mathew stared directly at the major artery in the middle of Teanna's wrist and concentrated. A moment later there was a sizzling sound and she let out a small moan. He repeated the procedure with the other artery as the doctor arrived.

"Oh, dear God," he said, taking one look at Teanna. "Someone get a stretcher. Let's get her inside."

To the astonishment of everyone, Mathew produced one, out of thin air, then he, Father Thomas, and Delain lifted Teanna up and placed her on it. Her head moved back and forth and her face was deathly pale.

As they started back toward the main building, Armand began to say something threatening toward him. Apparently he thought better of it after seeing the look on Mathew's face, spun on his heel, and headed in the opposite direction.

The first explosion hit them as they were passing the citadel's rear gate. The only warning Mathew had was the faintest tingling sensation, but it gave him no time to react.

A tremendous blast of hot air lifted Father Thomas and him off the ground throwing them backward fifteen feet. Instinctively, he placed a shield over himself, the priest, and Teanna. The second explosion destroyed the door along with a substantial portion of the Citadel's inner wall. More explosions could be heard at the outer curtain of Balengrath.

"To arms!" Delain yelled, drawing his sword. "We are under attack. Defend the castle."

Chaos broke loose in the yard. Orlocks rushed in through the opening where a gate had been blown open as the survivors tried to rally.

"Elgarians to me!" Delain shouted.

Father Thomas struggled to his knees and felt someone grab him under the elbow.

"Are you all right?" Mathew asked.

The priest was bleeding from a gash on the forehead.

"Yes . . . I think so. What happened?"

"Shakira's here. Can you get Teanna to safety?"

Father Thomas blinked to clear his vision. "Yes," he said.

Mathew stopped a soldier who was running by. "*You,* help Father Thomas get the princess inside."

The doctor was dead, lying a few feet from them; Teanna was next to him. Her head was no longer moving. Near the middle of the keep, Delain had gathered a contingent of soldiers who were locked in combat with the Orlocks. Mathew saw Armand and his Alor Satarans rushing back toward them. All along the wall their men had finally recovered their wits and were firing down into the keep, killing the creatures right and left. But their efforts weren't making much of a difference. For every Orlock that fell, two more seemed to take its place. Somewhere out on the valley floor trumpets were blowing. The attack had begun.

Despite the madness around him, Mathew forced himself to survey the situation. Two Orlocks carrying pikes focused on him and charged. They only got a few feet be-

fore being hurled backward into the wall. One fell unconscious; the other's neck was broken. Mathew turned away.
He saw that Father Thomas and the soldier were nearly
back at the castle with Teanna. He waited until they were
inside before turning back to the courtyard. There was no
sign of Shakira, but he sensed that she was close.

His first inclination was to draw on the ring and destroy
the Orlocks in the keep, but it was better to conserve his
power until he needed it most. Out in the valley the Alliance's cannons had finally begun to answer.

*At least our commanders weren't caught sleeping,* he
thought.

More explosions at the outer wall pulled his attention
away. He had no idea what was going on out there, but it
was time to see. Drawing his sword, he started for the gate.

Near the entrance to the main house, Darias Val was
engaged with two Orlocks. The Bajani's blade moved in
a blur, killing the first creature, which fell screaming. Val
went down a moment later with a sword in his side from
its companion. How Mathew covered the last twenty
yards, he was never quite certain. Val had lost his sword
and was struggling to get to his feet when he crashed
headlong into the Orlock. Before the creature could recover, Mathew plunged his dagger into the Orlock's
heart.

"Thank you, my friend," said Val. The Bajani was lying
on his side, trying to sit up.

"Stay where you are," Mathew said, restraining him.
He signaled to two of Val's aides. "Have your men cleanse
the wound as soon as possible. The infection will kill as
surely as the blade."

Val nodded weakly and motioned to his men, who
lifted him up and carried him inside.

Mathew looked to the courtyard again. Soldiers of the
Alliance were holding their own and actually appeared to
be gaining ground against the creatures. At the far end of

the complex he saw Armand and his people were involved in a fierce struggle in front of a small stone building.

*The armory.*

Whatever he thought of the man, Mathew had to concede that he was a valiant fighter. When they made eye contact, Armand broke away from the fight and came running across the yard to him.

"My brother betrayed us," he said. "One of my men saw him talking to Shakira earlier."

*"What?"*

"There's a tunnel under the citadel that comes out at the base of the hills. That's how the creatures got in. We need you; they're trying to take the armory."

Out of distrust, Mathew hesitated.

"I have good cause not to like you, Lewin," said Armand. "But if I ever come at you, it will be to your face and not behind your back."

"All right," Mathew said, and the two ran across the yard. They were stopped by a soldier.

"My lord," he said to Armand. "James of Mirdan has arrived and is attacking the enemy's rear guard, and the Sennians are in the outer bailey trying to break through to us."

"Good," Armand replied. "Tell Colonel Ranier I need two more squads of men out here."

The armory was a two-story building stacked with weapons. Crossbows hung on the walls, and every manner of pike, halberd, spear, sword, and axe that Mathew had ever seen were stored in row after row of barrels. Eric and Armand had obviously anticipated this battle for some time. As far as he could tell, there was only one room, its interior lit by a series of gas lamps.

Why the Orlocks were interested in the armory made no sense to him. Surely they had an ample store of their own weapons. Then he noticed the wooden kegs lined up along the back wall. Stacked one on top of another, they were at least four deep and rose nearly to the ceiling. A residue of black powder on the floor left no question about what their contents contained.

Mathew's eyes widened and his heart nearly skipped a beat. The fools had no idea what they were dealing with. Alor Satar might well have cannons now, but their lack of experience with black powder was obvious. The nearest keg was no more than three feet from a gas lamp. One spark would blow the armory and half the citadel into the next province. Even a stray spark from walking on the floor or a dropped sword could do it. He remembered the lessons that Felize had learned. In the beginning, they had lost two ships and a score of men before they started making the sailors who handled black powder wear felt slippers around it.

Even as the danger dawned on him, a contingent of creatures rushed through the rear gate, carrying torches. The nearest Orlock heaved his torch at a window near the front of the building, shattering it. A second torch followed it.

"Get your men out!" Mathew snapped.

Through the windows he could see that the Orlocks had surrounded the building and were throwing torches at it. A crash at the back of the room caught his attention. A single torch had just landed at the base of a powder keg. Without hesitating, he shoved Armand out of the door.

Father Thomas was at the bottom of the steps of the main house when he saw it happen. The building blew to pieces. Miraculously, none of the debris struck anyone in the courtyard. Incredibly, the fragments of stone shot outward and hit an invisible wall. The priest squinted through the smoke in disbelief. The armory was gone, but the air where it had stood seemed to be moving. On the other side of it he could see that an entire section of the citadel's outer wall was gone. One lone figure stood there.

He recognized Mathew and started running. The moving air had dissipated by the time the priest reached him.

Of the armory, only a shallow depression in the ground and its foundation still remained.

Mathew walked unsteadily toward Father Thomas. "I couldn't get the shield around the entire building in time," he said.

Father Thomas caught him as his knees gave way.

The fighting continued in the courtyard, though the Orlocks appeared to be falling back. Armand joined them.

"Are you all right?" he asked Mathew.

Mathew nodded.

"I owe you my life," Armand said stiffly. "You have my gratitude."

"It was nothing," Mathew mumbled.

"Nothing?" Armand said drawing himself up.

Mathew made a dismissive gesture with his hand. "Haven't you people ever heard of humor? You're welcome."

It took several seconds before Armand's face softened. "I'll remember to laugh when this is over. We're going to need you at the outer curtain. The Vargothans will attack there now that the wall is destroyed. Are you strong enough to fight?"

Mathew closed his eyes, then opened them. "Yes, I think so."

The battle continued through the night. When the sun rose the next morning, the valley floor was a sea of Orlocks and the black and silver cloaks of Vargoth. Mathew was physically and mentally exhausted. He went from place to place helping where he could, each use of the ring draining him further. One thing had become clear to him during this time. Despite their valiant efforts, the Alliance was losing ground. Clearly, Shakira was willing to sacrifice thousands of her people in order to weaken him, and her plan was working.

In the meantime, Gawl led three successive charges against the enemy's flank. The last forcing the Vargothans to regroup. Throughout the night catapults and cannons on both sides of the valley kept up a steady stream of fire. Mathew watched the Sennians' final charge from his vantage point on the wall. Twice Gawl was unhorsed, and twice the giant fought his way to his feet, his broadsword cleaving death in all directions. It was an incredible thing to see. Each time, Mathew held his breath, fearing the worst, yet Gawl each time emerged and remounted. At the opposite end of the valley, James and his Mirdanites continued to fight their hearts out.

It was close to midday when Father Thomas, Delain, and Armand came to see him. He was sitting with his back to the wall, drinking a bottle of water.

"Our center will not hold against another enemy advance, my son."

"What do you want me to do?" Mathew asked. His voice sounded thick even to him.

"We must find a way to stop their momentum," said Armand.

Mathew looked at each of them in turn and could see the truth in their faces. If the Vargothans broke through, they would overrun the citadel and that would be the end of it. He still had a vivid picture in his mind of what the Guardian had shown him, but could not yet bring himself to consider it. There had to be another way.

"All right," he finally said. He took Delain's offered hand and let the prince pull him up. "How much time do we have?" he asked.

"Not much," Delain told him. "They've been massing for an attack for the last hour."

*Shakira won't even have to raise a finger,* he thought.

Mathew leaned on the battlement and stared out at the valley. The Vargothan and Orlock armies stretched across all two miles of it and all the way back to the Roeselar River. Apparently, James and his people had still not been able get across.

He watched the enemy formations on the field for nearly a minute before Delain prompted him again.

"Mathew."

Mathew started but didn't turn around. "When is the best time to attack, Father?" he asked the priest.

Father Thomas didn't reply immediately, not because the question was a difficult one; on the contrary, it was elementary. The answer had more meaning to him and Mathew than to Delain or Armand.

"When your opponent is preparing to attack you," Father Thomas said. It was one of the first fencing lessons he had taught Mathew.

Armand and Delain appeared puzzled.

"We need him to help defend against the next attack," said Armand.

Mathew nodded, still looking out over the field. "The enemy will eventually get through, won't they?"

"Eventually," Delain replied.

"Then let them defend against us," Mathew said, his voice little more than a whisper.

What none of them could see was that the Roeselar River had begun to rise. For several minutes the change was not apparent, but it was becoming rapidly so. On the far bank, James Genet looked up from the conversation he was having with his commanders and stared at the river in disbelief. Four years ago at Ardon Field he had seen firsthand what Mathew Lewin could do, but still this was difficult to accept. His mouth dropped open as a wall of water sixty feet high rose out of the river and came crashing down on the Vargothan rear guard, flooding the end of the valley. A minute later the waters began to recede.

Closer to Balengrath, trumpets began to blow. At first James thought they were in response to what was happening. Then he reached for his farsighter and trained it on the citadel. A series of flags were flying from the central watchtower. That was his signal.

"Get the men ready!" he shouted. "The second, third, and fourth divisions will attack."

On the valley floor, Gawl was taking a drink of water when he saw the men around him pointing. Unable to make out what the commotion was about, he scrambled up a nearby tree for a better view. What he saw stunned him. The enemy soldiers who hadn't been killed when the wave crashed down on their heads were being pulled back into the river by the receding waters and swept away.

"What is it?" Jeram Quinn called up to him.

"Not what, Jeram—*who*."

"Fire wall!" someone screamed. The sound pulled Mathew back to the moment.

"Here it comes," said Armand.

Mathew felt it when the Orlock queen reacted, and he barely had time to prepare himself. A massive wall of blue fire sprang out of nowhere a half mile from Balengrath and started creeping forward, destroying everything in its path. On the wall they watched it advance for three minutes and then, without explanation, the fire's progress suddenly halted.

"It stopped moving," the priest said.

Everyone saw the same thing. Mathew's eyes, like theirs, remained fixed on the roaring flames a mere hundred yards from the citadel. So intense was the heat, he could feel it up on the parapet.

He had finally managed to bring the fire wall to a stop, but the effort was draining him. Time passed and the minutes crawled by, one into another.

*"Weakening. You are weakening, human,"* Shakira's voice said inside his head.

Some part of Mathew's mind was aware the trumpets were blowing again, and he heard a man shout, "Nyngary has arrived."

Whoever said it seemed very far away.

The voice might have belonged to Delain. Mathew was no longer certain. At some point he became aware that Lara and Collin were there with him, though he knew he could have been hallucinating. His strength was ebbing and there was little he could do about it.

Shakira's fire surged again and began to spread across the valley, yet she continued to speak to him, her dead white skin and the blue veins in her face floating in his mind's eye. She was sitting on a chair atop a flatbed wagon in a small glade at the far western side of the field, protected from the battle. A rapidly flowing stream moved through the trees behind her. A number of her subjects and Vargothans surrounded the Orlock queen, all of their attention focused on her. One of the humans was a thin-lipped man of about sixty who wore a thin circlet of gold around his brow. He was well-groomed and had white hair that came down to his shoulders.

That must be Seth, Mathew decided.

He took all this in at a glance, though he was not sure what good the information was. Strained almost to the point of collapse, he refused to give up. This was his world, and the Orlocks would not have it without a fight. Fear gnawed at the pit of his stomach, and he sensed that Shakira knew this. The effort she was expending was obvious from her face.

When the fire wall halted for a second time, he felt rather than saw it. Mathew gripped the edge of the battlements to keep himself from falling.

"Look!" someone yelled.

Shakira's fire wall continued to crackle and dance, rising higher into the sky, but on the western end of the field an opening had just appeared, as though someone had parted a curtain. A man on horseback rode through. Delain took a farsighter from one of his men and trained it on the rider.

"Hold your fire!" he yelled. "He's carrying a white flag."

It took the rider nearly two minutes to reach the citadel's main gate.

"My lords," the man called up. "His majesty, King Seth, and her Royal Highness Shakira of the Orlock nation, would have words with you."

"Tell them to go to hell," Armand yelled back.

The soldier smiled up at him. "Your feelings are understandable, Lord Duren. But it would be in your best interest to hear what they have to say. We are prepared to offer you and your people your lives . . . provided certain conditions are met."

"And what conditions would those be?" asked Delain.

"It would be better to hear them directly from their majesties, your highness. If you give me your word, I will signal my lords to come forward."

"I'll give you this," Armand said, and he grabbed a crossbow from the nearest soldier.

"No," Delain said, stopping him. "He's here under a white flag. I will not see him harmed."

"It's a trick."

"Trick or not, he has a white flag. Tell your men to hold their fire."

Armand held Delain's eye for a moment, then handed the crossbow back to the soldier. "State your conditions," he called down.

"If I have your words that you will honor a truce, my lords will meet with you in one hour in the town of Stewart Vale to explain their plan in person. You may bring an escort if you wish. There is a tavern in the village where you will be able to speak in private.

"I am instructed to say further that Mathew Lewin and the priest, Father Siward Thomas, must also be present. If you wish to have your people check the area first, we will understand."

Delain and Armand both turned to Mathew, who nodded. Father Thomas did the same. He was standing off to

the side, next to Collin. Lara was also there. She joined
Mathew and put an arm protectively around his shoulders.

"Why do Mathew Lewin and Father Thomas need to be
present?" asked Delain.

The emissary responded with an elaborate shrug.
"Their majesties did not choose to share their reasons with
me," he said, brushing some dust from one of his sleeves.
"They did, however, ask that I convey this letter to you."

"I'd like to know as well," Mathew called out, "so ride
back to your masters and get the answer."

The man drew a long suffering breath then twisted
around in his saddle and waved at the fire wall. "That
won't be necessary. If you will train your glasses there,"
he said, pointing, "perhaps that will answer part of your
question."

Mathew took one of the farsighters from a soldier and
focused it in the direction the Vargothan had indicated.
Another opening appeared in the fire wall and the wagon
bearing Shakira pulled through it. She was still seated, and
holding a small child on her lap.

Mathew's heart sank the second he realized who it was.
The farsighter slipped through his fingers and fell over the
edge of the wall, shattering on the ground below.

"What is it?" Lara asked.

Unable to speak, the stricken expression on his face
conveyed volumes.

"A child," Armand said. "She's holding a child."

Lara snatched the farsighter out of Armand's hand and
trained it on the wagon. She took a step backward,
stunned, the color draining from her face.

Delain turned to Father Thomas. "Is that . . ."

The priest nodded slowly.

"All right," Delain called back. "Tell them we'll come.
We'll meet them in four hours."

"Four hours, my lord?"

"This is something that involves the entire Alliance.

I will send word to both Gawl and James. Part of the decision must come from them as well." That is my answer.

The soldier smiled pleasantly and inclined his head,
then turned his horse toward the opening in the fire wall.

Before he left, he tossed a packet on the ground.

## 59

## Stewart Vale

FOR THE FIRST TIME IN OVER A HUNDRED YEARS THE KINGS of Alor Satar, Nyngary, Elgaria, Sennia, Mirdan, and Bajan all met under one roof. It took less than a half hour for the discussion to become heated. Mathew and Lara, on the parapet directly above the main house, heard the angry voices. Though trying to remain calm, Lara was in a near state of panic over Bran. She kept stealing glances at Mathew, wanting him to tell her that everything would be all right, that he had a solution. He knew he had to do something, he just didn't know what. He didn't want to consider what Bran's presence said about whether Martin and Amanda Palmer were still alive. He knew neither one would have given the child up without a fight.

Earlier, while they were waiting for Gawl and James to arrive, Delain had shown him the letter that was in the packet. The enemy's demands were straightforward. Seth wrote that he would send Bran's head back on a plate if Mathew did not surrender his ring. Moreover, if he failed to do so, everyone in the citadel would be exterminated and their countries razed.

Seth's proposal was somewhat different from the one Shakira had laid out in Rivalin, though it hardly mattered. Seth also wrote that Delain and Armand would be allowed to keep their thrones, provided they swore oaths of loyalty to Vargoth and became its vassals. Their armies were to be disbanded, of course. In addition, the Orlocks would assume two-thirds of Elgaria and one-third of Alor

Satar as their permanent home. James, Gawl, and Darias Val would then be free to return to their homelands, where they would work to normalize relations with the new regimes.

There were other demands, but it all came down to capitulation. The last part of the letter stated that Mathew and Father Thomas were to be turned over to the Orlocks, which didn't surprise Mathew at all.

The point, which was not so subtly conveyed, was to get the Alliance leaders to achieve Shakira's ends for her. Mathew saw through the ploy immediately and had little doubt the others would, too. He knew the leaders would not let him walk out the front gate and hand his ring over to the enemy. They would kill him before that happened, which was Shakira's goal.

"Do you realize what you're asking?" Gawl's voice drifted up to him from the gathering. "No man can be asked to give up his son."

"I realize it," said Armand. "But it's the boy or us. I'll see them in hell before I kneel to that bastard Seth and his creature friends. It's better to go down fighting."

"And what are we going to do if Mathew decides to leave?" asked James. "There's no one here who can stop him."

"His son's life is at stake," said Gawl.

"Look, I'm under no illusions about the garbage they've presented. It might not be next week, or next month, but they'll come for us as surely as the sun rises."

A silence followed.

"You know I'm speaking the truth," James went on. "We owe Mathew Lewin a great deal, but he cannot be allowed to hand his ring over to Shakira. Their victory would be a foregone conclusion so I agree with Armand on this point. I would rather go down fighting and end it now."

"As would I," Delain said. "But there must be an alternative. Is there some way we could mount a rescue attempt for the child?"

Abruptly, Mathew took Lara's hand and they started walking. There wasn't much time, and it was imperative that they act now. He looked around the complex for Collin, but he was nowhere in sight. The last he had seen of his friend, Collin was talking to Father Thomas. He assumed they were still together. Unfortunately, there was no more time to waste.

Mathew explained his plan to Lara: They were going to rescue their son. He had considered going alone, but knew it would be useless to try and keep her from coming.

The tunnel the Orlocks had used to enter Balengrath was fairly easy to locate. None of the guards reacted when Mathew and Lara approached. "Any activity, men?" he asked.

"Nothing," replied a sergeant who had seen more than his share of battles. "How are you and your lady holding up?"

"Fine. And you?"

"As well as can be expected."

"Where does this tunnel come out?" Mathew asked.

The sergeant shrugged. "Never been down it. In fact I didn't even know it was here until today, but Davis here says that it runs into town."

Davis nodded in confirmation.

"Is that right?" Mathew asked.

"Yes, sir," Davis replied. "It's about a fifteen minute walk."

"Thanks. The king should be here soon. Tell him that I've decided to go and pay our ugly friends a little visit."

"With your woman?" the sergeant asked, surprised.

Mathew moved closer and lowered his voice so that only the man could hear it. "I promised I'd show her how the ring worked." He added a wink for emphasis.

The sergeant clearly didn't think much of the idea, but he was not about to challenge Mathew, so he shrugged and stepped aside.

"Just don't go getting yourselves hurt," he cautioned.

"It looks like we're going to need you. Best take one of the torches."

"It's not me who's going to get hurt," Mathew replied.

The pursuit started eight minutes after they entered the tunnel. Shouts and the sound of men running echoed down the long corridor. In the distance they could see the glow of torches reflecting off the walls. Mathew and Lara began running, and by the time they reached the opposite end, were out of breath. Then he drew his sword.

"Take this," he said, handing it to her.

"What are you going to use?"

"My hands, if I have to."

"Mathew, what if they've already—"

"They haven't. Shakira needs Bran for leverage."

"But—"

"We'll figure it out once were there. Right now we need to gather some brush."

"What?"

"Just get it and I'll explain later."

He considered collapsing the tunnel behind them but rejected the idea. Stealth was the most important weapon they had. If he drew on the ring, it would alert Shakira to their presence. Also, he didn't want to injure the soldiers who were following them.

It took several minutes for the two of them to block the ntrance with brush, and when they were through, Mathew lit a match and set it on fire. Smoke began filling the tunnel. Some of it billowed outside, but that didn't matter. If the Orlocks or Vargothans came to see what was happening, they would assume the Alliance was trying to seal the tunnel off, and he and Lara would be long gone by then.

Satisfied that the wood was burning freely, they moved on. He considered the possibilities as they neared town. Negotiating with Shakira and the Vargothans was out of the question—neither could be trusted. The only thing he was certain about was that he had to save his son.

They were about a quarter mile from the village of Stewart Vale. It was little more than a collection of shops and buildings with forest on either side. A single road ran down the middle. The village sat close to the border between Elgaria and Alor Satar and was the last place travelers emerged after the passes. Near the end of town Mathew saw a building with a sign hanging in front and knew it was the tavern.

No one was in sight yet, which was fortunate. It would give them time to get into position.

The meeting wasn't set for another hour, and he intended to catch Shakira by surprise. He knew the Orlock queen would not come alone, but if Lara could distract her, even for a moment, it might give him enough time to get Bran to safety. It wasn't much of a plan, he conceded, but it was the best he could come up with.

Crouching low, they made their way toward the tavern using the trees for cover. Fifty yards from the front entrance they stopped.

"Do you see anyone?" Lara whispered.

Mathew frowned and shook his head.

The main street was deserted. Except for the sign swaying in front of the tavern, there was no movement at all. Images of what he had found on the *Daedalus* flashed into his mind.

"Something's wrong," Lara said. "Where is everybody?"

Before he could reply, the sound of horses and a wagon at the north end of the street drew his attention. Moments later a group of Alliance soldiers came into view at the south end of town. He made out Delain, Armand, James Genet, Eldar d'Elso, Gawl, and Father Thomas.

"Damn," Mathew said. "They got here faster than I thought they would."

"Oh, my God," Lara whispered, "there's Bran." She very nearly stood up but stopped herself.

Shakira was in her chair atop the wagon, Bran sitting at her feet. He appeared to be all right. Next to them rode King Seth.

"This doesn't change anything," Mathew said. "As soon as they pass us, scream at the top of your lungs, then get back under cover as fast as you can. That will be my sign—"

He stopped abruptly as the point of the sword pressed against his neck, and at the same time, his hand went for his dagger.

"Don't even think of it, lad," a voice behind him said. "There are three crossbows trained on you and the lady right now."

Mathew started to turn.

"Uh-uh," the soldier said, putting more pressure on the point. "Keep your hands where I can see them. And if you try using that ring of yours, the lady and child both die."

Mathew's heart sank when he heard the accent. It was unmistakably Vargothan.

"Now get up nice and slow. You, too, mistress."

They did as they were told and turned around. Four Vargothans looked back at them. Like a complete fool, he realized, he had just led them into a trap.

"Let me relieve you of that weapon," the soldier said to Lara, taking the sword form her. "There's a good girl. I'm Captain Ferrier of King Seth's guard, and I'm assuming you are Mathew Lewin."

Mathew said nothing.

"Cat got your tongue, eh? Well, it doesn't make a difference. I believe their majesties would like a word with you. Let's go."

The moment Seth saw them emerge from the trees, he raised his hand, halting the wagon and his men. Farther down the street the Alliance soldiers began to take up position along the block.

"I told you he would try something," Seth said to Shakira.

Shakira nodded slowly and stood up. One of Seth's men dismounted and helped her down off the wagon. Seth also got off his horse. Delain and the alliance soldiers drew to a halt about twenty yards from them.

"Come forward, your highnesses," Seth called out. "We have business to conduct."

"I have waited a very long time for this, Lewin," Shakira said. Her voice was little more than a whisper. "Do not try anything or the child dies."

The soldier who had helped Shakira off the wagon picked Bran up and walked over to Seth, while another kept his crossbow trained on the boy. Lara started to go to him, but Captain Ferrier raised the sword, aiming the point between her breasts, and she stopped.

"What is this, Seth?" Gawl rumbled, getting off his horse.

Delain, Armand, and Eldar did the same. Only James and Father Thomas remained in their saddles.

"An ill-conceived rescue attempt," Seth explained. "I will assume you had nothing to do with it."

"No, we didn't," said Delain.

Seth gave him a thin-lipped smile then walked up to Mathew and struck him backhanded across the face. The blow snapped Mathew's head sideways. He slowly raised his wrist to his mouth and wiped blood away.

"Enough," Shakira said. "Bring the child."

The smile faded from Seth's face. Not taking his eyes off Mathew, he motioned with his fingers and the soldier carrying Bran came forward.

Mathew's eyes darted from Father Thomas to Bran and then to Lara.

"I know what you are thinking, human," said Shakira. "Even you are not fast enough to stop the bolt from a crossbow. Remove your ring and hand it to me."

When Mathew hesitated, a blow to the back of his neck drove him to his knees.

"Kneel," said Seth.

"Goddammit, Seth," Delain exploded. "That wasn't necessary. We're here to talk peace."

"He doesn't want peace any more than she does," Mathew said. "Tell them where the people of this town are."

"What?" Delain said, looking around.

A second blow struck Mathew behind the ear.

"Speak when you're spoken to, boy," Seth snarled.

Gawl took a step forward. "What's he talking about, Seth?"

Two of the mercenaries reacted by training their crossbows on him.

"Tell the priest to get off his horse and come over here," Seth replied. "He's part of the bargain."

"I asked you a question," said Gawl, his tone becoming dangerous.

*"Enough,"* said Shakira. "We finish this now. Give me the ring or the child dies." She held out a gnarled hand.

Despair threatened to overwhelm Mathew. He had failed. He looked at his son and then at Lara. Because of his stupidity he had killed them all. The moment his ring was gone they were as good as dead.

*What have I done?* he thought.

When Mathew slowly began to remove his ring, all eyes were on him. A look of unconcealed glee played across Shakira's face and she put the knuckles of her hand to her mouth. Mathew prayed their deaths would be quick.

Twenty yards away a rider suddenly burst from the trees at a full gallop. Collin Miller charged directly for them. "Hang on, Bran, I'm coming!" he shouted.

Before Shakira could react, Collin drove his horse headlong into the mercenary holding the crossbow on the child, running him down. A bolt fired from the nearest soldier hit Collin in the back and another hit him in the chest. Collin yanked sideways on the reins and horse and rider went down.

Everyone started shouting at once.

Collin staggered to his feet as a third bolt struck him in the chest. And with the last ounce of his strength, he drew his sword and hurled it like a javelin at the man holding Bran. Lara dove for her son.

Then mercenaries rushed out of the homes and buildings on both sides of the street, screaming.

*"Ambush!"* roared Gawl, drawing his sword.

Shakira's first blow came out of nowhere, driving Mathew backward. He felt like he'd been hit by a boulder. The air was being crushed out of his chest.

Father Thomas leapt from his horse and ran to Collin. A soldier loomed to his left. The priest barely slowed as he drew his sword. He deflected the man's lunge, spun and beheaded him. The Vargothan's companion died of a broken skull caved in by Gawl's massive forearm. Roaring like a bull, the giant waded in among the enemy, his broadsword moving like a scythe. James dug his heels into his horse and crashed into a man who was trying to stab Eldar d'Elso, knocking the blade loose.

*"Defend the king!"* a soldier yelled, as the Alliance soldiers rushed to help. *"Defend the king!"*

Part of Mathew's mind registered it, wondering whether the voice belonged to a mercenary or to one of their own men. He knew he had to do something, but he couldn't remember what. He was in agony and it was impossible to think.

Snatching a sword from a fallen soldier, Lara placed Bran behind her and fought like a woman possessed. The nearest mercenary died when her blade pierced his throat, and the second to come at her found his weapon parried to the ground as she swept her line from high to low and left the point in line with his heart. Delain and two other men reached her a moment later.

In the years after that battle, Mathew rarely spoke of what happened, and then only if pressed.

*Get up, Mat. That was it. I heard Collin's voice as clear
as a bell in my ear. I knew he was dead and it wasn't possible, but I swear to God, I heard it.*

Mathew Lewin got up. First onto his knees, then to his
feet, as Shakira stared at him in disbelief.

"You cannot win," she told him. "I have waited for this
all my life. Even if I die, my people will prevail. We are
too many, too many."

Delain and Lara meanwhile, had backed up the steps of
the tavern. She was holding her child, trying to get him to
safety. She desperately wanted to do something to help
Mathew, but Bran was her first concern, as they had
agreed. Mathew had made her swear to that.

Two Vargothan soldiers coming out the entrance nearly
knocked them down. Delain went for the first one. The
second turned to Lara with a snarl on his face, raising his
sword. With Bran in her arms she knew she would never
get to her sword in time so she turned her body to the at-
tacker to protect her child.

The blow never arrived. Father Thomas did. Where the
priest came from, she never knew, but somehow he was
there. There was no expression on his face as he drove the
Vargothan into the street, the blade coming at the mercenary from everywhere at once.

Then disaster struck. An arrow caught the priest in the
back and he went down on one knee.

Lara screamed.

The mercenary immediately seized the opening. And
he raised his sword above his head with both hands. At the
last moment Father Thomas lowered his shoulder and
thrust his legs forward, coming in under the blade and hitting the man in the stomach. The pommel of the weapon
struck the priest's back. Before the man could recover, Father Thomas landed two punches to the side of the soldier's head, stunning him and knocking his sword to the
ground. The mercenary stepped back and drew his dagger,

but the priest moved with him, catching his wrist. Both men grappled for control of it, and then slowly, inexorably, the dagger began to turn until the point was at the base of the mercenary's throat. The Vargothan tried to pull away as the blade started downward. After a second the man's knees gave way and both men collapsed to the ground. Neither moved.

Mathew's head was clearer now, though Shakira was still talking to him, telling him to give up, and that he couldn't win. From somewhere, he heard Lara shout his name. The pressure on his chest lessened by a degree and then another.

This was not possible, Shakira thought. The human should be dead already.

Mathew struggled to his feet as Shakira increased the power of her attack. Thirty feet apart from each other their eyes met, and it seemed to Mathew that she looked very old. Collin's body lay nearby, his eyes staring blankly up at the sky.

The tears that rolled down Mathew's face were hot and his anguish became an all-consuming fire. Everywhere around them people were dying, and the reason for it stood before him.

The rage built until a roar burst from his lungs. On the steps near the tavern Delain and James drew back from the heat of a massive fireball that appeared out of nowhere.

In desperation, Shakira struck again. Two beams of white light shot from her fingers at Mathew. They never made contact. Ten feet from him the light rose straight into the air; and his own fireball hurtled forward.

A deafening bang shattered windows all along the street and was heard by people more than twenty miles away. When the smoke cleared, Shakira was gone. All that remained was a crater in the ground twenty feet deep.

"Dear God," said James.

The prince scanned the street for Seth, but there was no

sign of him. The mercenaries continued to fight, but the Alliance soldiers made short work of them.

Lara and Gawl reached Mathew as his knees gave way. He was struggling to remain conscious.

"My son?" he whispered.

"It's all right, boy," Gawl said, catching him around the waist. "I've got you. Bran's fine."

Another series of explosions snapped Gawl's head around. They were coming from the battlefield nearly two miles away. What no one in the village could see was that, one after another, the enemy cannons had suddenly begun to blow up.

Satisfied his work was done, Mathew lost consciousness.

## 60

## Balengrath

MATHEW OPENED HIS EYES AND LOOKED INTO LARA'S face. She was sitting on the side of his bed. It was such a beautiful face, one he could stare at for hours. He had always loved her eyes. Then he realized where he was.

"Bran," he said, sitting bolt upright.

Lara threw her arms around him. "Shh," she said. "He's all right." She began kissing his face.

"What happened?"

"You were magnificent, darling. He's all right, I swear."

"The others . . . Collin, Father Thomas—"

Father Thomas is wounded, but the doctors say he'll live. He saved my life. Mine and Bran's, just as you did. You have to rest."

"Collin?" he said, grabbing her by the shoulders.

Tears welled up in Lara's eyes and Mathew sank back down onto the mattress turning his head away.

"How long have I been out?" he asked.

"A few hours. They brought you back here. We're in Balengrath."

When he tried to sit up again Lara held him back. "No. You have to rest."

There was an urgency in her voice that made him look at her sharply. "What's happened?"

Lara took a breath. "Seth and a few of his men escaped. The Orlocks and the Vargothans began an attack almost immediately. Our people are fighting back and we're holding. That's why you have to rest."

Mathew threw the covers off and swung his feet over the side of the bed. And as he did so the room began to spin. He put a hand on Lara's shoulders to steady himself. "Help me up."

"No. You have to rest. Delain and Armand said we can hold them for quite a while yet."

"Help me up," he repeated. This time his tone left no room for argument.

He felt weak and unsteady on his feet, and the headache that always followed when he used the ring was there again. Bran was asleep on a cot in the corner. Mathew walked over in his stocking feet and looked down at the boy. He looked at him for a long time and then took Bran's small hand between his thumb and forefinger and gently rubbed the back of the boy's hand.

"He's so beautiful," he whispered.

Lara came up to him from behind and put her arm around his waist.

At a light tap on the door, they both turned. Gawl and Delain entered the room.

"How do you feel?" Delain asked.

"Well enough, your highness."

"Are you strong enough to come up to the parapet?" Delain asked.

Mathew nodded, but even that slight movement made his head throb. "Give me a moment to pull my boots on."

"You can come, too, Lara. I'll have one of the women stay with your child, if you wish."

"Mathew's still weak," she said.

Both men looked at him, but he waved her comment away. "I'm fine."

The statement earned him a severe look from Lara. "I'll stay," she said. "If your highnesses will excuse us for a moment . . ."

Delain made a half bow to her and withdrew and Gawl bent down and kissed the top of her head.

"We need him now, Lara," he said softly.

Mathew wasn't sure what Gawl was referring to, but he knew the situation had to be urgent. As a test, he reached for the power. He could still feel it there, but it was very weak. In time it would build again. That was a given. He just needed to find that time. The sounds from outside the window told him that a battle was in progress. He walked over to it and looked out.

What he saw was a shock. Shakira's fire wall was gone, but in its place was a mass of Vargothans and Orlocks. He had never seen so many bodies in one place. His heart sank.

*We are too many.* Shakira's words echoed in his mind.

Gawl reached out and squeezed his shoulder, then withdrew into the hallway to wait for him.

"I thought it would be over," Mathew said as the door closed.

Across the battlefield, Shakira turned to Seth and said, "He's awake."

"Can you take him?"

The Orlock queen fixed her eyes on the citadel and slowly nodded.

"Then do it."

"We must wait for Lewin to show himself. There will be no problem this time. He is afraid. I felt his fear when he drew back in the village."

"Then why didn't you destroy him?"

"He was strong—very strong," Shakira said quietly. "But it will make no difference now. I have seen his weakness. Fear gnaws at him like a disease. The day will be ours . . . at last."

Seth looked at her for several seconds then let out a long breath and turned to the soldier next to him. "Tell the second army to bring up the catapults."

* * *

Lara didn't want to tell Mathew that neither Seth nor Shakira were dead. He looked so tired and drained, but there wasn't any other choice. When she did, his shoulders slumped and he sat down heavily on the side of the bed.

"I understand," he said, reaching for his boots.

"There's something else you should know. You'll find out soon enough. The enemy sent a message saying they will take no prisoners if we don't surrender."

Mathew reached out with his mind and made contact with Shakira. She didn't bother trying to block him. The cold smile he saw sent a shiver up his spine. Lara knelt down and put her head in his lap.

"What are we going to do?" she asked.

Mathew stroked her hair and didn't respond immediately, then he looked across the room at his sleeping son. A dozen thoughts came and went in his mind. Collin was dead, Father Thomas and Daniel wounded, and the enemy was about to destroy everything his people had fought so hard to build.

*We improved the science, but not the people who used it.*

Those were the Guardian's words. It was three thousand years later and they were still at war.

It was a full minute before he spoke.

"Lara, I want you to listen carefully to me. I want you to take Bran and get as far away from this place as possible."

"What are you going to do?" she asked, looking up at him.

"Something I didn't have the courage to do before."

"Tell me."

Mathew slowly shook his head. "Take our son and go now. I must know that you're safe."

"Go *where*? And do *what*?" she said. "There won't be any place to go." Lara grabbed him by the shirt. "I lost you once before. I won't do it again."

Mathew thought his heart would break. Twice he opened his mouth to speak, but the words wouldn't come. When he finally found his voice, he said, "You'll never lose me, nor I you."

Suddenly she was in his arms again, and they clung to each other desperately. Walking out the door was the hardest thing he ever had to do.


On the walls of the citadel the faces of the defenders were grim. A few nodded to him as he passed by; Armand and two of his generals were near the main entrance watching the enemy movements through their farsighters. Armand's head was bandaged and one of his arms was in a sling. Spread across the valley floor before Balengrath were the troops of the Alliance. Banners marking the various divisions and armies flapped in the breeze. On the north side of the field were the Sennians and army of Bajan, and to the south, the troops of Nyngary. Alor Satar and the maroon cloaks of Elgaria held the middle. Somewhere near the base of the mountains were Akin Gibb and his people. Mathew tried to make them out for a few seconds and gave up. His heart was beating heavily in his chest.

He'd already seen the forces opposing them from his window, but looking out at them from atop Balengrath was even more depressing.

"They tell me you're spent," Armand said without preliminary. "Is it true?"

Mathew remained silent. He thought of Devondale and of growing old with Lara and watching their son grow up. Little memories like shopping in the market or listening to Akin play his violin in the square came and went in his mind. All that was about to change forever.

"Is it true?" Armand repeated. "I have to know what you're capable of . . . what we can count on."

Before Mathew could reply, one of Armand's generals pointed toward the field and said, "My lord, another white flag."

The enemy center opened to allow four riders through. One of them was on a white horse and wore a circlet of gold.

"Hold," the general called down to his men. The order was quickly relayed along the ranks.

"What now, Seth?" Armand shouted down.

"I've come to offer you one last chance to surrender the citadel. Once the attack begins, there will be no quarter."

"We read your message earlier. Your word is as meaningless now as it was this morning. Get out of my sight."

"Armand, you cannot win this fight. Delain already knows that. Get some sense for once in your life and look around you. I'll see to it the women and children aren't harmed."

"You're a liar."

Seth turned his palms up. "I'll give you ten minutes to think about it."

Gawl grabbed a spear from the nearest soldier and raised it to his shoulder. "This will give you something to think about."

Seth watched the spear fall twenty feet short of him and shook his head.

"He's not interested in whether you accept his terms or not," Mathew said. "They'll kill everyone here the second they have the chance."

Everyone turned to look at him.

"Seth wanted to know the same thing Lord Duren just asked me . . . if I can still fight."

"Well?" Armand asked.

Mathew looked at him for a moment, then turned toward the mercenary king. "Seth, tell your men to leave the field," he called out.

"Ah, there's the young man Shakira and I were discussing earlier. Well, she was right, I see—you are still alive. Perhaps you have more sense than the gentlemen next to you. If you surrender now you'll find us merciful."

"I've seen examples of your mercy. Tell your men to leave the field. If the Orlocks want a home, we'll find them one, but the killing has to end here and now. I don't want to see anyone else die."

"Particularly yourself, eh, Lewin? It's a generous offer, to be sure, but I'm dubious their lordships have elected you their spokesman. Personally I think you're bluffing. Shakira is still strong, and it'll be days before you can use your ring again. Unfortunately, I'm not going to give you that time. What I do give you is one hour."

Mathew watched Seth ride back. "I need our people off the field," he said over his shoulder.

Armand and Delain looked at each other.

"You don't just ask a half million people to move," Armand said. "It would take time and we'll lose field position."

"How long?" Mathew asked.

"An hour, two hours, but that's only part of—"

"Get them to move," said Mathew.

Armand took Delain under the elbow and pulled him aside and the two began arguing in vehement whispers. It was clear that Armand thought Mathew has lost his mind. Asking them to give up the ground they had fought so hard for was no small request and it could easily spell disaster. In the end it was Gawl who settled it.

"Mathew, are you still capable?" he asked.

Mathew's nod was almost imperceptible.

"Then I say, move them, Armand. I trust the boy."

"So do I," said Delain.

"But we'll be giving up field position," Armand insisted.

"It won't make a difference," Delain said. "You know that as well as I do. If they don't get through this time, they will the next."

Armand held his gaze for a long time before he said, "Give the order to retreat."

When the Alliance's trumpets sounded, a great cheer went up from the Vargothans and the Orlocks. Their commanders waited the appointed hour and then ordered their soldiers to advance.

Their progress, however, was short-lived. The doors to the citadel opened and a lone figure walked out. Most of the Alliance soldiers had already left the field and were marching along the road to Stewart Vale. Lara and Bran were among them. James and the Mirdanites had also pulled back to a position three miles from the battle site. Only Gawl and Delain still remained on the walls. Inside the citadel a breeze blew swirls of dust slowly across the courtyard. Gawl could almost feel the silence hanging in the air, heavy and foreboding.

After a hundred yards Mathew stopped. A half mile distant across the valley the Vargothan and Orlock commanders continued their advance, with Shakira and Seth in the vanguard.

"It's him," said Shakira.

Seth shielded his eyes from the glare and squinted across the field. "Alone?" he asked, incredulous.

"Alone."

In the west, just above the mountaintops, dark clouds had begun to gather and the wind was picking up. Not noticeable at first, it increased in strength over the next few minutes. Delain and Gawl, having the advantage of a higher position, saw the tops of the trees moving along the upper ridge of the valley and exchanged a glance.

On the field, Mathew remained where he was, feet wide apart, a mere three hundred yards separating him from Shakira, King Seth, and one of his generals. Hundreds deep the Orlock and Vargothan armies marched behind them.

"We end this now," said Shakira.

She extended her arm at the two nearest catapults and the chains suddenly snapped. Without warning, they lifted off the ground and shot forward at Mathew. Both exploded fifty yards from where he stood.

Rage twisted Shakira's feature's. "Kill him!" she screamed to her commanders.

Seth snapped his fingers twice, and looked at his general, then he pointed at the lone figure opposing them. He drew his sword and yelled, "Attack!"

*No more,* Mathew said to himself.

* * *

From the walls of Balengrath, Gawl saw a hundred yard section of ground in front of Mathew buckle and rise up like a wave. Rocks and dirt flew into the air as it started forward, gathering momentum, as though someone had just shaken a carpet. The mercenaries charging at Mathew were knocked to the side like so many rag dolls and confusion erupted in their ranks. Seth saw it coming, wheeled his horse around, and galloped to the side of the field. On her wagon, Shakira's lips pulled back into a snarl and she hissed.

The explosion that followed was deafening.

On the battlements Gawl and Delain both ducked out of reflex and watched as the armies of Vargoth and the Orlock nation regrouped. Across the valley floor over a thousand horsemen moved into an attack formation, lowering their lances, and charged.

"He's got to get out of there," said Delain.

Other than Mathew's arm coming up, he made no other movement. A shock wave rushed outward in an arc spreading across the valley. Horses, men, creatures, and catapults were flung into the air as the wave slammed into them.

Mathew knew that his first blast hadn't killed Shakira. Her life force was still strong. It was also possible that Seth was alive, too. Either way, it made no difference.

*"You fear to use the ancient weapons, human. I do not."* Shakira's voice spoke in his mind. *"Surrender now and you can save your people. Fail to do so and I will destroy them to the last. Their deaths will be on your head."*

The talking, he knew was an attempt to break his concentration. It was true that he had pulled back in Stewart Vale. Whether out of fear or because the images the Guardian had shown him were too horrible to contemplate, he didn't know. The death and destruction his ancestors had created was on a scale he could never have imagined in his wildest dreams. Even as he deflected Shakira's bolts of light, he sensed the hatred radiating from her—hatred for all that was human, hatred three millennia in the making.

He had seen death for so long now—on the battlefields, on the Great Southern Sea, and in towns and villages. It was time to put an end to it, even if it meant his own demise. The thought that he might never see Lara and Bran again nearly overwhelmed him, but it was something that could wait no longer.

He considered trying to reason with Shakira and Seth one last time, but knew that would do no good. Their hatred existed for its own end.

When Mathew's voice popped into Gawl's head, he started and looked around. One glance at Delain told him that he had just heard the same thing.

"We need to go," said Gawl.

Delain nodded and took one more look at the solitary figure standing on the battlefield before they ran down the steps. Shakira had continued to unleash bolt after bolt of the killing light at Mathew. Each time one struck, a fountain of earth shot up into the air, yet none had any effect on him.

Overhead, the sky grew darker and the wind rose to a shriek.

"How much time do we have?" Delain asked.

"Less than three minutes," Gawl said.

Both men mounted their horses and tore past the main gate toward the town of Stewart Vale.

The first clap of thunder caused both the mercenaries and the creatures to flinch. It seemed to come from directly over their heads. They could see that Shakira and Mathew were locked in some sort of titanic struggle. The bolts of light she was sending against him tore away enormous chunks of earth and sent shock waves through the ground.

The commanders had long since given up trying to urge their men forward. All were watching in fascination as the battle unfolded.

Mathew Lewin finally moved. Exhausted from his efforts over the last few days, his strength was fading. He knew it was now or never.

Somewhere, in a long forgotten cavern built by Mathew Lewin's ancestors, the needle on a gauge moved. Sporadic at first, it steadied itself and began to climb. A half mile away from the main complex, a series of orange lights that traveled along the center column of the Ancients' machine suddenly increased in intensity. The giant crystal that rose out of the ground near the laboratory and disappeared into the ceiling took on an angry red glow, throwing back the surrounding darkness. After a minute a second gauge began to register, and then a third, as Mathew drew more power into himself. A nimbus of light appeared around him.

The tremor was barely noticeable at first.

When the Vargothans and Orlocks felt it, they stopped talking and looked across the valley in confusion. Seconds later another tremor coursed through the ground.

The next was stronger than the first two. Two miles away, Gawl and Delain felt the vibration communicate itself through the ground and they looked toward Balengrath.

When the trees along the edge of the valley began to topple over, no one on the field was able to fathom what was happening. A few of the mercenaries started moving back toward the river, but their commanders ordered them to stand their ground. The tremor grew into a rumble and a terrible groaning sound could be heard coming from the earth itself.

Mathew Lewin finally dropped his shield and sank to his knees, his head bowed.

Shakira was nearly beside herself with glee. The human was spent, she thought. "Victory," she hissed.

Then Mathew raised his head and their eyes locked.

On either side of the valley two giant crystals erupted from the ground. And a bolt of blue light shot from them tearing into Orlocks and the Vargothan armies. When the two columns of light connected it felt like someone had suddenly opened the door to a giant furnace.

At the east and west two more crystals erupted at the far ends of the valley and a series of explosions began that moved with frightening speed directly toward where Shakira was standing. She never saw them coming. The first one obliterated her, and Mathew was hurled backward. He hit the ground heavily.

Those of the enemy who had survived seemed frozen in place.

The tremors then became so violent that men and Orlocks were knocked to the ground. And when the valley floor dropped by several inches, they began to scream. It continued falling away, and the screams took a long time to stop.

When Delain, Gawl, and Armand returned to Balengrath, they were speechless. A deep canyon now stood where a valley had once been. The earth's groaning continued for some time before silence settled over Stewart Vale.

It was late in the afternoon.

# EPILOGUE

## Devondale

SPRING CAME EARLY THAT YEAR TO DEVONDALE. THE ICE floes that drifted on Westrey Stream gradually grew smaller and smaller and eventually disappeared altogether. Green buds appeared on the trees and new sprouts pushed their way up through the ground in the flower beds on the square.

Mathew sat under an oak tree and reread the last line of a letter he had received that morning. It was from Akin Gibb. His friend had accompanied Teanna back to Nyngary. He wrote that the princess was doing well, and according to the doctors, her injury was almost completely healed. She was compensating for having one hand as well as could be expected. She also sent her regards and invited them for a visit.

It was strange, he reflected, that a princess and a commoner should have taken to each other as well as Teanna and Akin had, but Teanna was far from an ordinary woman, and he was far from an expert in such matters. The image of them together brought a smile to his face.

On the lawn, Lara and Bran were playing with each other, and Mathew leaned back against the bench and watched them.

After the battle, Gawl had returned home to his beloved Sennia along with Jeram Quinn, to set up the court system he promised his people. James had left for Mirdan. News drifted back that Edward Guy had been killed during the battle.

No one seemed to know what had become of Rowena.

Collin Miller was laid to rest behind the church. Delain attended the funeral. Mathew made it a point to visit the grave whenever he came to town. Lara did, too, always bringing fresh flowers. The last time they visited, she and Bran placed two letters on the grave. Neither offered to tell him what was in them, and he didn't ask.

Daniel Warren also came home to Devondale to recover from his wounds, at least for a while. Delain rewarded him by placing him in charge of building a new astronomical observatory in Anderon. It was a project that would take more than two years to complete. According to the letter he sent back, he had taken a house in the city and was getting to know Anderon. Like Teanna and Akin, he also urged Mathew to come and visit.

Father Thomas and Ceta Woodall were formally married after the battle. The priest recovered from his wounds and resumed his duties in the local church. He even took up teaching fencing again. The classes were well-attended by the boys in the village. Every now and then Mathew stopped by to help. So far, Bran had shown no interest in the sport, but there was no rush. Eventually, Lara came over to sit with him on the bench, and they watched their son doing somersaults on the lawn. She slipped her hand into his and rested her head on his shoulder.

Bran appeared to be a perfectly healthy little boy. Only Mathew knew that his son was able to work the ring. A few experiments one night left no question about it.

As the Guardian had predicted, people did seek him out. Some curried favors and some simply wanted to meet him or ask his advice. When they did, he handled the situation as best he could. Most were deferential; a few were not. Fortunately, the ones who weren't were in a distinct minority or too afraid of him to press matters when he turned them away.

Mathew folded Akin's letter and put it back in his pocket. It was a pleasant, mild day, and the square was alive with people. Hints of honeysuckle floated in the air. He tilted his head back and looked up through a network of branches into a cloudless blue sky. They would soon be covered in leaves.

*New beginnings,* he thought.

He recalled his last conversation with the Guardian. It was possible the day would come when he would have to make the decision they spoke about, but for the time being his views of humanity remained the same—hopeful.

## So Ends the Last Book of The Fifth Ring

# GLOSSARY

| | |
|---|---|
| Adrosta | Town in Alor Satar where Mathew and company stop for the night |
| Balengrath, Citadel of | Located in Alor Satar and site of final battle |
| Bell's Ferry | Town in Elgaria where Mathew and company stop for the night |
| Bokras | Where the Coribar priest was dropped by King Seth's galley |
| Brown | Coxswain and member of the *Daedalus* crew who took the guard boat with Mathew |
| Corrato | Capital of Nyngary |
| *Daedalus* | Name of the ship Mathew was serving on |
| Dobbs | Master's mate on the *Daedalus* |
| Edrington, Phillipe | Captain of the *Daedalus* |
| Epps Crossing | A place in Alor Satar where Vargoth, the Orlocks, and the Durens fought |
| Fikes, Elton | First Officer on the *Daedalus* |

| | |
|---|---|
| Giravele | A port city twenty miles from the Vargoth capital where Teanna is attacked |
| Henderson | Ancients' town under the earth |
| Holt, Andreas | Governor of Sheeley Province, Vargothan mercenary and captain of the *Maitland* |
| Kennard, Tabbert | Aide to Governor Andreas Holt |
| Kelsey Church | Place in Elgaria where the Vargothans and Orlocks turned on Alor Satar |
| LaCora, Raymond | Captain of the Vargoth ship, *Revenge* |
| Lane, Thaddeus | Name used by Mathew Lewin while in hiding |
| Lipari | A small town in Nyngary where the Vargothans had been hired to protect the textile guild |
| Maddox | Member of the *Daedalus* crew who took the guard boat with Mathew |
| Mardell | Name of the town in Sennia where Gawl landed on his return |
| Marek, Terrence | Head of the Coribar Church |
| Oridan | Elgaria's new name in honor of Armand and Eric Duren's grandfather |
| Palandol | Capital of Vargoth |
| Pruett, Glyndon | Third officer aboard the *Daedalus* |
| Rivalin | Teanna d'Elso's summer palace, located on Leola Bay |

| | |
|---|---|
| Selmo, Artemis | A brutal monk at the Monastery of Saint Anne who tortured Father Thomas |
| Stewart Vale | Site of the final battle |
| Thierry, Julian | Alor Satar major Mathew and company meet on the road |
| Walsh, Dermot | Devondale resident and informer |
| Warrenton, Fred | A midshipman on the *Daedalus* |